THAT FIRST *Date*

JENN MCMAHON

BOOK TWO OF THE

Firsts in the City

SERIES

Cover Design: Emily Wittig

Copy Editing: Caroline Palmier

Developmental and Line Editing: Kelsey Muller

Proofreading, Formatting: Cathryn Carter

AUTHOR'S NOTE

I needed to start this book by saying a huge THANK YOU to my readers for the outpouring of love and support from my debut novel, That First Night. Never in my wildest dreams did I think so many of you would read and fall in love with the characters the way that I have. Every bit of success that book saw, was entirely because of you. So thank you for giving me the platform to be able to write book two. I'm so happy you are here and continue the series as I grow as an author.

These books are meant to be light, but if you have any trigger warnings you can check my website at www.jennmcmahon.com

I hope you enjoy Marc and Avery!

Jenn

For the girls that have been told they're too loud, too wild, and too much.

It's not a you problem, it's a them problem.

CHAPTER ONE

Avery

You have got to be kidding me, I think to myself as I see an incoming call from my boss.

"Marc?"

It's not unusual for Marc to be up my ass when I'm off work. When I accepted the position as his assistant a few weeks ago, I didn't know he was the brother of my best friend's boss. I use the word *boss* loosely, though. Peyton and Thomas have certainly blurred some of those lines in the professional workplace and are leaning closer and closer to an actual relationship.

Peyton met Thomas briefly a few years back at a charity event. Fast forward five years after no communication, she accidentally becomes the nanny for his son, James. Let's just say, fate dealt its cards for her, and I wouldn't be surprised if they got married soon.

Unfortunately for me, fate was not in my favor when I landed my new assistant job with Marc Ford. Who just so happens to be Thomas' brother, and the biggest pain in my ass to ever exist.

An assistant might not seem like someone's dream job, but it's certainly something that I actually enjoy doing. What's that saying? If you love your job, you'll never work a day in your life? Something like that. Keeping people organized and together makes me weirdly happy. Plus, I've worked my ass off to climb the ladder in assistant positions when I started off as a nobody after I moved to New York. I answered phones for a popular fashion magazine making next to nothing until I worked my way up to higher paying assistant jobs like this one with Marc.

"Avery," Marc cuts through my thoughts. "I need your help."

"I'm not working today. I'm off."

My best friend, Kali, and I took Peyton for her first experience at a waxing center. We spent the better part of the day getting her pampered so she's ready for her big night at a charity gala with her boss. Except tomorrow she's actually going as his date.

"Thank you, Captain Obvious," he scoffs. "You know how I knew that? I'm here at the office and I'm looking at your empty desk."

"Are you always this rude to all your assistants?" I ask him. "No wonder you needed a new one. The last one probably ran for the hills the second she learned how *charming* you were."

Listen, Marc is hot. There's no question about that. The day I walked in for my interview, my jaw fell to the floor as I stood in front of all six feet of him. My first impression of him left me speechless as I fielded all the questions he asked me. He's way more relaxed than your typical rich boss. He walks around the office in the classic white button up dress shirt, with his sleeves rolled up to show off his thick, corded forearms that are every woman's wet dream. Don't even get me started on his tousled hair that begs me to run my hands through it.

However, he has the personality of a wet mop. He's basically a grump one hundred percent of the time, but that doesn't make my job miserable. I can hold my own with a man who has a permanent scowl on his face. Plus, I make it a mission to piss him off any chance I can. Why? Because I just love to see him clench that perfectly chiseled jaw in frustration.

I am fairly confident that I'm the best assistant he's ever had.

His office was in shambles before I stepped in. Frankly, he needed me.

"Cute," he deadpans. "Back to why I called. I need your help."

"What *ever* can I help you with, Your Majesty?"

"As you know," he starts, but pauses to let out a long breath, "Bill wants to pass down the agency to someone when he retires, and I'm up for consideration."

"I don't see how this is something I can help with."

"Bill wants a family man to run the place. He wants someone settled down in an established relationship. Not necessarily with kids—"

"I'm not pushing a Marc Ford spawn out of my vagina for you," I interrupt him. "Can you imagine how grumpy that child will be? No thanks."

Peyton must have been taking a sip of water because I can hear water spray out of her mouth and Kali starts to giggle as if they're eavesdropping on my conversation. I rush a few steps ahead, only to be stopped dead in my tracks by his next statement.

"And I'm not sticking my dick in you to create said spawn," he quips. "I need you to be my date to that charity event Thomas and Peyton are going to. Bill is going to be there, and I just need to make a small show out of it so he can see that I'm who he's looking for."

"So let me get this straight…" A laugh sneaks out of me as I think about what he's asking and how he might actually be drunk right now. That's the only explanation. "You need me to be your fake girlfriend for the night to show your boss that you're in a long-term happy relationship so he can pass the baton down to you?"

"Well, no. It's not a baton, it's a company. And more like fake fiancé so I can—"

"No, I will not be your fake fucking fiancé. Are you drunk?" I exclaim. Out of the corner of my eye, I see Peyton and Kali practically doubling over laughing.

"Avery." I can practically feel the desperation in his voice. "Trust me, I hate to ask you this. You're the last person on earth I want to be engaged to. Let alone *fake* engaged to."

I throw my head back with the phone still pressed to my ear. "This sounds like my nightmare coming true," I mutter. "Marc, I don't do relationships and I have never had the desire to be in one." I can't even lift a single finger to show how many relationships I have been in. Because the answer is zero. I know this wouldn't be a *real* relationship, but even just the idea of faking one has my skin crawling.

It's all so painfully cliché. Let's say it together on three… 1, 2, 3, *daddy issues*. When I was four, my dad walked out on my mom with his mistress. We haven't heard from him since and have no idea where he even is in the world. He could be in Egypt for all we know. My mom hasn't dated anyone since then. I saw the damage my dad did to her, and I never want to give anyone the chance to do that to me.

"Please, Avery," he pleads.

"You owe me the biggest raise of my life, Marcus." I abruptly hang up the phone because I don't feel like entertaining this wild facade anymore than I already have.

This is the worst idea in the history of all bad ideas. He's literally my boss. Not just the boss that works higher up and, you know, sometimes you see. No, I'm literally his personal assistant. My desk is five feet from his, separated by a huge wall of glass windows.

"Looks like I'm coming to this shindig," I laugh to the girls as I stuff my phone into my purse while we wait on the sidewalk for the Uber.

Peyton and Kali are my two closest friends. Probably my only friends. They befriended me when I first moved here to the concrete jungle and, honestly, we have been inseparable ever since. We're like thighs, we stick together. *We're the three best friends that anyone could have.* We sing-song that to each other almost on a daily basis, mostly because it fits us so well.

Kali is the older one and makes sure we know it. Despite her being just one year older than us, she's the most mature and levelheaded. She keeps us in our place, and has the best, most logical advice when you're in a predicament.

Peyton is the sweet one of the group. She's grown a lot since moving to the city. She lost her parents in a tragic car accident and was forced to try to fend for herself. That's what landed her in our apartment. She needed to get her life started again after she had to sell her childhood home. Since Thomas walked back into her life though, I have watched her blossom into the badass woman I always knew was deep down.

I won't sit here and give all the credit to Thomas. Because that shit is supposed to come from within. He just gave her that confidence back. Which elevated all the other aspects of her life.

And I'm a typical Aries. High energy, fiery, and passionate. At least that's what I'm told are some of my best traits. Sometimes my high energy can be taken the wrong way by people, but I could care less about what they think about me or say behind my back. I keep my chin up, head held high, and plaster a wicked smile on my face and move on with my life.

Peyton's Gigi always tells me, '*If they won't matter to you in five years, then don't spend more than five minutes letting them get to you.*' Wise words from the best adopted grandmother.

"What the heck was that?" Kali finally asks.

"And why are we acting so casual about this right now?" Peyton adds. "We didn't catch what he said, but from your end, that sounded pretty intense."

"Am I supposed to be freaking out because my boss, the grumpiest man on the face of the earth, asked me to be his fake fiancé to this charity event so he can get *his* boss to love him and *gift* him an entire company?"

"Yes," they both say in unison while aggressively nodding their heads to emphasize their answer.

"Stop it." I laugh as I wave my hand in the air to blow them off. "It may be a *really* bad idea because we work together, but I could honestly give two shits at this point."

"We're not saying it's a bad idea," Kali says first.

"It's just that..." Peyton rolls her eyes. "You two can barely stand each other outside of work. Plus, you have never even been in an actual relationship. How are you going to sell this to his boss?"

"And here I thought you knew me, babe." I huff out another chuckle. "I'm immune to this shit. I don't fall for all that corny charm. It'll be hard work because he's Marc, but my acting skills are top tier, like Oscar worthy. I can also fake an orgasm like no one's business."

"Stop it," Kali scoffs. "You've never faked one. No way."

"Sometimes a girl's gotta do what a girl's gotta do." I waggle my eyebrows. "Unfortunately, there are some men out there who still don't know the female anatomy or how to work with what they've got."

"She's not wrong, Kali," Peyton says. "Before Thomas, I have had to fake it plenty of times. Mediocre sex at best. But it's a whole new world when you find the right one."

"Woah there." I wave my hands in the air and sigh. "Don't spit my own words back at me. That's not what this is. This is a one date thing as I play the role of my overbearing boss' doting fiancé. There will be no sex."

"Come on, Avery." Kali bends over in a fit of laughter as she rests both hands on her knees to steady herself. "No sex for you? You're like the female version of a playboy. *Playgirl,* if you will. I don't know if that's a thing, but let's make it an Avery thing."

"Nailed it." Peyton emphasizes with a fist pound to Kali. "No pun intended."

She did, she nailed it. That's who I am and who I have always been because I love sex. If it's done right, it takes you to a whole new world. I am certainly not a female version of a playboy, but feel free to call me a dirty little slut in the bedroom anytime. It's kinky.

Most of the time, I keep it casual. I will see the same guy for a while until one of us gets sick of the other. More often than not, it's me because I don't do the clingy shit. Plus, I have yet to find anyone worthy enough to break down my walls and make me *want* to move forward with a relationship.

Marc has kept me insanely busy with work anyway. Which means I haven't had my itch scratched in a while. My little purple vibrator is going to have a broken motor if I keep up this dry spell any longer. Despite how long it's been, I most certainly am not going down that road with Marc.

"Listen, ladies. I never asked to be the shit." I lift my shoulders with a shrug.

I finish up my day with the girls and we go our separate ways. I need to get my last-minute things together anyway for this event that is happening in less than twenty-four hours.

It isn't until now, as I'm staring into my small closet, that I realize I have nothing to wear, nor am I mentally prepared. Before I go crazy looking for something, I shoot Marc a quick text.

How do you expect me to be ready for the holiday gala in 24 hours?

MARC

Does that mean you're going to be my fake fiancé?

Do I have a choice???

MARC

Yes.

But I'm still hoping you will help me out here.

I said I would, didn't I?

MARC

Actually, you didn't. You said I owe you a raise.

You do 🙃

Just as I'm about to type out another response to him, I get a notification at the top of my phone screen from my bank that a deposit has been made. I open it to see what this is all about because it's not payday.

My jaw drops to the floor when I see a deposit made for five thousand dollars.

The sender? Marc Ford.

Of course he has quick access because he's the one who personally deposits my paycheck each week.

What in the actual…?

Was that necessary? 🤦‍♀️

MARC

That's not your raise. Don't worry.

That's also not payment for coming with me. I know you're not an escort. 🙄 That's so you can find something to wear for tomorrow night. I asked you to be my date and I'm putting you out with all this last-minute shit, so it's the least I can do. You have no idea how much this means to me you're willing to help me out here.

Seriously, thank you.

I don't respond right away because my brain isn't wired for this type of generosity. I'm not used to guys actually being nice to me. Okay, maybe that's not the right thing to say. They are nice to me, but I can tell when it's actually genuine, and when it's fake. Most guys put up the fake nice guy act to try and get what they want out of me.

Yes, Marc needs my help with something, but it's all for

show. He's not getting anything else out of it. I can tell he's being genuine in his gratitude. I know by just that one text, that he feels bad for putting me out on such short notice like this.

Now I feel bad for being an asshole.

Who am I? I never feel bad about my attitude.

I can do this though.

I can be a fake fiancé for one night.

It's just one date.

CHAPTER TWO

Marc

I must have been drunk when I agreed with my brother, Thomas, to his idea to ask Avery to be my date to this charity event. Don't get me wrong, she's amazing at her job and drop dead gorgeous. However, she's a wildcard. A ticking time bomb if you will. The girl has no filter and a dirty mouth. She's about five foot four with a six-foot five attitude on her. Which I shouldn't find so damn hot because she is so far from being my usual type.

The first time I saw her was when she walked into my office for her interview. She was the last candidate of the day, and I was already aggravated over the others. Every single one of them had no experience working as an assistant. Some of them were secretaries previously, but that wasn't what I was looking for.

She had every qualification and experience I was looking for, but she had to show up filling my office with some kind of floral aroma I couldn't quite pinpoint at the time. She was wearing the tightest, black pencil skirt that stopped just below her knees and didn't leave a whole lot to the imagination, with a white button up blouse that was so slim fit, it could have easily been painted on her. Her buttons were open just enough to expose the top curves of her breasts. My eyes couldn't help but look.

I'm not ashamed to admit that I scanned her body up and down the moment she stepped foot into my office that day. A petite woman with sun kissed skin that complimented her blonde hair perfectly, and an innocent face that I'm sure gets her carded in every bar she goes to. She truly didn't look a day over twenty, but her high school graduation date on her resume told me she was in her late twenties.

She had temptation written all over her. My mind doesn't normally go right into wanting to know what a woman would feel like underneath me, but it did in this situation. I love sex, but I'm more of a relationship kind of guy. Casual hookups and one night stands just don't do it for me. I like having the comfort of a woman around to take her out on dates and spoiling the shit out of her. For me, consistency is key.

Despite my hesitation, I had to hire her. Because the next day, I interviewed four more candidates and again… not a single one met my requirements for the job. Avery was everything I wanted in an employee. Her references and love for organization were a dream come true for an employer.

Now here I am, stuck with my best employee who apparently "doesn't do" relationships, having to make her my fake fiancé for the night to impress my boss in hopes he sees me as a family guy.

That's just the thing. I *am* a family guy. I love my brothers, Thomas and Oliver, as well as my little sister, Emiline. Family is everything to me.

Thomas is a successful investor in the city and we partner on a lot of deals together. He became a single dad after a one night stand that he used to get *the one that got away* out of his head. We all always thought I would be the first to give our parents a grandkid, but it turns out James was the greatest thing to happen to all of us. He's the coolest and smartest kid you will ever meet.

Oliver is a free bird. After our dad died, we were all left an inheritance from him. Oliver decided to take his and travel the world. We thought he was out of his ever-loving mind, but he started documenting his travels on a blog site and now he makes a shit ton of money doing it. His trips are mostly sponsored by companies and fully covered as long as he blogs about wherever he is staying.

Emiline is the baby out of all of us. She was a surprise to mom and dad after they thought they would have a family of all boys. She's successfully working her way through an accelerated nursing program. We all couldn't be prouder of her.

I'm going to admit, I grew up as a mama's boy. I was always the closest to her, out of all of us. Things changed a lot after our dad died unexpectedly from complications of pneumonia, and she was never the same person. Now she spends her time traveling the world with her girlfriends, and we're lucky if we hear from her once a month other than a couple texts to tell us she's okay.

I work in real estate. Not just any residential real estate, but high-end commercial real estate. We don't sell houses, we sell buildings, skyscrapers, and all the other luxurious buildings you could think of. Thomas and I have our names on half the city. He invests, and I make the deal come to life. It's the perfect duo that makes us both rich.

It's just total bullshit Bill is looking for someone to take over his company who is a "family man." I am the biggest family man in this city, but I just haven't found *the one* yet to create my own family. However, his top two contenders don't have a wife or kids. It's between Todd and me. I've heard through the grapevine that he's been engaged to his girl for over a year now and plans to get married this winter.

Me? I don't even have a girlfriend. That's why I'm in this situation with Avery Woods. There's no reason it shouldn't work. Bill lives in Florida for the majority of the year and only comes to the city in the summer. Todd oversees Brooklyn and

Queens, while I oversee Manhattan, the Bronx, and Staten Island. And they don't know she's my assistant.

My thoughts are cut short when I feel my phone buzz in my pocket and see a phone call from my best friend, Logan.

"What's up?"

"Is that any way to answer the phone when I call you?" Logan chuckles. "You sound moody."

"I am moody," I scoff. "I don't want to do this shit tonight. Plus, I just dropped eight grand on an engagement ring for a fake fiancé."

"Ohhhh. I can see how that would make someone moody." He laughs.

"Don't start with me, Logan."

Logan is one of our best friends. He's been more like a brother to Thomas, Oliver and me for as long as I can remember. He's a cop here in the city, and damn good at what he does. He comes to these events with us to represent New York City's finest, and to get access to the open bar. He just so happens to be the biggest playboy of all of us, and always happens to leave these events with someone. My younger brother, Oliver, comes in a close second to him.

"Oh stop," he snickers. "It's not going to be that bad. Avery is hot, dude. She's an animal as long as you don't feed her too much tequila. You certainly don't need her breaking out in song and dance singing "Breakfast at Tiffany's" again."

I groan thinking about our trip to the beach house where Avery, Kali and Emiline got drunk off tequila and started belting that song while dancing on top of the kitchen counter. It was a sight to see, that's for sure.

"I think she will control herself for the night."

"I sure hope so," he huffs. "Do you want me to pick you up on the way tonight?"

"No, I'm good, brother. I have my driver taking us tonight because I have to pick up Avery. I don't think it would look good if we showed up separately, you know?"

"That makes perfect sense," he says with conviction. "Well, I will see you there. You got this in the bag. Bill would be stupid to give this to Todd. You're the man for the job."

"Thank you, Logan. Appreciate it."

"Anytime. See you there."

The ride to Avery's apartment has me more nervous than I have been in a long time because I know deep down, I have to treat it as a real date. I have to make a show that we're happy and in love.

I feel my leg bouncing in place and my heart is pounding a mile a minute. Will people around us know it's fake? Can I really prove to everyone inside of the Edison Ballroom that I am in love with Avery? I huff out a groan in the back seat as I think about the fact that this is going to be impossible. The two of us genuinely can't stand each other.

The problem is that our personalities are total opposites of each other. Don't get me wrong, I love getting her riled up when she throws her snarky comments at me. But that's really all we have going for us.

Pulling up in front of her building, I pause as I adjust my suit jacket before I make my way to her apartment. I stand outside of her door for what feels like minutes before I finally find the courage to knock. Within seconds, the door swings open and Kali is standing in front of me.

"Well, hello there." She scans me up and down as if she's approving of her friend's date for the evening.

"Hi, Kali." I fake adjust the cuff links of my suit jacket that I already fixed to avoid her stare. "Is Avery almost ready?"

"Yup. She will be out in a second. Come in. Come in." She steps aside and opens her arm to signal I can enter their space.

Their apartment is small. I don't know how two people can live here. It's crazy to think that there were almost three people in this space before Peyton took the nanny job with Tommy and moved in with him. The place is big enough for a loveseat sofa and two barstools at the kitchen counter. There isn't even enough room for an actual kitchen table.

"Are you judging my apartment, Marcus?" Avery says from behind me, cutting through my thoughts.

My head snaps in the direction of her voice and it's as if the whole world stops spinning on its axis. I feel my breath lodge in my throat as I take in the sight of her. I drink in her body from head to toe as she stands in place. Her long, bleach blonde hair is pulled back into a slick ponytail. She's wearing the most stunning bright red dress that hugs every curve of her body and matches her personality. There's no doubt in my mind that—

"I'm not wearing panties." She laughs. As if she can read my mind.

"I wasn't—"

"Yes you were, Marcus," she cuts me off as she takes a few steps closer to me and I feel the heat of her body as she steps into my personal space. "Your face just told me that you were wondering if I was wearing panties under this." She takes one final step closer. Our bodies are so close, and I feel a shiver run down my spine. She leans in to whisper in my ear. "The answer is no… *babe*."

Babe. She's playing the game of doting fiancé.

I stuff my hands in my pockets and force my mind to think of anything other than the way she just cooed the word *babe* from her soft pink lips and how breathtaking she looks in this dress.

Or the fact she isn't wearing any goddamn panties.

I clear my throat. "We're going to be late. Are you ready?"

"Ohhh, the sexual tension." Kali giggles from the kitchen island. "I can feel it from here."

"Let's go." I turn and walk towards the door, completely ignoring Kali's comment. She's not wrong, there is sexual tension. It's likely one-sided because that small interaction with her just did something to me I can't explain, yet Avery looks completely unphased.

This. Is. Not. Real. I repeat in my head as we exit the apartment and make our way to the car.

"Are you going to be a grump all night, Marcus?" she asks once we're settled in the car.

"Stop calling me Marcus and I might not be," I say as I unbutton my suit jacket. Avoiding every bit of eye contact with her perfect light blue eyes. "My name is Marc."

"Marcus suits you best."

A couple minutes pass by when I reach into my suit jacket to give her the fake, but very real diamond ring for her to wear tonight.

"Here. Put this on."

Slowly I hand her the ring, still trying to avoid eye contact with her. I can't take a chance by looking at her before we get there. But I hear a small gasp come from her lips which causes my head to snap in her direction. Her hand is on her chest as her eyes bounce from the ring in my hand to my eyes.

"Is this real?" she asks barely above a whisper.

"It's the realest fake engagement ring anyone will ever have," I scoff.

"Are you going to put it on me?"

I feel my jaw harden as I practically grind my teeth together. "We don't need to make a whole show of it."

"Relax, you big goof." She rolls her eyes. "I know this isn't a real thing. But once we step foot from this car, it has to be. You're the one needing this, not me. I'm just here to play the role of a happy fiancé." She plasters a smile on her face at the same time she puts her hand out in front of me. "Why don't you make me the happiest fiancé and slide that rock on my finger."

I can't help but shake my head. This girl is unreal.

My stomach bottoms out as I slowly slide the diamond onto her left ring finger. This feels *too* real. I have always wanted a wife and a big family. Never did I imagine that the first time I slid a ring on that finger would be for this stupid situation I got myself in.

I look up at her face as I watch her melt in the seat next to me. Her hand up in front of her face while she studies the diamond. Moving her hand side to side as she watches it glisten in the city lights as we drive.

"It's beautiful, Marc."

It is. But it's ten times more stunning on her finger. *Fuck me.* I need to tone these thoughts down.

"You look beautiful tonight, Avery."

"Did you just..." She gasps with her hand to her chest in shock. "Did you just compliment me?"

"Don't let it get to your head."

"I'm absolutely letting it get to my head," she says with conviction. "And that compliment went straight to my lady bits too."

"Avery," I growl.

"Just saying." She shrugs. "You just do something to me, *babe*."

I can't tell if this is her with no filter or if this is part of the show. But regardless, it's making me feel off, and I don't like it one bit. I can't feel off.

The rest of the car ride, we sit in silence, and I think about how this could end up being the best and the worst idea I have ever had.

CHAPTER THREE

Avery

"Marcus is a pain in my ass, Peyton." I groan in frustration at Peyton.

I'm so thankful that she is here with Thomas because I don't think I could do this shit tonight without her being close by. The ride here was awkward. I tried to practice my skit as a fiancé, and he wasn't catching on. He seemed more annoyed with me than anything. However, there's something so insanely sexy about a man when he clenches his jaw in frustration.

"Stop it." She waves me off with a laugh. "He's not that bad."

"He's lucky he's so fucking hot, otherwise I wouldn't be doing this." I take another sip of champagne. It's going down like water tonight as the nerves continue to dance in my stomach.

"Are there benefits to this arrangement?" Peyton asks with a raised eyebrow.

It's something I didn't even think about. There's a very small part of me that hopes there is a benefit to this arrangement. It's been so long since I've had sex, and I'm itching for it at this point. But Marc is also the last person in the world who I would want to have sex with. We work together, he's grumpy as sin, and he's probably a total softy in the sack. I like to be spanked here and there, and I'm not ashamed to admit it!

"Doubt it," I scoff. "But I'll do whatever I can to get a chance to ride that hot bologna pony."

"You're incorrigible."

"I'm horny, Pey."

"I can see that." She laughs.

I briefly glance down to my left hand where an engagement ring now glistens in the dim ballroom lights. It's the most beautiful piece of jewelry I have. Something I never pictured myself wearing.

I look back behind us and slowly start to scan the room. This place is extravagant. In the center of the ballroom there is the largest Christmas tree I have ever seen, besides the one in the center of New York, decorated with white and red twinkling lights. There is garland scattered everywhere while the hum of holiday music filters through the mix of people engaging in conversation.

My eyes finally land on my *fiancé,* who is talking it up with some older man. I have seen Marc in action at work, and he dominates every room he steps into. He means business especially when it comes to work. There is no denying that.

As if Marc can sense me staring, his head turns to the side and we make eye contact. He doesn't smile, but just stares at me. Giving me a look that could completely incinerate me from across the room. The room slowly starts to cave in on me as the heat from his gaze sends cold shivers down my spine. A mix of hot and cold, which is exactly what Marc is. Hot as hell with a cold personality.

Without wanting to, my mind wanders to the thought of him on top of me. Caging me in with his arms. Naked. Thrusting in and out of my soaking wet pu–... My thighs clench together in my seat at the thought of it, craving the small friction. *I would allow this man to break my back,* there's no doubt about it.

Suddenly, the whole *no panties* plan feels like it's backfiring on me.

His eyes travel up my body and stop when they land on my legs where I have them clenched together. *He knows*. I watch closely as his jaw hardens before he turns his eyes back to the conversation he was having.

"I have to go to the bathroom," I announce to Peyton as I hop off the barstool. "I'll be right back."

My eyes never go back to where Marc stands as I make my way across the room to the restrooms. Once inside, I lock the door behind me and take a deep breath. This is a wildly strange feeling for me because I do NOT allow men to have this effect on me. I can't, because then it leads to complicated shit and feelings that I absolutely want no part of.

Of all people, why does it have to be *Marc* making me feel like this right now.

While I filter through my thoughts, I decide to shoot Kali a quick text.

This was a terrible idea.

KALI

No it wasn't.

He can't stand having me around him.

KALI

The way he looked at you when he was here tells me otherwise.

I can't stand you.

KALI

I love you too.

I groan in frustration before I quickly give myself a once over in the mirror. As I step out of the bathroom, I see Marc waiting for me and looking as sexy as ever. His back is pressed against the wall. His suit jacket is unbuttoned, and he has one foot propped up behind him. Christ, he looks good.

"Marc." I blink. Heat rushes to my cheeks that I'm sure are now tinted pink and giving me away.

"Let's go." He pushes himself off the wall and comes over, stopping when he's standing directly in front of me. Our difference in height causes me to have to tilt my head up to maintain eye contact with him, being that I'm a whopping five foot four and he's a six foot one Adonis.

His hand finds the side of my neck and my body tenses from the unexpected contact. Without a doubt, he can feel my pounding pulse in his palm. His thumb gently strokes the apple of my cheek as he continues to stare into my eyes. His light brown, almost whiskey-colored eyes are making me feel dizzy and drunk, like I just downed a fifth. My hands grip his waist to steady myself from this uneasy feeling.

I close my eyes and suck in a deep breath. I actually think he's going to lean in and kiss me. Instead his lips brush my ear as he says, "we have to go meet Bill. Try to act like you're in love with me."

My eyes shoot open as I take a step out of his hold.

That wasn't at all what I was expecting him to say.

"You got it, boss man," I manage to choke out as I break eye contact.

He grabs my hand, interlocking his fingers in mine as we make way towards the main ballroom. Bill is standing there talking with a goofy looking dude. He looks like a total dickwad if I have ever seen one. I wonder if that's his competition for this little ruse.

"Ahh, look who showed up," the goofy looking dude mutters before taking a sip of his whiskey.

Marc smirks. "I've been here, Todd. I was on time for something, for once."

It's confirmed. Goofy looking dude is in fact Todd. The competition.

"Good evening, Marc." The older man extends his arm for a handshake with Marc. "Good to see you."

"Same to you, Bill." He lets Bill go and the same hand reaches behind me to land on the small of my back, which happens to be exposed from the open back dress I'm wearing. His featherlike touch sends shivers down my spine. "I would like you to meet my fiancé, Avery."

"I had no idea you were engaged." Todd grins. A smug grin like he's onto us within three seconds of standing here.

"I like to keep my personal life separate from my work life."

"It's nice to finally meet you, Bill." I've had enough of Todd's bullshit. "I have heard such great things about you." Marc grips my waist tighter at my remark. "How was your trip up from Florida?"

He nods. "It was a quick flight, but I already can't wait to get back to the warm weather. It's too cold up here for me."

"I understand that," I chuckle. "I am not made for the cold weather myself. Give me the sun, warmth, and a beach any day of the week."

"I absolutely agree with you, Avery." Bill laughs. "Are you originally from New York?"

"Would you believe I'm actually from Vermont? The cold weather should run in my blood with all the snow they get. Yet here I am, still not used to the snow or cold weather."

"Wow," Bill nods. "I love the mountains myself but can understand the cold being too much," he says before turning his direction back to Marc. "I'm pleased to meet your better half."

I feel Marc turn his head to look down at me, which causes me to tip my head up to him. He's putting on an excellent show of affection. I can see the adoration in his eyes that pairs perfectly with the smile on his face. He looks down at me with lust, like a proud fiancé would. His acting is so good that it's confusing me as to what's real and what's not. An uneasy feeling creeps into my gut as he pulls me in closer to his side and tightens his grip on my waist.

"I'm happy she's here," Marc adds.

"How did you two meet?" Todd asks.

"Well—" Marc begins but is cut off when Todd's phone starts ringing in his pocket. We are literally saved by the phone because this wasn't something we discussed. What is our story on how we met?

"I have to take this." He holds up his finger as if to say *hold that thought*.

"I should go check on my wife," Bill adds. "Enjoy the night, Marc. And it was lovely meeting you, Avery. I look forward to seeing you around more."

Marc interlocks his fingers with mine as we begin walking towards the bar. My body is buzzing with a mix of adrenaline and nerves.

"You were amazing, Avery." Marc smiles.

"I have to use the restroom," I announce, ignoring his praise. I realize I didn't actually use the restroom the first time I went. I have what I like to call a nervous bladder. Right now, that shit is acting up and I have to *GO*.

"Didn't you just go?" Marc chuckles.

"Yes. Sorry. I have to go again." I don't wait for his response before I beeline it to the restroom hallway again. Not only do I need to pee, but I need to catch my breath. I don't like these feelings that I can't control, and his swoon I can't escape.

Once inside, I do my business and find myself feeling the same way I did a little bit ago. Staring at myself in the mirror, figuring out a way to calm my erratic breaths. It's just Marc, I remind myself. He's the grumpiest of all grumps. This is all an act. It's all fake.

When I finish up and exit the restroom, it's like déjà vu seeing Marc standing right outside the door. Except this time, he has one arm holding himself up on the door frame and his head stares at the ground. He doesn't lift his head to speak and doesn't move from the position he's in. He's a brick wall that has me trapped in the doorway.

"What's going on in that head of yours, Avery?"

"That you're in my way, Marcus," I snap back, trying to ignore how hot the man standing in front of me is.

I take a step towards him, thinking that he will move out of my way but he doesn't. My body heats up as I stand inches away from him, so close that if I move any closer, my body will brush up against his. As if it happens in slow motion, he removes his hand from the door frame and rests it on the hollow of my neck. His thumb grazes my cheek again before his gaze meets mine.

"That's not what you're thinking," he says barely above a whisper. "Tell me what's going on in that pretty head of yours, Princess."

"You don't want to know what's going on in my head."

"Oh, but I do." The corner of his lip tips up.

I tilt my head up to meet his stare, and I watch his eyes turn from a light brown to gray. I bring my face as close to his as I can and feel him suck in a breath. He wants to play this game? Then I'll play along, and I'll play it better.

"I'll tell you exactly what I'm thinking," I taunt. "I'm thinking how I'm stuck here at this event with you, playing your game… when I could be somewhere else right now having someone rearrange my insides. I'm horny, Marcus." I take note that he has yet to release the breath he sucked in. "I'm doing this and quickly realizing that I'm getting nothing in return."

"What do you want?" he quickly interrupts my ramble.

I huff out loud before I pull myself out of his orbit. "Nothing that you can give me."

I sidestep him and begin to walk down the hall when a strong hand circles my wrist and pulls me back towards him. The force of the pull causes my body to collide with his. My hands instinctively land on his chest to brace myself. I feel nothing but rock-hard muscle beneath the palm of my hands.

"Just tonight," he says on a drawn-out exhale.

"Yes," I groan in frustration. "I'm only playing your fiancé for tonight."

He shoots me an award-winning smirk. "That's not what I mean, Avery." He pauses. Just before the grip on my waist tightens. "Just tonight. I will give you exactly what you need."

My heart races at the thought of him pleasing me the way I want. Desire courses through every single inch of my body. My nipples pebble under my dress, and my clit begins to throb. I want that, I really do. But can Marc give that to me?

"I'm not the girl who wants a soft fuck in the bathroom," I tell him.

Mentally, I know I can keep this a one night thing. I don't allow myself feelings for any man and sex certainly won't change that for me.

"Afraid you'll catch feelings for me?" he teases, as if he can sense my thoughts.

"If you haven't figured it out yet, I'm not looking to ride off into the sunset with you. I'm looking to be thrown around a little so I can wake up tomorrow feeling sated," I tease back, raising my chin to him with confidence.

His eyes bounce between both of mine before he leans into my ear, "Since you've been such a good girl… let me take care of your needs."

I suck in a breath, blinking at him as I consider what he's offering me.

I don't think about it long before I grab his wrist, dragging him down the hall to the first unlocked door I can find. Pushing him inside of it, I see a table sitting in the middle of the room. Probably the cleanest supply closet I've ever seen. I smile to myself while simultaneously shaking my head in disbelief at the universe being in my favor right now.

"I was thinking more along the lines of bringing you home with me," Marc says, while stuffing his hands in his pocket and laughing.

"No, here's what's going to happen…" I skate my hands

seductively from his wrists and up his arms and rest them on his chest before I continue. "You're going to hike this dress up." I start unbuttoning his suit jacket. "And you're going to bend me over this table and fuck me. Hard."

With one step forward, both of his hands cup the side of my face as if he's going to lean in to kiss me. But I quickly move my head to the side.

"No. No kissing." I press a finger to his lips. "That's not what this is."

"Enlighten me then, Avery. What is this?"

"This is just you scratching my itch." I shrug my shoulders. "You're simply returning the favor for me helping you out tonight."

I watch his eyes go from gray to black right in front of me. His hand finds my hips as he grips them forcefully and pulls my body flush with his where I feel his already hardened cock press into my stomach.

"It's cute that you think after I fuck you senseless that you won't come running back for more."

He presses his lips to the sensitive spot at the shell of my ear and my head tips to the side, allowing him full access to my neck. My hips press into him, craving any sort of friction as he continues to trail kisses along my bounding pulse, stopping when he reaches my collar bone.

"Do I have to keep repeating myself?" My body betrays me as I shiver under his touch. "You don't have to worry about me getting attached to this."

"We'll see about that," he says right before he spins me around. His hand grips the back of my neck, pushing me down on the table with a thud. He's rougher that I expected he would be, and that sends desire coursing through my body like a freight train.

"You liked that didn't you?" he asks. Removing his hand from my neck, he runs his knuckles along my spine until he reaches the curve of my ass. "Now, I know when I hike this tight little dress up, you'll be dripping wet for me. Won't you?"

I swallow as I try to control my already wild breaths. I can already feel that I am.

"Use your words. Tell me that your tight little pussy is craving this cock."

"Yes," I say with a hint of desperation in my voice.

He pulls my dress up and rests it over my lower back right before he takes a small step back. I feel cold air as he steps away, forcing me to turn my head to look at him over my shoulder. I watch as he runs his tongue along his bottom lip. His eyes meet mine, and my clit throbs in anticipation. My eyes never leave his as I arch my back to press my ass higher in the air. Swinging my hips side to side as if I'm putting on a little show for him.

"I don't even have to touch you. I can see you're soaked for me, Avery," he growls before he takes one step forward and within seconds, he has two fingers deep inside of me. I can't help the gasp that escapes my lips.

He doesn't go easy on me as he pumps me with one hand while the other wraps around my nape and grips my hair as he holds me in place. I already feel close to an orgasm, and it's definitely not his hand that I want right now.

"Fuuuck, yes," I pant.

"Ahhh, you like it rough. Don't you?"

"Marc," I beg. "I need you inside of me. Right now. I don't want to come anywhere but on your cock."

"Damn, Avery." I can hear the smile in his voice. "You're something else."

He removes his hands from me, and I tilt my head to the side as I watch him reach into his pocket and pull out a condom. I flip around and lean my elbows on the table as I fully take him in while he's unbuttoning his pants. My eyes widen as I watch his huge cock spring free. He's hard as steel as he rolls the condom on.

"Someone came prepared," I tease him. "Do you always have

those in your back pocket ready for a quick fuck in the supply closet?"

"You should know by now that I'm always prepared," he says back before he takes a step towards me and brings his hand to my throat. He forces my gaze up to him, and my eyes flutter closed from the intense feeling of him putting just the right amount of pressure against my neck that I *crave*.

His hand is still wrapped around my neck, and I am sure he can feel my rapid pulse under his touch. "If this is a one-time thing," he hovers so close to my mouth that I can taste his mint and spice infused breath on my lips. "You can guarantee I'm going to watch you as you come on my cock."

He lifts my dress, fully exposing me to him. My legs open without him having to ask, and I lean back on my hands. He takes one small step between my legs, lining himself up with my entrance before he swipes through me. Rubbing it up and down on my clit a few times, teasing me before he plunges into me full hilt.

"Fuuuuck," I cry out, my back arching from the fullness.

My hands claw at his flexed forearms gripping my hips so tight I'm sure I'll have a bruise tomorrow. I don't even care because I have never felt something so good.

"Jesus Christ, Avery." He throws his head back as he slowly thrusts in and out of me. "You feel better than I imagined."

"Move. Faster," I moan. "Harder."

He lets out a primal growl before his hand is on the base of my neck again, and he's pressing my body back down on the table. My legs wrap around his waist, heels digging into his back. I grab his forearm, ensuring that he keeps his hand wrapped around my neck.

"Harder, Marc," I scream out. "I can take it. Give it to me."

I watch as his eyes darken. "My girl is a dirty little slut, isn't she?"

My body tingles at him calling me *his girl*. I guess tonight, I am his girl. His *fiancé*.

His pace quickens as he does what I ask.

Fucking me relentlessly as my hands claw at his arm. The sound of slapping skin echo in the small space, mixed with loud breaths and moans of each other's name.

My eyes trail to where his body meets mine.

He smirks. "Look at you watching my cock disappear into this tight pussy. You're gripping me so fucking tight right now."

His pace slows as I hear a string of curse words come out of him and I can tell he's close and I'm seconds from seeing stars.

"Fuck. You're too perfect. I'm going to come if I don't slow down."

"Don't fucking stop," I whimper under him. "I'm—"

His pace halts, and I whimper. "If you want to come, ask nicely."

I buck my hips eagerly into him. Forcing his cock to bury deeper inside of me. Hitting the spot I am craving him to detonate.

"Please," I beg. "Please don't stop. Please let me come."

He thrusts hard into me. I can't help but scream out in pleasure while he fucks me harder and faster with each move. A mix of curse words on my tongue as I reach my peak.

"Come with me," he breathes out, the same time his hand moves to put pressure on my clit. "Come on my cock, Princess."

My body does as he asks. I come harder than I ever have in my life. My body convulses around him as I moan his name over and over again, and watch as his orgasm takes over his body at the same time. My name under his breath, so low I almost miss it.

There is nothing hotter than watching a man come.

Actually… there is nothing hotter than watching Marc Ford come.

His hands fall to the sides of my head as he falls on top of me. Both of us spent, our breathing out of control and neither of us wanting out of this bubble we've found ourselves in.

"Holy shit," he finally chokes out. Lifting his head so his eyes meet mine. "What the hell was that?"

I have to ask the same question.

Because… *what the hell was that?*

For someone who doesn't feel things, I sure just felt a lot.

There is a really good chance that I'm ruined.

CHAPTER FOUR

Marc

Six Months Later

Being a person with type A personality, Mondays are a mix of both anxiety and motivation. I love the start of a fresh week because it's a day to set new goals to conquer the week. But lately, it's been giving me more anxiety than anything. It's been six months since I saw my boss, Bill. He has yet to decide about who he is passing down Prestige Horizons to.

This is a huge deal for me because Prestige Horizons is one of the top real estate companies in New York. Our name is attached to hundreds—no, thousands—of buildings in the city.

Today, I'm on edge more than usual because Bill landed in New York for the summer. He and Todd are both coming here for a meeting. I haven't been in the same room with them since the charity event in December.

To top it off, Avery comes back to work today. She took a small leave of absence after Peyton's grandmother passed away. Everyone took her loss very hard. I wish I had gotten more of a chance to know her. From our trip to the shore house, I could tell she was an amazing woman and lived a fulfilling life surrounded by people who loved her.

Avery's leave was only supposed to be for a month, but right before she was scheduled to come back to the office, her mom called her after a terrible fall down an icy flight of stairs. Her mom ended up with a broken hip and fractured leg, which needed three surgeries to fix it. So, Avery's spent the last few months in Vermont taking care of her.

I needed the distance from her if I'm being honest. That night of the event, I lost control with her. We ended up having sex in the supply closet. If that's what you even want to call it, because if that was sex, then I've been doing it wrong all my life. The thought of her convulsing around me, the sound of my name falling from her lips, and the face she made when she lost control is permanently ingrained in my brain. There's no way I can replicate that feeling with anyone else.

Beyond that… the office feels different. It's quiet and sullen without her. She's got the personality that lights up any room she's in. I had hired a temporary assistant who was punctual and organized, but no one goes above and beyond the way Avery does. I found myself staring into her office space more times than I can count forgetting that she wasn't there. Making me question so much during our time apart.

I'm saved from my thoughts of her with a knock on the door.

"Hey you," Jessica says in her flirty tone she uses with me.

Jessica is one of my agents in the Manhattan office. She does *not* hide her attraction for me very well. She keeps it permanently painted on her face, along with the gallon of make-up she wears every day. She's a pretty girl, don't get me wrong. It's just that her eagerness to drop to her knees in front of me is just *too* much. I don't do desperate chicks. Especially the ones that I can tell are only after my money.

"What's up?" I reply with a flat tone. Yes, I'm a grumpy bastard at work.

"I have the reports from last week for you," she says in a playful tone. Then throws in a wink for good measure.

"You can email these to me, Jessica."

"I know." She pauses, fluttering her eyelashes. "But I thought I would see if you needed anything this morning with Bill and Todd coming in."

"No, thank you. Ms. Woods will take care of it when she gets in."

Her eyes travel to the other side of my office that has floor to ceiling glass doors connecting to Avery's office. As my firsthand assistant, her office is separated from mine with nothing but a glass wall, which offers neither of us privacy. Another reason I am thankful she took some time off.

"Looks like she's not here... yet again," she says that last part barely above a whisper and proceeds to roll her eyes.

"Is there a problem, Ms. Klein?"

"No, *sir*," she draws out the last word in a very seductive manner. It should make my cock twitch, but it doesn't when it comes from her lips.

"That's what—"

"I'm sorry I'm late, *sir*." Avery smirks from the doorway. Her hands are crossed over her chest as she leans on the frame.

Now, when it comes from *those* lips, it has my cock ready and standing at attention.

Every effort I have made to get this girl out of my head has gone out the window as I scan her from head to toe across the room. The first thing I notice is her long blonde hair and her natural beauty showing in her face. Almost like she decided on no make-up for today, which she most certainly doesn't need. She's wearing a tight pencil skirt, similar to the one she wore in her first interview. Her white button up blouse might as well be invisible, because I can see her black lace bra right through it.

The spunk has returned, that's for sure. She looks almost refreshed from her time off.

Deciding to look away from her before my face gives away my thoughts, I look to Jessica. "Anything else you need, Ms. Klein?"

"No, that was all." Her eyes bounce between Avery and me in question.

"Thank you for these reports. Next time, you can email them to me." I move to stand from my seat. "If you will allow us a moment, please. I have to get Ms. Woods caught up."

She nods and says nothing as she walks out of my office, closing the door behind her.

"She reeks of desperation." Avery laughs as she moves to take a seat at the chair across from my desk. "She wants what's in your pants so bad."

Wait... is she jealous? Or am I just imagining this right now?

"You're late." I ignore my own thoughts and her jab at Jessica.

"Actually." She grins. "I am right on time. I was just watching the show take place here in your office for a few minutes. Quite enjoyable might I add."

"Cute," I deadpan. "Listen, I have a big meeting today. Bill is flying in from Florida and Todd is coming into this office."

"Perfect." She rolls her eyes. "Happy first day back to me," she says sarcastically as her fingers squiggle in the air. "Is he going to finally tell you that you won this little game? It's a little ridiculous that he's taken so long."

"What's it matter to you? I haven't asked you to keep up the charade since that date."

"Thank God," she groans. "That night was excruciating."

I can't help the pained look that comes over my face or the fact that my eyes go wide. She doesn't miss it either, by the way her wide eyes match mine. The hottest sex of my life was excruciating to her. I sure hope she is talking about just playing her role as a fake fiancé, because that would mean that the chemistry I felt in that supply closet was one-sided.

"I didn't mean it like that." Her cheeks heat up and I watch as they turn a shade of light pink. "Acting like we were in love. That's what I meant." She moves to stand from her chair and points to where her desk is. "I will… uh… get to my desk. I have work to catch up on."

I'm silent as I watch her head to her desk. She walks away with her tail between her legs, not realizing the only thing separating us is a glass window.

Leaning back in my chair, I lift one leg and rest it on my thigh as I intertwine my fingers together under my chin. I don't know how long I am staring at her getting settled in her desk, but when she finally looks up, I can't help the shit-eating grin that covers my face.

Clearly, that night was not as excruciating as she claimed it was.

My lunch meeting with Bill and Todd was scheduled for eleven am. But it ended up being pushed to one in the afternoon, and I would be lying if I said that extra two hours waiting decreased any of my anxiety for this meeting. It only made it worse.

I like to think I'm ruthless in business meetings. It's why Thomas and I make such a good pair. Right now, all of my confidence flies out the window as I wait for Bill to deliver the final verdict.

The door to the boardroom swings open and Bill walks in with Todd not far behind. He's a lost puppy with a spot of brown on his nose from his head being so far up the boss's ass.

"Bill." I stand from my chair and meet him halfway. I extend my hand for a shake. "It's good to see you again. I take it you had a nice flight?"

"I did. Thank you."

Bill takes his normal seat at the head of the table.

"Todd," I greet him curtly.

"Marc," he greets me back in the same cold manner.

"Sit down," Bill says. His voice is in full business mode. "Let's get started. I want to take my wife to dinner tonight for some Italian. The Italian in Florida is not the same as it is up here."

"I agree with you," Todd says enthusiastically like he's trying to win brownie points. "Can I recommend anywhere for you two?"

"No. I'm from here, remember?" Bill laughs. Almost annoyed with him.

"Right." Todd nods.

"I called both of you here today to discuss the future of Prestige Horizon." His eyes bounce back and forth between Todd and me. "I started this business when I was just twenty-one years old, and it means a lot to me. As you know, I don't have children, which also means I don't have any grandchildren. There is no one in my direct family that I can pass this legacy down to. The decision I am making is strictly between the two of you. You both have been with me since graduating college and are my longest standing employees, which shows me your dedication to the company."

Todd and I show agreement as we take in what he is saying. I can feel the grip I have on my pen hardening and sweat forming on my palms as he continues.

"I know how you two work in the boardroom. You're both ruthless and dominate any sale that's put in front of you. You handle your employees with respect, which is why we have such a low turnover rate. However..." He pauses. "I don't know much about your personal lives."

Shit. I can feel the color begin to drain from my face.

"I want to learn about who you are outside of work. Family is a big deal to me. I want to know that the future of this company, that I built from the ground up, is in good hands and can eventually be passed down for generations to come. I don't want someone else to be in this position with no children or grandchildren to pass the legacy down, which is why I've decided to wait until the end of summer to make a final decision."

That does it right there. I know without a doubt I am white as a ghost as I take in what he's saying. He hasn't made a final decision because he wants to learn about our families.

"I know neither of you have children right now." He laughs. "So that isn't a factor in my decision. But I'm staying in the city and would like to spend some time with both of you outside of work. Basically what I'm saying is, I won't be in the office at all. I would actually like this to be my last time here. I am here strictly on a *vacation*." He uses air quotes as he says the word.

"That's great," Todd interjects. "I would love to have you and the wife over to the lake house one weekend. We can even take the boat out."

"That sounds great, Todd," Bill says before turning to me. "And how is wedding planning with Avery going? Would you two be able to fit in some time with Cathy and me this summer?"

I swallow the lump in my throat. "Yes, sir. We'd love to. We planned a long engagement. We didn't want to rush into anything so our schedule is wide open. We aren't getting married until next spring."

"Excellent." Bill beams.

"We're getting married this winter," Todd says without being asked.

"Okay," Bill says flatly. "We will touch base and figure some things out."

"Awesome." There's a little too much excitement in Todd's tone.

The three of us stand from our seats, shake hands and say our goodbyes before Bill and Todd exit the room. I'm eager to follow but my feet don't move from this spot in the boardroom.

I have to tell Avery that the deal is back on.

She is not going to like this one bit.

CHAPTER FIVE

Avery

You know that saying, *it's been a long week, but it's only Tuesday*? That's me today.

Yesterday was my first day back to work. At first, it was because I took some time off to be with Peyton. Gigi was like a second grandmother to me. Well, more like a first. Both of my grandparents died when I was a baby. All I have ever known in the form of a grandparent figure has been her. She adopted me into her life, and I was changed for the better.

Of course, right before I was scheduled to come back to work, my mom fell on some ice and broke her hip. Marc was nice enough to let me take some more time off so I could spend it in Vermont with her while she recovered.

Now here I am, back in the city and back at work. Don't take that the wrong way, I love my job, and I actually love working. It's because of my personality that my bosses have never walked all over me as an assistant. I am no one's coffee bitch. The work I do as an assistant is meaningful and helpful. My obsession with organization has been one of the highest praises from past employers. Marc knows this. I will not fetch your dry cleaning, but I will do things in the office that help you with business like keeping records in order and having contracts ready to go.

However, being in close quarters with Marc has me wound up tighter than an Olympian's spandex. He's the only man that has crossed my path who has the potential to melt my icy heart. It's *definitely* not love. I'm not sure what it is, and it freaks me the hell out. I'm calling it physical attraction because I get these weird butterflies in my stomach when he's around. I just don't get it, *why him?*

My phone buzzing in my purse pulls me out of my thoughts. I look down and see its Dean. We met before I left for Vermont. Everything with him has just been casual. They say the best way to get over a guy is to get under another. That's all that Dean was supposed to be. When I returned back, he was adamant on getting together more often.

"Hey, Dean."

"Hey, babe. Good morning." He sounds way too damn chipper for this early in the morning.

"Morning."

Why Dean sticks around is beyond me because I'm really not that nice. The sex is mediocre at best, good enough to hold me over. But there is nothing exclusive about us. It drives me crazy because I have made it *very* clear countless times. He claims the whole calling me 'babe' thing can work for friends with benefits. Never in my life has a casual hook up called me that.

If I were a normal person, Dean would be up high on the list as my type. Not quite a top spot contender, but he's up there. He's a true Prince Charming, he's caring and treats women with respect. He's also good looking, has washboard abs, and a stable job. He has a lot of boxes checked on the pro side. The con side, however, has just as many. He's blonde... which isn't my ideal type. They just don't do it for me. Give me tall, dark haired, and handsome. I can't even wear heels around the guy and that bothers me more than I care to admit. The biggest nail in the coffin is that the man chews like a cow. I don't want to see *or* hear your food being crunched around in your mouth.

These make me picky and shallow, don't they? But listen, if a girl is going to give in and give a *real* relationship a try for the first time in her life, she needs to be picky.

"How did you sleep last night?" His question cuts though my rambling thoughts.

"Fine," I say, just as I push open the car door to head into the office.

"That's good." I can feel the smile on his lips through the phone and that just annoys me. Clearly this is a one-sided thing.

"Listen, I'm heading into the office."

"Wait, really quick," he stops me. "Are you free for dinner tonight?"

I sigh. "I can't tonight. I'm hanging out with the girls," I tell him, which is a partial lie. It's just me and Kali like it always is every night.

"One of these days, I will get you to agree to an official date with me."

"We will see," I laugh. "I'll talk to you soon."

"Talk so—" he starts before I end the call just as I step foot into the building.

After I grab a coffee from the cart in the downstairs lobby, I make my way to my office. Marc's door is open so I can see that he's here already which is unlike him to be this early.

Stepping into the office, all the air leaves my lungs as I see Marc again. Remember those checkboxes? I am pretty sure all of Marcs are on the pro side of perfect boyfriend material. He can keep up with my back-and-forth banter. I know, for a fact, that he's the sweetest guy under his grumpy exterior because I have seen the way he is with the people he cares about. He's tall, with perfect dark hair I can comb my fingers through and he's handsome as hell. There is no denying that. To top it off, I know what he's like when he has sex. It's explosive. It's dominant. It's dirty. It's *everything*.

"Good morning, Avery." He smiles at me as I continue to stand in the doorway. "Are you going to come in? Or are you going to stand there all day?"

"Thinking I might stand here all day." I let out the breath I was holding before I make my way into the room.

Part of my routine when I come into work is that I stop at his desk before I even head to mine to put anything down. I get a quick rundown of the day, what meetings are scheduled and priority tasks I have to complete. It's something we started when I first began working here and it works well for us.

Placing my coffee on the desk and my bag on the floor, I take a seat in the chair in front of his desk. My eyes meet his. He looks a tad bit distraught this morning. His scowl is deeper than it normally is, and he has his fingers interlocked under his chin as if he's deep in thought.

"You look like your cat ran away, Marc."

"I'm more of a dog guy," he responds. No hint of joking in his tone.

"Noted."

"I'm going to cut to the chase." He leans forward, resting his elbows on the desk. His eyes never leave mine. "We need to talk."

I nod and swallow the lump in my throat at his serious tone. My eyes scan his face to assess his features. They are mixed with panic and worry. His eyes are heavy like he hasn't slept much in the last twenty-four hours. I can tell whatever it is, it has been bothering him all night long.

"As you know, Bill flew in yesterday and I had a meeting with him and Todd in the afternoon." He pauses. His eyes bounce between mine before he continues. "He and his wife are spending the summer here in the city."

"This is the last place I would want to vacation for the summer," I huff. My attempt to ease some of whatever tension he's got going on.

"He's only partially here for a vacation," he says with the most serious expression on his face. "He's really here for the summer because he still has not made a decision about who he's going to hand the company keys over to."

I don't like where this is going.

"I hate to put you in this position, Avery. I know you do a lot around here to help me out as it is. You're probably the best assistant I have ever had." He offers me a small smile. "But… I need to ask you if you would consider being my fiancé again."

"What?" I practically scream as I stand up from my chair.

"I know, Ave." He winces as he stands just as fast as I did and strides around his desk to stand in front of me. His hands lightly grip my biceps as he stares at me before continuing. "Trust me, I want to do this as much as you do. But this company means everything to me. Taking over Prestige Horizons, would mean the entire world to me. It's the only thing in my life that hasn't tried to break me down."

I am silent, my mouth still open in shock.

The only thing that hasn't tried to break him down? I want to know more about that, but I don't want to open that can of worms right now.

"This was supposed to be a one-night thing, Marc." I shake my head as I release myself from the hold he has on my arms. "I can't play your fiancé for *months*."

"Why not?"

"Marc…" I groan. "I just can't. There is no way we can convince him. We did fine the first night thanks to some champagne confidence and a room full of people. There's no way we can pull this off because we are two totally different people. You're used to this lifestyle." My voice grows louder with each word I spit out. "Besides, what if I'm seeing someone?"

"Are you… seeing someone?"

Shit. If you asked Dean this question, his answer would be that he's seeing someone exclusively. I wouldn't call us boyfriend and girlfriend but I'm not out with other guys either.

"Yes," I decide to answer. "It's nothing serious, but yes, I am seeing someone."

"How long?"

"Not long. It's new."

"You need to break it off with him."

"Excuse me?" I snap. "You can't tell me what to do and just order me to break up with the guy when I didn't even agree to this."

"You just said it wasn't serious." He grins.

"Marc…" I pinch my eyebrows together, and my hands land on my hips.

"I'm desperate, Ave. Whatever you want, consider it yours. It's only until the end of the summer because Bill promised a decision by then. Besides, he seems to think we're still planning our wedding."

"That would have been a good time to tell him that we called it off. You know, make something up."

"Yeah, because that would *really* make him want to pass the company to me," he scoffs and adds an eye roll for extra measure.

I'm stunned speechless for the first time in my life. I am not the girl who is ever speechless. In fact, I am the girl who always has a lot to say and a quick come back for everything. *Dammit, Marc.*

"Here's what's going to happen, Marcus." I take one step towards him with my hands still glued to my hips. "I'm going to walk my ass into that little box of windows over there, sit at my desk and finish my work for the day like the good little assistant I am. Then I'll think about this. I mean, *really* think about this because it's a lot to ask—"

"I know, Ave. I am so sorry to have to put you in this position. But—"

"Don't cut me off." I raise a finger. "I will think about this and decide by tomorrow morning when I come in. Got it?"

"Yes," he sighs. "But I hope you say yes."

I don't say anything back to him as I grab my bag and walk over to my desk to get my work done for the day. Once I'm settled, I decide to shoot a quick text to the girls.

SOS. Old Jose for dinner tonight.

KALI

Duh. It's Tuesday.

PEYTON

I can meet up tonight.

We're going to need margaritas with a side of tequila shots.

KALI

Oh boy...

My boss has lost his mind.

PEYTON

I can't wait to hear this one...

The day dragged on slower than usual. Marc had back-to-back meetings and then had to oversee a project downtown, so our paths didn't cross before I left the office for the day.

I headed straight for Old Jose. When Peyton moved to the city, we made it our weekly thing to get together for girls' night. What better day than Tuesday right? We quickly learned that tacos help solve all our problems.

Peyton had already texted us that she was running a few minutes late. With her living outside of the city now, sometimes it takes a little longer for her to get in with traffic.

I gasp when I see Kali sitting at our usual booth, I almost didn't recognize her.

"Kali! Your hair!"

"Do you like it?" She smiles and twirls her loose curls around in her fingers.

She must have had her hair done today while I was at work. This morning it was a light brown and tonight, it's a bright, coppery-orange shade. It's literally the most perfect shade for her.

"I freakin love it." I beam. "It's the perfect color for you."

"Thank you," she says confidently. "This was the first time in my life where I dyed my hair red and it *wasn't* because I was having a mental breakdown. Every time in high school or college if the hair was red… it was because I was unwell."

I can't help but laugh. "Peyton is going to lose her shit. In the best way possible of course."

As soon as the words leave my mouth, Peyton comes walking into the restaurant.

"Kali Peterson!" she shrieks. "I didn't think you would do it, but you did! I AM OBSESSED!"

Kali places a hand on her stomach and gives a little bow from her seat like she's done good.

"You can totally pass as the muse for the main character of that cowboy romance I just finished and passed down to you. Your personality totally matches hers too."

"I take that as a compliment," Kali chuckles from her seat. "Now that we're all here. Avery, what was with the SOS text earlier today."

I groan as I fall back in my seat.

"This morning when I walked into the office, Marc was in a total mood. No joke, it looked like his fucking cat ran away," I huff. "But he doesn't have a cat."

"Clearly," Peyton pipes up. "He's a dog guy."

"I know that now. But his problem was that his boss Bill is *vacationing* here this summer," I say using air quotes to emphasize that it's indeed not a vacation. "And said boss, has not made a decision about the future of Prestige Horizons."

"Oh Christ." Kali shakes her head. "I see where this is going."

As soon as the words leave her mouth, the waiter arrives with our margaritas that Kali had ordered for us.

"Perfect timing for the best part." I pause for dramatic effect because, why not? And take a long sip of the tequila infused beverage. "He's asked me to play the role of his fake fiancé for the entire summer."

"Shit." Peyton sighs. "I saw that coming."

"What do you mean?"

"Thomas met up with Marc for a late lunch yesterday after his meeting." She sighs. "He said something about how Marc was going through some shit in his head with having to let you know the arrangement would have to be back on."

I feel a pinch in my chest hearing that. Which is oddly strange because normally I just don't care. But I remember the look on his face when I walked into the office this morning. He was clearly beside himself with worry. I have known from day one as his assistant, that this job means the world to him.

"I don't know what to do if I'm being honest," I admit while shaking my head. "I know Marc and I have this strange relationship packed with sarcasm and the fact we can't stand each other because we are polar opposites… it's just who we are." I shrug. "But faking an entire relationship?"

"Your feelings are totally valid," Kali chimes in.

"And to add… I've been seeing Dean casually," I laugh. "I mean I'm pretty sure he thinks we are exclusive. Which would be news to me."

"You've done casual things before and ended it amicably. This won't be any different." Kali shrugs.

"*And* not to sound like I need something out of this… but what do I get out of this arrangement? I have to put my dating life on hold—"

"You don't date," Peyton cuts me off. "So, scratch that from the record."

"You know what I mean," I groan. "I am putting my life on hold for him. He's asking me for the entire summer to basically be at his beck and call. That's a lot to ask of someone. You know?"

"Oh, I know," Kali says matter of factly. "We totally get that, girlfriend. But what if… you figured out something that would benefit you both mutually?"

"It can't be sex," I add quickly. "That would be a double benefit for him. It's like getting the cake and eating it too."

"Hear me out here." Kali sits up higher in her seat as if she's ready to propose the best idea she has ever had. "I know you love being an assistant for him. You love your job because you have this sick obsession with keeping things organized. Which we love about you," she adds to not hurt my feelings. "You have mentioned a couple times in the past about wanting to get into real estate yourself."

"That will never happen. I can't stand school or the thought of spending the money on it. That's why I skipped college."

"It's not an actual school." She shakes her head. "It's a course you have to take. What if, in return, you ask him to send you to this real estate course. This way you get something out of it, *and* also a chance to excel in your career."

"I agree with Kali," Peyton says. "You have the personality for being an agent. I've said that all along. Don't get me wrong—you're an incredible assistant and anyone is lucky as shit to have your psycho organizational skills on their team. But imagine your skills, paired with being an agent? You'd kill it out there."

It's been so long since I mentioned that to anyone. It's not that I ever gave up on my dream of wanting to get into real estate, but like Kali said, I truly love my job. I have never been the type to set out to climb any corporate ladders and shit. I was raised to be proud of my work. Why do people have to add more titles to their name, go to more schooling, or whatever the hell people have to do to advance in life?

I'm sick of the "I find it hard to believe she's twenty-seven years old and hasn't advanced her career" speeches I hear so often on social networks about people who choose to do what they do. Why can't people be happy where they are in life? I'm twenty-seven years old and have never been happier with where I am in life.

I look at my best friend for example. Peyton had a tough run when her parents died. She worked in a daycare center where she barely made ends meet. She *loves* kids though. That's just what she wanted to do with her life in some way, shape, or form. That's why she took on a nanny role in the city because it's what she *wanted* to do.

This makes me think of my mom and how she raised me all on her own. Once my dad walked out on us, she was forced to get a job after being a stay-at-home mom for years so that she could raise me. She was lucky to be able to get a manager position at the local supermarket. It wasn't much because we lived in a small college town in upstate Vermont. But you know what? She was happy. Which in turn, made me happy.

"I like your idea. I really do," I say with conviction. "But... doesn't that seem weird to ask him for something monetary in return for being his fake fiancé for the summer? This is me asking him to *pay* for me to take a real estate agent course. I feel like that's a lot."

"You don't think that him asking you to give up your life for the summer is a lot?"

"No, you're right."

"I think it's something you should consider," Kali says.

"Those Ford brothers have all the money in the world." Peyton laughs. "A little real estate course would be pocket change for him. I think you could totally do this."

"What makes you so confident about that?"

"There're no real strings attached. When the deal is done, it's done."

She's got a point.

It's definitely something I can walk away from with no problem.

CHAPTER SIX

Marc

About 48 hours have passed since Avery has been back to work and she's consuming my thoughts more than she fucking should.

It really boils down to the fact that I want this deal to work out in the worst way possible. I meant it when I told her that Prestige Horizons means everything to me. I started here when I graduated college with a business degree. I immediately dove into a real estate class where I worked my way up the ladder.

I had trouble sleeping last night because I fought every urge to send her a text to see what was going through her head. Playing everything over forced thoughts of my one serious relationship into the forefront of my brain. It's something I never wanted to think about again.

My longest, most serious, relationship lasted about six years. I truly believed I was going to marry her. I *thought* I loved her. For as long as I can remember, I've known I wanted a wife and a big house filled with a couple kids. Probably because I was a total mama's boy. I wanted all of it. But Becky burned me. The night of my graduation from my master's program, I found her with someone else.

Have you ever looked back and replayed pivotal moments in

your life and thought about all the things you wish you said or wish you did? That's me whenever these thoughts creep back into my mind. I remember so vividly opening the door to her apartment and seeing her riding the dude on the couch like she was a champion rodeo rider. She was screaming his name and moaning so loudly that she hadn't even heard me come in. My mouth hung open as I stared at the two of them. She finally met my gaze right before I stormed back out the door I came in from, slamming it behind me. She tried to run after me, but the elevator door was closing before she could catch up with her bullshit apologies.

She tried to call me for weeks afterwards, assumingly to make things work. I ignored every single phone call. The reality of it was, I know my worth and what I bring to the table. She didn't deserve a second of my time listening to her explain how his dick ended up inside of her.

After that, I realized that I don't even know what true love is. But I know someday, I'll find it with a woman that I deserve and that deserves me. I'll find someone who will break down the walls I put up, the walls that Becky caused me to put up in the first place.

When I finally forced myself out of bed around five in the morning, I decided to run on the treadmill at the gym I had built in my penthouse. I swear I've never run so hard in my life trying to sweat out the stress of this whole ordeal and the past creeping back into my thoughts.

This morning when Avery came into work, I decided not to push the subject. We did our normal rundown of the day before she retreated into her office to get her work done. I can tell that the wheels in her head were still spinning trying to figure out if she's going to say yes to the deal or not. Or at least, maybe it was just me hoping she's thinking about it.

I wish I knew what she wanted so I could offer her something, anything, for helping me with this. I decide to shoot her a text even though she is sitting at her desk right near me.

Have you given any consideration to helping me out?

I keep my head down, facing my phone but lift my eyes to watch her through the glass walls. Her phone chimes on her desk, and she stops what she's typing to look at it. She doesn't lift her head to look at me and does an exceptional job at keeping a poker face as she types back.

AVERY

I've been thinking about it.

Can you elaborate on that?

AVERY

It means the organ inside my skull called the brain has been considering it but hasn't made a decision yet. 🙄

You have to know that this is a lot to ask of me. Pretending to be your fiancé for one event wasn't a big deal, but now you're asking me to fake a relationship for the entire summer.

She's right. Dammit, she's so right. I am such a dick to not think about how this is a lot to ask and how this would affect her life. She would be giving up her summer of doing whatever she normally does, with whomever she normally does it with… for me.

But I would be a lying son of a bitch if I said the thought of her doing whatever with whoever doesn't have the temperature of my blood rising with jealousy. I haven't been with anyone since Avery. I don't do casual hookups, like Oliver and Logan. That night with her in the supply closet was outside of the norm for me.

I know. You're right.

If you consider it... I'll give you whatever you want, Avery.

AVERY

About that...

I don't waste another second after her text hits my phone before I am out of my chair and storming into Avery's office.

"Name it, Avery," I tell her. "Whatever you want. It's yours."

She looks up at me with a shocked look on her face that quickly morphs into a smirk. She leans back in her office chair while she crosses her leg over the other.

"So... I've been looking at this building—"

"Done," I cut her off.

"You didn't even hear the rest of it, you wack job," she snorts.

"I don't need to."

"Let me get this straight," she sits up straighter. "You just want to give me some two hundred story building across town that is probably worth millions of dollars to play this game for the summer?"

"First of all, there are no buildings in the city that are two hundred stories high." That earns me an eye roll. "Second of all, if that's what it takes to make you say yes, then I would find someone to build you one tomorrow." I shrug my shoulders.

"You've completely lost your mind!"

"Avery." I scowl.

"Okay, Marc." She sighs. "Relax. I will do this for you... under one condition." I feel my shoulders relax and the stress from the last couple of days starts to drift away just hearing the words slip from her tongue. "I have a favor of sorts. Something you can help me with while I help you this summer."

"What do you need?"

"I would like to take a course so I can obtain my real estate license."

I feel my head whip back and my eyebrows pinch together at her confession. This *can't* be all she's asking for out of the deal. I had no clue that she ever wanted to become an agent or that it was ever part of her future plans.

"You want to become an agent?" I gape at her, surprised by her admission.

"It's not something I ever *dreamed* of, or anything. But lately… I have been thinking about it more and more since working here. I just can't stand school and all that bullshit. That's why I have never pursued it," she admits. "But… if you're willing to help me, then I think this can work."

I can't help the grin that forms on my lips as it takes over my face. There is no denying that Avery can read everything I am feeling right now. Relief mixed with appreciation.

"What does the building have to do with this though?"

"Oh, that." She throws her head back and laughs uncontrollably. "You know how many millionaire theme books I've read where the guy just buys the girl buildings? Don't answer that. I'll tell you… the answer is a whole damn lot of them. I just wanted to see what your reaction would be." She slows down her laughing and changes to a more serious tone. "Don't even think about it. I don't want a building."

"Lucky for you… I'm a billionaire." I wink.

"Cute." She shoots me a cheeky grin.

We both laugh for a moment as some of the tension between us slips away.

"I will set you up with the same course I took, if that works for you."

I cross the room until I am standing inches away from her. I take a minute to really take in her features. Her light blonde hair flows freely over her shoulders and her light blue eyes twinkle under the fluorescent office lighting. Avery truly is one of the most beautiful women I have ever seen. I've known this since the first day she stepped into my office, but being this close to her has my heart pounding in my chest.

I gently tuck a strand of her hair behind her ear, and I can hear her breath hitch at my touch while her shoulders stiffen.

Slowly, I lean in to whisper in her ear, "Did you break up with your boyfriend?"

She gasps before she takes a step back away from me and rounds her desk to sit back in her chair. "No, Marcus," she says, annoyed. "First of all, he was never my boyfriend. I've just been seeing Dean casually."

"Dean? What a stupid name," I say to which she rolls her eyes.

"And I planned to cut ties with him soon, anyway. He's a little... clingy."

"Well..." I can't help the smile that forms again. "So we're really doing this, Avery? You're going to help me out here?"

"I'll do this for you. But we have to lay down some rules here."

Knowing Avery and how she functions, I am willing to bet that this list of rules is longer than a CVS receipt. And it's probably handwritten and color coded.

I move to take a seat in the chair on the opposite side of her desk. I can't help but watch Avery as she moves her chair closer to her desk, leans on her elbows and stares at me intently. Avery exudes confidence and thinking back to her idea to become a real estate agent, I can see it being an ideal career choice for her. I would bet every dollar to my name that she would dominate a board room and close any sale that's placed in front of her.

She has this wildfire inside of her. My dick should not find that so appealing.

"You look good behind that desk."

"Nope. I know where this is going. Not happening." She waves me off before putting her fingers in her ears. "Blah blah."

"You didn't even know what I was gonna say." I can't help the child-like laughter that comes out of me. She totally knew where I wanted to go with that.

"You were going to say, '*but you would look better on top of it.*'" Bingo. She caught me. "And the smug grin on your face tells me I'm right."

"You're wrong..." My eyes scan her briefly. "But now I'm *definitely* thinking about that."

Her cheeks turn a shade of red right before she shoots me a scowl that screams, *I'm going to chop your balls off.*

"Alright, alright. Back to your rules. Let's hear them."

"I have a couple of ground rules that I've been thinking about," she starts, holding her pointer finger in the air. "The first one is the biggest. Absolutely *no* kissing."

"How do you expect we sell the fact that we're in love if we never kiss?"

"Simple," she retorts. "How often do you see couples making out in public? Don't answer that. It's hardly ever. If you ever see a couple making out in public, it is probably because they're drunk or in that honeymoon stage I hear so much about."

Touché.

"If you feel so inclined to show any sort of public display of affection, a simple kiss on the cheek or on the forehead will work."

"I can work with that." I nod. "Anything else?"

"Yes. Another big one," she adds with a grin, holding up two fingers. "No seeing other people."

I almost feel anger bubble up inside of me. Is that the kind of guy she thinks I am? Does she think I would ask her to be my fiancé while seeing someone else? I know my brother Thomas used to be like that. So *maybe* I can see her thinking like that from conversations with Peyton. My youngest brother Oliver is definitely like that. But me? Absolutely not.

Not to mention... I haven't been with anyone else since her.

But I am not about to admit that to her.

"I'm not that type of guy, Ave," I say as I shake my head. "When I'm in, I'm all in. When you're mine, you're all mine. There will be no one else." Her mouth is slightly parted at my words before I continue. "That goes for you as well. You see no one else during this arrangement."

I stare intently at her and watch as she swallows what I

assume is a lump in her throat. I can feel my body tense up as I prepare for what she might say to that.

"There will be no one else, Marc."

"Great." I relax as I stand from the seat. "Saturday night, we're going out."

"What do you mean?"

"I'm taking you out on a practice date." I wink and my body instinctively moves closer to where she is now standing behind her desk. "It's a good opportunity for us to learn a little more about each other, get our story down and make sure we're good to go before we do anything in front of Bill."

"Right," she huffs out with a laugh. "I guess we do need to make sure we have our ducks in a row."

"Speaking of ducks… Is there any chance you still have the ring I gave you?"

She offers me a smile. "I do."

The thoughts of her still having that ring send my heart rate up. I don't respond back because I can't find the words I should say back to that. I simply send her a wink before I retreat out of her office. As soon as I am crossing the doorway, I hear her call out my name.

"Marcus," she says. "One more thing."

Slowly I turn from where I'm standing and my gaze locks with hers.

"Don't fall in love with me."

Any words I had to say back to that are out the window. All I can do is stare at her.

This entire situation might be my idea.

But she is certainly the one in control here.

There's no doubt in my mind that I am going to need to keep my head on straight with Avery Woods.

CHAPTER SEVEN
Avery

"I could use a fucking drink," I mutter.

"It's not even two in the after—"

I shoot Kali a look before she can finish that sentence. I have *never* in my life been on edge the way I have been this week. If I really stop to think about it, there is absolutely no reason for me to feel like this because Marc isn't acting any different.

It's most definitely the idea of this whole thing.

Marc and I have our first official 'date' tonight. Deep down, I know I can rock this fake fiancé shit. On the surface it's hard to ignore how my body reacts to him when he's close. My heart rate seems to pick up speed, and my body tingles with… *desire* for him to touch me again. Something I have never felt with another guy before. It makes me feel insanely uneasy.

"Oh! You have that date tonight with my brother!" Emiline exclaims.

Emiline is the youngest of the Ford siblings. She's only twenty-two years old, but she acts mature for her age. She's even the youngest student in her accelerated nursing program and on track to being top of the class. The day Peyton introduced her to us, it's like we instantly became best friends because she fits in so perfectly with our little girl gang.

I let out an aggravated groan. "Don't remind me. I am looking forward to this the way I look forward to my monthly visits from Aunt Flo. And you know she's a bitch to me every time she visits."

"Oh, we know," Kali and Emiline say in unison.

"Hey! You two just be thankful that Aunt Flo isn't as mean to you. I wouldn't wish those cramps on my worst enemy."

Kali laughs. "Why do you think we leave you alone that week?"

"Yeah, yeah." I roll my eyes. "In summary... I am not looking forward to this."

"Why are you two even going on a date?" Emiline asks. "Is this a meeting with his boss?"

"No." I shake my head. "He wants to go out and get to know each other more, get our story right and you know, make sure this works."

"I mean..." Kali pauses. "It's a little late to decide if it's going to work, isn't it? The boss already thinks you two are getting married. He can't just show up with a new fiancé for the summer."

"You're kind of locked in regardless," Emiline adds.

The conversation is interrupted when my phone chimes with a text message on the kitchen counter.

DEAN

Whatcha up to, Sweet Cheeks?

"It's Dean," I huff.

"You haven't broken it off with him yet?" Kali asks.

"Truth be told... I've been avoiding him." I snort. "How the hell do you break up with someone when you weren't even official to begin with?"

I actually haven't spoken to Dean since the morning he called me on my way to work. This is my defense mechanism to avoid confrontation. I avoid and avoid until eventually they take the hint and just stop contacting me all together. Is it wrong? Sure.

Do I give a shit? Never. They know my stance on not making things serious when we first start.

"It's funny if you think about it. I have no filter and give no shit what comes out of my mouth. But I can't *break-up* with a guy to save my life."

"That's normal." Kali shrugs. "You don't like the cry-baby shit. I've only met Dean a couple of times, but I can tell that he would be the whiny type of guy who doesn't want things to end."

"*That* would make you uncomfortable," Emiline adds. "For the sake of argument here, I never saw that going anywhere to begin with."

"How come?"

"Because you don't need soft. You don't need sensitive." She sits up straighter in her seat and flexes an arm muscle. "You need masculine. You need someone who matches your attitude and gives it right back to you."

"I don't have an attitude," I snap.

"Attitude is the wrong word," Kali cuts in. "You're strong-willed. You're not afraid to share those wild thoughts in your head, regardless of what others think. You respect yourself enough to stand up for yourself. Which you definitely learned from your mom growing up."

"You don't like to be coddled either." Emiline laughs.

The girls are *not* wrong here. Could that be the reason I never let any guys close? It can't be. I know deep down my dating issues stem from my childhood. It's definitely daddy issues and the fact that I was raised by the same exact woman they describe me as.

"That's why my brother couldn't be a more perfect fake fiancé for you."

"Right," I scoff. "I have no doubt that Marc can handle my shit. He does every day at work. But I can also read him like a book. Deep down, he wants romance and a happy ending."

"You're good at the happy ending." Kali winks in her seat.

"We are *not* fucking going there."

"Stooppp it," Kali drags out the word. "You've already had his dick inside of you and you have been weird around him ever since."

"First of all." Emiline makes a grossed out face. "I don't want to know who, what or where my brother sticks his dick. Seriously gross." She shivers in her seat with disgust. "Secondly, you both certainly have been odd around each other. I have to agree with Kali here."

I throw myself back on the couch as I tip my head to the ceiling. Has it been that obvious? No fucking way.

"Is it really that obvious?"

"Yes," both girls say in unison.

"Dammit," I mumble under my breath. "This is exactly why this won't work out in his favor. Em cover your ears," I say to her before I look back at Kali. "You have no idea how hot that night was. He's the exact kind of dominant and dirty man that I like."

"You gave me no time to cover my ears and now this might be my cue to go."

"Don't leave me," I plead as I throw my hands together in prayer. "You can't leave your fake future sister-in-law hanging like this. Besides we know you're into kinky shit. You basically admitted during that card game on our trip to the shore that you want to be tied up."

"Now that you bring that up," Kali chimes in directing her attention to Emiline. "Was it just me or was I feeling some sort of sexual tension between you and Logan."

"I felt that shit," I nod repeatedly. "Isn't he old?"

"God no. He just turned thirty. That's only eight years older than me."

"Is this you admitting *something*?"

"No. Absolutely not." She shakes her head. "He's my brother's best friend. Not just any brother... my oldest brother. We grew up together, so I've known him for like ever. Besides, he's a cop. You know what they say about cops."

"That they like handcuffing in the bedroom?" I wiggle my eyebrows.

Emiline wrinkles her face. "Ew. No. It's that they all cheat!"

"Not all cops cheat on their spouse, Em," Kali says. "Totally an inaccurate stereotype."

"I agree. The small town I grew up in, everyone knew everyone. I knew dozens and dozens of cops there. Not a single one ever cheated on their wife or girlfriend. That shit would have been the talk of the town, if any of them had."

"And Logan doesn't seem like the type," Kali adds.

"You two clearly don't know him the way I know him." She snorts. "Logan is the biggest playboy there is. I don't think I have ever seen him with the same girl more than once. Tommy will tell you the same thing. Even *he* thinks his friend is a playboy."

"Well, shit." I do a little dance in my seat. "I picked the wrong man for this situationship."

Emiline barks out a laugh. "You have lost your damn mind. Situationship?"

"Girl, I lost my mind when I agreed to be the future wife of your brother," I huff out a sarcastic laugh. "And yes. It's not a relationship... It's a situationship. Now help me figure out what I am wearing tonight. And while we're at it, someone help me break up with Dean."

Kali swipes my phone from the kitchen counter and begins texting a mile a minute with a smug grin on her face.

"There. Done," she says as she places the phone back on the counter.

I shake my head at her as I pick up the phone to see what she sent to him.

I'm just hanging out with the girls.

Hey listen... I think it's best if we don't see each other anymore. I have a lot on my plate for the summer with work and I think it's best if I just focus on that for the time being. You're a great guy and I don't want to string you along.

"Oh my gosh, Kali!" I bellow. "I can't believe you just said that."

"What?" She raises her hands in the air defensively. "That's how you take care of it. You guys aren't even official. Relax will ya."

My phone dings almost immediately.

DEAN

You're seriously breaking up with me via text message?

I raise my phone to show Kali the text. All she does is grin and shrug a shoulder.

"He'll be over it by tomorrow. Now let's find you something to wear."

Over the next few hours, we blast our favorite 90's hip hop station while we dance around the apartment. I love these girls with every fiber of my being. Kali, Emiline, and Peyton, even though she isn't here right now, they just have a way of making anyone feel better. Thomas coming back into Peyton's life brought Emiline to us and she's been the perfect addition to our friend group.

That's the thing about our girl gang, when one person is having weird feelings about something – whether it's good or bad – we just blast some music and dance it out. Probably something we picked up from our years of binge-watching *Grey's Anatomy* on repeat.

I don't know jack shit about dating, what to wear or how to approach this. Thankfully, Kali lives in a romance world with Peyton, and she knew exactly what I should wear tonight. We settled on the standard *little black dress.* It's got spaghetti straps and reaches mid-thigh with a little bit of flow to it. Really, it would be a great dancing dress for a night out.

I opt to pull my hair back into a slick ponytail. I can't stand when my hair dangles in my face, so it's my favorite hairstyle. Paired with a set of stud diamond earrings and it's a perfect dressed up look.

Just as I sit down on the kitchen stool to slip on a pair of black heels, I hear Kali shuffle into the kitchen with a low whistle.

"Damn, Ave." She winks as she grabs two wine glasses. "You look fucking hot."

"I'm pretty sure that's my line." I chuckle.

Kali doesn't get a chance to respond when the doorbell rings. I'm expecting Marc on the other end, but when I open the door I see Marc's driver, Fred, standing there.

We had first met the night of the charity event in December when we couldn't find Thomas to get out of there after the hospital called Peyton about Gigi. Marc was quick to have Fred pull the car around front and we were out of there in seconds.

"Oh… hey there, Freddy." I give him a fist bump.

"Good evening, Ms. Woods." He gives a little half bow. Despite whatever is thrown at him, he always remains at the peak of professionalism. "I was asked to pick you up and bring you to the restaurant."

"Works for me," I tell him as I turn around to grab my wristlet off the kitchen counter. "Hey, Freddy. Since you seem to know where we are going, can you tell me if this outfit works for the restaurant?"

"You look lovely, Ms. Woods," he replies.

"Oh my god, Avery!" Emiline shrieks as she enters the kitchen space.

My eyes widen in shock wondering if I'm forgetting something or if I have lipstick all over my cheek. I look at myself up and down in the hallway mirror to see if anything is out of place.

"You're..." she pauses as she shakes. A small grin forms on her lips. "You're going to be my brother's undoing."

An uneasy feeling creeps into my gut.

Because the truth is, he might become *my* undoing.

CHAPTER EIGHT

Marc

I'm late to just about every single thing in life. Yes, this also includes meetings. My secretary knows to relay messages to my assistant that meetings start thirty minutes before they actually start so that I show up on time. It's a bad habit I'm struggling to break.

When I first asked Avery to dinner tonight, I had no plans as to where I would take her or how to approach this night. After a quick phone call with Oliver, who knows all about these places from his time blogging, we settled on a more upscale Bar and Grill on Park Avenue.

Now here I am, twenty minutes early to a practice date for our little ruse this summer. Twenty. Minutes. Early.

I'm standing on the sidewalk outside of the restaurant and trying to control my urge to nervously pace the sidewalk. Looking up from my watch, I see my car that Fred drives, pull up to the curb and my nervous energy spikes again.

I can't even pinpoint why this entire thing makes me as nervous and jittery as it's been making me. I know Avery won't fuck me over. She may be a little on the wild and loud side, but she's not a woman who would do that. If I had to guess… It all stems from having your sight set on something you want so badly and wanting it to work out the way it should.

It has nothing to do with Avery, because this arrangement will never amount to anything.

My thoughts are cut short when Fred opens the back door to let Avery out of the vehicle.

My breath hitches when she emerges from the car in a little black dress that is just short enough to expose her toned legs.

The air is physically trapped in my lungs as I stare at her.

Talk about taking your fucking breath away.

"Is this outfit not okay?" she says, pulling me from my thoughts.

My eyes slowly scan her from head to toe as I take in every feature. Her thin dress straps expose her shoulders and collarbones that I *should not* want to let my lips graze. Don't get me started on the curvature of her breasts that I'm just craving to touch. The dress flows around her thighs like she's ready for dancing around town.

I don't miss the diamond on her finger that glistens in the city lights as she moves her hand. I never asked for the ring back after the night I gave it to her. I didn't even know she kept it all this time until I asked her about it in the office.

"It's fine," I manage to choke out the lie so easily. It's more than fine, it's perfect. "Let's go, we're going to be late."

"Late?" she scoffs. "If the hostess knows you at all, she might keel over in shock when she sees you walk through the door this early."

"Actually…" I shoot her a smug grin. "I have never been here before."

"Great," she says with an exaggerated eye roll. "So we know nothing about how good the food is here?"

"Oliver says it's one of the best in the city."

The hostess escorts us to a private booth in the back corner of the restaurant. I wanted a spot that wasn't too intimate, and what do I get? A spot that's the definition of intimate. It's tucked into a small concave that has dim lighting and a U-shaped booth which forces us to sit next to each other and not across from each other.

Avery scoots into the booth first and I follow on the opposite side. The booth is small and our thighs almost brush against each other. I don't miss the intoxicating smell of her after I slide into the booth. I can't tell if it's lavender or lilac, but, being so close to her, it takes over every bit of my senses.

"I thought this was supposed to be a simple dinner to lay down the groundwork?" she asks.

"It is. I didn't expect this place to be so..."

"Romantic?" she finishes my sentence with a grin.

"I guess you can say that."

"Hey." She shrugs. "At least if anyone sees us here, we look like two love birds."

Nerves shoot down my spine while an uneasy feeling churns in my gut.

Love.

That is not even close to what this is.

I wipe the palms of my hands on my pants because I can feel them getting clammy, when thankfully the waiter approaches to collect our drink orders. I go for my usual top shelf whiskey, and Avery goes for a glass of champagne. I could have sworn she was a tequila girl after our trip to the shore. Champagne seems to be her drink of choice after the charity event and now this.

"Alright, gummy bear." Avery crosses her arms on the table and leans forward to engage in conversation. "Where should we start?"

"I'm going to ignore that god awful nickname you just gave me. Please for the love of all things... don't use that in front of my boss."

"Whatever floats your boat, honey bun." She winks.

"How about we start with an appetizer?"

"That's not where I was suggesting we start. I'm talking about this. Us."

I clear my throat. "Right. Okay. Tell me about yourself. Other than your professional resume that I already know, or the fact that you have the attitude of a lonely cat lady."

"I do not have the attitude of a cat lady," she retorts. "And you're one to talk. You act like someone pisses in your cheerios every morning."

"This is going to work lovely." I grin as I take a sip of whiskey that the waiter finally delivered.

"Okay, fine. I'll start," she says. "What do you do for fun?"

"It's hard to have fun when you work as much as I do. But when I'm not working, I enjoy running."

"Dammit," she huffs. "I knew you were a psychopath."

"How so?"

"*Nobody* runs for fun. If you ever catch me running, you better start running too. Because something is either chasing me, or something is on fire."

"Hmm..." I take another sip of my whiskey. "I bet I can make you fall in love with it. It's peaceful."

"There is nothing peaceful about being completely out of breath, soaked in sweat, and wanting to die. To each their own. I mean... if you're into torture, just say that."

"I started running after I finished my master's program in college, and..." I pause. Not sure I am ready to tell her about my biggest failed relationship. This isn't a real date, it's a fake one. Fuck, even on a real first date I probably wouldn't overextend my personal life like this.

"And?"

"I started running as a form of therapy after I graduated."

"Everyone has their vice." She offers me a somewhat sympathetic grin.

God, it's the most beautiful smile I have ever seen. This can't be the first time I have ever noticed that smile, can it? I shouldn't be finding her this attractive right now, but a part of me is going to run with it for now to help us sell this to Bill when we get together with him.

"What happened that caused you to start running for therapy?" she asks reluctantly.

Thankfully, the waiter shows up with some sliced bread and butter, allowing me some time to think about how to approach this heavy, and very real, question that she just asked.

"The night of my graduation, my girlfriend at the time told me she wasn't able to make it due to a conflict with her work."

"What a piece of shit." She makes a disgusted face. "I would have called out."

"One would think," I softly chuckle. "After I left the ceremony, I went to her apartment to wait for her to get off work. It was only going to be another thirty minutes or so. Except when I walked in..." I shake my head. The memories are flooding me.

"You don't have to tell me, Marc." She places her hand on top of mine. "You don't have to tell me any of this. I'm sorry I asked."

The contact of her hand on top of mine feels like I stuck a knife in an electrical outlet. If I wasn't sitting down, I would have been jolted backwards. The electricity I just felt with one single touch shot through my body at rapid fire. Unlike anything I've ever felt from another person.

She pulls her hand away quickly as if she felt the same thing. Both of our eyes shoot to where our hands just were. The same hand that was just resting on top of mine for a split second is now in her hair, twirling the ponytail around her finger.

I clear my throat, ignoring the weirdness of what that just was. "Needless to say, she was not at work. She was in her living room, naked, on top of her coworker, screaming his name."

She doesn't respond, but simply stares at me, her lips slightly parted. I swear I see her eyes start to glisten, but then she blinks them away, shaking herself out of it and looks down before I can confirm.

"Alright." I let out a laugh to try to get out of this conversation. "Now you tell me your story."

"I wish I had anything remotely interesting to share," she

says right before she takes a sip of champagne. "I told you I've never been in a relationship before."

"Never?"

"Never." She shakes her head. "Call it daddy issues, or whatever you want. My mom has been my entire life since my sperm donor walked out on us when I was young. I've never seen my mom in a relationship since. She's the strongest and most independent woman I have ever met. All my life, I have just wanted to be like her."

How is she going to sell a relationship with me, let alone an engagement, if she's never even been in one? I didn't think she actually meant it when she told me this before.

As if she can sense my anguish over the situation, she continues.

"I know that's the last thing you want to hear when we're supposed to be *in* a relationship." Her hand makes contact with mine again. The same energy courses through my body at her touch. This time, neither of us make a move to escape the feeling. "But I will let you know that I have read hundreds of romance novels. It's part of being friends with Peyton. She will legit force you to pick up her latest favorite read against your will."

"You know most of those aren't real life though? They are works of fiction."

"They might be." She grins. "But they are packed with all things romance and swoon. So don't worry, sweet cheeks. We got this."

"Alright. Alright." I raise my arms up in a small surrender. "Next topic. Where do you see yourself in the future?"

"What is this a second job interview?"

"Real funny. I know you mentioned becoming an agent. But like… where do you see yourself in say… five years?"

Avery sits back in her seat at my question as if she's deep in through. Her hands go to her hair to give her ponytail another twirl. Her eyes meet mine in a silent battle of uncertainty.

"I don't know how to answer that, Marc. Can I be serious for one minute?"

My hand lands on my chest with over dramatic shock. "You? Serious?"

She playfully swats at my arm. "Stop that. I'm being serious."

"Okay." I keep my voice steady and sincere. "Tell me."

"Did you know that no one has ever asked me this before?"

I can't help but stare at her. With every glance in her direction. With every look into those blue eyes. With every little laugh she lets out. With every word that comes out of her mouth.

I am completely terrified that my heart is going to fall for this girl.

I *cannot* fall for Avery Woods.

CHAPTER NINE
Avery

No one has ever asked me this question before.

Not my mom. Not my friends. Not a job interview.

The question takes me by surprise because I have never given my future much thought. I am certainly a fly by seat of my pants kind of girl. I go with the flow of life and where it decides to take me each day.

"If I had to look that far into my future," I finally admit. "I would definitely see myself as a successful real estate agent. Doing something like you do."

"My next question for you would have to be, why are you messing around as an assistant then?"

"I love being an assistant. I know that sounds like I'm downplaying my skills. I just have an insane obsession with organization. I will literally reorganize a friend's pantry if I go to their house and see that it's a mess. No questions asked."

That earns me a laugh from him. This date, or whatever you want to call it, has been the first time I have ever seen Marc laugh for *real* and not be his normal grumpy self. It's like a breath of fresh air. His laugh, and even his smile is hypnotizing. One could get lost in it if they were someone who was looking for a serious relationship.

"With that being said," I continue. "I also love the idea of people finding their dream home. I feel like if I were an agent, I could bring people around to see the houses and help them visualize themselves in it. For example, I could show them where a couch would be so that they could see themselves sitting and sipping their coffees while watching the television hung on a particular wall."

Marc simply nods but remains silent.

"That sounds dumb, doesn't it?"

"Not at all," he answers without an ounce of hesitation. "That right there is how you close the deal. You could be showing a multimillion-dollar home, and people will have reservations about spending that much money, despite them having plenty of it. Helping them visualize how they would live in the home, can really help them tip over the edge to say yes to the deal."

"Hmm…" I take a sip of champagne. "So maybe my idea of becoming an agent isn't so far-fetched?"

"Not one bit," he assures me. "Outside of work, any big dreams?"

Is this how real dates go?

When I first stepped out of the car when I arrived at the restaurant with Fred, my stomach swarmed with nerves. Most of the surface level things, like do I look okay? Am I too dressed up? What will Marc think of my outfit?

But deep down inside, I was also worried about things that would come out of my mouth. I only have a small handful of friends because my mouth gets me in trouble. I'm a lot as a person. I will be the first to admit it. I don't give a fuck what people think of me, so why do I care what he thinks of me?

It's a completely new feeling for me.

"Avery?"

"Sorry, I spaced out for a second," I lie. "Big dreams, huh?"

"Yeah… everyone has big dreams. What's yours?"

"Paris," I answer without missing a beat. "Someday, I'll travel to Paris."

"It's beautiful there. I can't believe you have never been."

"My mom never had much growing up." My throat goes dry as I share more personal information than I want to right now. For a fake date, we sure are sharing a whole lot of real shit with each other. "Don't get me wrong, I never went without. She made sure of that. I'm an only child so the two of us lived in a very small college town. She was the manager at the only supermarket in the town. My dad walked out on us with his *mistress*, and he never paid child support. Everything she ever had, she gave to me to make sure I had the best life possible."

Marc remains silent at the admission of my life growing up. I never want to open up like this with someone. The girls know a little bit about my childhood, but we avoid oversharing because it makes me feel extremely vulnerable. Like I do right now.

"Needless to say, I would love to take my mom to Paris. I took too much of my teenage years with her for granted for all she did for me. Even now, she's working so hard just to make ends meet. I hate that I've barely spoken to her since I've been back because she had to pick up a second job. Stupid disability barely paid her when she was out."

"You should've told me. I would have found a way to help you both out."

"You're my *boss*, Marc. Why in the world would I ask you to do that?"

He doesn't answer me but lifts a shoulder to his ear with a shrug before he takes a sip of his whiskey.

"Anyway, someday I'll earn enough to help her with her own bills the way she helped me for all of those years, and then bring her the trip of a lifetime."

"I like that." He smiles.

Not just any smile—an award winning, panty dropping one.

There's something about it that makes my insides flutter

being on the receiving end of this particular smile. It's real. It's genuine. It's *perfect*.

I shift in my seat, until my body is facing him. "Okay. My turn. I have a random question for you now."

"Hit me."

"What's one thing you've never seen before and one place you've never been?"

"Hmm," he hums over his glass of whiskey. "You're right. That is random." I watch intently as he thinks about his answer, eyes boring into mine. "I've never seen a dinosaur." He laughs.

I can't help the cackle that comes out of me as my body shakes with laughter. "That's really the answer you're going with?"

"It's the truth." He shrugs. "And I've never been to Florida."

"Florida? Hasn't everyone been there like once in their life?"

"Not me." He winks.

The laughter and my smile come so easily with him. Before I get lost in his charm any more than I already am, and the way my body is reacting to it, I decide to change the subject before he tells me more. "So, what are the plans for this summer? Do we have parties and meetings to attend or something? How are we making this happen? When is the expiration date for this?"

Marc's head jolts back as if my words just offended him.

"Well," Marc starts, but pauses to clear his throat. "Bill would like to just get to know our relationship. He's not here to work, he's here on a vacation of sorts. This will probably include a couple of dinners with him and his wife."

"Is that douche, Todd the toad, going to be there too?"

That earns me a laugh. "Unfortunately, yes. He will probably be at one or two of them. He mentioned inviting Bill to his lake house for the day. I'll probably be inviting Bill and Cathy to my penthouse one night for dinner to show some effort too."

"Great. We've got this."

"Do we?" he asks with a raised eyebrow.

"Why wouldn't we?"

"I just worry…" He stops his own thoughts and takes a sip of whiskey.

"Listen Marc," I cut through whatever he's thinking. "I know you're nervous about all of this. I also know I'm not your first choice here. But after really thinking about it more, I want to help you. After all, you're going to basically be family in the fall."

He barely gets the word out when whiskey sprays out of his mouth. "Family?"

"Duh," I snort. "Peyton and Thomas are getting married. She's like a sister to me."

"That doesn't make us remotely close to being family, Princess."

That nickname sends a cold chill up my spine, but also sends heat to my core. The last time I heard that word out of his mouth was when we were doing very inappropriate things in a very inappropriate supply closet in December.

"Tell me what you're worried about," I say, trying to not think dirty thoughts about Marc freakin' Ford.

"How can we make this work? Like how we will show affection?"

"There're plenty of ways to show affection that don't involve making out in front of your boss, Marcus."

"I understand that, Avery. I'm just worried we won't sell this."

Inside, I am screaming with nerves that I am about to do this. However, my history tells me in my head that I am immune to charm and what I am about to ask Marc to do, won't change that. Besides, he's just my grumpy-gills boss.

"Okay, pudding." I sit up straighter in the seat. "Show me right here, right now, how you would sell it if Bill was sitting right across the table from us."

"Avery—"

"Show me," I cut him off. "How would we prove this love story to them?"

Marc silently stares into my eyes from beside me. It only takes seconds before I watch his eyes darken. With hunger? I'm not sure what just shifted in those seconds, but my entire body lights up from his stare. What the fuck was that?

The corner of his lip turns up just the slightest, as I feel his body shift beside me. He scoots just an inch closer to me, causing our thighs to touch. The same, weird electric current that I felt when I placed my hand on his earlier, courses through my entire body at his contact. Then he delicately places his arm around the back of the booth, his hand grazing my exposed shoulder and I can't help but get tipsy off of his masculine scent taking over my space.

"This is how I would start," he says. "We would sit close together as if we can't get enough of being close to each other."

I simply hum in approval while air remains trapped in my lungs.

My gaze moves to where his hand sits on my shoulder as he brushes his pointer finger in soft circles. His eyes remain across the table as if there really was someone sitting across from us that he should be engaging in conversation with.

At that moment, the waiter comes over to ask us if we would like anything for dessert. I'm about to say no, when Marc cuts in.

"We'll take a chocolate mousse cheesecake with two spoons, please."

"Marc, I'm so stuffed." My hand finds my stomach. "I am going to pop out of this dress if I eat anything else."

"I'm not sure if I told you tonight or not." He smiles down at me, ignoring my protest and the fact that I truly can't eat another bite of food. "This dress looks absolutely stunning on you, baby."

The way he says *baby* makes wetness pool between my legs.

But it dawns on me, he's showing me what we would be like with his boss.

"Thanks, babe."

His smile grows wider when his hand that was around the

back of the booth comes in front of us as he places it on my upper thigh. There's no doubt that he can feel the goosebumps on my bare skin under his touch. They happen almost instantly as his hand makes contact.

Slowly he leans into my ear, his mild scruff on his chin brushing against my jaw line.

"But it will look better on our bedroom floor when we get home."

"Marc." I suck in a breath. "What—"

His lips remain by my ear. I can feel the heat of his breath. He shifts his body slightly while his opposite hand cups my jaw line. My heart is beating so fast, I'm willing to bet he can hear it. My eyes flutter closed at the touch. My goosebump-covered body is now erupting in a wildfire of flames.

"Marc," I whisper in a mix of desperation and pleasure.

"Yes, baby?" His lips hover dangerously close to mine. For a brief second, I think he's going to kiss me. He's going to break the very first rule I laid out on the table when we were making this deal. "What do you need?"

There's a small part of me that wants to feel his lips touch mine. I want to know what he tastes like. I want to get drunk on his whiskey infused breath that mixes with my champagne-flavored tongue. But I can't allow it.

I pull myself back from the trance he managed to put me in.

"Well..." I release a breath I didn't know I was holding. "I think you've got it down pat."

He sits back in his chair, and I watch as he adjusts himself with a small grin on his face. A grin that I know is packed with so many different emotions. Surely, he's feeling the same way I was feeling. There is no way *whatever* that was, was one sided.

Not only did he make me feel things.

He made me forget why I don't want to feel things.

If he's going to act like that the rest of the summer... I am so completely fucked.

CHAPTER TEN

Avery

PEYTON

Have you been avoiding me, Ave?

KALI

I live with her and I literally have the same question.

EMILINE

I've been wondering why this group chat has been so quiet. Normally you three are blowing up my phone while I'm studying or trying to sleep after work.

PEYTON

knock knock. IS ANYONE HOME?

Can't a girl be busy?

PEYTON

No.

KALI

Absolutely not.

EMILINE

What did my brother do now?

KALI

oooh the plot thickens.

Listen, I'm not intentionally avoiding my best friends. But dammit, they know me better than they know their favorite book, which says a lot.

Our "date" Saturday night left me feeling uneasy. I don't ever fucking feel uneasy, and that's left me shutting out my best friends. I can't open up to them about something before I even know what it is.

The way Marc faked, *whatever that was*, for those few minutes had me feeling very real things.

There was nothing fake about the way my body reacted to him.

There was also nothing fake about the feelings I felt with him either. There was an overwhelming sense of happiness at his words, his touch, and the way he smiled at me.

I was thankful that the universe aligned perfectly so that Kali was gone all day Sunday. She got an offer at work to write an editorial for the magazine she works for, which is a huge step in her career. I'm not sure if she wants to be a columnist. A while back when she was in college, she had joked with the idea of writing a book someday. We never pushed her on the subject because she gets cringy over it. I can't even begin to imagine how hard it is to write a book and the process that goes into one. Not to mention you'd have to have crazy thick skin because people can be downright vicious.

So writing an article for a magazine is a huge step for her. That's the reason she was gone all day Sunday. She was busy around the city doing research on the best restaurants to attend for bachelorette parties.

The universe stayed in its alignment yesterday when Marc had to work out of the Staten Island office for the day to attend meetings and close two big deals. It worked out for both of us, really. I was able to avoid him and let my body relax before I saw him again, and he got to see Bill in that office without questions about him marrying his assistant.

This morning when I arrived at the office, Marc was his usual chipper self. I say that with as much sarcasm as possible. He was his normal killjoy self and wanted everyone around him to feel it. It was like his Monday blues carried over into Tuesday. For once, I know it wasn't me who put him in that mood.

But the scowl I keep seeing him shoot me from his desk just about every hour tells me that there's a chance I might be the cause of it.

My phone chiming on my desk rips me from my thoughts, and I pick it up assuming that it's still the girls wondering what's wrong with me. But I gasp when I see the name Dean.

DEAN

Is this really how it's going to be?

You break up with me via text message and I just don't hear from you?

I let out an audible sigh to myself at my desk because, seriously?

I've been busy with work.

DEAN

You don't work on the weekends. I tried calling you Sunday to give you some time to think about it.

Dean... we were never officially together.

DEAN

But I wanted to see where things would go.

This right here is exhibit A why I never let myself get too comfortable with a man. This whole text encounter is ridiculously awkward and unnecessary.

This is really unnecessary, Dean.

Besides, I told you. I'm busy with work. This isn't what this was supposed to be.

DEAN

I wanted to be the exception, sweetheart.

For whatever reason, that causes a slight grin on my face. It would be cute if I was into that sort of thing. But my heart is anything but sweet.

Just as I'm about to reply, my email notification dings on my desktop, and I groan.

This is too much fucking communication from too many devices for a Tuesday before noon.

To: avery.woods@prestigehorizons.net
From: marc.ford@prestigehorizons.net
Avery,
I would like to remind you that you are at your place of work. At the same time, I would like to remind you we have a deal for the next few months that you will not be seeing anyone else. From my understanding, you were breaking up with your boyfriend. So please enlighten me as to why you have a shit eating grin on your face at your text messages all morning.
Sincerely,
Marc

He can't be serious right now.

Also, okay… I have been on my phone all morning. It's not my fault the group chat with the girls has me laughing at how well they know me. That stupid grin with texting Dean was dumb on my part. But who is he to say who I can and can't text. I crack my knuckles at my desk before I send him an email back.

To: marc.ford@prestigehorizons.net
From: avery.woods@prestigehorizons.net
Marcus,
I am dedicated to all aspects of my job and take it very seriously. You have received everything asked of me today in a timely manner, and our deal is still very much on.
I will have you know, I never had said boyfriend from your previous email. However, I have cut ties with my casual fling. My group chat with the girls has been a little haywire this morning which explains the phone dinging like crazy.
But I won't lie… Dean contacted me about the 'break up' I did via text message.
What can I say, I'm a difficult person to get over.
All the best,
Avery

I can't help but laugh at myself. That last line was kind of unnecessary, but that's also just who I am.

I pick up my stress relief putty on my desk as I lean back in the chair and wait for a response. But instead of a response, I find Marc standing in the door of my office. He's leaning against the frame with one leg relaxed over the other and his arms crossed over his chest.

He's also wearing his signature scowl that has his eyebrows pinched together.

"What can I do for you, boss man?" I smirk as I continue to squeeze the stress putty in my hands.

"What are you doing, Avery?"

"I'm working. What does it look like I'm doing? And I'm relieving some stress from emails my boss is sending me. You should invest in this for your desk."

"I don't need a stress ball," he huffs. "I need you to stop smiling and laughing at your phone for ten seconds and keep working."

"First of all, it's not a stress *ball*. It's called stress putty." I toss it over to him and he catches it despite being caught off guard. "More specifically a dill dough."

"Excuse me… what?" he practically yells in my office.

"Relax, you heathen." I snort a laugh. "That's the brand of the putty. Clearly it's not a dildo."

"You are not right in the head." He shakes his head. A smile doesn't reach his face though.

"I know this already. I work for you, remember?" That earns me a slight lift in the corner of his lips. "Back to my points I was making that you rudely interrupted… Second of all, the group chat I have with the girls was a little chaotic because they haven't heard from me in a few days and–"

"Why? Where have you been?"

He presses off the door frame and fully enters my small office, his face laced with… concern? Jealousy? Wondering not where, but *who* I've been with? There're so many things washing over his features right now.

"Well, honey," I draw out the term of endearment. "I spent Sunday curled on the couch with junk food and rewatching old episodes of *Friends*. Rainy weather makes me lazy, and after the week I had, I needed a day to just relax."

His shoulders visibly relax, and he nods but doesn't say anything else.

"Then yesterday, I worked here all day doing what I do every Monday. Pulling new listings from over the weekend for you. Gathering last week's sales reports from Jessica." I throw in an eye roll for extra measure when I say her name. "And then I color coded your appointment calendar because that shit was a mess."

"I was wondering why it was so colorful this morning." He smiles. "Can you please explain the Avery color coded system to me?"

I squeal in my seat, completely forgetting I was annoyed with him in the first place. Organization and things like this, make me way too happy for my own good.

"Here. Come. Sit," I ramble as I stand up from my chair a little too excited. I pat the seat for him to sit where I was just sitting.

Reluctantly, he sits down as I turn the chair for him to face the screen and I click open the virtual calendar.

When I lean down beside him to toggle through the apps on the desktop, I'm hit with an overpowering scent of a man. That's the only way I know how to describe it. I can't tell if it's his soap, aftershave, or cologne. But it's powerful enough that my body propelled forward to live in the scent as I start to show him what I did.

I rest my elbows on the desk, while I remain bent at the hip. I can feel Marc's gaze move from the computer screen to the ring on my finger until it lands on my face. I swallow the lump in my throat because I can't look into his eyes. Just the thought of his eyes on me right now has my legs feeling weak.

"I organized your meetings based on location," I say on a shaky breath. "Light blue is the Manhattan office, green is the Staten Island office, and yellow is the Bronx office. Each one is scheduled to allow you travel time to each location as well so you're not rushing around."

I don't see it, but I can feel him turn to look towards the computer.

"Each meeting is also scheduled fifteen minutes earlier than the actual start time because we know you can't be on time for a single thing in your life."

"Hey," he says defensively. "I can be on time for things."

"You're never on time for work meetings, Marc. Don't kid yourself."

I hear a small huff of air come out of him as if he just laughed, which causes me to turn my head and finally meet his stare. A smile instantly forms on my face without thinking anything. Hearing Marc laugh is probably the greatest thing I've heard and I want more of it.

I can tell by the way we are both staring at each other with such intensity, that his mind is swirling the same way mine is right now. As if the world has just started spinning on its axis in slow motion, Marc takes his hand and brings it to the side of my face. Gently brushing his thumb along my cheek bone, his eyes trail down until they land on my mouth.

"Marc," I breathe out. It's the only thing I can say right now because I have no words for what's happening here.

"I seem to recall…" He's so close to my face and I'm sure he would try to kiss me if I didn't have that firm rule in place. "I was on time when I picked you up for our date."

"That's because Freddy picked me up." My face leans into his hand on instinct. But I quickly pull myself back to reality. There isn't a hint of amusement on his face though. His features are serious, and his eyes are dark.

"I beat you to the restaurant that night. But I'm talking about the charity event." He grins. "I was on time when I picked you up. In fact, that was the first time I was on time for anything in the last few months."

"It was?"

"Yes," he says confidently. Brushing my hair from my face while still maintaining eye contact with me. His stare and touch reigniting a fire inside of me. "Something about you… The anticipation of seeing you… just causes me to show up where I need to be on time."

Tension rapidly fills the small space between us with his admission. Reluctantly, I move to stand up where I was leaning over and break free of the hold he has on me. However, Marc stands up quickly, his hands grip my hips and he presses his body into mine. The move backs me into the windows behind my desk.

"Avery," he says my name as if it's laced with desperation.

"Yes?"

He traces my jaw line with the tip of his nose until he reaches my ear. I hear him suck in a small breath as if he's trying to memorize my scent. The combination of his touch and close proximity sends shivers down my spine, a feeling impossible to hide because it causes my body to quiver the way a person would if they were cold.

Before I can do anything, realization passes through Marc, and he quickly takes a step back as if he's caught himself doing something wrong. He adjusts the sleeves of his button-down shirt, while looking down at the ground—looking anywhere but at me.

I cross my arms over my chest as my eyebrows pinch together with confusion, unsure of what the hell is happening between us. My eyes glance down, and I can see his budding erection forming behind the zipper of his pants.

"Thank you for setting up my calendar, Ave."

His final words are filled with affliction before he's out my door, not stopping at his own desk as he retreats out of the office.

I can't help but stand there, staring through the glass windows wondering what the hell that was.

CHAPTER ELEVEN

Marc

I don't know what hell looks like, but I can imagine it looks like my situation with Avery because this past week has been a true test of my self-control.

Ever since last Tuesday when I stormed into her office after I gave her shit for laughing on her phone, and allowing myself to get way too close to her… I don't know what the hell it is that just pulls me into her.

My. Fucking. Mistake.

Touching her, being near her, pinning my body to hers sent me into a full heat. It made me want more from her, but more I can't give her, despite the fucking ring on her finger that she has yet to take off. I spent the week reminding myself that this is all for show. It's all for Bill.

Her new color-coded system on my schedule has worked flawlessly, though. I will give her that. I wasn't late to a single meeting and my employees actually asked me if I was feeling okay when I showed up.

My schedule also kept me away from the office more than I wanted to be.

However, we're back to the same song and dance today. Let's

just say, my normal Wednesday drink night tonight with my brothers and Logan can't come fast enough.

This morning Avery was late. Not by much, but it was enough that I could bust her balls for it. For the first time in as long as I can remember, she didn't give me shit back. It was the weirdest thing in the world that had me tense all morning. She hasn't left her office once today and kept herself busy replying to emails and getting my notes ready for a big meeting I have tomorrow. It's with the owners of a high-rise luxury complex Thomas wants to invest in. He's interested in buying and renovating it, upgrading it with more luxurious amenities, and flipping it for a profit.

I pull up the listing to get my personal notes together for it when the intercom on my work phone buzzes.

"Mr. Ford?" my secretary calls out.

"Yes?"

"I have Bill Jones on line two."

"Thank you." I take a deep breath and click through to the line. "Marc Ford."

"Marc, it's Bill," he announces. "How's it going?"

"It's going," I laugh. "Typical Wednesday here."

"That's what I like to hear. Listen, I have a question to ask you."

Every time he talks like this, I can't help but feel a sinking feeling in my gut. I want this to go right *so badly* that it's fucking with my head. The very last time I swore things were going right in my life, only to be shit on, was when I found Becky cheating on me. I know that sounds pathetic, but I saw my future with her. Ever since then, Prestige Horizons has been my life.

"Anything." I clear my throat. "What can I do for you?"

"Are you and Avery free for dinner on Friday night?"

I pull the phone away from my ear to let out an audible sigh that's mixed with pain. This will be it, our first official outing.

"I can double check with her to make sure we don't have

plans," I reply in a much more uppity tone than intended. "What did you have in mind?"

"I was thinking of keeping it casual and having you two over to the house. Cathy is making ham and scalloped potatoes and has been dying to have you two over. She also wants to make her famous apple crisp for dessert."

"My mouth is watering thinking about all of that," I only partially lie. The food sounds great, the act we have to put on is what makes my mouth go as dry as the desert. "Let me call Avery and confirm we're free and I will send you a text. Does that work?"

"Sounds perfect. We can shoot for dinner at 6:30."

"Great. I will confirm with you shortly. Was that all you needed?"

"Yup," he confirms. "You're killing it in the Manhattan office, Marc. Proud of you."

I swallow a lump in my throat. "Thank you, sir."

After I hang up with him, I allow myself no time to sit with these nerves of having to ask her to go to dinner before I make my way to Avery's office.

I'm about to knock on the door frame when I find myself pausing to take her in. God, she's so beautiful. She's much more relaxed in her outfit choice today. She is wearing a pair of dress pants and a flowy blouse. It's not her usual look of skirts and a button down. She is typing out an email, but she doesn't have a smile on her face. Something is definitely bothering her today.

"Knock knock," I announce with a smile. "Can I come in?"

"Sure."

I take a seat in the chair across from her desk, feeling edgy because this isn't the Avery I am used to. Normally, she would hit me with a smart-ass response back.

"Is everything okay?"

As soon as the words leave my mouth, she directs her gaze at me and I can see tears forming in her eyes. She blinks aggressively to attempt to hold them back.

"Talk to me, Avery."

"It's nothing, Marc." She swipes a tear that escapes. "What can I help you with?"

"Nothing until you tell me what's going on?"

"It's nothing," she snaps as she averts her gaze to anywhere but me. "I'm sorry. But it's nothing."

"Avery."

"If you must know, I got my period yesterday and I always get extra emotional on the second day. My stomach is killing me, I'm bloated as fuck, and I just want a bag of salt and vinegar chips but the stand downstairs was out of them when I was on my way in."

"Is that why you were late today?"

"Yes. I had to have a cry session in the bathroom over a stupid bag of chips. Is that okay with you?"

I try to hold back my laughter over the emotional outburst, but I know what women go through each month. I feel for them, because it must be so difficult to go through such a range of emotions.

I decide not to reply to her at all, instead I pull out my phone to make a phone call.

"Fred," I say into the phone from her doorway. "I need you to do me a favor. Can you run to the local pharmacy and pick me up a few things?"

"Marc—" Avery starts, but I cut her off with a finger in the air.

"Yes. Thank you," I continue. "I need a heating pad. Get the fancy one that wraps around the stomach that is designed for cramps. I also need a box of the Midol tablets. Lastly, I need you to get me a giant bag of salt and vinegar chips. If they don't have it there, find it somewhere else."

I turn to look at Avery while Fred confirms the few things I need in my ear, and she is swiping another tear from her eye.

"That will be all. Thank you so much, Fred." I hang up and pocket my phone.

"You didn't need to do that." She shakes her head. "I was going to go on my break."

"I saved you a trip."

"Thank you, Marc."

"Of course." I nod. "If it doesn't help, I think you should take the rest of the day off. I would send you home right now, but I know you and your insane work ethic, and you won't leave unless I shove you out this door."

"You'd be right about that," she scoffs. "I'm used to this. Happens every month, remember? I just got a little bat shit crazy over the chips not being available the *one* day that I want them."

"I got you."

Three words. They slipped out but they hold so much more meaning than I meant for them to hold. I meant that I got her on the chips, but does she know I've got her in all other aspects? I think she feels the same way because the look she shoots in my direction is one mixed with lust and confusion.

"Listen, I hate to bring this up today when you're going through what you're going through..." I hesitate to continue. The small smile on her face tells me I can though. "But Bill called."

"Where do we need to be?"

"First of all, thank you for being so good with all of this and willing to jump at what he needs." I smile. "He invited us to dinner at his house Friday night. Cathy wants to make ham and scalloped potatoes. Plus, she apparently has a famous apple crisp recipe that she is dying to make."

"You don't have to tell me twice. I'm there," she squeals. "I can fuck up some scalloped potatoes and some apple crisp. I'll bring a tub of vanilla ice cream, because you can't have warm apple crisp without vanilla bean ice cream on top."

"I've never had it."

"OH MY GOD, MARC! How have you never? It's an orgasm in your mouth."

That makes my dick twitch.

"Noted." I adjust myself in my pants hoping she doesn't notice. "I will let him know that we are good to go. He said 6:30 for dinner."

"Got it," she confirms. I simply offer her a smile and begin to leave her office. "Oh, and Marc?"

I turn my body back towards her. Her arms cross over her midsection, and her toe fiddles with the hem of the area rug in her office. "Yeah?"

"I just want to say thank you. For that. With Fred."

"I told you, Avery. I got you."

After I leave her office, I shoot off a text to Bill to let him know we are good for Friday.

But "*good*" is stretching it.

Moores bar is packed tonight. I don't even know how long we have been coming here but we made it a point to get here every Wednesday to meet up for drinks mid-week. Sometimes it's both of my brothers plus Logan and other times it's just one or two of us. Basically whoever can make it, shows up.

They know us so well too, that our table tucked in the back corner is always ready for us despite how busy it is.

This week, Oliver is home from his birthday week, so he's meeting Logan and me.

"Oliver." I smack a hand on his back. "Happy belated Birthday. Long time no see. Where are you getting back from?"

"Thank you. I spent my birthday in Cali this year." He laughs. "There's nothing like that California sun, my brother."

"I bet." I nod.

"Don't forget the waves and babes," Logan adds.

Oliver lets out a low whistle. "You are not wrong, Logan."

"Logan, aren't you getting a bit old for that?" I ask.

"I've only been thirty for a month." He laughs. "That hardly classifies me as *old*. Besides... aren't you joining the thirty club at the end of the year?"

I shake my head at Logan before directing my attention back to Oliver. "How long are you in for?"

"Just a few days," he shrugs. "I'm heading to the mountains next week. Somewhere in bumblefuck Montana I think. I have no desire to go there, but a backpacking company wants me to get some pictures in the mountains for my next blog post. They're fully funding my boarding and the flight there and back."

"That's awesome, Oliver. You've got a good gig going."

"I do love it. It's exhausting, but I truly can't complain because who else can say they get to travel for work like this?"

"Jealous as shit, dude." Logan shakes his head. "You're out traveling the world and I'm just trying not to get shot or punched in the face by drunk assholes."

"Hopefully if you land that promotion to Chief, you won't have to worry about being in the streets anymore. You can sit pretty behind a desk instead."

"From your mouth to God's ears." He laughs. "How's your thing going with Avery?"

I can't help but groan.

"I don't know, bro." I take a sip of my whiskey. "It's so hard to read her and figure out where this will go. Bill called me this morning and invited us to dinner at his house Friday night. Our first time getting together with them."

"Technically," Oliver states. "They have seen you together before."

"Yeah, but in a crowded event where we could go off and do our own thing." I shake my head at the memory of that night. "This time, it's going to be just us two with him and his wife. Much more intimate setting."

"How does Avery feel?" Logan asks.

"She's ready to run with whatever we have to do. Which I have to say, surprises me a lot for how reluctant she was when I first presented her with the idea of keeping this ruse up for the whole summer. Except I don't know how she will actually react when it's time to put up the act."

"That girl is a fucking trip." Oliver laughs.

"I allowed myself to get way too close to her at the office, and she seems hesitant with the way she responds. Almost like she's holding back."

It's like she wants to touch me back, she wants me close. I can also feel the wheels in her mind spinning circles trying to figure out what's real and what's fake. Maybe hesitation is the wrong word to use? But it just felt… off.

"How was it when you two kissed?" Logan asks.

"We haven't—"

"Don't even fucking tell me," Logan cuts me off. "You mean to tell me, that you two are set up to be this fake engaged couple for the summer and you haven't practiced kissing yet? How do you expect this to work?"

Oliver leans back in his chair, crossing his arms over his chest before he says, "I'm with Logan here. This won't work."

"Would you fuckers let me finish?" I throw my arms out in defense. "No kissing was actually her number one rule for this agreement. She was dead set on it and explained it in a way that sort of made sense."

Logan leans in with a grin plastered on his face. "Explain it to me. Because I'm not following."

"She asked how often you see people making out in front of their boss or out in public. You don't, really. She said there is no need to practice it or make it a thing because we won't need to kiss or make out in front of him."

"That still doesn't make sense to me."

"She did say if I felt completely pulled to show affection of any kind, that I can give her a kiss on the forehead."

"Ohhhh," Oliver coos with an eye roll. "So spicy."

"I'm just thankful as shit she's even agreed to doing this for the entire summer with me. I'm running with whatever she gives me."

"Yeah, you got a point," Logan agrees. "She's missing out on hot girl summer being tied down to your ass."

"Asshole." I punch him in the shoulder. "I won't lie, though. I am nervous as hell about how this night will go down. We laid down the groundwork of what we will say and do, but we truly don't know what will happen when we get there."

"You think it's gonna be awkward?" Logan asks.

"Without a doubt." I nod aggressively. "It's going to be awkward as fuck."

"Color me curious," Oliver interrupts, leaning in close with his elbows on the table, chin perched in his hand, with a smirk on his face. "What were her other rules to this agreement?"

"No kissing was her first rule," I say after taking a long sip of whiskey. "No seeing other people was number two."

"Avery set that rule?" he asks, surprised.

"She did."

"Look at the queen of casual being all exclusive. Go Avery." Logan raises his glass as if to cheer with a toast to her when she's not even here. "Was that all the rules?"

"Her final rule was…" I pause, rubbing my forehead uncomfortably. "Don't fall in love with her."

Both men look at me with shock in their eyes before they turn to look at each other with knowing smirks.

"What's that look for?"

"Does she know who she asked that of?" Logan starts.

"She asked the man who would give anything to have a wife and kids, to *not* to fall in love with her," Oliver adds.

"And not for nothing… as wild as Avery is, she's easy to fall in love with." Logan shrugs a shoulder. "She's fun to be around and hot as fuck. Hell, I think *I* love her."

"Watch yourself," I snarl. "That's my fiancé you're talking about."

"Relax, you neanderthal." He laughs. "I don't love her like

that. It's just that Avery has this personality that makes you feel like you've known her forever. You can't help but have a smile on your face, laughing at her loud craziness."

"I have to agree," Oliver adds. "I haven't been around her as much as everyone else, but the times that I have been, she's a trip and funny as shit."

"See." Logan tilts his head to the side and opens his arms very matter of factly. "She's easy to love."

I don't say anything back other than nod to acknowledge what they are saying.

The truth of the matter is that they're right.

She is easy to love.

And that's what terrifies me the most about our situation.

CHAPTER TWELVE

Avery

Of all Friday nights… you all choose THIS Friday night to be busy?

PEYTON

Sorry boo. We're taking James to the shore house this weekend for some carnival they are having.

EMILINE

I'm working, girlfriend.

KALI

My boss asked me to stay late. I wish I could be there.

I let out a drawn-out groan and toss my phone on the bed as I stand in front of my open closet trying to figure out what to wear to dinner tonight. It's not out at a fancy restaurant or anything, but it is at his boss's house. I don't know if we're walking into a little cottage or a crazy large mansion. What the fuck do you wear when you have no idea what to expect?

I decide to forgo getting dressed for a moment and head into the kitchen to pour myself a glass of champagne. Listen, I'm not one for drinking alone. But desperate times call for desperate measures right now.

I gulp down the first glass and then pour a second before I retreat back into my room to get ready.

I decide I need to be my own hype girl for tonight.

"I'm a bad ass bitch," I repeat the words of affirmation to myself.

"Marc Ford has no effect on me, and I can do this," I add for dramatic effect.

The truth of the matter is, Marc Ford *does* have an effect on me.

One that I never asked for nor wanted.

Unfortunately for me, he's the first guy I have ever been close to that causes my body to melt into a puddle when he's near me. No matter how hard I try… his touch, the way he looks at me, and his heaven-sent smile, just causes chills to spill down my spine.

I don't want the chills.

I don't want to lose my breath when he touches me.

I don't want butterflies to swarm my stomach when I think of him.

Why are my thoughts lately consumed with only him?

I went into this agreement completely confident I could keep feelings out of this, based on my history with men.

Then on Wednesday, he had to go and be *the* most perfect guy in the world and have Freddy pick up and deliver some things to help alleviate my period cramps. I hate how I can't control my hormones when Aunt Flo comes to visit. She's always so nasty to me and she makes me want to curl into a ball with a pint of ice cream.

I fought all morning that day to hone my emotions so Marc didn't see me lose it. Except when I stopped on my way in to grab a bag of chips, the cafe downstairs didn't have any salt & vinegar chips. Of course, The ONE time I want them is the ONLY time they don't have them.

Cue tears I didn't ask for.

Don't get me started on the special heating pad he got me that's perfectly designed for period cramps. Like, it has a belt that wraps around my waist. How have I been a female for twenty-seven years and didn't know these existed?

All of this does *not* help my case of not feeling things for this man. Talk about swoon.

Heading back into my closet, I decide on a casual summer dress. Now that Aunt Flo went back into her cave for the month, I feel less bloated and more like myself. The dress is a flowy deep maroon colored dress with short sleeves. Since this is dinner with his boss, I want to keep it casual and respectful.

I rarely ever wear my hair down so tonight I decide to let it down with its long, natural waves. My hair isn't straight but it's also not curly. It's got the perfect amount of natural wave to it that works for this dress and occasion.

I glance at the clock and see that Marc should be here in the next fifteen minutes, but the doorbell rings just as I glance down.

There is no way Marc is fifteen minutes early. I assume it's yet another package of books that Kali ordered online.

When I answer the door, I'm shocked to see Marc standing there.

"Missed me so much that you had to show up fifteen minutes early, boss man?"

I open the door without looking at him and retreat to the kitchen.

Marc gives me no response, but I hear the door close behind him.

As soon as I turn to look at him, all my affirmations that I chanted not long ago of *I can do this* are thrown out the window.

Marc stands there looking suave as ever with his hands tucked in the pockets of a pair of black dress pants. He's wearing a light blue button down that has a black suit jacket to cover it. He decided on no tie which is so on brand for him. His dark chocolate brown hair is the perfect mix of sexy and sophisticated mess. Purposely unruly as if he runs his fingers through it several times during the day. The things I would do just to be able to run my hands through it.

I tell myself to stop thinking about that, but my eyes scan his body slowly from bottom to top. The world might as well have stopped spinning right then and there. I think my mouth is hung open, but I don't have the right mind to bring my lips back together. I can't help but pat myself on the back for deciding to put on panties with this dress.

"Are you checking me out?" his voice cuts through my own thoughts.

"Do you want the truth or a lie?"

"Obviously I want the truth, Avery."

I swallow a lump that formed in my throat, feeling dryer than the Sahara Desert all of a sudden. How did that happen?

"You're making it very hard to look away right now," I admit.

The signature smirk forms on his face, as his gaze drops to the floor, and he shakes his head. My eyes never leave him as he walks over to meet me in the kitchen.

He's now standing directly in front of me, barely an inch away, which forced my head to lift up to meet his intense stare. I think I've stopped breathing, but I can't tell.

I might actually pass out and die from lack of oxygen to the brain.

Cause of death: the man standing in front of me.

Both of his hands come up to brush my hair flowing down my chest to behind my shoulders so it all lays on my back. The light brush of his knuckles on my shoulder as he does it makes me feel weak in the knees and I swear if I didn't have bones holding me up, I'd be a puddle at his feet.

"Now you know how I feel," he says. Barely above a whisper.

There is no one else here.

This is all Marc Ford and his charm.

God dammit.

"We should go." I take a step back from this bubble he has me trapped in, allowing myself to breathe again. "You know, before we're late and all."

"It's a good thing I was early for once then, huh?" He grins before he walks off.

"You're such a motherfucker. You know that, right?" I laugh as I watch his most glorious backside walk away from me. Fuck, he has a great ass. "Even the initials of your name match it."

"You're the one marrying this motherfucker," he snickers as he opens the front door of the apartment and extends his arm. Signaling it's time for us to go.

My steps falter as the word *marrying* leaves his mouth. I catch myself before he sees the ways his words hit me though.

Was what he said to me before real?

Or is it just the start of our acting for tonight?

It's starting to become very fucking hard to decipher what's what anymore.

CHAPTER THIRTEEN

Avery

Marc surprised me when he hopped into the driver's seat of his fancy, and very expensive looking car. I had assumed Fred would drive us to Bill's house since I have never seen him drive himself anywhere before. The car screams *Made for Marc Ford*. It's a sleek black sports car that can barely fit someone larger than a toddler in the backseat. The inside was all black to match the exterior. I'm willing to bet this thing can drive itself.

The drive took us over an hour. I didn't realize his boss' place would be outside of the city on Long Island. Traffic at this hour, on a Friday, in the summer… talk about a nightmare.

"Are you ready for this?" he asks after we pull into the driveway.

This isn't a cottage, a penthouse or a house. This is a full-blown mansion right on the lake. The life of luxury has never been on my vision board. Can you imagine having to clean a place of this magnitude? No ma'am.

"Born ready, *babe*. Am I dressed okay? I didn't expect a place like this when you said dinner."

He takes a moment to scan my body. The corner of his lip tipping up just the slightest bit before his tongue swipes slowly along his bottom lip. Once again, pouring gasoline on the fire that he ignited inside of me.

"Perfect."

Then he's out the car door.

Leaving me there gaping at the *one word* he left me with.

But it wasn't what he said, it was how he said it.

That word dripped with lust, and not a single ounce of sarcasm.

Reluctantly I exit the car and as soon as I do, the extra-large double doors of the mansion swing open and Bill greets us from the top of the steps leading up to the door.

"Hey, kids!" He beams. "I'm glad you made it. I was afraid you would get lost. We're tucked away back here in the woods and sometimes it's hard to find."

Marc takes my hand in his as if we do this every day.

"Hey Bill. No issues at all. Thank you so much for having us." His hand doesn't leave mine as he uses his opposite hand to give Bill a welcome handshake. "Before I forget, we brought some ice cream for the apple crisp. Avery says we can't have apple crisp without it. I would throw it in the freezer, because it got a little soft on the ride here." He hands him the small bag with the tub of ice cream.

"Oh perfect! Please come in." He signals with his arms. "Cathy is just about done."

Marc removes his hand from mine, and I feel like I can take a breath again. Except… he places his palm on the small of my back. I feel my body quiver in response to the touch.

"Are you cold?" He leans in to whispers in my ear.

"No," I answer a little too quickly, shaking my head.

I need to snap out of this right fucking now. I can't let Marc know that he's getting to me.

Cathy breaks my thoughts by greeting us in the entryway.

"Marc!" she bellows before she wraps her arms around him for a hug. "It's so good to see you again."

"You too, Cathy," Marc replies. "Thank you for having us.

Your home is beautiful, and I can already tell dinner is going to be amazing. It smells so great."

"You're in for a treat!"

"I would like to introduce you to my fiancé, Avery." His damn hand is on the small of my back again.

"It's so lovely to meet you, Avery." She wraps her arms around me for a hug.

I don't immediately hug her back, my arms are plastered to my sides at this almost awkward encounter. Hugging isn't my favorite thing in the world. Anyone close to me will tell you all about that too.

My eyes meet Marc and he gives me *the eye* telling me that it's rude to not hug back. I roll my eyes at him as my arms reach up to gently pat her back.

"It's so nice to meet you too," I finally reply back to her.

She releases me from her hold and takes a step back as her eyes bounce back and forth between Marc and I. Shit… did I already blow this?

I shuffle to the side to wedge myself under Marc's arm. As if he can sense my uncertainty, he wraps his arm around my shoulders and tugs me tight into him.

How am I just getting a whiff of his scent right now? I just spent an hour in the car with him and didn't notice anything. Now that he has me close to his chest, pressed against him, I'm hit with the aroma of his rich, masculine cologne. He smells like he belongs on a page of a *Giorgio Armani* magazine ad.

"Come in. Come in." Bill pulls me out of my thoughts. "Let's get you two something to drink."

We follow closely behind them as they guide us into the kitchen. If that's even what you want to call it. This isn't a kitchen… it's almost double the size of my apartment.

I scan the room and notice dozens of cabinets from the floor to the tall ceilings. I'm sure they need a ladder of sorts to get to the stuff high up at the top. It's probably where they put stuff that they only use once every six months. That's what I would do.

There isn't one, but two islands in the middle of the room. Each one with four bar stools on them. There's a huge farmhouse sink under the window overlooking the backyard. Okay, maybe *that* would be on my vision board if I had one.

I have never in my life seen something of this magnitude as far as a kitchen goes.

"What can I get you guys to drink?" Bill asks.

"We're fine with whatever," Marc answers for us.

"We have whiskey and wine on hand. Both red and white."

"I'll have a whiskey," Marc says. "What about you, baby?"

I never thought I would be the girl who likes being called that. I can't stand it, if I'm being honest. The way he just so casually called me *baby* without skipping a beat has my thighs clenching together though.

"I'll have a glass of white, please."

It's almost as if Marc can sense the awkward tension that's currently filling the kitchen. It's not something I believe Bill and Cathy might pick up on, but the two of us know this is fake. I think our subconscious thoughts are equally nervous to make sure that they don't know it.

He makes his way over to me on the opposite side of the island that separates us right now to stand directly next to me. His body hovers close enough to me that the hairs of his arm brush over mine. It's barely a touch but the electrical current coursing through me is enough to make me think his hands were all over my body.

"How was the drive in?" Bill asks.

"It wasn't bad at all." Marc shakes his head. "We hit a little bit of traffic but not enough to set us back at all. Thankfully we made it on time."

"I was surprised at that." Bill laughs.

"See, babe." I laugh with Bill. "I'm not the only one who notices you're late for everything."

I watch as uneasiness washes over his face.

I wish I could take back my words. Not for my sake, but for his.

How is Bill going to trust him to run the company when he's not on time for anything?

"Thankfully," I spit out quickly in an attempt to save his ass. "You're only ever on time for the things that really matter to you." I shift my attention to Bill. "When we first started dating, he was twenty minutes early to pick me up for our date. My best friend is actually dating his brother, and from what I understood, he was late for just about everything they always planned. I guess something shifted when we first got together, and ever since, he's been on time for everything."

"When did you two officially start dating?" he asks.

"Just under two years ago," I lie.

"Wow," Cathy exclaims as her eyes bounce between us. "You two are the definition of *'when you know, you know.'*"

Welcome back, awkwardness. Long time no feel.

Between Bill and Cathy, I can already tell that she's the one I think we have to watch out for. Maybe it's just my guilty conscience but I am starting to feel like she's already onto us.

"I certainly knew alright," Marc replies to Cathy.

My stomach flutters and I can't help the smile that comes to my face.

It's not a forced smile to show that we're happy, this smile comes naturally and without thought. Because *he* said it about me.

"Right back at ya, babe." I lean into him and rest the side of my head on his shoulder.

The world was already moving slowly around me, the way it always does when he's this close to me, but it stops the second I feel his lips connect with the top of my head for a brief kiss.

It was quick.

Like he does it every day.

But that one small kiss felt like… everything.

For a brief moment, I want to live in that feeling. Frozen in time with a feeling so foreign to me but feels so damn right. It felt like he was silently communicating the words he repeated to me in his office... *I got you.*

"Come sit," Cathy announces, popping the Marc Ford bubble I keep finding myself trapped in. "Dinner is ready, you two love birds."

Marc and I sit next to each other while Bill and Cathy sit across from us. The same way two couples would if they were on a double date.

That's when I realize, this is about to become a game of twenty-one questions. I feel like I'm going to need stronger alcohol for this.

"So, Avery," Bill starts. "What do you do for work?"

I know from talking with Marc that Bill has no idea that I'm his assistant. I was really only there for a short period of time before I took the month off after we lost Gigi, which led to months off to take care of my mom.

"I work as an assistant right now." I don't lie about that. "But I'm hoping to attend a real estate course soon and become an agent."

"No way." Bill grins from ear to ear as he passes dinner rolls to Cathy. "Marc, did you know that Cathy and I met as agents? Back in the day, we were the power couple of the city!"

"I had no idea." Marc smiles. "I can see how everyone would call you that. You two have done a great job with Prestige Horizons."

"I am certainly very proud of what we have built together. The company means the world to me. But I must say..." He pauses his thoughts to make sure Marc is watching him. "I'm even more excited for the future of the company and where it's going to go."

I continue to butter my roll, but my eyes discreetly scan to the side to watch Marc's reaction to that statement, without making it known that I'm looking for his reaction. As an outsider looking into this conversation, you would think that Bill just handed him the company right then and there.

But Marc's demeanor shifts to nervousness, and I watch as his body tenses next to me. I know how bad he wants this.

His hands find his thighs as he rubs his probably sweaty palms on his dress pants.

I place a hand on his thigh to help ease the unwanted feeling that I can tell fills his body. His muscular thigh tense up under my unexpected touch at the same time that he takes a sip of the whiskey.

I got you.

His hand finds the top of mine under the table. He gives me three small pulses, signaling that we're both on the same page.

"But let's not talk shop." Bill claps. "Tell us about the wedding!"

"My favorite topic." Cathy wiggles in her seat with excitement. "I love weddings so much. I am one of those crazy ladies who loves the planning aspect of the whole night."

I start to quickly think of some of Peyton's wedding planning things because I clearly don't know the first thing about planning a wedding, let alone what goes into one.

"It's really so much fun," I say with an enthusiastic lie.

"When is the big day?" she asks.

"We decided to have a longer engagement because of her taking the course," Marc intercepts the question just as he swallows a bite of his dinner. "We're hoping for a date in the spring."

"Oh my word." Cathy gasps in shock. "You two must set a date. You need to pick a location because they fill up quickly. The vendors, the music, the food, the flowers, and everything else do as well. Didn't you two get engaged last year."

"We did," I cut in. "Unfortunately, the night of the event I met you at in December, Bill, I had to leave abruptly because my best friend's grandmother was really sick. She ended up passing away the following morning. She was like a grandmother to me."

"I'm so sorry to hear that, Avery," Bill says.

I nod. "Thank you. Right after that we were going to attempt to get the ball rolling. And then my mom slipped on some ice. I had to go back to Vermont to help take care of her because she ended up with a broken hip and a fractured leg."

"Wow." Bill shakes his head, just as he takes a sip of red wine. "It sounds like it's been a rough few months for you."

"It was a lot," I agree. "But I'm happy to be back in the city. I missed this guy." I tip my head in his direction before I smile. "He was such a trooper for putting up with me being away."

As if he's pleased with my response, Marc stares down at me with adoration in his eyes, and a megawatt smile crossing his lips. His arm reaches around the back of my chair to pull me in for a brief side hug. Giving my shoulder a light squeeze when he does it.

"How did you guys meet?" Cathy asks.

"Through my brother, Thomas," Marc answers, directing his gaze to her to answer her question. "This one is his fiancé's best friend."

"That is so sweet," Cathy coos.

"I knew I wanted to make her mine from the moment I first laid eyes on her," Marc responds with his eyes on Cathy. He slowly shifts his gaze to mine, causing him to have to look down to me. Our eyes lock when he says, "Best decision of my life."

My heart beats wildly in my chest at his response, as his words flutter through me.

Mine.

"Well..." Cathy claps her hands together as if she's ready for the main event. "We need to plan this wedding. Do you have a location in mind? Here in the city? A destination wedding?"

"We haven't really discussed that much," I answer honestly, poking the scalloped potatoes on my plate.

"I have a few places in mind," Marc interrupts. "I've been looking into *Penthouse 45* in the city or *Sound River Studios* in Long Island City."

"Look at you go, Marc." Cathy beams. "But both of those locations are very different. The first one you mentioned holds less than one hundred people, where the second location can make for a large, beautiful wedding overlooking the city skyline."

"I want to see what Avery decides as far as a big or small wedding goes." Marc clears his throat. "Since we never fully discussed it. I wanted to have a plan for both."

Like I said... I don't know the first thing about wedding planning or how any of this goes. If I'm being honest, I have only ever attended two weddings in my life. Both of them were backyard style weddings in Vermont for two of my high school friends.

The only thing I know about weddings at the moment comes from Peyton planning hers. I have been the worst bridesmaid in this one though, because I haven't been here for the bulk of the planning because of my mom. Then again, Peyton and Thomas seem to have the whole thing covered.

This would be a great moment for my brain to remember where the fuck Peyton said they were getting married. I vaguely remember something about a yacht club and a beach. But for the life of me, I can't remember the location.

Worst best friend award goes to me.

"I'm good either way," I lie. "I like the idea of a small, intimate wedding." That's not a lie. If I really was to get married, that would probably be my style.

"Seems like you two have a lot to figure out," Cathy concludes. "Are your parents around to help you out, Avery?"

"I don't know my dad," I admit. "I mean I know who he is, but he hasn't been around my whole life."

"I'm sorry to hear that. I didn't mean to ask such a personal question."

"No. No. Don't be sorry, Cathy," I assure her, wiping the corner of my lips with my napkin. "It's really just my mom. Unfortunately, she lives in Vermont. It's hard for her to get down here to help other than over the phone because she works a lot and struggles financially."

Cathy tips her head in agreement as she sips on her wine. "I can understand that. My offer still stands. I'd love to help you with the planning of anything you could possibly need. I know how stressful a lot of brides find planning the actual day."

"I really appreciate that. By the way," I say, making an effort to change the subject and get the spotlight off of us. "This dinner is absolutely delicious. My God."

"Isn't it? My mom used to make this for me all the time as a kid, and I've continued to make it for years and years. It's a once-a-week staple in this house."

"I can see why." I laugh.

The dinner topic changes to small talk about living in the city. Bill asked me a few questions about living in Vermont and how I liked living down here. It was very refreshing to talk about something other than a fake wedding that we're planning.

When dinner is done, Cathy rises from the table and grabs a few empty plates.

"Here, let me help you," I offer.

I grab the few plates she didn't and make my way over to the sink. Cathy starts to clean the dishes, but I jump in and offer while she gets dessert ready.

Marc jumps in next to me, and we begin the process with me washing and him drying.

"You two don't have to do that," Cathy starts. "You are guests here."

"My mom always taught me that if someone is going to invite you over for dinner and feed you a delicious meal." I smile as I scrub the plate. "The least you can do is help clean up the dishes."

"It's not necessary at all." Cathy laughs. "But it's greatly appreciated. I'm going to warm up this apple crisp."

Marc and I continue our mini assembly line. His arm gently brushes against mine with each pass of a dish. No words are spoken between us. In fact, Marc has been a little too quiet tonight.

My curious thoughts wonder if he's alright. If I'm playing along well enough.

As if he could sense my thoughts he whispers, "You're doing great, Avery."

"Right back at you, boss man." I blush.

We finish the dishes and I excuse myself for a quick bathroom break. Then I open my phone to see the group chat from the girls.

PEYTON

We just got to the shore house. How's it going, Avery?

KALI

Curious minds want to know.

PEYTON

Keep your panties on tonight.

Avoid any closets and bathrooms tonight.

KALI

Or don't...

PEYTON

Kali, don't egg her on. It will start to make things weird.

KALI

Avery has been on edge for the last few weeks. Girl needs a release, Pey.

PEYTON

You got a point.

EMILINE

My eyes are bleeding. This is one of those instances that you guys need to make another chat...

WITHOUT ME.

KALI

Oh stop, you kinky little minx, you.

EMILINE

leaves group chat

I can't help the laugh that escapes me as I catch up on these messages. They just know me so well.

My vibrator works just fine.

PEYTON

I used to think that myself... 😉

KALI

You deserve the D, girl.

EMILINE

ME WRITING *LEAVES GROUP CHAT* DOES NOT MEAN I REALLY LEFT.

THIS. IS. MY. BROTHER. We're talking about. 🤦‍♀️

I laugh as I pocket my phone and wash my hands. When I reenter the kitchen, Cathy is setting the dessert plates on the table and serves us a scoop of the apple crisp.

If you have never had apple crisp, you're missing out. It's probably the most delicious dessert I have ever had. It's mandatory that you scoop a heaping spoonful of vanilla bean ice cream on top though.

"This is my all-time favorite dessert." I moan as I take a bite of the warm goodness.

"You've had it before?" she asks.

"It's been a while since I have." I wipe my mouth with a napkin. "But it tastes even better than I remember."

"I've never had it before," Marc says, scooping another bite into his mouth as if he can't eat it fast enough. "This is heaven."

"I will have to give you the recipe." Cathy laughs at him.

"Please," Marc begs. "I could eat this every day of my life."

"Avery, looks like you have to make it for him very soon."

A laugh bubbles out of me. "I'm not sure I can. My kitchen is way too small. There isn't enough space for all the steps to making this. Which is probably why I haven't had it in so long."

"I thought you two lived together?" Bill asks.

Shit. Shit. Shit.

My laughter dies down quickly, and I refuse to turn to look at Marc to know what he's thinking about how much I'm fucking up right now. I'm fairly certain that my face is now ghost white.

Marc should fire me right on the spot from the title of fiancé.

"We uh…" I start, but can't find words.

"We actually didn't live together," Marc cuts in. I can hear the nervous tone in his voice. "Well, technically we still don't at this moment. We're in the process of packing up her apartment to move into the penthouse with me."

Penthouse?! Of course I forgot that Marc Ford also lives in a penthouse. I wonder if it's anything like Thomas'. If it is… woah nelly. Move me the fuck in.

Or don't.

That's weird.

I think the wine is starting to talk.

"I'm sorry." Bill laughs. "I don't know why I assumed you two lived together already. Cathy and I moved in together before we even got engaged. That was way back in the day though. Different times."

"We had planned to move her in months ago." Marc nervously laughs. "Everything with her mom set us back a little. But no matter what…" He pauses and his gaze sweeps over my body. "I know I will be spending the rest of my life with her. Whether we started living together months ago or this week. She's it for me, no matter where we live."

I can no longer differentiate between the wine making my

skin heat up, and the words that sound very fucking real. I really need to rein in my wandering thoughts right now. The wine is causing my brain to actually wonder what it would be like to be the girl that Marc spends the rest of his life with.

Can I see this becoming more than what it is?

Can I see me *actually* being in a relationship with Marc Ford that isn't fake?

I had three rules when I agreed to doing this.

And one of us is going to break the most important rule of them all.

CHAPTER FOURTEEN

Marc

My palms have been clammy since the second I stepped out of the car when we got here. I know how to sell the relationship because I've been in a relationship before. Nerves are racing through me because I'm trying to sell a relationship with someone who doesn't know the first thing about being in one. I am praying like hell that Bill doesn't catch on to any of the awkwardness between us.

Living arrangements?

Why the fuck didn't I ever think about discussing this prior to coming here?

We laid the groundwork of how we met and a brief overview of the wedding and what not. She handled it so perfectly by saying that the plans got set back because of her mom.

I think both of us were shocked over the topic of us living together being brought up.

Avery refused to look at me, but I looked at her.

I feel like I'm always looking at her lately.

In ways I don't want to… ways I shouldn't be looking at her.

Her face went pale, and she didn't know how to respond.

"What an exciting next step for you two," Cathy says, cutting through my thoughts.

"I can't wait." Avery half smiles, looking my way.

"When are you planning to start taking that real estate course, Avery?" Bill asks her.

"I'm not actually sure." She shrugs. "I'm hoping to get it started soon."

"I'm going to try and set her up with that same one I took before I started," I add. "I think with her personality, organization, and love for making people see things clearly… that she needs to get it done sooner than later. The next class starts in September so I'm going to push her to register for that one."

"That program is one of the best for sure." Bill nods enthusiastically. "When I saw that on your resume, I knew you learned from the best and would be an asset for Prestige Horizons. Now look at you." He throws his arms out. "You're the top agent I have on my team."

"Thank you, Bill." I clear my throat. "I have the best mentor."

"Seems like Avery is going to have a great mentor as well." Cathy winks.

"I certainly will," Avery replies.

"I'm hoping you plan to join Prestige Horizons after the course." Bill throws in. "I can see this power couple taking over the city. Right, Cathy?"

Cathy's eyes bounce between Avery and me. The way she has done so many times tonight. It makes my skin crawl if I'm being honest. You can tell just by being around the two of them for a short period of time, that she wears the pants in this relationship. Bill is a force to be reckoned with in business, but when it comes to Cathy, he willingly bends to her. I firmly believe that the final decision will be up to her.

"I can see it," Cathy says hesitantly.

"The organization skills are a big plus too," Bill says.

"I've never seen anyone more organized than Avery. The first time she came over to the penthouse, she reorganized my pantry." I laugh remembering she said that tidbit about herself.

Bill covers his mouth to laugh, while his eyes widen in shock. "She did not! That is hysterical."

"What can I say?" Avery says with conviction. "I love organization. I'm sort of a freak when it comes to it. I like seeing things neatly in a row on a shelf and easy to find. One day, I even color coordinated his work calendar based on the location of his meetings. Different color for different locations of his three buildings he works out of. His schedule was a mess before me."

"Doesn't your assistant do that for you?" Bill questions.

Avery is *not* supposed to be my assistant. Bill has no idea that she already works for Prestige Horizons, and I want to keep it that way. Office romance is frowned upon in a lot of the city. Once we're "married", the terms change, though.

"She does. She was out for a couple weeks when she had surgery. Some kind of carpal tunnel surgery that put her out for a few weeks," Avery lies, knowing damn well *she's* the assistant. "I wanted to help ease some of the stress he had at work during that time."

"Seems like you two make a great team," Bill states confidently.

"We really do."

Cathy moves to clean up the dessert dishes. She made a whole tray of the apple crisp and put extra in a to-go container for us. I already can't wait to have more when I get back home tonight.

"We should probably head out," I announce as I stand from the kitchen table. "It's getting late, and we have an hour drive back to the city."

"Of course." Bill stands up from his seat. "We can't thank you two enough for coming over for dinner. It's been a great night."

"It really was. Dinner was delicious, Cathy. Thank you so much."

"Of course, honey. You are welcome here anytime." She goes in for the goodbye hug. "Besides, it seems like we have a lot of wedding planning to do."

Avery stands and is immediately at my side. I wrap an arm around her so naturally. Something my body did without thinking earlier tonight. This time, my body betrays me again as I dip down to drop a quick kiss to her head.

I feel her body melt into my side more. She wraps her arm around my waist as if she were hugging me, and not wanting to let me go. Not wanting me to leave her side at the moment.

A feeling so new for the type of relationship we have.

"That we do," I say with a smile. "We'll have to have you over to the penthouse one night very soon to help us with some details."

"I would love that!" Cathy beams with excitement as she clasps her hands together. "I know you two don't know me very well at all. But consider me your unofficial wedding planner."

"Cathy." Bill's tone is much more serious. "You can't just plan their entire wedding."

"She absolutely can." Avery chuckles next to me. "I am not good at any of this stuff and I'd be beyond thankful for any help."

"How about we plan for you two to come by after the Fourth of July weekend? I don't have my calendar on me right now. But from what I remember off the top of my head, I'm free the whole week after that."

"Consider us there." Cathy beams.

"Drive safe, kids," Bill says as we walk out the door.

Once inside the car, I feel the tension thicken. It doesn't help that this car is small, she's closer to me in this car more than she would be in a regular sedan. It's not the most practical car. But it's been my dream car since I was a kid. The thing even drives itself.

I'm not sure what shifted from the time we got here until right this moment on the drive home.

That's a lie. I know what shifted.

It was me.

The entire time we were there, it was an act for Cathy and

Bill. However, there was no part of me that felt like it wasn't real. It felt natural, comfortable even. It felt like I could do it every day for the rest of my life.

When she was close to me, there was a weird buzz in the air. It was electric and extremely difficult to deny. It was one that made me want to live in that feeling, to get closer to her. One that caused butterflies to erupt in my stomach like a high school boy who has his first crush. This isn't supposed to be a crush. This is just supposed to be a way to gain what I have wanted for so long.

We sit in silence for a good twenty minutes with only music playing from the car speakers. Neither of us make an effort to break it.

Avery shifts in her seat as if she's uncomfortable.

Her long, beautiful legs are almost rubbing together.

"Are you cold?" I break the silence.

"Nope." She pops the P as she says it.

"Is everything okay?"

"Yup." Another P pop.

"Great," I say, emphasizing the letter T to playfully mock her a little bit. Hopefully relieving some tension that's growing by the minute in this car.

"Are you mocking me, boss man?"

"Never in my life, Princess."

I hear an audible gasp come from the passenger side of the car. My eyes stay on the road, but I see her head turn in my peripheral vision. A smirk forms on my face as I take my hand off the shifter and place it on her thigh.

"You did so well tonight, Avery."

I turn my gaze completely to her when she doesn't answer and notice her cheeks flush with my praise. I don't miss the way her thighs pinch together as she wiggles in her seat, craving friction from one simple statement that was not meant to be sexual in any way.

Hmm… I'll keep a mental note of that.

She still hasn't responded to me but shifts in her seat again as she brings one leg over the other to cross them as her eyes trail out the window.

I decide to take it a step further and confirm it for myself since she's giving me the silent treatment it seems. "Just in case you didn't hear me the first time… you did so well tonight."

Her head falls back on the seat, and I don't miss the moan that comes out of her while she wiggles in the seat. Blood is rushing to my cock at the way she's reacting to me. I should not be turned on by this.

I feel the goosebumps erupt under my hand on her now bare skin from her dress shifting in the seat. "Tell me… do you like being praised?"

She laughs as if I'm joking around.

"Something funny?"

"Don't try to turn this into something it's not."

"I'm pretty sure you did that all on your own." My thumb delicately rubs back and forth on her thigh. Her eyes drop to where my hand is. "Now I'm going to ask you again, Avery. Do you like being praised like a good girl?"

"Being praised turns me on. Okay? Are you happy now?" She swats my hand from her bare leg and sits back with her arms crossing her chest.

Thank fuck she's staring out the front window, because if she were to look at me and give me a once over, she would see my cock trying to break free from my pants.

"That's very interesting."

I press two buttons on the dash without her seeing and keep one hand on the wheel. We're on the highway for the next twenty miles or so, and my little sports car is now driving itself. I don't think she knows my car does that.

"Tell me more," I coax her.

"Again, *Marcus*. Don't try to make this into something it's not."

"Again, *Princess*." I throw her tone back at her. My one hand remains on the wheel while the other is still on her thigh. I scoop my hand under her dress to find the exposed skin high up on her thigh. I'm so close that if I move my pinky the slightest bit, I can find out just how wet she is right now.

"I'm pretty sure you started it," I continue. My fingers brushing her inner thigh again. She doesn't move an inch to stop me. Her eyes on my hand, mouth partly open as she watches to see what I will do next. "But I'm confident that I'm going to finish it."

My hand makes a move to cup her pussy and I feel wetness seeping through her panties on the palm of my hand.

"Marc," she breathes out. "What are you doing?"

"I want to feel what my words did to you. I want to feel how wet you are sitting here like the passenger Princess that you are." My fingers gently rub her pussy with the only barrier being her panties right now. Giving her the friction I know she is craving. "You did so fucking good tonight, Avery."

That wasn't a lie.

That wasn't a coax for more out of her.

That was me telling her that she did, in fact, do a great job tonight.

Her head falls back on the headrest of the seat as a moan escapes her lips.

I continue to rub her clit as the car continues to drive itself.

"You're so wet for me." My jaw clenches as I stare out at the road ahead of us.

"Fuck it," she snaps, quickly raising her dress up. Hooking her fingers in the sides of her bright pink panties and pulling them down off her legs. Tossing them to the floor of the car as fast as she can. "I need more than that, Marc. I want your fingers inside of me. I want you to feel how hot your words make me."

Jesus fucking Christ.

I don't waste another second before my hand is back on her bare pussy. My middle finger dips inside of her while my palm begins to rub up and down over her clit. She moans in response at the same time she opens her legs more for me to gain better access.

This was a terrible idea on my part. My eyes are on the road when they should be on her. I take a quick glance at her and notice her head is tipped back and her eyes are closed. Feeling every bit of pleasure I am giving her as my circles on her clit grow faster.

"Watch," I order.

"Huh?" she hums.

"Watch. I want you to watch me fuck your pussy with my fingers. I want you to watch as I make you come with just my hand."

"Oh please," she scoffs. A mix of pleasure and attitude laced in her words. I wouldn't expect anything less from her. "You really think you can make me come with just your hand while you drive this fancy sports car?"

My two fingers plunge inside of her. Her hips thrust forward into my hand as I do and she lets out a squeal of pleasure. I can feel her head turn to look at me, but my eyes remain on the road. I can't look at her right now because I am three seconds from pulling this car off to the side of the road and fucking her properly.

The smarter side of my brain knows that's a horrible idea since this shouldn't even be happening right now. I can't watch her face as she comes because I know I'll become an addict and want to see it over and over again.

She shifts her position, showing me she wants this. She wants more. One leg is resting on the dash and the other spread as wide as she can go, allowing me better access. I thrust my fingers in as far as they can go. Reaching the spot that I know will set her over the edge.

"Marc," she moans. Her eyes flutter back to the spot where my fingers enter her. Her hand clutching my forearm like her life depends on it. Keeping me in place and ensuring I don't stop.

"God dammit, Avery." I clench my jaw as her hips meet

every plunge of my hand. "Your pussy is so wet. So tight. So fucking perfect."

"Fuckkk. Please don't stop."

I pump my hand faster. Her hands are clawing any part of my body she can reach. I know she's close by the way her body is squirming in the seat. It's when her hands connect with my thigh that I lose it. I dive in as far as I can go, hooking my finger the slightest bit.

"That's it," she practically screams. Her hips start bucking harder into me. "That's the spot."

"That's it, Avery. I want this pretty pussy to be dripping onto the passenger seat with your cum."

"God." She lets out a low, guttural moan of pleasure. "You're going to make me come just talking like that."

"My girl likes it fucking dirty, huh?"

"God, yes."

She's right there. I feel her pussy begin to pulse around my two fingers.

"I can assure you, Avery." I release my fingers from her pussy, to tease her clit one more time. "God does not talk like this. The only two people in this car right now are me and you."

She groans in annoyance. "Marc!"

"Now be the good little slut that I know you are." I tease her clit with slow circles. "And come for me. But when you do, I want it to be my name that comes out of your mouth, not the Lord's."

I don't allow her a second to respond before I dive my two fingers back into her pussy. Leaving them there as I let her hips ride my hand. Her eyes never leave the spot where we connect while she bucks her hips into me. She quickly contracts around me, and that does it.

"I'm coming," she screams.

"Yes you are, Avery."

She screams out a mix of curse words and my name laced into her orgasm. Her pussy squeezes my fingers as she comes all over my hand. Her arousal is dripping down my wrists and onto the seat.

It takes her a minute to catch her breath. I turn my gaze to look at her and she looks thoroughly sated. I can't help the grin that takes over my face as I release my fingers from the wet warmth of her.

"Pleased with yourself?"

I turn back to look at the road, the same time I bring my two soaking wet fingers to my mouth as she watches every move, chest rising and falling while her mouth parts open again. The second they touch my tongue, I swear I could come right here, right now. Like a teenage boy who just busted in his pants by simply looking at a girl for the first time.

Jesus. She tastes… better than I ever imagined.

"I'm pleased with something. That's for sure."

"I did not *ever* take you for being a dirty dog."

I smirk. "What did you take me as then?"

"I don't know, but it certainly wasn't… that."

I give my fingers one last suck as I lick them clean. "You taste fucking so sweet, Ave. Dare I say, you taste better than that apple crisp."

"You must have bumped your head," she cries out in laughter. She adjusts her dress to bring it back down over her legs. "Because there is nothing better than apple crisp."

When we left Bill's house, I thought the same thing.

And then I got my first taste of Avery Woods.

CHAPTER FIFTEEN

Avery

"I just want to know why we need this much fucking macaroni salad?"

I scoop out yet another tub that Peyton has made. I swear there is about four gallons of this stuff ready for this Fourth of July barbeque.

I love macaroni salad like the next person, but this is absurd.

"It's a staple for barbeque food," Peyton states.

"So are cheeseburgers and hot dogs," I add. "And you don't have three million of those."

She laughs. "I have most of them in the outside freezer."

I offered to help Peyton today by coming early to her house. They moved outside of the city a few months ago to the most perfect place for the three of them. Peyton was never a city girl. She has always wanted the house with a yard and a white picket fence in the suburbs.

From what I know of Thomas, he was a city guy until Peyton. I imagine it has been a tough transition for him since he works in the city. But in the end, it was a smart move for them. His son, James, is loving his new school and all the friends he's making.

"What's the status of the real estate course?" Peyton asks.

"Thomas told me that Marc was going to be setting you up with that soon."

"I haven't heard details myself… but Marc told his boss that the next course starts in September and wants to have me enrolled in that one."

"He told his boss?"

"Yeah, when we went to their place for dinner. He asked what I do for work and all that small talk." I roll my eyes. "It was brought up, and I'm not going to lie, the more I think about it the more excited I get about doing it. I think it will be a great step for me."

She sends me a beaming smile. "I think you're meant to do that, Avery."

"Thanks, Pey." I offer her a smile back. "I make good money now working for Marc, believe it or not. But I just want to really be able to help my mom out more. I feel so bad for her. She's done so much for me for so long, it's time I help her out, ya know?"

"Jan is truly a superhuman. I don't know how she does it, but you're right… she deserves a little break."

I smile as I stir more macaroni into the bowls. It's been too long since I talked to her. Our schedules this summer are making it damn near impossible to get on the phone with each other.

"What time is everyone showing up?" I ask.

"They should be here soon." She starts slicing up a massive watermelon. "I told everyone to come around noon. The weather is perfect today, and I want everyone to be able to enjoy it."

"Who exactly is *everyone*? Since you know, we have enough food to feed an army." I think I know the answer, but just feeling out the situation at hand.

I know Marc is Thomas' brother and all, but a major part of me is really hoping he's busy for this holiday weekend.

Since luck is rarely on my side… I feel like that won't be the case.

Ever since he dropped me off after his boss' house last week,

I have been so on edge at work. What happened in the car was very unexpected. I didn't set a damn rule for no touching. So technically, he hasn't broken a single rule from our agreement.

He did make me fucking feel things, though. Things I don't want to be feeling for my boss. I don't know what came over me when I ripped my panties off and threw them on the floor. Desperate for him to have his way with me.

He makes me want more. Not just more of what happened that night but more of *him*. It may have been an act, but at some point, I felt like we had stopped pretending. His charm was next to perfect in front of Bill.

"The usual." Peyton breaks my thoughts. "The Ford clan. Marc, Oliver and Emiline. Logan is going to drop by after his overtime shift that he picked up. Kali will be here too. Obviously," she states matter of factly. "Thomas' mom isn't going to make it because she's in Alaska for a month. Something about it being the best time of the year to travel there."

"She's not wrong. The temps are in like the low seventies and the days aren't crazy long. It really is the best time. I took a cruise there years ago, and strangely enough, it was the best cruise I have ever been on."

"I believe it," she agrees. "A mom from James' school is also coming by and bringing her daughter for James to play with. She's a single mom and I thought it would be fun to invite her over."

"Do we like her?" I tilt my head in question.

She laughs. "We do. She's super sweet. Your typical PTA mom."

"Great," I say with an eye roll to show my sarcasm.

"There's one more person coming," she states in a much more serious tone. Her eyes stay glued to the watermelon she's cutting, as if she's afraid to tell me.

My stomach curls around itself at the thoughts of who it might be. I don't think Peyton or Kali would invite Dean here if Marc is coming. He's been trying to contact me almost every other day and I deny it every time my phone lights up. The girls don't really know him well, but my mind can't help but wonder about the possibility that it's him.

"Just tell me." I place my hands on the kitchen island across from her. "Look me in the eyes when you hit me with the bad news."

"I mean…" She shrugs. "I don't think it's really *bad* news that your mom is coming here for the weekend."

My eyes widen with a mix of shock and happiness.

I have missed my mom since I left Vermont. We have *barely* spoken on the phone because she picked up a second job as a hostess at a local restaurant to make up for the lost income while she was out.

I try to help her as much as I can, but city living itself is expensive.

"Shut up, Peyton. Tell me right now that this isn't a joke."

"It's not a joke. Thomas and James should be back any minute from the airport. They went to pick her up."

I quickly shuffle around the island, to pull Peyton in for the biggest hug.

"Thank you," I murmur in her ear. "I've missed her so much. This is going to be the most perfect day ever."

"Honey, I'm home, a male voice bellows from the foyer.

"*Marc,*" Peyton yells annoyingly. "This is not your home, and I am not your honey. But she's in here."

"I am *not* his honey either," I whisper shout at her.

"But you're having so much fun pretending." She winks. "I'm going to get the rest of the food from the outside refrigerator."

And then she leaves the kitchen the same time Marc enters with grocery bags in hand full of cookies and potato chips. Looking like a whole snack while holding snacks.

His eyes immediately find mine and a wicked smile forms on his face. A smile that tells me that he's actually happy to see me.

Why do I get this smiley side of him at Peyton's house?

But at work, I get nothing but a scowl?

"There's my girl." He beams with a smile that reaches his eyes.

"Marcus," I playfully swat his arm when he reaches me. "You do know that everyone here knows that we aren't really a couple?"

His arm wraps around my shoulder as he pulls me in for a side hug. I want so bad to shift in his arms and wrap mine around his waist and hug him the way a hug should be. The thought of that terrifies me. He's had his fingers deep inside me, but we've yet to embrace in an actual hug.

Probably for the best.

"Let's pretend for today," he whispers down in my ear.

"Why?" I ask, pulling my head away from him to look up at him.

"I heard there's a single PTA mom coming today who's desperate for some rich dick. I am not about to be the one giving it to her."

"Peyton says she's sweet."

"Thomas says she's desperate."

I step out of his hold. Giving myself space from him that I need to breathe. Lately, whenever I'm in his presence, my brain feels like a pinball being bounced around from one side of the machine to the other.

"Listen." I stare down at my bare hand. Fiddling with my watch that sits on my left wrist. "I know I set the rule of seeing no one else. But I know first hand that a person has needs. If you need to take care of them, do what you have to do, boo."

He throws his head back and laughs.

"Boo?"

"Yeah, you know." I lightly laugh back. "It kind of rhymes. You do you, boo. Get it?"

"I get it." His laughter dies down. "But I like hearing it from your lips."

"Stop it."

"You stop it," he snaps back. Like a child on a playground with no comeback. "I will not be going after some PTA mom that I barely know."

"Do you really need to know her? Come on, you're a dude."

"I don't." He takes a step into me. Putting only inches in between us. "But I know you."

Gravity practically pushes me closer to him as if there is just a pull that I can't deny.

I lean into him, knowing damn well that I shouldn't.

His fingers reach up to my shoulder before he delicately trails his pointer finger down my arm. Why does my body betray me every single time by causing my skin to quiver with chills?

"I know how you sound when you fall apart with just my fingers."

His hand comes back up to brush the hair away from my face and tucks it behind my ear so delicately that it makes me lose all the air in my lungs.

He leans in close, almost as if he's going to kiss me. Except his cheeks brush mine, lightly until his lips come close to my ear.

"So… right now, there's only one person who I want to have this *rich dick.*"

Peyton comes skipping back into the kitchen, her normal happy self.

I pull away from Marc as if I'm a small child who just got caught dipping her hands into the cookie jar. Marc doesn't make any effort to move from where we just were.

"What are you two love birds discussing here?" Peyton asks playfully.

"Marc is just being his normal arrogant self." I give an exaggerated eye roll. "And we definitely are NOT love birds."

Marc simply shrugs and gives his best cocky grin.

"Oh, Christ." Peyton laughs. "Did Thomas tell you about Bianca wanting a rich dick?"

"He did." Marc joins her in laughter. "She's certainly not getting mine."

"Trust me," she snorts. "You're not her type anyway since she's more about the nerdy ones. That's the only reason I invited her. She won't want any of you Ford boys."

As if on cue, Thomas walks through the kitchen with little James in toe.

"Ave!" James screeches. His little body barrels into my legs and I almost topple over, completely bypassing Marc on his run into me. "I've misseded you!"

"What am I, chopped liver?" Marc throws his arms out.

"I missed you too, bud." I lean down to give him a hug. "What have you been up to this morning?"

"We had to go pick up your surprise!"

I look at Peyton and Thomas standing on the other side of the kitchen, lost in their own embrace.

"A surprise, huh?" I play dumb because he's just so cute and I don't want to ruin this for him.

"Yes. Yes. Yes." He jumps up and down, clapping his hands.

I'm smiling so big when my eyes connect with Marc. His smile almost matches mine as if he knew about this surprise too. Was I the last to know? I mean… I guess it was a surprise.

"Where's my girl?" my mom's voice shouts from the hallway.

"Surprise!" James shouts. "We picked up your mom for you! She's here!"

"Mom!" I shout as I run as fast as I can to her. She opens her arms and I run into them. "I missed you so much."

"It's only been a little over a month." She hugs me tighter. "But I missed you too."

"I can't believe Peyton convinced you to take off work."

"I know. She's very persistent." She sighs. "I was reluctant because of the cost of the flight and missing those days. But it was fully covered. I felt bad accepting the offer, but I wanted to see you so badly. Even if it's just for two days."

Offer? My eyes dart towards Peyton and Thomas. Peyton throws her hands up in defense as if to say it wasn't her and

Thomas shakes his head *no* right before he tips his head towards Marc.

Did Marc pay for her flights to have my mom come in for the weekend?

Marc smiles and tips his head down before James is pulling him outside.

My heart pounds in my chest.

This man.

"Do we have any more cheeseburgers left?" Logan asks as we all sit around the fire pit.

"Logan," Emiline snorts. "You ate three already! How can you possibly fit anymore in that stomach?"

"I'm a growing boy, Shortcake." Logan winks.

This is the first time since our trip to the shore for Thomas' birthday that we have all been together. This time Oliver and my mom are here.

My mom left Vermont early this morning to catch the first flight out, so she couldn't stay up any longer and went to bed. She is staying in Peyton's guest house at the back end of the property and tomorrow, we are going on a mother-daughter shopping date in the city.

When Peyton and Thomas first got together, I don't think any of us expected to gain such an amazing friend group. Not only does Emiline fit in perfectly with us, but Thomas' brothers and Logan just add to the dynamic that we all have with each other.

Thank God that PTA mom wasn't into any of the guys here today. She was very engrossed in playing with the kids. Peyton was right… no one here was really her type. She made no passes at anyone and left surprisingly early. She was sweet and nice. And she didn't try to get into my man's pants.

My man? Stop it.

There has been too much sangria here today.

As if he can read my thoughts, Marc walks out of the house with a whiskey in one hand and a glass of white sangria in the other. Despite a full day of running around in the yard chasing James and rolling in the grass, he looks devilishly handsome. He's wearing a pair of khaki shorts and a sage green polo that compliments his tanned skin tone. The short sleeves of his shirt barely hang where they are supposed to because of his hard bicep muscles. And seeing Marc's arms exposed like that, just does something to me.

I want to claw at his biceps, and have his thick corded forearms protrude while he has his hands wrapped around my neck.

I can't tell if that's my vagina talking or my brain at this point. Maybe it's both.

"I got you another glass of sangria," Marc says as he takes the seat next to me by the fire.

"Thank you."

"How's the daycare coming along?" Oliver asks Peyton.

"It's going." She exhales a long breath. "It's a lot more work than I ever expected. I am excited to see where it goes, though. We have had tons of applications for enrollment already despite not opening until the new year."

"New year?" Kali asks. "I thought you'd be opening sooner."

"I thought so too. But with the permits and renovations, it's taken longer than we expected. I wanted to wait a few months post wedding before the big grand opening."

"How's the planning going for that?" I ask.

"Eek!" She beams from ear to ear. "I am having the time of my life planning it, honestly. I feel like all my childhood wedding dreams are coming true."

Kali clasps her hands together at her chest. "I am so excited for you. I can't wait for the big day. It's going to be the wedding of the century."

"It's too big," Thomas groans.

"Oh, stop it." She playfully hits his arm. "It's a small wedding and you know it. Plus, you don't even have to do anything but show up in your tux looking as sexy as you always do."

"So you think I'm sexy, baby?" Thomas purrs.

"Can we for once not be a witness to this?" Logan throws his head back in annoyance. "There's too much love here today."

"Leave them alone, Lincoln Log." Emiline swats his arm with the back of her hand. "They are the only ones here oozing all the love. Get over it."

"Nah." He shakes his head. "We got these two over here too." He hikes his thumb in the direction of Marc and I.

"Oh no. No. No." I wave my hands in the air in defense. "You know this isn't real over here. Get the idea of *love* out of your head."

Marc remains silent as the words come out of my mouth. I watch in my peripheral vision as he brings his glass of whiskey to his mouth without so much as a smile crossing his lips. In fact, he radiates annoyance right now.

Have I offended him?

He's lost his ever-loving mind if this will ever be anything more than it is.

"You two are…" Logan pauses. "*Really* good at your act. That's for damn sure."

"Man." Oliver shakes his head on the other side of the fire pit. "I've been gone for way too long. I miss out on all the fun. I mean, I know you guys are doing the whole thing to impress the boss, but damn… I'm with Logan here. I feel whatever you two have going on from over here."

"I'm glad someone said it." Thomas laughs.

"Have all of you bumped your fucking heads?" I join in the laughter. Except, my laughter is laced with an edge that other people are seeing what I'm borderline feeling.

My feelings for Marc *are* there.

Do I want them there? Absolutely fucking not.

It's certainly more of a physical attraction than anything.

Which is the last thing I wanted or expected from this whole situation.

The two of us are like a rollercoaster. When we're at work, Marc is just Marc. He doesn't make passes at me, and we coexist with an employee and boss relationship. We spend the week climbing the first big hill of the ride, and then a few days later, my hands are in the air and we're flying down the hill with an orgasm that rocks my world. The highs are incredible, but when we're not flying down that big hill with our hands in the air, or hitting the loopty loop, it's just… stagnant.

"Leave them alone." Emiline leaps from her chair. "Let *them* worry about them. Let's play a game of cornhole!"

"I'm down with that." Marc jumps up.

"Girls against guys?"

"I am so in for that," Marc says, while Logan follows him. "Me and Logan against Emiline and Ave."

"You're going down, Lincoln Log."

"Don't you wish I was, Shortcake?" He winks before he starts off toward the cornhole set up.

The entire group freezes around the fire. Marc stands in place with a pissed off look on his face, while Thomas freezes with his whiskey glass at his lips as if he was just about to take a sip but thrown off by what Logan just said.

Kali and I look at each other with wide eyes before we shift our attention to Emiline who stands there with her mouth hung open. As if she didn't expect it herself.

He did *not* just say that out loud.

Logan turns around and makes eye contact with everyone in the group.

"Oh please," Logan rebuts. "That's not what I meant. I meant like… she wishes we were going down. Not." He stops his rambling and groans. "You all have dirty fucking minds."

"Do we?" Thomas' eyes narrow at him.

"I didn't take it the way you are saying it was meant to be taken," Marc adds.

"This is gold." Oliver laughs to break the tension.

His laugh causes Kali and I to break out into laughter.

"Let's just fucking play," Logan huffs as he continues to the cornhole.

The corn hole set up is off to the side of the fire pit. The sun has set, so it's not perfectly lit. The only thing that lights up the game is the glow of the deck lights and the fire illuminating the yard.

Since it's girls against guys, Logan insisted on being on the same side as Emiline, which doesn't help his case of his previous rebuttal. That leaves Marc and I standing on the same side.

The tension that radiates from everyone is almost too much to bear.

I glance over at the fire pit and notice Oliver typing away on his phone with a very serious look on his face. My eyes scan the rest of the group and I see Peyton sitting on Thomas' lap, deep in discussion. I have no clue what they are talking about, but the way Thomas looks at her is a look of pure adoration.

If I were a girl who believed in love, or craved even a slice of it, I would want it to be the way Thomas is with Peyton. There isn't a question of doubt when you look at the two of them. I'm so happy Peyton found her happily ever after.

"Ready?" Marc cuts my thoughts as he takes a step to stand next to me.

"Are you ready to lose?" I tease.

"In your dreams, Princess." He nudges me with his shoulder and then shoots me his devilish wink.

Logan and Emiline go first. I can feel some weird sexual tension coming from them, even across the game. She swears up and down that nothing is going on. Truthfully, the two of them fight like an old married couple would. They have such an odd dynamic, so it wouldn't surprise me if there was something they weren't telling us.

"You go first." He smiles in my direction.

"Such a gentleman." I smile back but watch as Marc's face turns to anguish at the *gentleman* comment.

I ignore it as I toss the bag across the lawn. I miss the hole by a long shot. It doesn't even hit the table.

"Oof," he chuckles. "That's a rough start."

"Let's see you try to do it better, boss man."

As if he is a part of some professional cornhole tournament in his spare time, Marc tosses the bag and it does an air shot right into the hole. It doesn't even touch the board.

God dammit.

"You should already know by now…" He brings his mouth down close to my ear as if he's telling me a secret that only I need to hear. "I always do it better."

"Oh please." I playfully push him away.

"You and I both know that's the truth, Ave."

"I know one thing you're not good at." I tip my chin in confidence.

"What's that?"

"Tacos."

"Excuse me?" He barks out a laugh as if that's not what I expected.

"You don't do tacos right," I say confidently.

"What in the world are you talking about? Since when is there a wrong way to *do tacos*."

"How in the world could you not like avocados, Marcus?"

"Are we still on this avocado thing from *months* ago?" He shoots me an exaggerated eye roll. "Fine. Tuesday at noon we have a lunch date. Let's get tacos, I'll even have mine with avocados. My treat."

Did he just set up a date with me?

I was only finding a way to joke with him about his hate for avocados. The truth of the matter is, Marc *does* do everything better. He's smart, he's funny, he can hold a conversation and he knows how to give me shit in the same way I give it to him.

Not to mention, I know how he fucks. It's dirty. It's raw. It's animalistic.

And I fucking love it.

"Again." I grin. "Always such a gentleman."

"So, what do you say?"

"It's a date," I blurt out. Shit. "I mean… not a *date* date. You know what I mean."

"You want to go on another date with me, Princess?" he says as he takes a step closer, invading my personal space. It's night out, but I can tell that his eyes have darkened. Using his pointer finger, he raises my chin to look up at him. His body leans in to press against my body at the same time the corner of his lip tips up. I swear, he's seconds away from kissing me.

I roll my eyes at him, despite the fact that I kind of want to, which is totally unlike me.

"And just so we're clear, there's nothing gentlemanly about the things that I want to do to you."

I can't help the gasp that comes from my chest.

With every move that Marc makes, I feel… *everything*.

When he takes any sort of step closer to me, my skin erupts in flames.

When he looks at me, it causes my stomach to flip flop and the butterflies decide to start fluttering.

When he winks at me, my pussy throbs.

And when he flashes me his megawatt smile, my heart betrays me and beats wildly.

I feel myself losing the control I thought I couldn't lose.

CHAPTER SIXTEEN

Avery

The sun pours in through the open windows, and I let out an audible groan.

The one thing I can't stand about staying in places other than my apartment, is that I love me a set of blackout curtains. It allows me to wake up when I want to wake up, and not when the sun tells me it's time to wake up.

I stayed at Peyton's last night in their guest room because it was just too late to trek back into the city so close to midnight. Plus, with my mom here for the weekend, I wanted to stay close to her.

Picking up my phone, I see that it's six in the morning.

Another groan.

How do people get up this early and go about their day not feeling tired by ten in the morning?

I pull myself out of bed because there is no way I can fall back asleep with the sun shining in the window the way that it is. This room must be directly on the sunrise side of the house. I don't even bother looking in the mirror before I head to the kitchen to make some coffee. Peyton and Thomas have *the best* coffee bar set up with all the fancy syrups that my heart craves in the mornings.

I regret my decision to not look in the mirror the moment I step into the kitchen.

My feet are stuck in place.

I can't move.

I can't breathe.

Marc is standing there in nothing but a pair of workout shorts and running shoes, guzzling water while looking like a tall drink of water himself... His very chiseled back is on full display for me as sweat cascades down it. How did I not know that he was built like a fucking brick? Oh, that's right... we've been mostly clothed.

He obviously didn't hear me enter because his earbuds are still in his ears.

He must have gone for a morning run.

Like a psychopath.

Slowly, he turns his body, allowing me a full view of the front of him.

I thought the back view was hot, but it has nothing on what I'm seeing now.

His strong pectoral muscles stare back at me and I'm gawking at him like a voyeur. My eyes scan down a little further to take in his toned six-pack of abdominal muscles. I fight every urge in my body to run over to him and run my hands along the contours of his abs. Maybe he should be pouring that water on me, because right now I need to be cooled down.

"Good morning."

How long have I been standing here with my mouth wide open? My eyes snap to meet his. He's enjoying this, judging by the look on his face. I can tell he's amused by me standing here stuck in place and drooling over him like he's a fancy steak dinner. Or maybe it's the fact that I haven't even brushed my hair yet.

Quickly, I turn my gaze to the floor and run my hands through my hair. It even feels like it's a fucking hot mess.

"Looks like you slept well, Princess."

"Very funny, track star. What in the world are you doing up before six in the morning?"

He smirks as he takes his workout towel and wipes the sweat off his face.

Jesus Christ, he's fucking hot.

"You already know I like to run. When I stay out here, I go longer distances because of the area. It's much more relaxing and therapeutic than running in the city. It's all farmland and suburbs out here. The most perfect location."

"Do you see yourself living out here in the future?" I ask. Trying to ignore the fact that he is still shirtless.

"I could." He shrugs. "I'm not sure, honestly. I love it out here, and I love it in the city. But eventually, I want to start a family. Out here would be the end goal if that's the route my life takes me."

I nod repeatedly, because it's really damn hard to think with him looking like… that.

"Can you like… put some clothes on?" I wave a hand at his body.

"Are you not enjoying the view?"

"I'm not saying I'm not…" I scoff. "But it's a little too early in the morning for all that muscle to be flashing in my face like that."

He stands in place as his eyes drink me in the same way I just did to him moments ago. His eyes remain stuck on my exposed legs for an extended period. I didn't think this through because I'm wearing nothing but a pair of silk sleep shorts and a matching silk tank top that I borrowed from Peyton. Obviously, I'm not wearing a bra either because I like to let the girls free at night.

I cross my hands over my chest at the same moment that his eyes trail up to my chest. I try my best to cover up the fact that my nipples are hardening under my tank.

The smirk on his face tells me I'm too late.

"Cold?"

"It's July," I huff. "Of course I'm not cold."

"I see." His smirk grows wider.

I roll my eyes as I finally move my feet from where they have been stuck for this entire conversation. I grab the cold brew from the fridge, trying my best to ignore the fact that I can feel his eyes trail me around the kitchen. I make myself a glass with some caramel flavoring and froth up some caramel vanilla creamer to top it off. It's basically a fancy coffee shop iced coffee done at home.

Just as I'm pouring the frothy cream on top of my cold brew, I feel Marc's presence directly behind me.

My nipples perk up again from feeling him so close to me.

If I lean back even the slightest bit, my back will collide with his chest.

"That looks yummy." His mouth dangerously close to my ear.

"It is," I choke out. Barely.

"I have a question for you, Avery." His hand comes up to brush the hair that was hanging over my shoulders to my back. Exposing my shoulder to him. Without thinking, my head tips to the opposite side. Welcoming him to my exposed skin.

"Yes, boss man?"

His fingertips feather my skin from my bounding pulse in my neck, down my shoulder to my wrists. "Do you always look this beautiful when you wake up?"

That does it.

I relax my body back into him. His hard body presses into mine as his hands drop to the counter to cage me in while his face presses into the hollow of my neck. I'm trapped in the swoony orbit of Marc Ford, and if I'm being completely honest… I don't think I ever want to leave.

"What is that smell in your hair?"

"Lavender," I breathe out. "It's my shampoo."

I hear a deep inhale before he softly presses his lips to my shoulder.

I suck in a breath and it stays there, trapped in my lungs like I'm drowning in the waters of him. The skin under his lips feels like a branded tattoo I didn't ask for. For the first time in my life, I want a man's lips all over me. Not just any man's lips —this man.

"Marc," I whisper.

One of his hands leaves the counter, and takes residence on my stomach, pressing me harder into the front of his body, and I've never felt so relaxed in a man's arms. I practically melt into him while my hand leaves my coffee cup to cover his hand, keeping him in place because I don't want him to release his grip.

"I went on a long run this morning." Another kiss to my shoulder. "I felt alive. My heart was pounding with every step that I took, while I breathed in the fresh air and the smell of fresh cut grass of the suburbs. It was the perfect way to wake up."

"Okay?"

"But then I saw you walk into the kitchen..." His words stop as he presses his hips into mine. His erection pressing into my lower back. I exhale the long breath in an attempt to regain some composure. "Not even pounding the pavement the way I did today, can get my heart racing the way being in your presence does."

My body turns quickly in his tight hold. The front of our bodies now molding together as his hand dips to the lowest point of my back, keeping me in place against him. My hands grip his biceps as if my life depends on this moment. Like I'll fall if I let go.

I already know he's turned on by the bulge in his shorts pressing against me.

I would be lying if I said I wasn't soaked standing here.

"You know that a high heart rate left untreated can lead to a lot of cardiac issues," I tease him a little bit, trailing my hands up his arms and sliding them around his neck. His pulse races under my palm.

"Unfortunately for me, the only way I can avoid that is by avoiding you, it seems."

"Hmm." I smirk.

"And you're delusional if you think that will ever happen."

I bring my mouth closer to his before I say, "What if—"

I'm cut off by the sound of the sliding door opening.

The two of us break away from each other as if we were just caught doing something we shouldn't be doing. Which is partially true. Neither of us should be letting this go further than it is because what happens when this arrangement is over?

"Oh hi, honey." My mom beams, before she looks at Marc who's still very much shirtless and adjusting his shorts. "Good morning, Marc."

"Good morning, Ms. Woods."

"Oh please." She waves him off. "Call me Janice. Or Jan."

"Why are you up so early, Mom?" I question her.

"I'm always an early riser. You know that." She makes her way to the kitchen to pull out the same cold brew that I just had out.

"Peyton has that hazelnut syrup you like for your coffee."

"Amazing," she moans, as if she's already taken the first sip of coffee. Any good coffee drinker will tell you, that first sip really is heaven.

"Well, I'm going to hit the shower," Marc says. Scratching the back of his head as if he doesn't know where to go from here. "You two enjoy your day." And he's out of the kitchen without a passing glance back.

My mom says as she stares down the hallway with a furrowed brow. "Is he alright?"

"He'll be just fine." I grin.

By mid-morning, I finally jump in the shower. I would be lying if I said I didn't get myself off. Marc got me so fucking worked up this morning that I was still feeling the throb in my vagina hours later.

However, I had to get ready quickly. We planned a girls' brunch for my mom, Peyton, Kali, and I since my mom goes back to Vermont later tonight. Peyton knew I wanted to spend as much time as I could with her since I most likely won't see her again until the wedding.

"I've never been here," Kali says. "What's good?"

"Just about everything," Peyton answers.

Peyton picked this spot because she claims they have the best waffles she's ever had, aside from the ones Tommy makes her. They have a wide variety of specialty pancakes and waffles that are either loaded with gooey hazelnut spread goodness or topped with fruit and whipped cream. Plus, they have a specialty vegan section of the menu, which of course caused her to fall head over heels in love with this place. It's rare you have places that cater to that.

"I'm such a hoe for pancakes," I groan as I read the menu.

"They have chocolate chip." Peyton winks. "I know those are your all-time favorite."

"The way to my heart is always food, babe."

The waiter comes and we order a round of mimosas while we each order different types of pancakes. No good brunch can go without a good mimosa. It's just facts.

"So..." my mom starts. "Is anyone going to tell me about this Marc character? He was a little odd this morning."

"What do you mean?" Peyton questions.

"I used the back door to come into the kitchen so I could make coffee and not wake anyone up. Thank you by way, Peyton. The hazelnut syrup you have is to die for." She smiles toward Peyton. "Anyway, he was acting all awkward. Kept rubbing the back of his head. And dare I say he seemed... nervous?"

"That's *very* weird." Peyton's eyes narrow towards me. "Was anyone else there? Or was he alone."

"This wild child." She giggles as she hikes a thumb in my direction.

"That makes sense." Kali rolls her eyes.

"What? Why?" Mom asks.

"I'm going to let you tell her." Kali sits back and crosses her arms over her chest. She can't help but laugh.

No. I, in fact, have not told my mom about the little situation with Marc and what's happening this summer. We have barely had time to get on the phone with each other, let alone discuss the fact that I stupidly agreed to be someone's fiancé for the summer.

"You see…" I start. And then the waiter comes with our drinks. "Oh, perfect timing, kind sir."

I take a long swig of the mimosa, chugging it like its water.

"Continue," my mom urges.

"Marc is in a little bit of a situation at work. He needed someone to help convince his boss that he's established enough to take over Prestige Horizons. And…I'm that someone."

"You are the fucking worst at telling things how they are," Peyton cries out in laughter.

"You left out the most important parts of that," Kali chimes in.

"You see, Jan." Peyton directs her attention to my mom. "Marc does need someone to help convince his boss he's in an established *relationship* so he can take over ownership of the real estate agency. They have to be fake engaged."

"Oh, my word." My mom's hand finds her chest. "That's…"

"A situation," I interrupt her before I shift my attention to Peyton and say through gritted teeth, "like I said."

"Oh, honey." My mom laughs before she rests her elbows on the table to lean in to the three of us. "Do you know how fine that boy is though?"

"Mom!" I whisper-shout.

"My ears," Peyton shrieks as she puts a finger in each ear to drown it out. "That's my fiancés brother!"

"But she's not wrong," Kali adds with a shoulder shrug.

"This is not one bit funny!"

"It is, though." Kali chuckles. "Besides, I don't see what the big deal is. You're immune to this shit. You won't be falling for him."

My lips form a tight seal as I sit there. My eyes travel to each person sitting at the table, unable to speak or say anything. The truth is, I *have been* falling for him. Not like I wanted. But it's starting to be harder and harder to deny feelings that are so obviously there.

"Avery Woods," Peyton gapes.

"How's wedding planning going?" I attempt to change the subject.

"You asked me this yesterday. Nothing has changed from then until now. Stop trying to change the subject."

"How's the daycare coming along?"

"Avery," she practically growls at me. "Are you catching feelings for Marc?"

"Kali, how's work?" I shift my attention to her.

"Avery Woods," my mom cuts in. "Stop trying to ignore Pey."

"Ughhhh," I groan in frustration. "Yes! Happy now? It's strictly physical attraction but something is there. The lines are blurred and although I don't know the first thing about being in a relationship there's no denying the way I feel around him. It's exhausting."

"Jesus," Kali mutters.

"Let me ask you something." Peyton sits taller in her chair. "What's the worst that could happen if you *do* feel something more than physical?"

I shrug in response because I have no other words.

"Honey. Listen to me." My mom places her hand on top of mine and grasps it in a reassuring hold. "I know you well enough to know that you are one of the most independent and strongest women I know. You're so much like me, and I'm so proud of you. I also know that your entire life you only know what you saw from me. I never met anyone else after your dad, as you know. I don't want that to be your life."

"I like my life the way it is," I cut her off. "I've always looked up to you."

"And I love you." She smiles. "But do you realize how lonely my life really was when you were growing up?"

"Huh?" My eyes narrow at her.

"I was alone for as long as I was because *you* were my entire world. I fought like hell to give you everything you needed. Getting into a relationship wasn't my priority. I had to work double the amount a normal mother would because I didn't ever want you to go without. There was no time for me to date."

"Mom." I frown. "I never once expected you to stop living your life for me."

"I know you didn't. But I'd stop at nothing to make sure your future looked bright. I was able to buy your first car and afford to send you to college. I never stopped thinking about your future. This is what parents do. They look out for their children."

Guilt stabs me in the chest.

"But again, it was so lonely. I don't want that for you. I've *never* wanted that for you."

Movement from Peyton catches my attention and I watch as she wipes a tear from her eye as my eyes land back on my mom.

"You need to know that you can be independent and strong, *and* open your heart to someone at the same time. What your dad did to us by walking out, not every man out there will do that. I forgave him a long time ago."

"How can you just forgive him like that? After what he did to you?"

"Oh honey." Her tone is much more sympathetic. "It's taken years of therapy."

"Maybe that's what I've needed all this time too."

She shakes her head. "I'm so sorry, Ave. I wish I knew back then this was going to affect you the way that it has, because I would've sent you as a child. You were so young when he left. I just assumed you weren't going to be affected by it."

"I wasn't. It's just, I only had you to watch growing up. I saw how amazing you were and I wanted to be just like you. I never want to give someone the chance to do what dad did to you."

"I wouldn't change anything. I've always had you."

"I love you, Mom." I lean over to wrap my arms around her.

"I love you too, honey." She returns my embrace. "I want you to be happy. I know you're happy with the way your life is. But you need to know that for so many people, having a *person* to confide in and be there through good and bad times, just adds to the happiness of life."

"I can attest to that," Peyton pipes up, wiping another tear from her eye. "Ave, you know I swore off relationships. I was cheated on and treated so poorly in my past and just had a bad taste in my mouth for men. I swore up and down that I would never do it again."

"And look at her now, Ave," Kali says.

"I have never been happier. Not every guy out there is Richard."

Richard. The bastard from Peyton's past who cheated on her and basically ruined her for all future men until Thomas came along. She was dead set on never doing a relationship thing after she walked in on him eating his secretary out on his desk.

"You mean Dick," I snicker.

"Po-tay-to, Po-tah-to," she repeats words I've said to her in the past.

"I mean it, Avery." My mom laughs at our banter. "If you feel any ounce of happiness with Marc, despite whatever this situation you two are in, you should go after it. Everyone is deserving of good in their life. Especially you."

My heart beats wildly in my chest at the thought of a future with Marc.

But for the first time, I don't feel uneasy about it.

CHAPTER SEVENTEEN

Marc

This is the Mondayest Tuesday that ever existed.

From someone who usually works seven days a week, taking three days off for the holiday weekend to spend at my brother's house outside the city was a lot for me. That means I woke up today with dread in my gut for all the work that I didn't accomplish over the weekend. Combined with anxious energy to see Avery again.

After our little... *what are we calling that thing that happened in the kitchen at six in the fucking morning?* I don't know, but after *that,* I didn't see her again.

She went to spend the day with her mom and the girls, and by the time they returned, I had already left to head back to the city to get ready for the week. I was exhausted to say the least.

I was up that morning before the sun because I couldn't get thoughts of my fake fucking fiancé out of my head. I tossed and turned until I saw four A.M. on the clock, and I finally gave up trying to sleep, and hit the pavement.

It worked. I felt more relieved until she walked into the kitchen wearing her little silk pajama set that sent all the blood in my body straight to my dick.

I almost kissed her.

I almost broke the very rule that she set for me.

I wanted to break that fucking rule, and all the other stupid rules she made.

Except seeing other people. There is not a chance in hell that I could ever see anyone else anytime soon now that I've learned how her body feels pressed against mine.

My desk phone ringing pulls me from the thoughts of the person I can't get out of my head.

"Marc Ford," I answer.

"Marc, it's Bill."

"Good morning, sir. How was your weekend?"

"It was great!" he excitedly answers. "We spent the weekend at Todd's lake house. Went out on the lake and watched the fireworks from the boat."

Dammit.

Fucking Todd.

"Sounds like a great weekend."

"It was. Hey, question for you?"

"Of course."

"Do you have the reports from the last two weeks? I'd like to see how the offices you oversee are doing."

I toggle through some screens on my computer to quickly open up my emails to see if I got an email from Jessica with last week's reports yet.

Shit. She didn't send them to me.

"I have the reports from two weeks ago, but it looks like Jessica hasn't emailed me ones from last week yet. I can have them for you within an hour."

"Great," he replies. "No rush. If you could just email them to me by the end of the day, that would be perfect."

"I can do that. Now, I also have a question for you."

"I might have an answer." He laughs back.

"Are you and Cathy free for dinner sometime this week? Now that Avery is all settled into the penthouse, she mentioned she'd love to have you over to help with some wedding questions she has. She can't stop talking about how great Cathy was with her wedding advice."

All lies.

I hate myself for everything that's come out of my mouth.

"She can't stop talking about it either! We could do it tonight, or tomorrow night."

"Excellent." I pull out my cell phone to shoot Avery a text message. She's not in yet because I told her to come in late this morning since she had to take her mom to the airport last night. "I will ask her which day works better and get back to you. If that's alright?"

"Works for me, boss."

Boss. In my dreams.

We hang up and I fire off a text to Avery.

I know you're not coming in for another hour, but I have a question.

AVERY

What can I do for you, boss man?

Why does it turn me on when you talk like that?

AVERY

That sounds like a you problem.

Was that your question?

No

AVERY

Well hurry up and ask. I'm trying to rub one out before I have to come in for work.

"Fuuuckkkk," I groan as I lean back in my chair. The thoughts of her touching her perfect pussy has my dick standing at attention. I refuse to touch myself here at work.

AVERY

You not responding tells me you liked knowing that... boss man.😉

More than you fucking know...

AVERY

Then you will be VERY pleased to know that you are the star of the movie in my head while I take care of myself.

Avery...

AVERY

Can't wait to hear you moaning my name.

I put my phone face down on my desk because I can't keep *sexting* her at work. She's going to be here within the hour anyway. I can ask her what day works best for her when she gets here.

Like throwing ice water on my head, Jessica knocks on my door.

"Mr. Ford," she purrs from the door.

"Ms. Klein." I keep my voice steady and professional.

"I have the reports for you from last week." She saunters over to my desk. Exaggerating every swing of her hips when she walks as if she's actually going to turn me on.

"I recall asking you a few weeks ago to email these to me first thing in the morning." I stand from my chair. Thankfully I already adjusted myself in my pants. "Is there a reason they're late today?"

"I wanted to hand deliver them myself."

"That's entirely unnecessary."

"Is it?" She gives me a slow, trying to be sexy, grin. "I feel like I haven't seen my boss in a few weeks. I felt this was overdue."

Hearing the word boss come out of anyone's mouth other than Avery's has my skin crawling. I'm quickly learning I want to hear anything out of Avery's mouth.

"What else can I help you with, Ms. Klein?" My tone filled with annoyance.

"I'm more so wondering what I can help *you* with," she purrs as she tries her best to round my desk and come closer to me.

"Jessica," I warn her.

"Oh." She giggles. Coming close to getting on her knees in front of me as I stand there shell-shocked. "I'd like it if you used my first name more often."

"And I'd like to connect my fist to your mouth," Avery bellows from the doorway.

"Excuse me?" Jessica turns her attention to Avery.

"You heard me." She stalks over to where the two of us are standing. "Back up."

"This is a private matter," Jessica snaps back.

"Seducing my fiancé is a private matter?" Avery quirks an eyebrow.

"F-fiancé?" Jessica's eyes snap to mine while my eyes snap to Avery's. Our plan was for people in the office to not find out about this so that it's not something that gets back to Bill. Except, I can't help but feel excitement coursing through my body that she just called me her fiancé *so easily*.

"That's her," I say, grinning as my eyes stay locked on Avery's.

"Well then." Jessica takes a few steps back from me. "I see."

"Will that be all, Ms. Klein?" Avery asks her as if she can sense that would be the next question out of my mouth.

Jessica drops the reports on my desk and grunts as she storms out of the office, slamming the door behind her.

"What the fuck was that, Marcus?" Avery throws her hands in the air. Clearly annoyed.

"You think I asked her to try and seduce me?"

"Is this your thing with her? Is that why she's always here so early on Monday mornings? Oh my god," she gasps and places her hands over her mouth. "Were you sleeping with her?"

"Avery." I let out a long exhale as I make my way to stand in front of her. She makes a move to step away from me as if she's appalled by me. "Avery," I repeat.

"I have to get to work."

She quickly tries to turn to head toward her office. My hand grasps her wrist to stop her, the force of my pull causing her body to collide with mine.

"Avery." My voice grows louder as I repeat her name again. Using my finger to lift her chin so she looks at me. The moment her eyes meet mine, a grin forms on my face. She doesn't smile back.

"It's hot when you get all jealous."

She tries to break free of my hold to stomp away, but my hands grip her upper arms to keep her in place, pressed against me. If she thinks for one second she's going to get away from this thinking that I'm fucking Jessica, she's sorely mistaken.

"Do you really think I would ever sleep with Jessica—"

"I mean," she cuts me off quickly. Not allowing me to finish.

"Stop talking, Princess. Let me finish."

Her lips form a straight line as if she just zipped them closed like an actual zipper was on her lips. I love how she looks when I call her Princess.

"Do you really think I would ever sleep with Jessica… when I can't get the thought of you out of my head?"

I'm met with a stunned look in her eyes at the same time her lips part, just the slightest.

"When I can't stop thinking about how fucking beautiful you look when you first wake up in the morning? Your hair a wild mess, and your pajamas wrinkled from a good night's sleep."

She blinks a few times, clearly unable to reply.

"When I can't get the taste of you off my tongue?"

"Marc," she murmurs as she closes her eyes.

"When I can't get the feel of your pussy pulsing around my cock all those months ago out of my head?"

She opens her eyes to stare back into mine. Her hands are now gripping the collar of my shirt.

"Tell me, Princess." I run my hand down her stomach, and over the hem of her skirt line. My fingers feathering the fabric on the outside of it close to her most sensitive spot between her thighs. "Did you think of me when you touched this sweet pussy of mine before you got here?"

"No." Not an ounce of hesitation in her voice.

"No?" I question, as my head jerks back.

"No," she repeats with a smirk. "I just wanted to get you going. I was already in the cab on the way here when you were texting me."

"Hmm," I hum. Unsure how to feel about that.

"But back to what you were saying…" She presses her body into mine. Clearly able to feel my hard cock bulging inside my pants. "*Your* sweet pussy? A little possessive now, aren't we?"

"For some reason, with you, I am."

"That kind of turns me on." Her hands trail down my arms, until they land on my hands. She takes a step back, bringing my hands into hers and holding them in front of her. "You have nice hands."

"That's… an interesting compliment?" My eyes narrow.

"They would look great around my neck."

"Avery," I growl. My cock ready to break through the seams. "Does your insurance know that you like being choked?"

"There's a lot that they don't need to know."

She drops my hands from her hold, and they find my belt almost instantly. Her eyes never leave mine as she moves to unclasp it. My mouth falls open, words stuck in my throat and air trapped in my lungs.

"Tell me something, Marc," she draws out my name. "Was it me or Jessica trying to put the moves on you, that made you as hard as you are right now?"

My fingers cup her chin hastily at the same time she cups my balls over my pants. I'm slightly more aggressive than I intend it to be, but she's lost her mind if she thinks my cock is screaming behind the zipper because of someone else.

My hold on her chin forces her eyes to widen as she looks deep into mine. "You should already know the answer to that."

"A girl likes to be reminded every once in a while."

She shrugs her shoulders as she unzips my pants, and my head falls back with a long drawn-out exhale. She hasn't even touched my cock yet, and I want to explode. There's no one else in the world, not even an ex, that can make me feel the way Avery makes me feel.

That scares the shit out of me.

"What are you doing?" I finally breathe out.

She reaches into my pants to free my tucked in shirt before she quickly reaches into my boxer briefs to grip my girth. Her face twists into shock as if she's never had my cock in her hands before.

Come to think of it… she hasn't.

If all the blood in my body wasn't already shooting into my dick, it sure as fuck is all there now.

Her face distorts from shock to pleasure as she quickly frees my cock from my pants. Pushing my pants down past my hips with her twinkling blue eyes locked with mine. She takes a small step backwards while I stand there, precum dripping from the tip as my cock stands fully erect and drinks me in momentarily.

"What are you doing?" I repeat, but it comes out hoarse like I'm stuck in the desert and haven't had a sip of water in days.

Her tongue swipes across her bottom lip as the sexiest smirk I have ever seen crosses her mouth. "You said you couldn't get the taste of me off your tongue," she starts saying, but pauses when she takes a step back towards me. Her hand immediately finds my cock again as she slowly begins to stroke it. She continues stepping into me, forcing me backwards until the backs of my knees hit my office chair. My pants drop to my ankles as I fall back into it, assuming she wants me sitting here.

"I did."

"But your taste is not on *my* tongue." She hikes up the skirt she's wearing which allows her to drop to her knees. She gives my cock a few languid strokes before she trails her tongue from the base to tip.

"Fuckkk." I throw my head back and moan as she takes me into her warm mouth.

My cock is already in the back of her throat because this is Avery we're talking about. She's a dirty girl and I know she likes to play rough.

My hand finds the side of her neck while I feel myself hit the back of her throat. "Look at you on your knees for me like a good little slut." I buck my hips the slightest bit as she bobs her head up and down. Her eyes are full of pleasure looking up at me. I can feel her pulse hammering against my palm. "You look so pretty with your feisty little mouth wrapped around my cock."

She hums in approval as she picks up the pace of her strokes, bobbing her head with each one. Twisting her hands just the right amount to bring me closer to the edge. A blaze of heat rushes through me and I feel like my body could combust at any moment. With one hand gripping the arm of the chair, I scrub the other down my face in disbelief that this is really happening right now. Anyone could walk in on us since the door isn't locked.

"Eyes on me, boss man. I want you to watch how much I'm enjoying sucking your cock."

My head snaps back down to look at her and notice the devious smirk plastered on her face. I grip the back of her head and plunge deep into the back of her throat. Bucking my hips and watching as she moans with each thrust. Not gagging even once.

I release a throaty moan. "You're a dirty girl. You like the idea of me fucking your face here in my office where anyone can walk in and catch us?"

Her eyes close in pleasure as I slow my hips. She doesn't let up though. Her head moves faster and faster as she strokes me harder. Her thighs rub together as she wiggles on the ground beneath me. Her other hand inches up her thighs in an effort to move the skirt she's wearing out of the way. Reaching her panties, she cups her pussy with her two fingers and begins rubbing small circles.

"Show me how wet you are, Avery," I growl, my eyes never leaving hers. "I know your pussy is dripping for me right now knowing that only *you* can get me this hard."

She moves her panties to the side and swipes two fingers into her heat. She must touch a sensitive part, because her eyes roll in the back of her head as if she enjoyed that. God dammit, I swear I am seconds from coming.

Then she does what I least expect her to do… keeping my cock in her mouth, she reaches the two fingers up and brings them to my mouth. Urging me to suck her arousal from the tips. I do because, fuck, the taste of her is my kryptonite. I want, *need*, more of her.

"Good girl, baby," I moan into her fingers. "Do not touch yourself again. That's my pussy to touch when we're done here."

As if she knows what's coming after, she grips my girth harder. Twisting more and bringing me to the back of her throat. Swiping her tongue from base to tip over and over again.

"I'm going to fucking come," I grunt.

She opens her throat for me, taking me deeper than she has, and I lose all control. A tear spills down her cheek at the same time that I spill down the back of her throat as she hums in pleasure. My breathing erratic as I bask in the ecstasy of her mouth on me. I have never in my life had someone suck my cock the way she just did.

"Mmm." Her finger wiping the side of her lips as she stands up from the floor. She leans on the desk next to me and I can't help but stare up at her. "Salty and sweet. And so fucking hot."

"Sit," I order.

She pushes herself to sit on the edge of my desk, while I wheel the office chair closer to her. A grin spreads across her face as she slides her panties off one leg at a time. My fingertips tap her inner thighs, telling her to spread them. She props her heels on each arm rest of my chair, while I lean back and stare at her glistening pussy on display for me.

"My turn." I lick my lips. Ready to devour her right here, right now.

"This wasn't about me, Marcus."

She leans back on the desk, while using both hands to prop herself up. I melt back in my chair and interlock my fingers under my chin wondering where she's going with this.

"I'm three seconds from coming," she exclaims. "Watch."

"Excuse me?"

"I want you to watch me make myself come." She positions herself so I have the perfect view. "I know you were thinking about me doing this before I got to work. Now you can see for yourself."

This is true Avery fashion. She doesn't listen and does what she wants anyway. Despite me telling her not to touch because it's *mine*, she's going to show me anyway how she plays with what's *mine*.

Her middle finger finds her clit and she starts slowly. Her head falling back in pleasure as she picks up the pace. I don't blink as I stare at her hand rubbing circles over the bundle of nerves I wish my tongue was on.

"Marc." She wasn't wrong. She's close. I can hear it in her voice.

"That's it, baby." I praise her. "Say my name when you make yourself come. Show me how you can dirty up this desk for me."

I run my tongue along my bottom lip as she rubs faster. Like she's a DJ on spring break scratching records for the world. But she's doing this just for me.

"I'm..." she moans louder. "I'm coming, Marc."

She does. Hard. Fast. Explosive.

Like nothing I have ever seen before.

My own personal porn show.

She takes a minute to steady her breathing as I stand to pull up my pants and fix my belt. I know I come to work in a relaxed fit more often than not, but right now, I look downright disheveled.

She does the same. Leaping off my desk, more perky than usual, as she fixes her skirt and fixes a button on her blouse that I didn't even realize came undone.

The urge to pull her into me and kiss her is stronger than ever.

After what just happened, I'm ruined.

I'm thoroughly fucked. In every sense of the way.

"This is probably a bad time to ask." She giggles, her hand brushing through her messy hair to try to fix it. "But you texted me earlier with a question. What was the question?"

The question?

I had something to ask her?

"Oh yes." I laugh back. Trying to ease the nervous energy flowing through me.

I'm not normally this way with women. But this one makes me as nervous as ever. She's a fireball. A wildcard, if you will. Feelings are inching their way into my brain. In no way, shape, or form should I have these feelings. That's not what this is supposed to be. I should not be thinking about her as much as I do.

"Well…?" she urges me.

"Bill called this morning, and I invited him over for dinner," I finally reply. Rolling up my sleeve that fell down at some point. "He said tonight or tomorrow work for him. I may have said that you can't wait for Cathy to help you with the wedding planning."

"You did not," she says, stunned.

I throw my hands out in defense, "I know. I'm sorry. But he talked about how he was with Todd all weekend. I needed to do something."

"I can't do it tonight. Tuesday night is girls' night. Let's do it tomorrow," she agrees without wavering a single bit.

"Yeah?"

"Yeah." She nods. "I hate that fuckwitt Todd. There's no way he's landing this company."

Avery picks up her purse and makes her way to her office.

"Oh, and don't forget to order the tacos for lunch." She hollers from her desk. "Extra avocados."

My heart rate picks up speed again.

I'm without a doubt falling for this girl.

CHAPTER EIGHTEEN

Avery

Have you ever had a day where you wish it had a reset button?

That would be me today.

My day started off with the smoke detectors in the apartment buzzing. Not beeping, but straight up buzzing as if there were a fire somewhere in the place. Nope, nothing. They buzzed for about thirty seconds before they stopped. Ten minutes later they went off again. We thought it was the toaster oven, but nope. No smoke or burnt waffles here. Then when they went off again for a third time, we thought it was the steam of the shower. Nope, not that either.

I spent my morning groaning in annoyance and it was the worst start to the day.

I left for work early because I couldn't take it anymore and Kali was handling it with the landlord. I grabbed a breakfast sandwich and a coffee from the local coffee shop on my way in. I dropped the sandwich, sending it flying everywhere. I was embarrassed when they made me another one. Only to walk out without my coffee. So I walked back in to grab the second one and what did I do? Dropped the sandwich… *again*.

It's like it wasn't meant for me to have the pork roll, egg and cheese goodness.

If you try to tell me it's Taylor Ham, I will fight you because I'm not in the mood today.

Taylor is the brand name for pork roll.

Pork roll is the most epic type of breakfast meat there is. The closest thing I can compare it to for you is Canadian Bacon, but better.

It's a New Jersey thing I picked up when Peyton lived there.

Anyway, I then proceeded to spill the entire coffee on the sidewalk as I left the deli.

Basically… by eight in the morning, my day was shot to shit.

A ticking time bomb if you will.

After my morning, I expected the day to explode in my face. However, it went relatively smooth. Everything was on time that needed to be. Marc was in the Staten Island office all day. The computers worked great and nothing backfired on me.

Hell yeah.

I had to know that it would be short lived, though… because after I got ready to head to Marc's penthouse for dinner with Bill and Cathy, my car decided it was an excellent time to not start. The fucking battery was dead. When I called Marc to tell him I'd be late, he said *"Don't worry about it. I'm sending Fred right now."*

As if Freddy could teleport to me, he was at my house in ten minutes. Does he have a special pass that he can fly through traffic lights and clear the streets? Because there's no way that he could make it across town that fast for me.

Clearly, I'm just in a fired up mood today.

That's why I'm currently standing in the lobby of Sunset Square, taking a few moments to steady my breathing. A little bit of woosah if you will.

Of course, Marc lives in the same luxury condo building that Thomas used to live in. This place is legit nicer than the Ritz-Carlton. The entire building is set up so that only one side of it has the windows. The side that's facing the direction of the sunset. You get the most amazing views in the evening.

My breathing finally calms down, and I adjust my mood from feisty to a little more calm, cool and collected.

This day has already been total shit, so what's in store for tonight, Universe?

Unlike Thomas, Marc's entrance is accessible via the regular elevator, while Thomas has some back door, hide-and-seek entrance hidden past the employee lounge. I take the elevator up to the very top floor as nervous energy dances around my stomach, because of course that's where his place would be.

Only the two Ford brothers would live in the only two penthouses in this place.

My hand isn't even on the door to knock before it swings open.

"Avery."

His eyes scan me up and down. An approving grin forms on his face and I can tell he approves of my outfit. I went with a pair of form fitting dress pants simply because I wanted to wear something as close to yoga pants as I could find. Marc said jeans would be fine but… fuck jeans. I paired it with a floral, form fitting blouse. The outfit screams comfortable, but also acceptable for guests coming over for a nice dinner.

Since you know… I live here and all.

"Does this look okay?" I'm still standing in the hallway when I put my arms out.

His head is already bobbing up and down before he says, "It's perfect, Ave."

"Are you going to let me into my new home, boss man?"

Marc waves his hand as he steps to the side to let me enter. He doesn't reply, but the grin hasn't left his face since he opened the door. I bite my lip to fight off the smile that I'm trying to hide. And then I'm left utterly speechless when I take in the view of his penthouse.

It's *nothing* like Thomas'. It's a little smaller, but has even more windows and a more open layout. The living room and kitchen all mesh together, making it a perfect spot for hosting a party, if he has them. You know the heart of any gathering in a home is in the kitchen.

"This place is..." My words fall short because it is truly so beyond perfect.

"It's a little too much for just me."

"You could say that again." My eyes are still scanning the massive wide open view. My feet take me to the windows as I look out and stare at the start of what will be a beautiful sunset sometime within the next hour overlooking Central Park.

"God, it's breathtaking," I murmur to myself.

"It's what?"

"Nothing." I shake off the daze I was captured in. He wasn't meant to hear that. "Do you want to give me a quick tour before they get here? I don't know where anything is and we kind of have to convince them I live here."

"Right. Yes. Uh. This way," Marc mumbles through his words as if he's caught off guard by something. By what? My presence?

The way he's been looking at me lately, the small glances in my direction, the stare as I entered his home just moments ago... it's starting to feel like there's nothing fake about this arrangement anymore. I don't know what to make of anything.

I've to get these thoughts out of my head immediately.

"This is the living room," he starts.

"You don't say?" My tone drips with sarcasm as if the couch and television doesn't give away the fact that this is the living room.

"That mouth, Avery," he spits back at me.

"What about my mouth, Marc?" I challenge, arching an eyebrow to see just how far I can push him. Clearly my feisty mood from the day is still lingering on my tongue.

"Watch it," he pushes back. "Before I find something to fill it with."

I simply hum in approval. Wanting nothing more than for him to fill my mouth with a certain something to flip this day around for me.

When I showed up in his office yesterday, I had no plans of dropping to my knees for him. I had no plans to *ever* drop to my knees for him. But there's this pull that I can't quite describe. Jealousy raged inside of me when I saw Jessica in there, ready and willing to suck him off under his desk.

Never in my entire life have I felt jealousy. It took me all afternoon after the incident in his office to realize that's what that strange feeling was. The way I reacted… I didn't want Jessica to have him. Hell, I didn't want anyone to have him but me. The feeling of possessiveness over him sent me over the edge.

It turned me on more than I will ever admit to anyone.

Just thinking about it turns me on right now.

"Avery, did you hear me?" Marc says, slicing through my thoughts.

"What did you say?"

"The kitchen is here. Can I get you a glass of champagne?"

I blink a few times, unable to tear my gaze from him. Maybe it's the fact I was thinking about yesterday, but shit, looking at him in the most relaxed state, in his own home is seriously fucking with my psyche right now.

I'm at a loss for words.

He moves around the kitchen with ease because duh… it's his house. He's wearing a pair of dark wash jeans and a pale yellow polo shirt. The color only accentuates his already bronzed summer skin. How he has a tan is beyond me. They guy does nothing but work all day long.

"How in the world are you so tanned for someone who works as much as you do?"

"I run every day, remember?"

"How could I forget?" I roll my eyes. "You seem like the type of guy who runs 5K's on Thanksgiving morning too. You know that's a major red flag, right?"

Marc lets out an amused chuckle before he changes the

subject. "I didn't have much time to cook or prepare for this dinner because I was running late from my meeting—"

I bring my hand to my chest. "You? Running late? Color me shocked, Marcus."

"Cute," he tosses back with a cheeky grin. "Thomas helped me out and had Rosie whip up some stuffed shells and garlic bread. She brought me the ingredients to make the apple crisp too." His hands scrub at his chin as if he's nervous. "I was thinking we could make it together before they get here."

"You're cute when you're nervous."

"I'm not nervous." His words stammer around the lump in his throat. He takes a sip of whiskey and I'm in a daze as I watch his throat bob when he swallows.

"It's okay if you are." I chuckle. "I'm nervous too. I've had the day from hell and I can feel my nervous belly kicking in."

"Why?"

"My stomach has been making weird twisty turns all day."

"Twisty turns?" He barks out a laugh.

"Don't make fun of me. When I get nervous my stomach hurts."

"Did you want me to cancel? Can I get you something? Want some water? Some medicine?" he spits out the questions in rapid fire succession. I can't help but giggle at him being so caring and thoughtful.

"Stop it. I'm fine." I round the kitchen island and start opening up some cabinets. "Help me get acclimated to this ginormous kitchen. Tell me where the bowls are."

"I keep them in the pantry," he says as he holds an arm out to guide me towards the sliding door on the side of the kitchen.

As soon as he opens it, my jaw falls to the floor. It's massive. I think it's bigger than my closet in my apartment. Just… messier. Bowls and kitchen appliances are scattered everywhere and mixed in with the assortment of snacks and cooking ingredients. This causes my organization receptors in my brain to fire a million different directions. My skin is actually crawling at the urge to reorganize this right now.

"It's too big."

"No, it's a damn mess."

"It's not that bad." Marc laughs as he makes his way to the shelf that holds the bowls. "See? I know exactly where the bowls were."

"You need to hand over your credit card immediately."

"For what?"

"I'm reorganizing this entire thing. You can't live like this." I shake my head as I fully step in and spin around the pantry. "Hell, *I* won't be able to sleep knowing you live like this."

He laughs again. "What do you need my credit card for?"

"I'm going to The Container Store and getting you some things to make this the best and most organized pantry you've ever seen."

Marc runs his hands down his face. "Ok, fine. Whatever makes you happy."

Whatever makes me happy.

My stomach swirls with butterflies at the man willing to please me with such a simple task. I mean, this would make *his* life easier. But my love for organizing things would make *me* really happy at the opportunity to tackle this.

"Let's get to cooking," I announce.

Within minutes we have all the ingredients ready to prepare. Marc pulls out a glass baking dish and begins to spread the apples in it.

"What in the world made you fall in love with organization so much?" Marc asks.

"I'm not sure," I answer honestly, stirring in the remaining ingredients in the bowl. "I just developed this sick obsession back in high school with seeing things neatly organized. I love color coded papers and pens, baskets sitting nicely on shelves, and clothes organized in the closet by the length of the sleeve."

He laughs. "The length of the sleeve?"

"When you walk into the closet, the first shirts you should see are tank tops. After that is a row of short sleeve shirts, followed by long sleeves. The back of the closet should be dresses and more formal attire that doesn't get worn very often. I've been organizing like that for as long as I can remember." I feel my cheeks heat up as I admit all of this, so I stir the dry ingredients in the bowl more than they need to be. "I know, I'm a total weirdo."

"I don't think that."

I look up to meet his stare without saying a single word, and I don't miss the fact Marc's features have softened. He's so close that if I leaned in just an inch, he'd suck me into his orbit more than he already has. The buzzer on the microwave pulls him away from me, and I feel like I've just been saved by the bell. Literally.

I continue to stir the ingredients as he grabs the melted butter from the microwave, and I feel his body press against me as his strong arms cage me on the counter. I watch as Marc reaches around me, pouring the butter into the bowl in front of me, his rock hard body, pressed against my back.

I try like hell to fight off the way my body reacts to him being so close to me until I feel his breath on my neck before he says, "I don't ever want to hear you call yourself a weirdo again. Understood?"

I nod in response, unable to form a coherent sentence right now. Marc doesn't leave the space behind me when he reaches into the mixture and scoops up a small dollop of oats, brown sugar, cinnamon and melted butter on his index finger. The other hand wraps around my throat, holding me in place as he brings the mixture to my lips. I open up for him, sucking the mixture off his finger.

"How's that taste?" he asks.

"Perfect." I swallow the mixture, my throat suddenly going dry. I press off the counter, which forces him to take a step back. "You try." I scoop up some of it with a spoon and bring it to his lips. His stare burns through me as he opens up and takes a bite himself. I can't help but smile at him as he does it.

He groans, his eyes fluttering closed. "Shit. That's good."

"We make a good team." I laugh, before I realize the words I'm saying hold more weight than intended.

"We do." He smiles. "We really do."

Thirty minutes later, the apple crisp is fully done and Thomas' housekeeper? Chef? I don't know what her title is... but Rosie had dropped off the dinner she prepared for us. We both feel more relaxed thanks to some champagne for me, and whiskey for him.

However, the sinking feeling in my gut that's causing my stomachache hasn't left. It's worrying me because I want to be able to enjoy dinner. I've had Rosie's food with Peyton before and it's elite cooking.

There's a knock on the door, and Marc snaps his head to me, as if to silently ask if I'm ready.

"Game time, baby." I clap my hands together.

Bill beams as soon as Marc opens the door to let them in. "Marc!"

"Welcome." He opens his arms allowing them to enter the door. "How was the drive in?"

"It wasn't bad at all. Lucked out with no traffic being a Wednesday."

"I brought goodies with me," Cathy chimes in, lifting a canvas tote bag she's holding in her hand. "It's got information about a couple of venues, florists and entertainment here in the city. If we're going to do this, we're going to do this *right*."

I look at Marc, forcing a smile that I'm sure looks as fake as ever. I had completely forgotten in my sexual haze of yesterday, that he said he told them I wanted to meet to discuss helping us with wedding plans.

"Amazing," I finally choke out. "I can't wait to go through all of this."

"We're so grateful for your help, Cathy," Marc adds.

"Oh it's nothing." She waves her hands in the air as she doesn't want the acknowledgements. "Like I mentioned, I love this stuff. I'm retired and have nothing better to do anyway. This will bring me joy!"

"Let's sit and get you guys something to drink." Marc motions to the kitchen where we all proceed to gather.

Within minutes, Cathy has everything spread out on the kitchen island. She has lists of florists in the city, venues that have great reviews and DJ's that play the best music. She takes the time to explain each one to me.

"This is all so overwhelming." It's not a lie. If I was really getting married, this would be so damn helpful. But it's overwhelming, even for a fake bride-to-be.

"Once you nail down the groundwork and check the big things off your list, it will be easy peasy." She giggles in her seat.

"Thank god we have you."

"What are your plans for after the wedding? Are you two planning on having kids right away or waiting a little while?"

The question throws me off guard. Kids? God, never in my life did I want to have kids.

"Oh no." I shake my head. "Kids aren't in the cards for me."

Marc wraps his arm around my shoulder, giving me a tight squeeze as if to silently say, *wrong answer*.

"Yet," I quickly add, forcing a smile. "They aren't in the cards for me yet."

Cathy's eyes bounce between me and Marc. "I see." Curiosity fills her face as she studies us and what is really happening here.

"We're going to wait a little after the wedding. I think it will be good to get some traveling in, maybe look into a house outside of the city and set some roots down before we start our family."

"That's such a good plan." Bill nods his head.

"Let's sit for dinner," Marc announces, cutting the conversation off.

My stomach churns with distaste. *Fuck, what is wrong with me tonight?*

There's nothing better than the smell of garlic bread mixed with Italian flavoring invading my senses. But my stomach is screaming, *don't you dare put that in your mouth.*

I just have to get through dinner, I tell myself on repeat.

I switched to water once Bill and Cathy arrived. Feeling like alcohol was not a good choice with the pain coursing through my midsection.

"I have to use the restroom really quickly before we sit down," Cathy announces. "Where is the ladies room?"

"Uhhh..." Fuck where is the restroom?

I look to Marc for help, but he's engrossed in conversation with Bill facing the windows overlooking the city.

I stand from my chair to guide her to the bathroom. Looks like we're taking a field trip in the penthouse and learning together, Cathy.

"Let me show you," I tell her. "One could get lost in this place. I still do."

She doesn't so much as laugh at me, but a nervous chuckle escapes my throat.

I walk slowly as my eyes scan the one hallway that's set off the main open living space. *It has to be this way.* I tell myself.

Why are there one hundred doors in this hallway? Okay, that's exaggerating. There's probably four. But which one is the ladies room?

I open the first door and see a perfectly made bed. The room is filled with cream colored accents and next to nothing on the dresser. This must be the guest room.

"Oops," I stammer. "Wrong one."

We move to the door across the hall from it.

Bingo.

"Sorry. I tend to get my left and right mixed up with these

two doors. There's just too many here." I'm waving my arms around like an Italian in a heated conversation.

She says nothing, but shoots me a questioning glare.

Dammit. I'm screwing this up for Marc.

I decide to see what the other two doors in the hallway hold while I'm on this little penthouse adventure.

When I open the third door, my jaw falls to the floor as I take in the exquisite home gym set up. There's a treadmill smack dab in the middle of the room that faces the floor-to-ceiling windows for the perfect running view, and the floors are a rubbery black feel as if you were at a real gym. The one wall is lined with weights that look like they range from five pounds to one hundred pounds, and the other wall has different heights of pull up bars. No wonder his body is built like a brick.

I close the door and move to the fourth door. Hesitation washes over me because there's only one possibility of what's behind this door. His bedroom.

I slowly open the door and take in the master suite.

This… is…

My jaw hangs on the floor as I gape at the room that's larger than my actual apartment. A theme of black and red paints the accents of the room. It's masculine. It's sexy. It's…

"Are you alright?" Marc whispers in my ear.

I spin to face him as quickly as I can, closing the door behind me with more force than I intended.

"Yes."

"Are you creeping into my bedroom?"

"Would never dream of it."

"If you wanted to see my bedroom…" He leans in close, placing his hand on my hip to press my body into the door frame. "All you have to do is ask. I'd be happy to show you every inch of that room."

I arch an eyebrow. "Would you now?"

"I would. In fact, it would bring me *great* pleasure."

"I'm starting to feel like it would bring *me* great pleasure too, boss man."

His face dives into my neck. I hear him groan as he inhales the scent of me while his arm scoops around my back. Pulling me close to him, erasing every inch that's between us.

"Marc," I practically moan out in pleasure.

"If you're a good girl," his breath is hot on the nape of my neck. "I'll give you an official tour of the room later."

"I'll be whatever you want me to be," I practically pant out the words. Pressing my hips into him, craving friction and forgetting the fact that we have guests here.

"Damn, Ave." He presses his body harder into me, as if he can't stand being disconnected from me. "So eager for my cock. Such a greedy girl, grinding your pussy on my leg when we have guests in our home."

Our home.

A smile touches my lips that I can't fight off.

"I can't help it. You have a perfect cock."

He growls. A deep rumble from deep in his chest. "Avery. I will fucking kick them out of this house right this second."

"I wish you would." I give him a devious smirk.

"Don't tease me, Princess. I'm not against spinning you around, bending you over and fucking you right here against this wall."

"I wish you would do that too," I repeat my words. Running my hand down his rock hard stomach, I can feel every muscle under my feather-like touch through his shirt. I trail the palm of my hand past the waistband of his jeans, until it lands on his cock. I moan as I feel the hardness under my skin through his jeans. "It would feel so fucking good, Marc."

"We have to get back out there." Marc takes a step back. Adjusting himself in his jeans. "This conversation isn't over."

He saunters back down the hall, and I follow like a puppy chasing after its owner.

The next hour is filled with awkwardness and tension. I can't help but feel like Cathy might be onto us. My little issue of not knowing where the bathroom was doesn't help our case. She has been badgering us with questions since we got back. Back to how we met, how he asked me out, how he proposed. At one point Bill even asked her to ask us anything else.

Marc is on edge, and I can feel it radiating off of him.

It's likely a mix of what happened in the hallway, and the questions being fired at us.

"What made you decide on a spring wedding?" Cathy asks.

"I love the flowers blossoming that time of year," I answer honestly. "A winter wedding runs the risk of snow and ice."

"Do you have plans for your honeymoon?" she asks without even acknowledging the previous answer. I feel like I'm in my own round of twenty-one questions.

"I—"

"Paris," Marc answers for me. "She's never been to Paris, and I want to take her."

"Oh, Marc." Cathy clutches her chest in awe. "That's the most perfect place. You're going to fall in love, Avery."

I think I just might… Dammit.

We cleaned up the dinner dishes from what was probably the most delicious stuffed shells I've ever had. Despite my stomach, I had to eat them.

We're getting ready to serve apple crisp when my stomach decides to stab me from the inside. The pain causes me to curl over myself in the kitchen. I rest a hand on the counter to steady myself, my other hand clutching my stomach as if that will actually ease some of the pain.

Cathy gasps from the other side of the kitchen. "Avery! Are you alright?"

"I…"

"Babe." Marc's calm tone brings me back to reality. "What's wrong?"

"My stomach. Fuck. It hurts so bad." Pain shoots through my

stomach again. Sending a wave of nausea through me. "I'm sorry for my language, but I think I'm going to be sick."

Cathy moves quickly to the fridge to grab a bottle of water for me before placing it down in front of me. One look at the bottle and thinking about drinking that right now makes me feel even sicker.

"Are you okay, honey?" she asks. "What can we do?"

"I-I'm fine." At the same time the words leave my mouth, my stomach twists again. Causing me to curl over my legs on the floor.

Marc doesn't waste a second before he scoops me up in his arms as if I weigh less than a pound. "I'm sorry, Bill," he shouts over his shoulder as he carries me through the living room.

"Don't be. Please let us know if you need anything."

"Feel better, Avery," Cathy adds, her voice carrying through the rooms.

We both hear the front door close shut at the same time he places me on the ground in his master bathroom ensuite. He places me down carefully, resting on the wall that's closest to the toilet as if I'm going to be sick any second.

"Marc. I'm fine," I choke out with pain laced in my tone. Bringing my legs to my chest, I'm feeling incredibly vulnerable right now.

"You're not." He opens a closet in the bathroom and pulls out a washcloth before he runs it under cold water. He crouches down beside me on the floor to run it across my forehead. "What can I do?"

I stare up at him, blinking in shock. No one other than my mother has ever taken care of me when I was sick. I mean… It's been *years* since I've been sick. I'm not sure what's come over me.

"You don't need to do this."

"Avery, for once in your life, shut up," he snaps at me. My mouth hangs open and tears sting my eyes. "I mean that in the nicest way possible of course," he adds.

"It's just… I'm just fine," I assure him.

Despite every part of my body *not* feeling fine.

"Let me take care of you."

"Why? I don't want you to see me get sick. Just call Fred to come get me. He apparently has some lightning speed on his car and can get places faster than anyone else in the city. He can take me home before I retch all over this bathroom."

He swipes the washcloth over my forehead again, offering me a soft smile. Brushing the hair that's fallen into my face out of the way with his knuckles. "Because whether you want to believe it or not, I care about you."

I give him a displeased scoff. "What if I'm contagious?"

"Then it looks like I'll be getting sick too."

"Did you bump your head or something?"

"Avery." He covers my lips with his pointer finger. "Stop talking."

I clamp my lips down together, succumbing to his demands.

"Good girl," he praises. "Here's what's going to happen. You're going to spend the night here."

I open my mouth to protest.

"Nope. Don't even try it. Something is wrong, and I can't let you leave here knowing that you have no one to take care of you."

"Kali might be home."

"I'm not taking any risks with you, Princess."

"Marc," I blow out his name with a sigh of resignation. I cross my arms over my knees and rest my head down on them. Defeated. Feeling more ill than I did three minutes ago.

Staying here is a horrible idea.

But the thought of standing up to walk out of here sounds even worse.

Sobs are begging to rack my chest, and for the first time in as long as I can remember, I break down in front of someone other than my best friends.

"I hate feeling like this," I cry. "Why does this have to happen to me right now? I feel so terrible and so gross and so—"

"I got you, Avery," he cuts me off when his arms are wrapped around me.

My body warms with the comfort of having a man take care of me. Not just any man, *this* man. I lean into his chest, sobbing harder as every emotion runs through my body.

Next thing I know, I'm hurling into the toilet.

Marc never leaves my side.

Showing me an entire new side of him that is awakening every feeling I didn't know I could have for another person.

CHAPTER NINETEEN

Marc

The light shining in from the living room windows wakes me from my half-assed attempt at sleep.

I really need to put some curtains in the living room.

I swing my legs off the side of the couch and groan as my bones snap in every part of my body it can. If you want to feel really old, sleep on a firm couch. It's enough to break your back.

I think I slept all of five minutes.

Avery ended up extremely sick all night. I even had to call my sister, Emiline to see if she should go to the emergency room or not. The consensus was that it had to be some sort of food poisoning.

When she's better, I'll have to remember to give her shit for how the green baby food looking fruit damn near took her out. Even though it was likely the chicken she had in hers, since I had the beef and didn't get sick.

Fred took a midnight trip to the store for me for some electrolytes and crackers for when she's ready to start eating again.

I really owe that man a raise.

Another mental note.

It's been a long time since I've felt wanted… needed by someone else before.

This was the most vulnerable state I've ever seen Avery in, and it made me see her in a whole new light. Behind that rough, independent exterior is a woman who will break down in a time of need. The way her body shook with sobs after the first few times she got sick and how she melted into me when I held her, told me that she needed me right then and there.

I wasn't planning on going anywhere.

I shuffle down the hall to creep into the room to see how she's doing. It wasn't until around four in the morning that she finally stopped getting sick.

My heart cracks behind my ribcage when I see her curled up in my bed.

My bed.

Her body looks even smaller tucked under the covers, right in the middle of the massive king size bed. She's wearing nothing but my oversized t-shirt I had put on her, and *fuck*, if that doesn't make my heartbeat faster. Despite being pale and weak, she's the most beautiful woman I've been this close to in a while. Watching her open mouth breathe, hearing her little snores come out of her is the cutest thing. I can't help the smile that crosses my face.

I close the door and make my way to the kitchen to make a cup of coffee when my phone vibrates in my pocket.

"Hello?"

"Morning," Emiline responds groggy and half asleep.

"Hey, Em. Just wake up?"

"Yeah. I was worried about Ave. How's she doing?"

I know that Emiline formed a close friendship with the girls after our trip to the shore house. Knowing my sister is worried about her tugs at my heart, though. It makes me wonder that if this became real, would she continue to approve of it?

"She finally stopped puking early this morning. It was horrible, Em," I choke out. Unable to control my emotions. Tears begin to gather behind my eyes. Emotions that I haven't felt in a long time. Maybe it's the fact that I'm beyond exhausted right now. "I have never felt so helpless in my life. Nothing I could do would help her."

"Aww, Marc." She sighs. "You care about her."

This is a statement, not her questioning me. My little sister is a lot like me, a softy at heart. When she feels, she feels with her whole heart.

I swallow the lump in my throat. "I do."

"I'm glad she's getting some rest. But you need to rest too," she scolds me the way a big sister would. For being my little sister, she's very mature and wise for her age.

"I know. It's just hard to sleep when I'm afraid she's going to wake up and need something. Did I already mention how helpless I already feel?"

"That's a very normal feeling, Marc," she assures me with her words.

I sit in silence with the phone pressed to my ear, scrubbing my chin and contemplating what I'm going to say back to that. I know deep down that I don't have to say much, because Emiline Ford can read people like a book. It's only a matter of time before she catches on that a big part of me doesn't want this to be fake anymore.

"I had a feeling this would happen."

"What? You knew she was gonna get sick?"

"No," she barks out a scoff. "I knew you were going to fall for her. I mean, what's not to love? This is Avery we're talking about."

"Now you sound like Logan."

"Ew, Marc! Do *not* say I sound like him. He's so fucking annoying."

"Stop it." I laugh at her. "You love him."

"Anyway... Back to what I was saying. You should probably consider telling her how you're feeling. Because this whole fake facade you two are putting on is starting to look a whole lot more real, from the outside looking in."

My heart rate picks up speed as if the air in the room has

shifted.

I feel her before I see her.

Avery clears her throat from the entrance of the hallway, rooted in place with nothing but my oversized t-shirt on.

"Listen, Em. I have to go. Avery just woke up."

"Tell her—" And I cut her off with a click of the end button.

"Avery." I suck in a long breath of air before I walk over to where she stands. Her hair is a mess from rolling around in the bed, and she has her arms wrapped around her midsection hugging herself. She looks on the verge of tears.

"Morning," she mumbles. Her voice is hoarse, probably from throwing up so much. "The baby monitor was a nice touch." She adds with a dramatic eye roll.

I was hoping she didn't see that. I wanted to make sure she was ok when I wasn't in the room with her. If she woke up, I wanted to be there to hold her hair up, rub her back and comfort her.

"I'm sorry. Just did it so I knew you were okay."

"You keep spare child monitors around?" She lets out a light chuckle.

I shrug. "For James."

I pull her into me using my hand to bring her head to my chest, and the other hand to bring her body flush with mine. Her body shivers under my touch. My heart beats erratically under her ear. I'm sure she hears it picking up its pace with each second that passes.

"Are you cold?"

"I am a little. I'm still so tired. I could sleep all day."

"Why don't you go back to bed? What are you even doing up already?"

"I heard you on the phone. I looked at the clock and saw it's almost time to go to work." She pulls herself out of my embrace just slightly. "I should probably head ho—"

"Don't even think about it."

"Marc." Her hands ball into a fist and they land on her hips.

"I have to get home. I need to shower and get this god awful smell of puke off me. I need my toothbrush. And most importantly, I need to get ready for work!"

"You're cute when you're flustered." I shoot her a devilish smirk." We're not going in today."

"We??"

"Yes… *we*," I repeat. "We're staying here. You're resting. And I'm going to try and get some work done while you rest. When you start to feel hungry, I'm going to cook for you. When you're ready, I'm going to draw you a bath. There's an extra toothbrush already on the sink for you. Anything I'm forgetting?"

"You should call Emiline back and have your head checked, because I think you're losing your mind."

"There's my little firecracker." I pull her back into me for another hug. "I was starting to think you lost that smart mouth of yours in the toilet."

"You think this is funny?"

I narrow my eyes at her. "When are you going to accept that I want to do this? I don't mind taking care of you. In fact, I enjoy it. I *want* to be the one to take care of you."

"That's not what this is."

I take a step away from her, smile on my face as I turn on my heels and walk into the kitchen. She's trying like hell to deny any sort of feelings she has for me. But there's no way the chemistry between us is one sided anymore.

"Do me a favor. Brush your teeth and take a long hot bath in that really fancy expensive tub I had installed with jet streams that come out of all angles. If you're up for a light breakfast when you get out, I'll make you something and then we can talk."

"Fine," she huffs out as she crosses her arms over her chest. "But we're talking about this." With her parting words, she storms off into the bedroom.

It's becoming more and more clear that this attraction I have for Avery Woods isn't just physical anymore.

CHAPTER TWENTY

Avery

Marc wasn't wrong.

There was a toothbrush set out on the bathroom counter for me to use. It was quite honestly the best teeth brushing I've ever had after the night that I had.

I woke up stretched out in a giant king size bed wearing nothing but Marc's t-shirt. I'm assuming Marc put this on me, because in my sick haze, I don't remember doing it. Inhaling his scent that was soaked into every fabric of the comforter, I won't lie and say I didn't snuggle deeper when the rich sandalwood smell that intoxicated my senses. I didn't want to move from the bed.

However, I knew I was ruining it with the overpowering smell of puke radiating off of me.

I've never been so embarrassed in my life with how sick I got last night in front of someone else. I've been hungover sick in front of Peyton and Kali plenty of times, but nothing compared to this. Fucking tacos from lunch yesterday. I'm scarred for life now.

He also wasn't wrong about the insane bathtub he had built. How did I not notice that when I spent half the night in this bathroom? It was the greatest bath of my life. I even sat in there ten minutes longer than necessary just to relax and breathe in the steam.

When I got out, I pinned my hair up in a claw clip without even bothering to care how it looked. Marc had a pair of sweatpants and a fresh t-shirt laid out for me. I decide to forego the bra and panties, because let's face it, he's seen all he needs to see, so there's nothing left for me to hide.

Making my way down the hall, I hear Marc on the phone. It's distant so I assume he must be in a room or something. Is there a home office here I don't know about? It's close enough though, that I can hear it's a work thing. They're discussing a house on the lake on Long Island. This is new for him because he really only deals with big buildings and sticks to the city limits. This must be a special customer.

I plop myself down on the oversized couch smack dab in the middle of the living room. The blankets are no longer lining the back of it, and pillows are strewn everywhere. Guilt makes the nausea creep back up, because it's obvious that this is where he slept last night.

That feeling is quickly replaced with hunger as my stomach makes the most awful growl.

The kitchen is packed with an array of food choices. I'm not going to lie, the choices are a dream for a person like me. Give me any type of breakfast food for every meal and I could live happily. Seriously though, what is it about breakfast food that is *soo* good any time of day? You can't have chicken fettuccine alfredo for breakfast, but waffles for dinner isn't frowned upon.

"Creeping through the kitchen cabinets now?"

Marc's voice stops me in my tracks. I turn to face him as if I had been caught snooping around. He stands there looking refreshed and… my eyes trail his body. A body that is wearing nothing but a pair of charcoal gray sweatpants that sit just low enough that his *fuck me* lines are showing. I've never seen a man more perfectly chiseled than the one standing in front of me.

"I wasn't creeping. I'm looking for a pan to make some scrambled eggs."

The corners of his lips tip up just the slightest as if he knows exactly what my brain was thinking. As if he can read every dirty thought running through my brain as I stand there, stuck in the middle of his massive kitchen.

"Allow me." He opens the one cabinet I haven't opened yet and pulls out a pan. "Sit."

I do as he says and perch myself right on the barstool directly across from the stovetop. I catch myself meticulously watching every move he makes. The way his muscles flex with every stir of the spatula. The way the veins in his forearm protrude as he grips the handle of the pan, mixing the eggs to make sure they cook evenly.

"You're staring again, Princess."

Annndddd... I'm busted.

"The eggs... they look... delicious."

A throaty laugh leaves his body. "I'm sure they do."

He plates the eggs and then pulls a slice of toast out of the toaster oven and slides the plate across the island in front of me.

"How are you feeling after your bath?" he asks.

"So much better." The words barely form with the food stuffed in my mouth like a starved bear just out of hibernation. "Sorry. These eggs are amazing."

"Glad to hear." He laughs.

"That soak in the tub and a good brushing of my teeth is exactly what I needed." He hums in approval as he cleans up the breakfast pan. "What about you?"

"My shower was... nice."

My mouth falls slightly open. "That's not what... Breakfast... What about you eating for breakfast?" When did things get awkward around here? Oh, I know. When he decided to walk around shirtless in front of me. I think every last brain cell I had is out the window.

"I ate already while you took a bath. I told you I'd make you something to eat when you were ready."

He did say that.

It dawned on me that the last twelve hours were much more tolerable because *he* was there. He never left my side, and here he is yet again, never leaving my side.

"Thank you," I manage to choke out. "For taking care of me last night and making sure I didn't croak."

He huffs out a laugh. "I wasn't going to let you croak, Ave."

I believe it too.

While this man standing in front of me is demanding in the boardroom, ruthless with his business and hard on every part of his body during sex… his soft side is what's causing my brain to swirl with so many different thoughts.

If he was any other man who's just trying to get a chance at my vagina, I would've been left high and dry, fending for myself over a toilet. Listen, puke isn't pretty. It's gross and makes people run for the hills.

But Marc did none of that.

"What do you need me to do for work today? From the sound of you being on the phone before—I promise I wasn't eavesdropping." I wave my hands in the air in defense. "It sounds like we have some work to catch up on."

"*We*." His fingers toss back and forth between him and me. "Don't have to do anything. I do have to make some phone calls, but your job is to sit your pretty little self on that sofa over there and rest."

"I'm rested," I say at the same time a yawn comes out of me.

"Hardly." He throws his head back with a scoff. "You we're up for the better part of the night. You may feel alright now, but it's only a matter of time before your body catches up and realizes how tired you really are."

I press my lips together realizing he's not wrong. My body is already tired. Despite being able to put food in my mouth, and keep it down, I feel weak. I feel like I could probably sleep all day.

"Put a movie on and get some rest."

"Fine." I stand from the stool. "You're the boss."

I throw myself on the couch, wrap the blanket around myself and switch to the channel that plays *Friends* on repeat. It's a guilty pleasure, really. It doesn't matter how many times I watch any episode, it's just as funny as if I were watching it for the first time.

"Come. Sit." I pat the sofa next to me. "You've been up all night too. Watch a few episodes with me."

Marc rounds the couch but doesn't sit down just yet. "What are you watching?"

"*Friends*. Duh." I playfully roll my eyes.

"I've never seen it."

My mouth falls open. "You're joking right?"

"Nope."

"How am I about to be married to a man who has never watched a single episode of the greatest show of all time. That's probably the biggest red flag."

Marc laughs at my antics before he sits down on the couch next to me, relaxing his legs on the ottoman in front of us. He takes the bottom half of my blanket and throws it over his waist. It's barely enough to cover him.

The episode on right now is the one where Ross is trying to find out who ate his sandwich at work. Marc becomes so engrossed in the episode, he doesn't realize his hand has been on my thigh over the blankets for the last twenty minutes. Every so often his thumb brushes back and forth. I can't help but wonder if he needs this connection with me after the night I just had.

He also hasn't stopped laughing at the show, and I realize I've missed half of it because I can't stop watching this man laugh. Marc doesn't do it enough, that's for sure. I never thought I'd actually *enjoy* the company of a man before. Doing the most mundane thing like watching a TV show.

After the second episode, Marc finally stands up. "Alright, time for you to rest."

I fight back a yawn. "Come on. I'm not even that tired."

"You're yawning. I have some work to catch up on anyway. Do this for me, Ave." He practically begs. I can't fight this man for anything, nor do I want to. The way he has the most caring heart I've seen in as long as I can remember.

"Ok," I whisper.

I lay my head down on the pillow as the third episode starts. Marc lifts the blanket from over my waist and brings it above my shoulders to tuck me in comfortably.

He leans down, pressing a quick kiss to my forehead. I look up, smiling uncontrollably at the man who would do anything to make me happy.

Then I fall asleep in the comfort of Marc Ford's penthouse.

The heat of the sun blaring on my face wakes me from a deep sleep. I reluctantly open my eyes and notice it's not just the sun shining through the windows, but it's the sunset.

Telling me I slept all day.

Shit.

I throw myself off the couch and jump up faster than I should have. Sending a lightheadedness through my head from going twenty-four hours with little sustenance in my body.

Strong arms are quickly wrapped around my waist from behind, steadying my balance from falling over. My hands gripping his forearms like my life depends on it.

"I got you."

Three words in my ear as he pulls my body into his, making me feel dizzy all over again. My feet feel like they will fall out from under me. My body tenses under his touch, forcing me to turn around and meet his stare. The eyes that look back at me are filled with so much more than I ever asked for.

He looks like he wants more.

He looks like he wants to devour me.

He looks like he wants to kiss me.

The worst part of it all is that there's a piece of me that wants him to. A part of me that wants to kiss him wildly in return as he claims my mouth.

Claims. Me.

I feel like I'm losing the control I need to keep my emotions in check. This place, his presence, all the swoony shit he keeps doing… it's overwhelming me in every way possible. I know we should probably sit down and talk about it, but my defense mechanism is to avoid it until it goes away.

The thoughts shoot through my body, forcing me to tense up.

I know for certain that I have to get out of here and get home.

"What's wrong, Ave? Are you sick again?"

"No. But I should probably get home."

He releases his hold on me, allowing me to step back and out of his space. My body is still not able to relax as the tension radiates from each part of my body. I've never let a man this close to me before. Every new feeling is honing in on me as fast as a lightning strike out of the sky.

"I'm fine," I continue through his silence.

Marc steps back into me at the same time his hand comes to the side of my face. He sweeps back a loose strand of hair that fell from my claw clip before his hand found a place on the side of my face. Cupping my neck while his thumb brushed softly over the apple of my cheek. The world feels like it's coming to a halt as we both stand here.

"Marc," I whimper.

"Stop trying to deny this feeling, Avery."

My eyes close. "I don't know what *this* is. But it can't happen, Marc. I'm not wired for whatever is happening here. You know this already." I make no attempt to release myself from the hold he has on me.

"You came with a warning."

"Huh?"

"You came with a warning," he repeats. "I know this isn't you. I know you don't do this. I know you set rules for what can't happen."

My eyes shoot open thinking about the rules that I set, wondering which one he's talking about right now.

No kissing.

No seeing other people.

No falling in love.

"But right now." He pauses. His eyes scan my features until they land on my mouth. "I can't think of anything else but my lips on yours."

I gasp. "You want to kiss me?"

"I might die if I don't, Avery."

Why does my brain short circuit around this man? One minute I need to get away from him, and the next I want his hands all over every inch of my body. This can't be healthy. Is this how relationships feel?

Who the fuck knows.

All I know is that I want to feel him claim me right here, right now.

I shoot him a cheeky grin. "What are you waiting for, boss man?

His jaw hardens, and his fingers tense around my face. "Tell me I can. Tell me I can fucking kiss you."

"Fucking kiss me, Ma—"

He eats my words when his mouth crashes down on mine. A groan vibrates from his lips and reaches every part of me. His lips, his body, all crash into me with a force more powerful than either of us can deny right now.

He pushes his body into me harder as if he's desperate to erase any space that's left between us. I push back with just as much urgency as I moan into his mouth from a kiss that sends electricity soaring to my toes. Marc kisses me like he would've actually died if he didn't get to do this.

I never once wanted this with another man before.

But now that I've had it with Marc, I can't imagine a kiss with anyone else.

He pulls away from the kiss. Just barely. His lips feathering over mine as he rests his forehead on mine. "Fuck, Avery," he pants breathlessly against my lips.

His hand tangles in my hair as he twists my head to the side, exposing my neck and allowing him access to any inch of exposed skin this oversized t-shirt allows him to have. He peppers kisses down the pounding pulse in my neck until he reaches the sensitive spot on my collarbone.

"What are you doing to me?" His breath is hot against my skin.

My hands grip his waist, pulling the fabric into me despite being as close to him as I can get. "I could ask you the same thing."

His lips trail back up my neck until they land on mine again with enough pressure that forces me to open up for him. The second I do, his tongue sweeps inside, forcing another moan out of me as he ravenously claims my mouth as his.

This isn't a normal kiss. It can't be.

This is wild.

This is unhinged.

This is everything I never knew a kiss could be.

Marc takes my bottom lip between his teeth. Just enough that causes my breath to catch in my throat before he releases it. The look in his eyes is downright dark as he incinerates me with his stare. His fingers play with the hem of my shirt, gently skimming the skin above the waistline of my sweatpants, sending pleasure right to my core.

"I think you've ruined me, Avery Woods." His words skate across my lips. "You've completely ruined me."

Same, Marc. Same.

CHAPTER TWENTY-ONE

Marc

My desk phone rings not even five minutes after I step foot into my office. I already have a feeling it's going to be *that* kind of day.

"Marc Ford," I answer.

"Marc. It's Bill." His voice is firm and serious which causes my hand to tense up around the phone.

"Good morning, sir. What can I do for you?"

"We have a meeting this morning."

God dammit. I quickly grab my briefcase and toggle through the open applications on my computer for my calendar to see where this meeting is. Clearly I'm about to be late for it.

"Are you there?"

"Yes. Yes. I'm here. Sorry, I'm just gathering stuff I need for it." I click faster to try and urge the computer to hurry the fuck up. "I hit some traffic coming in today and had to stop by the Manhattan office to pick up the things we needed for it."

"You don't need anything for it." Bill laughs. "The meeting is here on the phone. Are you okay?"

I slump into my desk chair and exhale a sigh of relief. *Close call*. But still, I'm on edge over the fact that I even forgot about this phone meeting in the first place.

"Oh, you're right." I run my hand down my face. "Sorry, sir. It's been a long morning."

Long morning? More like a long week. The last time I saw Avery was Thursday evening when she left the penthouse. I worked from home while she slept the day away on my couch. Clearly her body needed to recover from being sick all night.

What I did not expect was for us to end up kissing.

My god… what a kiss.

Never in my life have sparks flown the way they did when I kissed her. It wasn't planned. I didn't want to break the simple rule she put in place. But it's been getting harder and harder to deny how much I wanted her. This attraction we have towards each other *needed* to be explored.

We didn't so much as talk about whatever that was. Fred came to pick her up, and she went back to her apartment without a passing glance. Stupid me forgot that she used some paid time off for Monday and Tuesday to attend a couple of appointments with Peyton for some wedding things, so we still haven't had the chance to discuss anything.

"Is everything okay?" Bill asks. "Is Avery still sick?"

"She's better now. A stomach bug or some type of food poisoning wiped her out. We're going with the latter since no one else seemed to get sick from being around her."

"I'm glad she's alright. Poor Cathy was so worried about her when we left. Couldn't get Avery's pale white face out of her mind for the entire night."

I swallowed the lump in my throat, because if he only knew how worried *I* was that night.

"I'm sorry we worried you."

"Just happy to hear she's better now. Now tell me how last week went in your territories."

"Yes, sir. We did really well. Summer is always a busy time for us, as you know. Our Staten Island office is showing really good numbers. We've even expanded a little more doing big residential properties in that territory. There's a guy over there who was hired strictly for that, and it's been a game changer. Business is booming."

"That's what I like to hear." I can practically feel the smile on his face. "You're a smart man, Marc. You make wise business moves and I know that the future of this company will be in great hands."

My chest tightens at his words. It's almost as if he just handed me the keys to the company. I stay silent because I'm not entirely sure what to respond to that with. I want to say *Thank you* and ask what it all means.

He continues to discuss some other business aspects of things that go in one ear and out the other because I'm still stewing over the fact that he actually said the company would be in great hands. I reply, but I can't even tell you what I said back to him for any of this exchange.

"I've been meaning to ask you." he cuts my thoughts off. "The first week in August. You're taking the weekend off."

"I don't work the weeke—"

"Don't tell me you don't. You work seven days a week. I'm no fool, Marc."

He's no fool. Except I've been fooling him since last December. Showing him a fake relationship to earn this company. *Fuck. Me.*

"I know you're not, sir. What do you have planned?"

"I want to do something relaxing. Take a break from the hustle and bustle of the city. I figured we would head to my cabin up in the mountains for the weekend."

"The mountains?"

"Yeah, I own a house in the Catskills. It's about a two-hour drive from here.

"That sounds like a lot of fun. I will just have to run it by Avery to make sure she can get off work."

Lies. Lies. Lies.

Obviously she's going. *I'm* her boss.

"Excellent," he exclaims. "Todd and Vivian are already good to go. Just waiting on you two kids."

Todd. Vivian. My blood runs cold.

Great. This isn't just a trip for the four of us.

"I'm sure we'll be good to go." I barely get the words out because my throat is closing in on me. "I'll touch base this afternoon."

"Great. Talk to you then." And the line goes dead.

I've never been more thankful in my life than right now that I told Avery to come in at noon today. I think a subconscious part of me wanted the morning to take some extra space before every part of her invades my senses, my space. She's done nothing but consume me since this started. In both the best and worst ways possible.

The best... because nothing feels better than having her around. She brings me—dare I say? Happiness. Everything feels easier when she's around. I feel things I haven't felt in years since Becky built the wall around my heart. Avery makes me want to take a sledgehammer to every wall I've ever put up. I'm a glutton for punishment clearly because that life isn't for her.

Which brings us to the worst... she keeps saying she's not wired for this. All she's known her entire life is an independent and fierce role model. Her mom is amazing, no doubt about that. She looks up to her, and hell, a part of me does too.

That's why I made the decision to book the flights for her to come down here to spend the weekend with us. I didn't meet her until that weekend, but with a little help from Peyton, we arranged it and made it look like Peyton's idea, because she and I were not in a place for us to say it was me at the time.

Avery has talked a lot about how much her mom means to her. She told me the story about her dad walking out when she was young. And she briefly mentioned how her mom has always sort of struggled financially. It was the least I could do bringing her mom down here for after everything she's doing for me.

I thought my little breather this morning would help relieve some of this built-up tension by the time she gets here, however

I'm more on edge than I was before because there was just a huge ball dropped on me.

A cabin in the mountains.

A weekend.

With my boss.

With Todd and Vivian.

With… Avery.

I decide I need to take a walk around the block to get some air. I stop at the little coffee stand outside of the building and get myself a cup of black coffee. Don't ask me how a cup of caffeine can ease the tension, when most have the opposite reaction. But it works.

I don't know what happened from the time I left until the time I walked back in, but my front desk receptionist is on the verge of tears, and I can faintly hear a male voice on the other line shouting at her.

"What's going on?"

She covers the phone with her hand so the person doesn't hear her. "This man is angry. He's trying to get in touch with Avery. He keeps screaming and—"

I cut her off by yanking the phone out of her hands, more forcefully than I intended too. But anger shot through my blood at the fact that he was screaming, and it was about Avery.

"Hello?"

"Who's this?" The man on the other end huffs out.

"I'm about to be your worst nightmare if you keep yelling at my receptionist the way you have." I keep my tone steady and give the receptionist a small nod that she can go. She didn't waste another second before she was scurrying down the hall to the break room. "Who. Is. This?"

"I'm looking for Avery." His voice grows louder. "She's my girlfriend. I can't get in touch with her. Who are you?"

My anger turns to rage the second I hear him say *my girlfriend*.

There's no way Avery has been hiding a boyfriend all this time.

No. Fucking. Way.

"Name." I practically growl into the receiver, my knuckles turning white as I grip the phone in my hand.

"Avery. I'm looking for Avery."

"No," I snap. "*Your* fucking name."

He huffs out an amused breath like he thinks this is funny. "You're an angry elf, aren't you?"

"I don't have time for games. You're calling *my* place of business. Looking for *my* employee and yelling at *my* receptionist. So yeah, you could say I'm fucking angry right now."

"Christ," he mutters. "I'm Dean. Where is Avery?"

Dean.

My blood is mixed with anger, jealousy… pain as thoughts of Becky burning me so fucking bad come barreling into the forefront of my brain. Remembering that moment in her apartment so fucking vividly.

She wouldn't… would she?

Avery is not Becky.

She told me she was seeing a guy named Dean casually, but she also told me that she broke it off with him.

So why is he calling here?

Why is he calling her his girlfriend?

"Hello? The fuck. Are you there?" Dean raises his voice as if I can't hear him.

"What do you need her for?"

"I just told you," he rasps. "I'm her boyfriend and I need to get in touch with her."

"You know, it's interesting really." I pause as the pain is quickly transferred back to a blinding rage. "Avery has never mentioned a boyfriend to me."

"Why would she?" He laughs. The fucker laughs. "You're her boss. She doesn't need to disclose her personal life to you."

"When was the last time you've seen her, *Dean*?" I draw out his name like it's poison slipping across my tongue.

"Does it matter?" he tosses back.

"It does. Because if you've seen her recently then you probably noticed a very expensive piece of jewelry on her left ring finger." I'm such a bastard that I smirk into the phone as if he can see me. The other end of the line is silent. He's got nothing. So I decide to push it more. "I don't recall *you* being the person who put it on her finger though."

"Again. She doesn't need to share her personal life with her fucking boss. How do you know that I didn't put it there?" I feel the anger in his question.

Now you know how I feel, dick head.

"Her *fucking boss* also happens to be the man who put that ring on her finger."

"W-What. No. She. No. She's not engaged."

"She's very much engaged. The 4-carat diamond ring on her finger proves that to be very true."

"That fucking slut," he mumbles. Low enough that I know he didn't want me to hear it.

Except I did.

And now I'm seeing fucking red.

"Say that again?"

"Did you know that you're marrying a slut?"

"Listen to me closely, *Dean*. Let me hear you call her that again and I will end you. Understood?" When he doesn't respond, I check to see if the line went dead. "Keep my fucking fiancé's name out of your mouth."

"We'll see about that." He ends the call with his arrogant laughter ringing in my ears.

It's quickly replaced by a voice that I normally would welcome when I'm feeling like this, however I can't hear it right now.

"Morning, boss man."

Avery saunters in the reception area with a smile on her face, and I can't even look at her right now.

I can't get the vision of red... rage... and jealousy out of my head.

I know it's wrong to take it out on her, but I can't discuss the phone call I just had here in the reception area while my body is still shaking. My hands are balled at a fist on each side of me and I watch as Avery's eyes take in the feelings plastered all over my face, before she trails down to my hands and visibly sees it in my stance. Concern washes over her features.

"I'm leaving for the day." I turn on my heel back to my office.

"Marc," she calls out to me. I don't so much as turn around. I keep walking until I reach my office, not bothering to close the door behind me. I know she's not far behind me when I hear my office door slam with a thud that shakes the frames on the wall. "Who the fuck pissed you off this morning?"

"You!"

Fuck. I don't want to do this.

I'm silently begging the universe to have her drop this until I calm down.

"I just got here," she yells back at me, throwing her hands in the air. "Don't take your bullshit morning out on me."

I don't spare her so much as a glance. "I'm done with this conversation, Avery."

"Yeah, I bet you are," she scoffs. "I've never in my life met anyone more hot and cold than you."

"Get to work."

Her face falls again with something I can't quite explain. Disappointment? Worry? I'm not entirely sure but she does as I ask when she stomps into her office.

I refused to look at her the entire time she was in here. Deep down, I know that she did *nothing* wrong. She can't help the douche bag is obsessed is still trying to get in touch with her. I know for a fact that this is going to be one of those moments I'll look back on when I calm down, and wish I handled it differently.

I feel a strange crack in my chest thinking about it. My heart beats wildly behind my rib cage because I actually… trust her.

Which says a whole fucking lot considering my past.

"Have you guys heard what Oliver got himself into on his recent trip?" Thomas asks Logan and me.

Logan rubs his hands together in amusement. "I can't wait to hear this."

I've never needed a Wednesday at Moores the way I need it tonight. The lingering rage has been eating me up all day. I fully plan to talk to Avery about it first thing in the morning but decided on getting the guy's advice first.

"Oliver was on his way home from bumblefuck Montana, and he hit it off with the girl he sat next to on the flight." Thomas laughs. "Now he can't stop fucking talking about her."

"Oh shit." Logan gasps. "Oliver is the last person I expect to want to settle down."

Thomas full-on laughs. "There's no settling down when they don't even know each other's full names. He's got no clue where she's from, her last name, nothing."

"Sounds like someone we know." I offer a small smile and a wink to Thomas.

"No, he's straight up obsessed."

"And you weren't?" I challenge him. "I seem to recall you looking around the city *for a year* trying to see Peyton again. Don't think we didn't notice you watching people as you walked down the streets, in hopes you'd get *a glimpse of her hair in the wind or some shit.*"

"So romantic." Logan bats his lashes in sarcasm. "Hey, maybe fate will work in his favor too and they will be reunited."

"Doubtful. He has no clue if she lives in Montana and was just taking a trip here, or if she was coming home to the city. As you know, both states are pretty damn large. She could be from anywhere."

Logan smirks. "You never know. They could find each other and live their life like one of those romantic fairy tales in books."

Thomas shoots Logan a side eye. "Logan, I'm starting to think you're secretly reading romance books with the amount you know about them."

"No way." He puts a hand up in defense. "I just hear about them a lot. Besides, if you ever notice me catching feelings for someone, I need you both to punch me in the face."

"Hmm... sure." I laugh.

"Even if I'm reading... it's literature."

"Literature, cliterature. Same thing." Thomas winks. "Don't try to fool me, bro. Peyton tells me all about the books she's reading. I promise you... there's *no* literature in those pages."

"You've been caught, bro." I shrug a shoulder.

"So, Marc." Logan tries to change the subject. "How's it going with Avery?"

"Don't try to change the subject. Are you going home after this to read a nice little romance book, Logan?" Thomas teases him.

"Nah, I'm trying to get lucky tonight."

Whiskey almost pours out of my face from the sip I just took. "Lucky?"

"Yeah, I'm trying to suffocate tonight. Find someone who would like to use my face as their seat because their legs are tired. Catch my drift?"

Both of us are left gaping at the words spilling out of his mouth.

"Anyway." Logan attempts to change the subject a second time. "Avery. How's it going with her?"

I take a sip of my third glass of whiskey for the night before I confess, "I fucked up."

"Oh shit." Logan's face falls with concern.

Thomas takes a sip of whiskey. "Spill."

Shit. Where do I start?

"As you know, Avery was sick last week."

"Yes, Em told me."

"Yeah, she told me too," Logan adds.

Thomas shoots him a death glare. "Yeah, I fucking bet she did."

"Anyway… I forced her to stay at my place. I had this deep need inside of me to take care of her. It was bad. Like really bad. She didn't stop puking until around three in the morning. We concluded that it was food poisoning—"

"I don't see where you fucked up," Logan cuts me off.

"Can I finish?" Logan waves a hand as if to signal the floor is mine. "She stayed the night, but only after begging to have Fred take her home. She slept the day away on my couch, but when she woke up, something… shifted between us. I don't even know what it was, but I felt a strong need to kiss her."

My face must distort in anguish because Logan says, "That bad, huh?"

"Opposite actually. It was… everything. It was hot, explosive, and the kind of kiss that makes you question everything."

"I can see why you think you fucked up. Especially because it was one of those dumb rules she set," Thomas starts. "But that doesn't sound like a big issue to me. I mean, not for nothing, you two are already faking it till you make it. What's so wrong about the two of you having *very real* feelings for each other and just pursuing it?"

"We never got a chance to talk about the kiss, honestly. Yet, it's a kiss that I can't get out of my fucking head. It keeps me up all night."

Logan claps his hands together and plasters a grin on his face. "Welp. At least you're right on track for having a wife now. Just make the fake one fall for you. Bing. Bang. Boom."

"What is wrong with you?" Thomas shakes his head at him. "We should have Em check your head. Because you're not right up there."

Logan throws prayer hands in the air. "Pleaseeeee, let her check my head."

"I'm going to kill you. You know that, right?" Thomas leans over the table to threaten him.

"It's a joke! It's a joke!" Logan backs up in his chair. "Geez, tough crowd."

"There's one more very real problem," I interrupt these two, trying to get the thoughts of Logan and my baby sister together out of my head. The two of them stay silent but look at me urging me to continue. "Bill wants us to go up to his cabin in the mountains the first weekend in August. Todd and his fiancé included. I don't think Avery is going to go for it."

"Oh, I'm sure she will. If she hasn't run for the hills after your kiss, or ended shit, then I'm sure you're fine," Thomas says.

"Well… today didn't necessarily go very… *smooth*."

The understatement of the century.

"Her ex called the office today trying to get in touch with her."

"Dean is such a douche bag." Thomas shakes his head. "I always got creep vibes from him."

"You know him?" I ask.

"Not well. I met him briefly once, but mostly just from what Peyton has said. They met before she went to Vermont. He got really clingy while she was gone and texted her like every day. When she came back, they started this casual thing. Avery was never in a relationship with him." Thomas shakes his head. "I think he just assumed. Or wanted it despite her being very forward with him. Who the fuck knows."

"Interesting."

"Why? What did he say?"

"He was making my receptionist cry, so I took the phone. He said he was looking for his… *girlfriend*." The last word lodged in my throat. Anger rising again recalling the entire ordeal.

"Fuck, dude." Logan shakes his head.

"Marc," Thomas starts, as if he can sense the emotions I'm

working so hard to hold back. "Listen to me. As your brother, I know where your head is at. I know exactly what you're thinking because of Becky. It's anger and pain. Am I right?"

I nod as my hand grips the glass beneath my hand because brothers know best right?

"That's because you feel something for Avery. Despite not knowing exactly what the hell you're feeling, there's something there between you two. The jealousy stems from that too. You have always been possessive—"

"Gee, thanks." I roll my eyes.

"Not in a bad way, Marc." His tone remains serious. "You fight for what's yours and those you love. You always have. With me, with Oliver, with Emiline and with mom. It's just who you are. The pain you're feeling is because you've been fucked over greatly in the past that you put up these walls, and you're slowly starting to let them down. Day by day they've been crumbling as you let Avery in, letting yourself feel something for someone else again."

Logan pretends to wipe a tear from his eye. "Fuck, bro. Peyton made you soft as shit. This is the stuff Marc is supposed to be saying to us. Not the other way around."

"He's got a point." I offer a light laugh.

"I'm serious, though," he continues. "Avery is off her rocker a lot of the time. She's louder than a teeny bop concert some days when you get her going on stories. There're times when I want to just tell her to shut up." He laughs. "But for some strange reason… I trust her. I don't think she's going to hurt you. I don't think she's spoken to the guy since they ended it."

"I think I fucked up."

"We know," both of them say in unison.

"I raged pretty hard this afternoon and took it out on her. I couldn't even look at her after that phone call. Hell, I still feel it just talking about it. I know it was wrong, but I needed some time to cool down."

"Take the time you need." Thomas tips his head. "But then fix it."

He's right. About everything.

I decide to send Avery a quick text on my way to use the restroom.

Are you free Saturday night?

AVERY

Who's this?

Real cute.

AVERY

I didn't know we were speaking again.

Does this mean you're done being a grump?

I'll never be done being a grump.

AVERY

🙄

We need to talk in the morning.

AVERY

No, we don't.

Shit. This isn't going to be easy. Here I thought whiskey, and the boys would help subside some of this outrage I've had running through me all day.

AVERY

I don't know what happened this morning because you shut me out, but you need to know two things. 1. That shutting me out shit won't fly with me. 2. When you do get angry, take it out on me... in other ways... if you need to. 😉✋ <necklace>💦

This. Fucking. Woman.

CHAPTER TWENTY-TWO
Avery

Zero stars, do not recommend drinking away a bad day with tequila on a work night.

I also don't recommend sending texts to your boss that include multiple sexual emojis after you've been drinking that he doesn't answer.

I'm barely awake when my phone buzzes on the nightstand.

"Hello?"

"Hello, honey." My mom. "You sound like you're still asleep? Don't you have work today?"

I glance over at the clock. Yup, I'm probably going to be late. However, the realization doesn't make me jump out of bed any faster. The *Pearl Jam* concert in my head right now is pounding so hard that I don't think I can lift my head off the pillow.

"I do have work. I just have a horrible headache." I lift myself off the pillow with an aggravated groan. "But I'm getting up now."

"Oh, good, good."

"Everything okay, ma?"

"Everything is great. I just miss you. I haven't had a chance to call you because working both jobs has kept me kind of busy over here."

"I understand, mom." I sigh sympathetically, wishing I could do more for her. "You'll be caught up soon."

"Yeah, thanks to you!"

"What do you mean '*thanks to me*?'"

"You did *not* have to mail me that check you sent me. I'm seriously so grateful, but it was too much."

"Mom. I—"

My words fall short when she beats me to it. "I'm so, so proud of you, honey. You've been working so hard. I don't need you to take care of me. This was enough to cover three mortgage payments, Avery. You have no idea what this means to me."

I swallow the lump that's stuck in my throat. I feel like a cat right now, about to hurl up a hairball. My throat is dry, and last night's liquor sits right at the top of my stomach.

Making a mental note to call Peyton *asap* and see if she had anything to do with this.

"I love you, mom," I choke out. "But I have to get ready for work. Or I'm going to be late."

"Call me later. I want some updates on your situation with Marc."

"You got it, Ma." I keep my voice as cheery as possible in hopes that she doesn't sense my avoidance in wanting to talk about it.

Yesterday was enough to drive me to drink. I'm *not* the type of person that goes for the bottle of liquor during a time of stress. But desperate times call for desperate measures.

He refused to tell me what was causing the smoke to come out of his head, and I spent all afternoon in my little cubicle of glass walls wondering what the hell I could have possibly done that caused that. And if it wasn't me that caused it, who was it?

Now that I'm sober enough to think about it all, who the fuck does he think he is talking to me like that? Taking his rage out on me. When I'm over here helping *him* out! My hangover mixed with these thoughts now has *my* blood boiling.

As I get ready for work, I decide to go with the tightest black pencil skirt I own. The one that sits just above my knees, showing more of my legs than I ever have in the workplace. I pair it with an *almost* see-through light pink blouse, keeping the top button undone, exposing a little more cleavage. I can't stand my hair in my face most of the time, but today, I let it hang free with loose waves.

I know the moment I walk into the office and see Marc's face morph with anguish that I definitely chose the correct attire to really get under his skin. The same damn way he did to me yesterday.

I skip the morning chit chat with him, and head right into my work for the day.

It doesn't take long before my cell phone rings on my desk with a phone call from Dean.

This guy is relentless.

But I will say, it's been a solid week or two since his last attempt at getting a hold of me. Kudos to him for going so long, fighting the urge to call me.

I do what I always do, and deny the call immediately. Except it chimes seconds later with a text message.

DEAN

Pick up your phone.

No.

It's time I finally respond. I need to clear the air and end this for good, because he can't keep calling me the way he is. This is getting borderline stalkerish.

Dean, you have to stop calling me. You're a great guy, but I told you already… I'm busy. I don't have time to be involved with anyone right now.

DEAN

When were you going to tell me that you're engaged?

I can feel the color drain from my face at the same time my jaw hangs open. My eyes dart to Marc through the glass walls that separate us, but he's immersed in work. How the fuck does Dean know I'm engaged?

I ignore his text and fire a message to the girls.

How the hell does Dean know that I'm engaged?

KALI

I thought we ended it with him weeks ago?

EMILINE

Second that question...

I screen shot his message and shoot it to the group chat.

My hands are trembling under my phone. I don't know why my heart is racing the way it is. Dean means nothing for me to feel like this right now, but I can't help but wonder if this conversation I'm having right now has something to do with the outburst Marc had toward me yesterday.

KALI

He's such a baby back bitch. Why haven't you blocked his number yet?

PEYTON

Marc didn't tell you yet?

WHAT IS THERE TO TELL ME? I JUST GOT TO WORK!

KALI

This should be good.

PEYTON
You should really ask him.

When I pull my eyes away from my phone to look back at Marc, he's staring at me with his signature scowl. Only this one is darker. I hate myself at this moment, not because I've done anything wrong. I ended things with Dean, and he's just crazy. But it's because he has this unexplainable power over me to make me melt into a puddle regardless of how he's looking at me.

Marc briefly takes his eyes off of me to pick up his desk phone, pressing a single button before he leans back in his chair, and his eyes are back on me, burning through me like daggers.

My desk phone startles me when it starts ringing.

I shoot him a *'you can't be serious'* look with my eyes before I finally answer.

"What can I help you with, *sir*?"

His brows furrow, but he doesn't say anything right away. Instead, he watches me. His phone pressed to his ear, as his eyes incinerate me from head to toe while sparks skate across my skin. *God dammit, Marc.*

"We're going out Saturday night," he finally says flatly.

"Oh, are we back to the grumpy boss who thinks he can just order me around and tell me what I'm doing on my weekends off?" I keep my eyes locked on him before they trail down to his mouth when I catch his tongue roll over his bottom lip.

My thighs begin to rub together in my seat on instinct.

Now is not the fucking time, vagina.

"Like I said… Saturday night, we're going out."

"No. I'm busy," I lie.

His jaw tightens, and I watch as his knuckles go white, gripping the phone. Is that… jealousy?

"It wasn't a question."

"Maybe not." I lift my shoulder. "But I had an answer. And that answer happens to be a big fat *no*, in neon lights."

"Going out with the boyfriend you've been texting since you got here?"

And there it is.

That confirms that whatever is happening here, whatever happened yesterday morning, has to do with Dean. But how?

"You know what? Fuck you, Marc."

For the first time in days, I see a smirk form on his face. "Gladly, Princess."

I do my best to hide my face because he's still watching me. His eyes haven't left mine this entire conversation. One we could have *clearly* had face to face and not over the phone.

"Careful, Marcus... your jealousy is showing with all these little comments you keep making."

Slowly he lifts his pointer finger in the air, curling it toward his palm to summon me over to him. "Come here."

My cell phone dings on my desk at the exact moment with a text.

I hang up the desk phone with Marc because I will not be summoned by anyone. Doesn't he know anything about me by now?

DEAN

I feel bad for him really. It's only a matter of time before you put him through the same hell you've put me through.

I suck in a sharp breath as I read the message right before I click his contact and hit the block button.

This day is a fucking mess. When I got involved with Dean, I never expected any of this. He's the first man to even linger around like this and what? Cause drama? This is exhibit B on why I don't get too involved with men. Exhibit A is sitting at his desk right now.

This day makes me feel like a child on a seesaw. First I was down because of the epic hangover I woke up with. Then I was up in the air with the confidence I always have inside of me to gain control of the situation again and make Marc feel bad for being so dismissive of me yesterday. Every up has to go back down though, and these stupid text messages from Dean did that.

"Now, Avery," Marc shouts from his office as he beckons me with his finger.

I force myself back up on the seesaw of my day. Lifting my head up and channeling the inner strength that I know I have in me. That I've always had.

"What?" I snap as I enter his office.

"Damn." He shakes his head, grinning from ear to ear. "I made you come with just one finger. Imagine if I used two?"

The power. This man. Has over me.

I feel my resolve crumble at my feet.

Marc bites down on his bottom lip and I can't help but wish it was my lip between his teeth. "You're thinking about it, aren't you?"

My hands fall to my hips. "Are we done here? I have work to do."

"Work doesn't involve texting your boyfriend on my time."

My blood boils like a bomb ticking inside of me that was waiting for the right time to detonate.

"You have some fucking nerve, Marc. That's the second time in a matter of minutes that you made that snide comment about a 'boyfriend.'" I raise my hand to make some air quotes. "I seem to recall that *you* asked me to help you with this. *You* asked me to give up my summer and my social life to do this for you." I flash him the diamond ring on my finger. "I'm wearing *your* fucking engagement ring!"

His face remains stoic, staring at me as he scrubs his chin.

"I had an interesting phone call yesterday, Avery."

"Oh, was that what triggered your blinding rage?"

"Yes," he admits almost too quickly.

"Enlighten me."

"Dean called here looking for his girlfriend… looking for *you.*"

"And you should already know that I don't have a boyfriend. I was very clear at the start of this that he and I were nothing more than a casual thing that I ended when this started."

"He seemed pretty set on—"

I throw my hand in the air with a signal that says stop talking. "So instead of asking me– your *fiancé*– you just listen to a stranger on the phone?" I don't let him answer before I continue. "Yes. That nut case texted me this morning. I told him to stop contacting me. Then I texted the girls. Does that make you feel better?"

"No. I'd feel better if he didn't contact my future wife all together."

I stand there stunned.

My hands fall from my hips and relax at my sides.

The way he just so casually called me his *future wife.*

The way we just had this entire conversation as if we actually *were* an engaged couple.

It's like he just clipped the wire of the second bomb inside of me, stopping it from exploding before it caused even more damage.

"Marc." My voice is low and breathy. "You know you could've just talked to me yesterday, right?"

"I know." His face falls into a form of defeat. "I know."

He stands from his chair, rounding his desk until he's standing directly in front of me. The energy in the room has shifted the same way my body shifted to face him.

"For that… I'm sorry." He brushes my hair out of my face. "I wanted to, but I spent the better part of the day fighting myself to calm down. I knew this wasn't a conversation I could have in the state I was in. I had every intention of coming into work today, much more relaxed, and talking to you about this the second you walked through that door."

"That would've been a good time for it."

"You're telling me," he huffs. "Then you walked through those doors. Looking like the sweetest fucking sin. Something I shouldn't want. Shouldn't crave." He releases a heavy breath. "Then I had to watch you texting over there. The thought of another man touching what's mine, makes me see red."

My jaw falls open.

His.

"And it made me so god damn jealous over someone else having you."

I blow out a sigh. "You have me, Marc."

He shakes his head. "I don't, Avery. Not the way I want to have you."

His desk phone ringing breaks us apart. I don't even have a chance to respond before the receptionist tells him his scheduled client is here for the day over the speaker.

"I have to go to this closing." He picks up his stack of papers and tucks them under his arm. "I don't want to fight with you. Anyone but you…"

"It's fine, boss man," I tease him to try and lighten the mood. "We wouldn't be us if we didn't fight a little, right?"

He nods as he makes his way to the door.

"Marc." I stop him, and he spins around as if he's anticipating something big. I pause as he stands there, I want to rush to him and kiss him the way he kissed me in his penthouse. I want to tell him everything that I'm feeling. That deep down, he's slowly melting away the ice of this cold heart. But instead I blurt out, "I blocked his number. Dean's. He won't contact me again."

"Just do me a favor, and stop saying his name in my presence."

"It's cute when you're all jealous," I coax him.

He drops the laptop and the stack of papers on a small end table he has set right by his door and he stalks over to me. His teeth clamped down together, exposing the tick in his jaw.

"You think it's cute?"

I tip up the corner of my lip, trailing my finger over his perfectly sculpted jawline. "Your jaw gets all hard, and sexy."

He grips my hips, forcing my body forward until it crashes into his, grinding his hip into me before he takes my jaw between his fingers and thumb. "There's a lot of things hard right now."

I feel wetness pooling in my panties at the thought of that. Is make-up sex a real thing when you're not actually in a relationship? Right now, I'm so fucking turned on that I wouldn't be one bit mad if he bent me over his desk and fucked me like he still hates me.

"What are you going to do about *that*?" I press my hips back into him.

"Later." He takes a step back. "Don't forget, dinner Saturday night." He turns on his heel and picks up his stuff for the meeting off the table again. "You're coming to the penthouse after too."

"Why?" I act oblivious, as if I don't know the reason behind that.

I think he's going to leave without an answer to my question when he opens the door to walk out. Except he stops to look back at me with the door knob in his hand. "Because I'm going to fuck you until the only name you can say is mine."

CHAPTER TWENTY-THREE

Marc

I've had plenty of time to think about how I handled the whole Dean situation. I've barely slept since then, stewing over the way I reacted. It was wrong, I know this. I just could not for the life of me stop the rage that took over. My brain was screaming to *shut it down*, but my mouth just kept spewing ugliness to her.

"Listen." I nervously run my hands through my hair. "There's something we have to talk about."

She nods as she wipes the corner of her mouth with her napkin after finishing her steak dinner.

"First, I got you set up with that real estate course. You start at the end of September.

"Wow." She gasps. "That was really fast."

"Is that okay with you?"

"That's more than okay, Marc. You have no idea how excited I'm for this next step. I almost feel bad doing it, though."

"Why?" I'm taken back by her admission right now. "This was part of the deal."

"Yes. It was. But with everything that's happened… I just feel bad. You've given me more than I anticipated with this ordeal."

I sit stunned in silence. What have I given her?

She waves her hands in the air cutting off whatever is about to come next. "What else was there? You said, 'some *things*', plural."

I swallow the lump in my throat because fuck Bill and his plans. I want to learn more about what I've given her. "We have a trip planned for the first weekend in August." I watch her as she gives me a questioning glare. "Bill has a house in the mountains and wants to take a weekend trip to his cabin."

"I'm not sure that's such a good idea."

I cock my head back in question. "Why?"

"Do you think it's a good idea for us to be stuck in a cabin together? We can't exactly stay in two separate rooms in their cabin. They're going to know immediately that something isn't right."

Oops. I must have left out the detail that it's not just the two of them. I bite my lip to try and hide the tension in my body. "Todd and his fiancé will be there, too."

She groans in her seat. "I can't stand that guy. It blows my mind that this entire thing is between you and *him*. He looks like a fucking toad."

I can't help the laugh that comes out of me. Even the couple at the table next to us looks over with a funny stare. "He does look like a toad, doesn't he?"

"He does," she says and joins me in the laughter.

"I know it's not ideal. But I will try to figure out the room situation."

"Okay."

Okay? That's all she's got? My palms feel clammy. She shows no emotion to this right now and it's making me feel edgy.

"Is that good with you?"

"This is what I signed up for, isn't it?"

"I don't know," I admit. "After what happened Thursday... things have been..."

She cuts me off with a small laugh as she reaches across the table and places a hand on top of mine, sending heat racing across my skin. "That's all you. Nothing is weird here on my end regarding that. If anything..." she trails off, raking her hands through her perfectly curled blonde hair so that it's out of her face.

"If anything?"

"If anything, you're making this really easy."

My hands twist on the table under hers until I'm taking her hands in mine. "What does that mean, Avery?"

"It means that you're making this a lot easier to like you."

My heart rate picks up pace in my chest at her confession. I want nothing more than to reach across the table and take her face in my hands and press my mouth to her soft, pink lips and scream, *yes*!

"Are you developing feelings for me, Princess?"

Her face flushes as I watch her cheeks turn red. "I said I like you. Don't let that go to your head."

I'm so fucking gone for this girl.

I want to explore more on what that means. Does that mean she likes me more than a friend? Does she just like me as a person? As her boss?

The biggest question is... does she like me enough that we can continue this relationship when this is all over?

"Is it a bad thing if you like me? I mean I'm your boss." I shrug. "It might not be the worst thing in the world if we actually tolerated each other more than we have been."

She laughs. "It's that black heart, Marcus. You should already know I won't stop busting your balls at work—whether I like you or hate you."

She's mentioned having a black heart before and I can't help but think how wrong she is. She may have been dead set on never being in a relationship in her life, but who she is as a person tells me she's got a bigger heart than she makes it out to be.

This is the woman who color-coded my business calendar because she knows it helps me. The woman who sets my meeting times early so that I show up on time for them. The woman who dropped work to be there for her mom in her time of need. The woman who fights for what she believes in, like how she fought me this week to bring my jealous mind at ease that she's not seeing someone else. The woman who agreed to spend the entire summer convincing my boss that I'm worthy of having an entire company passed down to me. This woman definitely doesn't have a black heart.

My mind is spinning with an urge to tell her how I really feel. I want to admit that I want to explore this more, and I want her to be all mine, beyond this deal that we made. But now is not the right time because I know I need to tread lightly with her.

"I wish you'd still bust my balls." I decide to playfully admit.

"Is that so, boss man?" she coos. "You should know that I'd *gladly* bust them."

I groan in my seat at the same time the waiter passes by. I stop him in his tracks and say, "Check, please."

She sends me the cutest fake frown I've ever seen. "No dessert this time?"

I smirk. "Oh we're getting dessert. Just not here." She sits in silence, with a slightly stunned look on her face. "I'm taking you home."

Avery walks into the penthouse as if she lives here.

It's so much different than the first time I brought her here.. She knows this place now and I can feel how comfortable that makes her.

The feelings I have for her have been building and building over time, and this one small move of her walking into *my* home, only confirms how much I want her.

More of her.

All of her.

Which doesn't sound like it would be a breaking point for someone, but for me… it is. All of a sudden, I want her in my space at all times. I want her clothes in my closet, and her favorite scent of candle lit on the kitchen island.

After getting changed into sweatpants, I make my way to the living room to find her standing at the window with a glass of wine she poured for herself, overlooking Central Park. The city sky lights up from the thunderstorm that started as we were leaving the restaurant. She hasn't gotten changed yet, so she's still wearing that very tempting little black dress, and her hair is still damp from the downpour we got caught in.

I step into her space and stand directly behind her. I feel her body tense up without my hands even being on her, ss if she can sense me being so close.

"You didn't get changed?" I ask.

"I didn't get changed," she repeats as a statement, not a question. My fingers delicately brush the exposed skin on her shoulder before they trail down her arm. I press a light kiss to her shoulder, and she shivers at the touch before she places the glass of wine on the table beside us.

Blood rushes to my cock, and it's taking everything in me to hold back.

"Even a mess from the rainstorm we got caught in." My hands find her hips. "You still look just as beautiful as you did when you first walked into the restaurant tonight." My hand skates around her midsection until my palm is pressed on her stomach, forcing her body to melt into mine before I lean into her ear. "How is that possible?"

"It's possible that you need to get your eyes checked," she mumbles at the same time she presses her ass right into my bulging cock.

I grind my hips into her. "Fuck, Ave..."

She spins around in my arms until she's face to face with me. She reaches up to run her fingers through my hair. "That's what I'm hoping is going to happen tonight."

"That's not why I invited you back here."

"It is, though." She laughs as she brings herself to her toes so she can whisper in my ear, "Your exact words were, that you were going to fuck me until the only name I can say is yours."

Yeah... I guess I did say that.

I grin as I comb my fingers through her hair until I have a handful, tilting her head back with a forceful grip. "Is that what you want, Princess? You want to be fucked?"

Avery releases a long exhale of pleasure right before my mouth collides to hers in a kiss laced with so many real feelings of wanting more with her.

I press my body into hers until she's backed up against the windows. My one hand is still intertwined in her hair as I gently pull, while the other is gripping her ass, holding her close to me. She opens up for me as I slip my tongue past her lips. She wraps her arms tightly around my head and lifts her leg to wrap around my body as if she can't get close enough to me.

Just as she's about to pull away, I take her bottom lip between my teeth to tease her and I take a step back from her. Her lips are perfectly swollen from that kiss, and she's wearing her signature teasing grin.

The primal urge to claim her as *mine,* is taking over every part of my body.

"Take the dress off, Avery."

She doesn't hesitate before she reaches for the hem of the dress and pulls it over her head. I trail my eyes down her body and notice she's not wearing... *anything*.

I arch an eyebrow. "Nothing under the dress?"

"My mistake really." She bites down on her bottom lip. "I didn't expect to be so turned on by you when I decided to forgo the panties. I regretted it the second I saw you in the restaurant." Her hands reach for the band of my sweats as she crooks her finger inside of them, running them along the seam to play with me. "I'm pretty sure I left a wet spot on the booth we sat in."

"And the bra?"

"Another mistake." She slowly starts to push my sweatpants down past my hips. "I couldn't control my own nipples being in your presence. I'm surprised you didn't notice how hard they were for half of dinner."

I suck in a breath of air. "Avery."

She removes her fingers from my sweats, and goes for the hem of my t-shirt, lifting it over my head. Her eyes trail down until they reach my sweatpants. "Your fuck me lines are seriously so sexy."

I huff out a laugh. "Fuck me lines?"

"Yes. These." Her fingertips brush my lower abdomen where my muscles cut into a V-shape. "Because if I keep trailing my fingers along them." She does as she says, trailing her finger, forcing my sweatpants down with it, until she reaches the base of my cock. "They reach here."

Her hands fist my cock and my eyes flutter shut at the feeling of having her hands on me. She pushes my pants to my ankles with her other hand, and I spring free, fully erect with precum dripping from the tip just for her.

She pumps me with slow, languid strokes from base to tip as she stands there completely bare and exposed while thunder booms in the distance. The perfect storm is brewing everywhere around us.

"On your knees, Princess."

"Yes, *sir*." She drops to her knees for me. She gives my cock a few more pumps with her fist before she licks the precum off the tip. Her eyes fall closed, and she moans while she takes me fully into her mouth.

"This fucking mouth," I rasp as my hand finds the back of her head. "You take my cock so well."

She bobs her head faster, her hand pumping and twisting as I disappear past her plump pink lips. I already know I'm not going to last. Her mouth is too fucking perfect.

As if she can read my thoughts, her hands find my ass and she takes me deeper, my hips buck into her face as pleasure rushes through me.

"Oh, you dirty girl." I smirk down at her. "You like it when I fuck your face, don't you?"

She hums in agreement and picks up her pace. She doesn't dare release me from her mouth, sucking harder and faster while I stretch her throat. As if she's starved, and this is her last meal. With one last thrust, I reach the back of her throat and she hums, sending a vibration to the base of my cock.

"That's it, baby," I praise. "I'm going to come down the back of this perfect little mouth. You're going to drink up every last drop. Understood?"

She doesn't answer but moans around my length, gripping my dick with one hand while the other finds its place on my balls. Gently squeezing them just enough to send me over the edge. Her eyes prickle with tears and I think she's going to gag but doesn't. And that's when my orgasm crashes through me. I spill down the back of her throat. "Fuckkk..." Grunting and cursing as she swallows every last drop.

She releases me and sits back on her heels with a grin as she wipes the corner of her mouth, and then sucks her fingers clean.

I lift her up, and quickly spin her around facing the window.

She lets out a small squeal as I press my body into hers. Her entire naked body is against the window. I lean in to inhale her scent, bringing my one hand to her lower stomach, making my way to her pussy while the other hand goes to her neck. "How wet did that make you?"

"I'm fucking soaked, Marc."

I slide two fingers inside of her, not wasting another minute as I slide them in and out, her arousal already coating them. "You're dripping for me. Did sucking my cock turn you on this much?"

"Yes," she breathes out.

Her legs open for me and her back rocks into me. Clearly my dick didn't need any time to recuperate because it's already hard again.

She moans my name while she withers under my touch, as if

her legs weaken at my contact. I drop my mouth to her shoulder to pepper kisses on any piece of skin my mouth can reach while I move my fingers harder. "Marc," she screams. "Fuckkkk."

"I easily slid two fingers into this tight pussy, that's how wet you are," I grit out, tightening my hold on her neck, pumping my fingers faster in and out of her. "I'm thinking that if I bend you over right now, the whole city can watch as I fuck you until you come on my cock."

"Do it," she begs.

"What is it exactly you want me to do to you?"

Her grip on my wrist tightens. "Fuck me," she cries out. "Right here."

I reluctantly withdraw my hand because there's nothing more than I want to see her come, but the thought of her coming on my cock has me going feral at the moment. I bend down to reach for the condom I had put in my pocket because I was simply being optimistic that this would happen.

"You want the whole city to see you?"

"Yup." She doesn't waste a second with her admission. "Let them see you claim me as yours."

I bite down so hard on my bottom lip, I swear I break skin. "I don't have to fuck you for everyone to know that you're mine."

I roll the condom on quickly, before my hand cups the back of her neck, forcing her to bend at the hip in front of me. She presses into me, eager for me to be inside of her.

"So ready for me, Princess."

I don't let her get another word in before I thrust fully into her. The second her warm cunt is wrapped around my dick, euphoria takes over every part of me. I don't know how I went so long without this. Without her.

"Oh my god," she cries out, pushing back to meet every motion with her hips.

"You take me so well. It's like your pussy was made for me."

"Your cock was made for me," she rasps. "But fuck! You're too big."

"But you're such a good girl, Avery. So shut the fuck up and take this dick like the good girl that I know you are."

"Keep talking, Marc." Her voice hitching as her hands press firmly on the glass window. "It's so hot."

I bend over her, plunging into her as far as I can go, allowing me to get close to her ear before I whisper, "You want me to tell you how I'm going to worship every part of your body tonight until you're perfectly sated?"

"Please do," she pleads through uneven breaths.

My movements slow because if I don't, I'm going to come way too fast, despite just shooting a load down her throat.

"Move," she pants. "I need to feel you."

"Give me a minute, Ave. Having you here like this, with me stretching this tight pussy, filling you to the brim… it's going to be over before it even starts."

She presses harder into me, her breathing wild and uncontrolled, and I grip her hair in my fist forcing her head back to expose more of her neck. I trail kisses up her neck as she cries out my name, laced with pleasure as I can feel her begin to convulse around me.

"I can *feel* your warm cunt milking my fucking cock right now."

"Jesus Christ," she pants. "You're going to make me come just talking like that."

I pick up my pace, thrusting in and out of her, each time reaching full hilt to ensure I hit the spot that's going to send her over the edge. I move my hands to grip both of her shoulders and I can feel perspiration under my palm. She rocks back into me harder, our wet skin slapping together with every movement, while her hand reaches between us to rub circles over her clit.

"That's it, baby. Make yourself come using my cock."

"Harder," she begs. "Marc, fuck me like you hate me."

My pace slows again, and I'm taken back by what she just said. I swallow the lump in my throat, anger bubbling to the surface at the idea of her thinking I could ever hate her.

So I fuck her… hard and fast.

"Marc!" she shouts my name louder.

Giving her exactly what she's begging for, I look down and watch as I disappear inside of her over and over again. "Fuck, tell me you're close." My voice hitches.

"I'm there, Marc. I'm fucking comi—"

Avery can't even finish the sentence before her legs begin withering beneath her. A string of curse words pouring out of her as my own orgasm crashes down on me while I fill her. Our breathing is loud and intense. Her head falls between her shoulders, her hands never leaving the window as her back rises and falls with every rapid breath she lets out.

I slowly pull out of her, not bothering with the condom yet before I flip her around to face me. Bringing her face between my hands and forcing her to look me in the eyes, I crash my mouth to hers with more force than intended. Enough to show her that she's delusional if she thinks she isn't mine for real after this.

I pull away from the kiss, hovering close to her lips. "I'll have you know, Princess." I kiss her again with a quick peck. "That was *not* me fucking you like I hate you."

"Then what the hell was that, Marcus?"

"That was me making you *mine*." I scoop her naked body in my arms to head to the bedroom and she lets out a squeal. "I'm not done with you, yet. And I won't be done until you realize this isn't fake anymore."

CHAPTER TWENTY-FOUR

Avery

My body is buzzing on a high that I can't quite explain, but I know I don't want it to go away. He scooped me up and carried me to the room, but after that last orgasm, I don't know how he expects me to give him another round.

He places me down in his bedroom and I stand there, bare to him. "God, Avery. Do you have any idea how fucking perfect you are?"

I step into him, he cups my face and crashes his lips to mine again. The fire ignites inside of me once again. My hand grips his toned muscles at his midsection as he takes a few steps back until his legs hit the bed. As soon as he sits at the edge, his legs open for me to step inside of them, as his hands travel to gripping my ass until I'm pressed flush against him. His mouth finds my hardened nipples and he sucks on them as if he couldn't wait another second to have them in his mouth.

"Fuckkk," I moan, my head falling back, pleasure shooting right to my core again.

"I love the sound you make when you're turned on, baby," he purrs around my breasts. "You want this just as bad as I do, don't you?"

"Yes, Marc." I flutter my eyes closed as he sucks on the other breasts. "God, yes."

"Good." He releases me from his hold and backs himself onto the bed. "Now, come sit on my face."

"Marc," I gasp. "I can't sit on your face. I'll suffocate you."

"That's the point, baby." He laughs. "Now get up here and sit on my fucking face. I'm starving."

"That's a lie." I begin to climb on the bed above him, taking my time as I graze my skin over every part of his body as I do, wanting to turn him on the same way he turns me on. His cock rubs along my stomach as I make my way to the top of him like I'm climbing a goddamn tree. "We just got back from dinner. You can't be *starving*."

"But remember, we skipped out on dessert." I hover over his face, my arousal already pooling between my legs again, begging for his mouth to touch me. He grips my ass in his hands, before he says, "And there's nothing sweeter than the taste of you for dessert."

His tongue swipes through my wetness until he reaches my clit. My back arches on instinct and I'm already finding it difficult to sit up from being so sensitive from just moments ago in the living room. "Oh my… god," I scream out. "That feels so good. Don't stop."

He grips my ass hard, pulling me closer to his face but I resist. "Avery. Sit."

I look down at him between my legs, his eyes pinned to me and I lower myself more until his tongue drives into my pussy. He laps me over and over, my hips rock on instinct. Holy shit, I'm going to come again… already.

I lean back the slightest bit as I rock back and forth on his face, reaching behind me to drive him as wild as he's driving me. I cup his balls.

"Fuck, Ave." He stops himself. "You want that at the same time as you ride my face?"

"No, sir." I moan as I feel his tongue flick back and forth on my clit again. Sending me closer and closer to the edge. "I will gladly sit my little ass on your face and call it my throne. But if you think I'm leaning over and sucking your dick at the same time then you've got me fucked up."

I feel his laugh vibrate through my pussy and I lose it, I can barely sit up straight as his mouth attacks me. "Grab the headboard, Princess. Then I want you to ride my face until you're dripping."

"Dammit, Marc," I cry out, my hands gripping the headboard like my life depends on it. "I'm already close."

Pulling me even closer to his face–if that's even fucking possible–he sucks my clit and sends me over the edge. My legs quake under me as my orgasm rushes through me like a hurricane. Powerful, raw, dangerous.

"Holy shit, I'm coming."

And I do. I come harder than I ever have in my entire life.

He releases his grip on my ass and I fall to the bed beside him. My chest rises and falls rapidly as my hair splays in every direction on the bed, sticking to my head from the sweat pouring out of me.

"Fuck," I breath out, blinking a few times as my body tries to come back down to earth. "What in the world are you doing to me?"

He chuckles as he rises from the bed. "I told you there's nothing fake about this, Ave. It's about time that you realized that the way I already have," he says as he crosses the room and enters the ensuite bathroom.

He's back moments later with a washcloth and I've yet to move from my spot on the bed. Perfectly sated and fucked to oblivion.

"You've ruined me, Marcus."

He doesn't say anything back as he takes the washcloth and cleans me up. Carefully, like I might break if he touches me the wrong way. There's something about the way Marc cares so deeply that causes my heart rate to pick up again.

Marc finishes and goes back to the bathroom to discard the washcloth and emerges in a pair of gray sweatpants with no shirt. I bring myself up to my elbows to drink him in. There's no denying this man is a walking form of art. He really has to be the sexiest man alive. I'm surprised he hasn't made it on the cover of that magazine yet.

"You checking me out again?"

I bite down on my bottom lip and offer him a smile. "I might be."

He stalks over to where I lay on the bed, still naked, and still in the same spot that I fell after he ate me like a three course meal.

"You make it very hard for me to look away from you," Marc says, standing over me, trailing his fingers from my ankles to my thighs. Goosebumps erupt over every part of my exposed skin. My head falls back as he continues his trail past my hips, up my stomach and over the curve of my breasts. I feel my nipples harden immediately at his touch.

"That's supposed to be my line, boss man," I tease him, still leaning on my elbows. My head falls back when his fingers trail along my collarbone.

"Call me boss man one more time, Avery. And I'm going to spank you until you're coming on my lap."

"Oooh. Is that so... *boss man*?"

In one swift move, he's on top of me, spreading my legs apart with his thighs as I fall to my back on the bed. My hands instinctively wrap around his neck and I smile up to him. Marc pauses a moment as his eyes bounce between mine, and his eyes darken as I watch so many thoughts pass through his mind. Thoughts I want to hear him say out loud in the worst way.

"Tell me what you're thinking."

"I'm thinking..." He pauses before he dips his head into my neck. My pulse beats like crazy below his lips as he kisses my most sensitive skin. "I'm thinking how goddamn perfect you are, baby. Every part of you."

I tighten my hold around his neck, holding him close to me. I don't want this moment to end, if I'm being honest. "You're not so bad yourself," I breathe into his wildly tamed hair.

"I can't get enough of you, Avery." Marc presses his body down on top of me, I can feel his hardening cock between my legs. "You have consumed me for so long. I meant it when I said I was going to make you realize this isn't fake anymore."

I rake my hands through his hair, pulling him off of me so I can look him in the eyes and say, "I'm not sure it's fake anymore, either."

"Fuck," he says on a throaty breath before his lips crash to mine in a fury of relief. I open up for him, allowing his tongue to swipe across mine, gripping every part of his body my hands can grab.

I wrap my arms around him, and toss him to his back until I'm on top of him. Caging in his head with my hands, not releasing my mouth from his. The first fucking rule I set of not kissing each other, has turned into the one thing I don't know if I will be able to live without if this whole thing ends.

"Avery. Baby," he rasps. "I need to be inside of you again."

"Allow me." I grin as I hover over him. He puts both of his hands behind his head as he stares up at every move I make. Slithering my way down his body, until I reach the hem of his sweats. Pulling them down until his cock springs free, erect and ready for me.

I grip the base of it before giving it a few pumps, and I keep my eyes fixed on him as he runs his tongue along his bottom lip, watching fervently as he waits for my next move.

I move to sit on top of him, hovering over his thick length. I can feel it pressing against my already wet pussy. He moves to grip it, and I swat his hand away. "Nope," I smirk down at him. "You've already gotten your turn at fucking me tonight. It's my turn."

"Avery," Marc growls. "Condom."

"I'm clean, and I'm on the pill."

His eyes bounce between mine, unsure of what to do next. "Are you sure, Avery? I'm clean too. I've never..."

"I'm sure."

"I've never been with anyone without a condom before," he finishes. The admission makes my body vibrate with desire. The idea of both of us feeling this pleasure of nothing between us for the first time. 'Are you sure you want this?"

I reach down and line him up with my entrance before I slowly press down until he fully disappears inside of me, giving him his answer. His eyes flutter closed as his head falls back and he lets out a moan.

"Eyes on me, boss man." His eyes flutter open at me taking control of him in his bedroom. "I want you to watch me ride you like the stallion you are."

I rise up slowly, but not enough that his cock ever leaves me before I crash back down on him. His hands grip my hips tightly as I bounce up and down on him. His eyes are fixated on where we're connected, as he disappears inside of me, filling me to the hilt.

"You feel that, Marc," I moan out in pleasure. "Your cock is stretching me so well."

"Yes, baby," he says through gritted teeth. "Fuck yes."

I change direction as I rock back and forth on him, picking up the pace as an orgasm is ready to crash over me any minute again. He bucks his hips up into me, hitting me right in the spot as my body is just about ready to catapult over the edge.

"You want to come already?" His voice hitches as he grips my hips to keep his dick deep inside of me. I nod my head because I want to come so bad. "You may think you're in control here... looking fucking perfect on top of me with your tits bouncing in the air."

"Marc," I scream out, my voice rising as my movements slow because the pleasure is too much to bear.

"My rules, Princess. You don't get to come until I tell you to come."

I let out a groan, "I can't stand you."

"That turns me on even more." He grins up at me. His hands move to cup my breasts and he pinches my nipples between his fingers. I'm right… fucking… there. "Don't you dare come."

"Fuck you, Marc." My moans turn into a string of curse words, sitting at the edge of ecstasy, ready to explode any second.

"That's it, baby. Ride me. Make me come with you."

"Oh my god," I cry out, leaning down as I hover over his lips. Our hot frantic breaths mixed with each other as the only sound we hear is our wet bodies crashing together.

"I'm going to come, baby. Don't stop."

"Marc." His name comes out of me so loud that I'm sure the whole city hears me. "Oh my god, Marc." And then I come so hard I see stars.

"Baby," he grunts right before he pours his release into me, his hips jerking up as he fills me while my arms give out on top of him. He doesn't waste a minute before his hands cup my face and he kisses me with the most intense and intimate kiss I've ever experienced in my life.

"Fuck, Ave," he says breathlessly against my lips, his forehead pressed against mine and his eyes fall shut. "I…" His voice trails off as anguish takes over his features. "Stay the night."

I don't think that's where he was going with that sentence.

But I can't let this happen this fast.

I give him a soft smile. "Next time."

CHAPTER TWENTY-FIVE

Avery

"Okay ladies, what's the plan for the day?" Peyton asks as she drops the napkin on the table.

"I just have to pack later today."

I took the whole day off to get ready for our weekend trip to the mountains tomorrow. I'd be lying if I said I wasn't nervous about the trip. Not so much because of Marc, but because of being around Bill and Todd and trying to lock this in with one last hoorah before Bill makes his decision after this trip.

Then again, the feelings I have for Marc now, the feelings I've finally let consume me… they should make this so much easier.

In the last two weeks, I've only been back to his place one time when I managed to get there and rearrange his entire pantry. It was, without a doubt, one of my greatest projects. Marc wasn't home while I did it, which was both nice and disappointing.

I can feel a shift in his demeanor lately. He's been sweeter, more caring, and doesn't walk around work with a face that looks like a grumpy cat. He's only kissed me a few times but the times that he did, they were quick kisses, like a habit he does every day of his life.

I'm not saying that the sex was the reason my heart is feeling things more than my body is, but the connection, the chemistry, the *electricity* of that night... is just something I can't stop thinking about nor deny. There's something there. Something big and soul consuming.

I want him, with every fiber of my being.

I want to open up to him and let him in *completely*.

Break down every single wall I've spent my entire life building up.

But that all scares the shit out of me.

"Earth to Avery." Emiline waves her hands in the air.

"Yes," I reply, unsure of what they even just said.

"I'm happy to hear you're excited about your trip with my brother." Em laughs. "It's about time you two stopped denying this and made it official."

"Oh, wait. What? No."

Kali joins in with a laugh. "I saw you just space out, Ave. Your head went somewhere and it's time you spill. We haven't talked about this in almost two weeks."

"You're avoiding us," Peyton adds.

"I'm not intentionally trying to avoid you guys. I've just been busy with work."

"Riiiight," Peyton draws out.

"You went out to dinner with Marc and then you've just... ghosted us...for two weeks." Emiline rolls her eyes. "I talked to him the next night and he had things to say."

I bring my elbows to rest on the table. "Enlighten me on what he had to say."

"He told me things shifted between you two..."

"What?" Kali and Peyton both shriek at the same time.

"How could you not tell us?" Kali throws her hands out.

"I was going to tell you guys." I hold my hands up in defense. "But I just didn't know what was going on in my head after that. I won't lie to you guys. Something big is there. I want to explore it and see where it goes, I'm just trying to figure out how to do that."

Peyton's shoulders relax, her face fills with sympathy. "I know, girl. But this is all such a good thing. Whatever you're feeling here, it's a *good thing*!"

"Is it though? Because last I checked, opening your heart to someone just allows you the chance to have it broken."

Em shakes her head. "Marc isn't like that."

"You're obligated to say that because he's your brother."

"No, I mean it. I grew up with him, of course, but he's not the type of guy who takes a girl for granted. When Marc loves someone, he loves them with everything he has in him. He takes care of them and puts them first. He was only ever in love once, at least he thought that's what it was." She shakes her head at the thought of his past. "When Becky fucked up, he realized that maybe there was no love there in the first place. He was outraged by what she did. It fucked him up big time, but there was also a part of him that was thankful for it so he didn't have to fall deeper for her. Or hell, *marry* her and find out she was a cheating bitch."

"Marc didn't deserve that to happen to him."

"You're right, he didn't. You may be one of my best friends now, too, so I know deep in my bones that you wouldn't do anything to hurt him."

I cut her off, shaking my head and looking down as I wring my hands together on the table. "You don't know that, Em. What if I do something unintentionally to hurt him?"

"You won't because you two have already been through so much as a fake couple. He's seen the vulnerable side of Avery Woods that not many people get a chance to see. You've allowed him to see the worst parts of you and the best parts of you."

"I wouldn't classify a raging bout of food poisoning and puking all over the place as the *worst* part of me," I scoff.

"You know what I mean." She laughs.

"I do," I say, offering her a smile. "I want to tell him how I feel, but how the fuck do you even do that? I can't really just say *hey, I love you*, becau—"

"Woah woah…" Kali cuts me off. "Love?"

"Is our girl in *love*?" Peyton coos.

"Stop it. That's not what this is. That's why I just said I *can't* say that."

"But if that's how you feel, then yes! You actually can say just that."

I've loved before, but that list is short and it's never been with a man. It's my mom and my best friends.

Love for my mom is unconditional, a love like no other. She was my first best friend, and that forever type of friend. The woman who's been my biggest cheerleader in life, who's stood by me through good and bad, and pushed me to always believe in myself. I'm who I'm because of her and how she's loved me.

Love for my best friends is like finding the sisters you've always wanted. They may not have been there my whole life, but they came in and just made everything so much better. Shoulders to cry on, girls to sit around and laugh at the dumbest things with.

Love for Marc though?

Could that be what all these feelings are?

The more I think about it, the more I think that's what this is.

The uneasy churning in my stomach when he's around is just simply butterflies of excitement that he's in my presence. The all-consuming feeling of wanting him to touch me in any way, shape or form. Whether it's just his arm around me, his hands cupping my face before he leans in to kiss me, or his body pressed into mine. The smile that touches my lips when I think about a future with him. How safe my heart would feel in his hands.

Marc Ford came into my life like a wrecking ball, breaking down every single wall.

"I think there's definitely something there," I admit to them. "Maybe it's just lust or a crush at this point. But I can't say for certain that this is love."

"You're going away with him tomorrow, right?" Peyton asks.

"Yeah, that's why I took today off to pack."

"Well this weekend will be a way for you to find out. No pressure of work around you, a getaway to the mountains where it's just the two of you—"

"It's not just the two of us," I cut her off. "It's Bill and Cathy as well as Todd and his fiancé."

"Even better." Peyton claps her hands, and smiles widely. "You two won't have to fake a single thing. If this is really what we all already know it is, then you two can go to that cabin and be a *real* couple for once in front of everyone."

"Yeah... you have a point."

"I know. Let's get the check and head out for some last minute shopping for the trip," Peyton says right before she flags down the waiter to ask for the check.

"Shopping?" I snort. "I don't really need to shop for this. I just planned on bringing yoga pants and a couple t-shirts."

"You're going to the mountains," Kali chimes in. "You have to look the part."

"We're just going to get you a pair of hiking boots to go with those leggings you plan to wear," Peyton says. "The nights might even be a little cool. So we can get you a cute light vest to go with it. You will look really out of place rolling up to dinner in a flowery t-shirt and flip flops."

"Okay, fine."

"Lunch is on me," Peyton says as the waiter hands her the check.

"No, that's too much." I try to grab the check from her hands. "You've already done too much the last couple weeks."

"Me?" she exclaims. "What the hell have I done?"

"You know... helping arrange for my mom to be down here for the Fourth of July weekend."

"I didn—"

"Stop," I cut her off. "I know Jan is like a second mom to you, but you didn't have to send her a check to cover some of her mortgage payments. It was too much."

"Avery." She stops me. "I didn't do any of that. What the hell are you talking about?"

"Wait."

If Peyton didn't do it, then…

I cover my mouth with my hands, and my eyes go wide. "Oh my god!"

"What's happening right now?" Emiline looks worried.

"I think she's going to pass out. Her face looks white," Kali adds.

"Marc," I breathe out.

"I wasn't supposed to say anything, but he's the one who paid for your mom to come down for the holiday. However, I have no idea what you're talking about with the mortgage money."

I shake my head in disbelief. Why would he do something like that?

I down the rest of my mimosa in one gulp. "A couple weeks ago, my mom called me to thank me for sending her some money to help her with bills. You know she's been struggling since her fall. That's why I assumed it was you."

"But it was Marc, wasn't it?"

"Who else could it have been? He knows about her situation."

"Wow." Emiline lets out a long exhale. "Just wow."

"What?"

"Logan told me he asked him to help find an address in Vermont. They pulled some strings and were able to find it. That must be what it was for."

I swallow the lump in my throat.

My heart beats rapidly.

This man.

"Come on girls." Kali stands from her chair. "Let's go shopping. Ave has a big weekend with her future husband and we have to make sure she's ready for it."

"Yes! Let's do this," Peyton snorts.

I can't help but shake my head and laugh at these girls as we stand and leave the restaurant. I don't know how I got so lucky to have these best friends in my life.

I decide to shoot my mom a text when we pack into Peyton's fancy SUV.

Hey mom. I wanted to talk to you about something.

MOM

Of course, honey. I can't talk on the phone right now because I'm at work.

That's fine. But do you remember that money you called me about?

MOM

Yes. I still can't thank you enough for it.

Well… that wasn't from me.

MOM

Who was it from? That's a lot of money to not be from you.

I'm almost positive it was from Marc.

I watch as the bubble pops up that tells me she's typing, but it goes away when an incoming call comes from her.

"I thought you couldn't talk?" I laugh.

"Avery!" she shrieks on the phone.

I pull the phone away from my ear the second she does. "Mom, I think you just blew out my ear drum."

A series of more screams come from inside the car. Kali, Peyton and Emiline all say their hello's to her and I switch to speaker so she can say hello to them back.

"Anyway…"

"What makes you think it was him, honey?"

"I asked Peyton about it and she said it wasn't her. Who else could it have been?"

"Wow."

"I know."

There's a pause on the line before she says, "He loves you."

"Mom." I sigh sympathetically. "Don't."

"He does. And you should allow him to love you. Not because of the money. But because of what he did for me. Him bringing me down there for you to be able to see me alone, just proves that he cares about *you*, and the people *you* care about. That speaks volumes."

"I know."

"Do you? Because from my end, you don't sound so sure."

"I think I do, Mom. Something is there but I don't know how to move forward with the feelings."

"She's going away with him this weekend, Jan," Peyton yells from the front seat, loud enough so that she hears her over the phone.

"That's wonderful!" I can feel my mom smiling through the phone.

"I'm taking it one step at a time, mom. I don't want to screw this up."

"You can never screw this up." My mom sighs. "I don't want you to follow in my footsteps. I want you to know that. All I've ever wanted was for you to walk your own path and go even farther than I could ever dream. So far… you've done that."

A tear threatens to spill over. Feeling *things* has turned me into the biggest sap.

"Don't let the fear of what your father did to me stop you. Go after what your heart truly wants."

"Thanks, Mom. I love you."

"I love you, too."

We end the call and I slump back in my seat. Staring at my phone, my mind spins with everything the girls said at brunch and what mom just said on the phone.

Go after what your heart truly wants.

I think my heart truly wants Marc Ford.

CHAPTER TWENTY-SIX

Marc

Have you ever been so excited for something that you find yourself pacing your home waiting for the hands on the clock to move just so you can go to whatever has you feeling that way?

That was me this morning. The anticipation of seeing Avery again had me walking around with a giant smile plastered on my face.

I don't know what's shifted between us, but I can confidently say I'm so far gone for her. I mean, I almost spilled the words *I love you* to her the night she was at the penthouse. But I don't think that's what this is… not yet. We were in the heat of the moment with each other, I think anyone would've almost spilled it after the greatest sex of someone's life.

I find myself wanting to be around her, to kiss her, have my hands on her, and craving to see her smile.

She's spun my whole world around.

When I finally picked her up earlier, she answered the door wearing black leggings that had a flannel shirt wrapped around her waist, and a white tank top that was cut just enough to show her toned midsection. Her hair was braided into a messy side braid, topped with a baseball cap that read *NBU*. Looks like a college logo, but I've never heard of it.

She then leapt into my arms and kissed me. As if she does it every day. I wrapped my arms around her and kissed her back. It wasn't the most explosive kiss I've ever had with her, but it erupted something inside of me. A desire to say fuck this fake shit, this weekend will be all real. All us.

But I decide to tread lightly, because I've come to learn a lot about Avery and who she is as a person. Opening up to someone will not be easy for her. Part of caring for someone so much is allowing them that time to process their feelings until they're ready.

The ride to the mountains has been effortless. We talked about the most mundane things. From her latest episode of *Friends* to trying a new restaurant in the city that Oliver says we need to go to. Everything with her is just so carefree.

The GPS interrupts my thoughts when it says, "*Your destination is on the left.*"

"Wow." Avery sits up from the passenger seat to look at the cabin out the window. "That is *not* a cabin. That's a full mansion in the woods."

My eyes land on the home and it's truly beautiful.

However, it's not quite a mansion. The driveway has two dirt road entrances that are in the shape of a horseshoe. The house is perched on a curve in the mountain, showing that it's a three story home. You can see all the land, and I notice the giant pond behind the house, and a massive two car garage off to the side of the property. It has one large opening that would be where someone would park an RV for their stay, and the other is large enough for a truck to fit in.

"This place is stunning," I say as I put the car into park.

"It really is."

"Bill was right about one thing, this will be a great spot for a weekend away from the busy city. There isn't a neighbor in sight."

"What do you expect? We're out in the middle of nowhere."

"Are you going to survive, Princess?"

"The chances are slim." She laughs.

God, her laugh is the greatest sound. My head snaps in her direction the second the sounds left her mouth. I can feel my face morph into lust as I watch her chuckle in the seat next to me staring out the front window. As if she can feel me looking, she twists her head until she's looking right at me.

"What's that look for?" She begins to wipe her face. "Do I have something on my face?"

"No." I shake my head, smile growing wider. "You don't."

"Why does your face look like that then? It's all weird and smiley." She laughs again.

"That laugh, Ave."

She waves me off. "I know, it's obnoxious. I can be a lot of a person. Most of the time I don't realize how loud I really am."

"That's not what I'm talking about." I place my hand on her thigh. "It's perfect."

"You don't have to lie to make me feel better."

"I'd never lie to you. You have the most beautiful smile, and most contagious laugh. I don't know who made you feel like your laughter was anything less than, but let me be the first to tell you that it's perfect. It's everything."

A knock on the window doesn't give her the chance to respond. When I whip my head towards the driver side door, Bill is standing there waving.

"Come on, kids. Are you going to sit out here all day?"

"Sorry, sir," I say just as I open my door. "I was busy admiring the view."

It isn't a lie, except the view I was talking about wasn't the mountains. When I look towards Avery rounding the car, I see a blush of pink creep into her cheeks as she tucks a loose strand of hair from her braid behind her ear.

"It's a real sight out here. If you ever want to invest in a getaway house for you two, I recommend the mountains over the beaches."

"Over the beaches?" Avery's hand lands on her heart. "But my sun and sand, Bill? You wound me."

Bill lets out a laugh. "I know. I know, Avery. You're all about the sun and sand. But after this weekend, I think you will change your mind about the mountains."

Avery stands next to me, resting a hand on my shoulder before she says to Bill, "We'll just have to see about that, won't we?"

"Let's go, kids." Bill waves a hand signaling for us to follow him. "I'll show you your room."

I feel Avery's hand tense up on my arm. I know this was what she was worried about this entire trip, but there's a piece inside of me that hopes she changes her mind. There's nothing more I want than to wake up with her in my arms this weekend.

I scoop my arm around her neck, leaning in to whisper in her ear, "We'll figure this out." Before I press a kiss to the side of her head.

Bill gives us a grand tour. He confirms his home is three floors. Technically, the bottom floor is a basement, but it's finished as if it's a living space. For how big the house is, it's a very cozy space. It even smells like the woods. Pine and cedar fill the rooms, while the lingering smell of firewood looms in the air from the last time it was lit.

The first floor has a standard kitchen with a dining room off to the side. There's an archway that leads to a spacious living room that has a beautiful wood burning fireplace and a television mounted on the wall. The upper floor has two bedrooms and a bathroom, while the basement floor has another living room and a single bedroom.

"Since you two beat Todd and Vivian here, you get first pick of the rooms," Bill says at the end of our tour.

"Upstairs works," I say at the same time Avery says, "Downstairs."

We both look at each other, and I can see the silent look in her eyes that says downstairs would be the better choice. Considering it would leave us alone from the others… and there's a living room right outside of the bedroom.

"Downstairs it is," I say to Bill, but smile at Avery.

"Good choice." He nods. "I'm going to check on Cathy. She was just getting out of the shower. Todd should be here within the hour. I'll leave you two to get settled."

"Thank you," Avery says as we walk down the stairs into our space. "I figured this would be better for our… sleeping arrangements."

I swallow the lump in my throat and bite my lip to ward off the tension. Choosing not to answer her right now because that's certainly not how I want this to go. Instead, I place our bags on the queen size bed in the room and start to unpack.

"Is this okay?" she questions as she plops down on the bed next to the bags.

I stay silent because the truth of the matter is that it's not okay. I pick up a stack of t-shirts I brought with me and place them in a dresser drawer before I unpack my shower bag and place it on the bathroom sink.

"Marc." She stops me just as I'm walking out of the bathroom. "Stop."

"I'm just trying to unpack, Ave."

"No, you're avoiding me. Did I say something wrong? Did I do something wrong? Help me out here."

My shoulders relax as I hear the worry in her voice.

Fuck. I don't want her to think she did anything wrong because she didn't. This is all me. This is me wanting this to be more than it is.

I have to give her time.

My hands cup her face as I stare intently into her eyes. Her hands find my shirt and she grips it like she never wants me to let go. I bring my mouth down to hers and hold it there as she melts into me.

This right here. *I want this every day for the rest of my life.*

I offer her a smile after I release my lips from hers. "You did nothing wrong."

Her grip tightens on my shirt, her body flesh with mine as her blue eyes gaze up at me behind her long eyelashes. "Then what's the problem?"

"My problem is that I've never in my life wanted someone as bad as I want you," I admit and press another quick kiss to her lips so she doesn't have a chance to answer. "I don't want us to be a fake couple anymore. I know I have to take my time and allow you to feel that too. I'm trying hard not to push you into anything that you—"

"Okay."

"What?"

"I don't know when things changed between us. But I can't fight off the chemistry we have anymore. It's fucking explosive."

"So, you've felt that too?"

She laughs. "Oh, I felt it, alright. And I'm not just talking about the couple orgasms you gave me that night."

"Couple?" I scoff. "More like a handful… I lost count after the first two."

She playfully swats my arm, before she turns on her heel. "You're such an asshole."

I grip her wrist, forcing her to turn back around and crash into me. My one hand reaches around to place itself on the small of her back and holds her to my body, while the other hand gets lost in her messy hair. "Tell me you mean all of that, Ave. Tell me you want to see where this goes between us."

Her hand comes up to hold my chin between her fingers and thumb. "Yes, boss man."

I bring my lips to hover over hers, so close that I can feel her ragged breath on mine. "What did I tell you about calling me that?"

"It's not necessarily a threat that I hate… boss man," she says with a wink.

"You're something else, baby." I pull her into my arms for a long embrace.

"Say that again," she murmurs against my chest.

"Say what?"

She pulls her head back to look up at me, a smile across her lips, "What you just called me."

"Baby?"

"Yes that." She shivers under my embrace. "So totally swoon."

"I'll tell you anything you want to hear, baby."

"Oh will you?" she teases, her hands skating down my arm until she reaches the hem of my t-shirt. "Will you tell me all the dirty things you want to do to me in that massive shower behind you?"

"I'll do you one better," I say right before I grip her ass and pick her up in my arms. She lets out a squeal as she wraps her legs around my waist and I carry her into the bathroom. "I'm going to show you."

CHAPTER TWENTY-SEVEN

Avery

"Remove the clothes," Marc orders, unbuttoning his jeans and sliding them down his toned legs. He's wearing nothing but a pair of navy blue boxer briefs, and my eyes take a minute to trail his body. "You asked me to tell you all the dirty things I want to do to you in this shower. I plan on doing just that. So take off your clothes."

There's something about his dominant side that makes me melt to my knees.

"You're so bossy." I roll my eyes playfully before I pull my crop top over my head and slide my leggings off. "It turns me on."

"All of it, Ave. I want to see all of you."

My hands reach behind me to unclip my lace bra, but my eyes stay fixed on his. His bottom lip disappears between his teeth as bites down and watches me intently. I hook my thumbs inside my panties and slide them down to the floor.

"Good girl," he says before he swipes his tongue over his bottom lip. He takes two steps into me, and his hands find their way tangled in my hair as he tips my head back so that he can claim my lips as his. "On your knees, Princess. I want to see your pretty lips wrapped around my cock."

I do as he says, and drop to my knees. I hook my fingers into his boxer briefs and push them down. His cock springs free, hard as steel, precum dripping from the tip. I grip the base of it and give it a few pumps.

"Suck, baby."

I bring the tip to my lips, smearing precum across my bottom lip. He lets out a moan as I lick from base to tip before I take him into my mouth. Pumping my hand at the same time my head bobs up and down, Marc brushes the hair out of my face, looking down at me. He bites his bottom lip and I hum in satisfaction that I'm turning him on this much.

"Fuck, baby," he grunts. "I don't want to come in your mouth but seeing you on your knees for me, with a mouthful of my cock, knowing your pussy is soaked right now has me ready to blow down your throat."

My eyes fall closed, and I nod my head, pumping harder as I bob my head for him, hoping that he does as he says. But then he pulls himself out of me.

"Nope." He pulls me to stand. "The only place I'm coming is inside of you."

He lifts me into his arms with one fast move and I wrap my naked body around his while he steps into the shower. I think he's going to place me down, but instead he backs me into the wall. The steaming hot shower water cascading down his back as I claw at him.

I reach below us, gripping his cock and lining it up with my wet entrance. "Get inside of me now, Marcus."

"You look so good when you put me inside you like that." He smirks, and with one move, he thrusts into me, filling me to the brim, and stretching me with his thickness. "Slick and ready for me, baby."

"Always," I moan, clawing at his messy hair as I run my fingers through it, forcing him to look up at me. "Always ready for you. God, I don't think I will ever get used to your size, though."

He fucks me hard, raw, and fast. Like the primal need inside of him has been completely unleashed inside of this shower. My heels dig into his back, his mouth kissing any part of my skin along my neck and shoulder that he can. My body bounces up and down against the shower wall, and I know I'm close because I can feel my legs begin to quake around him.

"Tell me you're close, Ave. I need you to fucking come because I'm not going to last."

"I'm so close," I cry out. He leans back just a little bit to look down at where we're connected. I reach my hand between us and feel the spot where we connect. "Fuck."

"Rub your clit for me. I want to see you get yourself off while my cock is buried deep inside you." I begin to rub slow circles, putting just the right amount of pressure that will set me over the edge while he pumps me full. "That's it, Princess. You're such a good fucking girl."

"Your good girl. Only yours."

"Come for me," he growls. "Right. Fucking. Now."

"Yes!" My moan mixed with curse words and his name as my orgasm crashes over me.

He lets out a series of grunts as his abdomen clenches and his movements slow while he spills into me.

"Holy shit."

His chest rises and falls as he slowly pulls out of me, placing me to the ground and under the showerhead. He silently grabs the sponge and begins to wash me from behind. Taking special care of my lady bits after he just pounded me into oblivion.

He leans in to whisper in my ear, "I'm going to worship every single part of you later." He trails the sponge between the apex of my thighs, peppering kisses along my shoulder. "Every part of you belongs to me."

And I've never wanted a statement to be truer in my life.

We spent the better part of the afternoon engaging in small talk on the back deck of the cabin. There's nothing like it here, not even in Vermont. The air is crisp and it's a state of calm that brings you peace. The backyard has a pond, and a spectacular view of the mountains. You can even see the slopes of what would be a ski resort in the winter.

Todd and Vivian finally showed up. Vivian is a lot quieter than I thought she'd be. She almost seems... sketchy or nervous. Like something is off with her. But my spidey senses haven't picked up on what exactly that is yet.

After a drink on the deck, Bill suggested we head down the mountain to a little bar and grill that he often frequents when he comes. He says they have the best wood fire pizza and beer. While beer isn't my jam, we agreed to go with the rest of the group.

"This place is adorable," Todd exclaims. The word *adorable* should not be used by a grown business man when talking about a hole in the wall pizza joint on the mountains.

"I reserved a spot on the screened-in porch off the back for all of us. I figured since we're here to relax, we didn't need to do the whole sit down dinner. The room has a couple of couches and a bar right inside."

"This place is awesome." I beam as we enter the private porch. "Did you find this place just driving around or did a local tell you about it? I would've gotten lost finding it since it's so tucked away."

"The locals," Bill answers, making his way to a high top table that has two chairs. "We try to come up here at least four times a year. This spot is always non-negotiable during our stay."

"The pizza is *to die* for," Cathy says. "I could melt just thinking about the pizza we're about to eat." She takes a seat on one of the couches.

Todd follows Bill to the high top because he can't remove himself from Bill's ass, and Vivian hesitantly takes a seat next to Cathy.

Marc interlocks his fingers in mine. "We're going to head to the bar for a drink. Can we get anyone anything?"

Bill jumps off his stool and pulls his wallet from his back pocket, "Grab a pitcher of sangria for the ladies and a pitcher of beer for us."

Marc waves him off. "On me, Bill. Don't worry about it."

"Here take mine, Marc," Todd interjects, flashing his credit card in front of Bill. "Open a tab on me."

"That's not necessary, Todd," Marc grumbles, before he tightens his hold on my hand. "We've got it."

Turning on our heels, we leave the patio and make it to the bar right inside. It must not be their busy season because every seat in the bar is open.

"Hey there," a young girl—who doesn't look a day older than twenty-one—greets us. "What can I get for you, tonight?"

"I'll have whiskey neat and she'll take a glass of champagne," Marc answers.

"Coming right up."

Marc swivels his chair so that my legs are between his thighs. "We're having ourselves a drink before we head back there. Todd is driving me insane."

"Is it just me or does Vivian seem a little… off to you?"

"She really is. Something doesn't sit right with her. I just can't pinpoint what it is."

"Here you go," the bartender interrupts us, and I don't miss the sleeve of tattoos cascading down her arm. "Whiskey neat and a glass of champagne. I filled it to the tippy top because you look like you need it." And then she winks at me.

"You're a gem." I offer her a smile. "Can you tell us a little bit about this town? We just got here this morning and were wondering about it."

"I wish I could," she scoffs. "I just moved here myself. From one small town to another."

"Where are you from?" I ask.

"Montana. I had to get away from that state." She has a sad

look on her face. She looks way too young to have that look in her eyes like she's been through hell and back already. But then she lets out a laugh. "Anything to piss my parents off."

"I like this girl," I tell Marc before I direct my attention back to her. "Do you mind if I ask how old you are?"

"I'm twenty-four," she admits. "I'm here to find a little bit of serenity and peace. It's just a stepping stone until I can afford to make it to the big city."

"New York?" Marc asks.

"Yes. It's always been my dream to make it there as a chef. I've wanted to cook for as long as I can remember. Life threw me a couple curve balls before I even turned eighteen, but I figured now's a good time in my life to try and pursue it."

"Wow. Good for you, girl. It's never too late to pursue your dreams." I cheer her on. "We're from the city."

"Are you?" She beams. "That's amazing. Is it as cool as everyone says it is?"

"I wouldn't go that far," Marc grumbles.

"I think it's pretty awesome." I shoulder bump him. "Don't listen to this grumpy cat."

Marc looks down at his watch after he finishes his drink in record time. "We should get back to the group. Can we get a pitcher of sangria and a pitcher of beer to bring to the patio?"

She wipes the counter. "You got it."

Marc leans into me, whispering in my ear. "I can't wait for this night to be over to crawl into bed with you."

"Oh yeah?"

He presses a kiss to the spot right below my ear. "Yes. You look so fucking beautiful in this little dress. You've been tempting me all afternoon, wishing I had my head buried under this dress and eating your tight, wet cunt."

"Marc! You can't talk like that in public."

"You're lucky I'm only just talking about it and not actually doing it." His hand slides up my thigh and under my dress, inching his way closer to my core, sending desire coursing through me. "You're thinking about it too, aren't you?"

"I'm always thinking about it with you." I exhale a long breath, taking a long swig of champagne. "You are very good at working that tongue of yours."

"Mmm," he murmurs into my throat, before he grips the back of my neck pulling me in for a kiss.

"Ohh, la la," the bartender coos. "Newlyweds?"

"Oh no." I shake my head.

"Just engaged," Marc answers for me, in a deep steady voice that makes my heart flutter.

"Adorable." She offers us a smile. "Here's the pitchers."

"You can put it all on our tab…" Marc starts. "I'm sorry, we never got your name."

"Macey."

"Thank you, Macey." He hands her three crisp hundred dollar bills. "Keep that for yourself."

Her mouth falls open and tears prick her eyes. "Thank you. So much."

"It was so nice to meet you. If you're ever in the city, look me up. I'm Avery Woods!"

"Avery Woods?" She tilts her head in question. "That name sounds so familiar, but I can't pinpoint right now where I know it from."

"I'm not sure. I've never been to Montana." I laugh.

"Hmm. Not sure either." She shrugs a shoulder. "Regardless, it was nice meeting you guys. Thank you for the tip and I hope you two have a fun trip."

"Thank you," Marc says before he wraps his free arm around my shoulders and we head back to the patio.

"'Bout time," Todd snickers. "Thought you two got lost."

"The bartender was new," Marc deadpans.

"How hard is it to make a pitcher of sangria and beer?" he scoffs.

"Hey," Bill cuts him off. "If she's new, give her the benefit of the doubt, Todd. You never know what's going on with people."

Todd nods. "You're right, sir."

"So Vivian," Cathy changes the subject, a weary tone in her voice with how she says her name. "Tell us about your upcoming wedding? We never got a chance to talk about it on the lake trip."

"Oh… uhhh," Vivian stutters. "Planning is going really well."

"When are you planning the big day for?"

"Summer," she answers at the same time Todd says, "Winter."

The two of them exchange a look. Todd is looking at her with an, '*I thought we discussed this,*' look. If anyone can point out a fake relationship, it's me because I've been in one all summer. I'm pretty sure my jaw is on the floor and my eyes flash to Marc who's standing to the side of the table. Clearly, he has come to the same realization.. His eyebrows are pinched together and he has a smirk on his face.

"We're working out the details." Todd clears his throat and lets out a small cough.

"Yes. The details," Vivian repeats, taking a sip of her beer.

Sitting here with Vivian for the first time, I can tell she doesn't fit the mold for whatever this is playing out to be. These two don't have any chemistry whatsoever. I noticed it sitting on the back deck of the cabin, and it's been made clearer now.

While I can't knock them for what they're doing because Marc and I are doing the same thing… At least we have some sort of explosive chemistry happening between us.

My gaze travels to Bill to try and assess his thoughts of the situation and his eyes are bouncing between Todd and Vivian as he tries to piece the pieces of the puzzle together himself.

"How about you, Marc?" Todd taunts, as if he's trying to catch us in the same thing.

"Spring," he says with conviction. "We decided on *Sound River Studios* in Long Island City."

"It has the most perfect view of New York City as the backdrop for our ceremony. I can't wait to make this man my husband there." I glance over at Marc and I've never seen a wider smile on his face at the admission of me looking up the location from the first time he mentioned it at dinner. A smile that tells me that he'd like that too. My heart rate picks up, because the more and more we put on this show, the more I wish this was all real.

"I can't wait to dance with my wife on their patio," he replies back.

"Gosh," Cathy coos, with her hand over her heart. "I truly love your love."

"I hope you and Bill will be there. Plus I need some help with booking a DJ for the event. I haven't forgotten your offer."

Cathy shoots me a wink. "You better take me up on that."

Our conversation is interrupted when the waiter delivers a couple of pizzas, placing them on the coffee table sitting between the two couches. Over the next half hour, the men talk about work, and the women talk about wedding things. When I say women, I mean Cathy and myself. Vivian was very tight lipped on plans.

"So, Avery." Bill sits back in his chair, crossing one leg over the other. "Could you ever see yourself with a place out here?"

I laugh at his very serious question. "You know how I feel about my beaches, Bill."

"I do, but has this day changed anything for you?"

"If I'm being honest with you… it absolutely has. I know we just got here and haven't seen much of the town, but it truly is such a peaceful place for a getaway. It almost reminds me of home, but better." I take a sip of my sangria. "So to answer your question, I could totally see us having a place out here in the future. Plus it's way closer to our home in the city than Vermont is."

"You better get on that, Marc." Bill laughs at Marc.

"One thing at a time, sir." He laughs back at him over the brim of his drink. "Maybe after the wedding and honeymoon."

"We saw a house for sale on the way up the mountain when we were coming in today," Todd says, breaking into the conversation. "I sent it over to my assistant to see if she can get me more details on it."

"I bet you did," Bill mumbles against his beer. "It's a great town."

I look at Vivian whose face is now beet red with embarrassment. Is she as embarrassed as we are, watching him suck up to his boss the way he is? You're not alone, girlfriend.

"We're going to head back to the house if that's okay with you guys?" Marc asks. "We left early this morning and I'm exhausted already."

"Of course. Of course." Bill stands. "We'll be back there within the hour ourselves."

Marc tips his head. "Sounds good. See you back at the house."

After exchanging goodbyes, we're out the door. Marc stopped by the bar to see Macey again and pay the entire tab without Bill knowing. He kept saying it was the least we could do since he opened his house up to us for the whole weekend.

"Let's get you to bed, Princess."

Excitement bubbles up inside of me.

However, exhaustion wins the battle and the last thing I remember on the ride home is the darkness of the winding roads of the mountains before my eyes close for the night.

CHAPTER TWENTY-EIGHT

Marc

Everything on this trip with Avery has been easy since we hit a turning point and both admitted that we want this with each other.

Around Bill and Cathy, there's no faking it anymore. The only lie we find we're telling is the wedding planning. The two of us have that down perfectly, though. There's a small inkling in my chest that hopes she's full of smiles while talking about it because down the road she actually wants that too.

That's just the inner me who looks far into a dream though. A wife and kids are a big part of the future for me. I'd be a lying bastard if I said I didn't see Avery as my wife. Which is wild. It's too soon, right? There's just no denying the way sparks fly when she's around, the way I lose my breath when she walks into a room, and how every kiss with her tastes like the last first kiss I'll ever have with a woman.

Yesterday, after her admission, when we got to the cabin, I wanted nothing more than to fall asleep with her in my arms and head pressed against my chest. The sangria must have gotten to her first, because she was sound asleep in the car five minutes into the drive back to the cabin. I decided to sleep on the couch in the living room space in the basement after I carried her to bed. She didn't confirm or deny that she wanted to share a bed, so I didn't want to wake up to an angry Avery.

I could barely sleep though, thinking about the beautiful blonde girl laying in the bed one room over. Needless to say, I was up at five in the morning and I set out for a morning run. It was the most challenging thing I've done in a while. The hills, mixed with the difference in altitude was a good change up from the flat city sidewalks I'm used to running.

I didn't want to wake the house, so after I cooled down on the back deck, I used the back door entrance that leads to where our room is. When I walked in, Avery was sitting on the couch with her legs under her and the same blanket I slept with covering her body.

"Good morning."

"Morning," she mumbles, her tone laced with disappointment.

I move to sit next to her on the couch, placing a hand on her thigh. "Are you alright?"

"Yup," she says, popping the P with her lie.

"Did you know that I have a sister, Ave?"

"Obviously." She rolls her eyes. "Emiline is one of my best friends. *Remember*?"

"Great. So you also know that I can pick up on the fact that when someone answers in the tone you just used… that I know it's a lie?"

"It's not a lie," she answers, shocked that I called her out.

"Mmm." I lean in to press a kiss on the side of her head before I stand up from the couch. "You keep telling yourself that, Princess. But for now, when you're ready to tell me what's bothering you… I'll be in the shower." And I retreat to the shower without another word from her.

As I walk away, I find myself saying *"I love you"* under my breath because… I really fucking do.

"Whose idea was it to go on a mountain hike?" Avery asks, bent over with her hands on her legs trying to catch her breath.

"It's not that bad." I laugh. "We're going up the bunny slope, for crying out loud."

"It's only called that when there's snow on the ground for the kids to glide down slowly. It should be called death mountain when you're forced to hike up it."

"Come on, Princess. If Bill and Cathy can do it, you can too."

She groans as she pulls herself up and starts hiking until we're caught up with the rest of the group. For someone who hates this type of outdoor activity, she is dressed perfectly for the part. She must have bought a brand new pair of hiking books that she paired with her signature black leggings that are… chef's kiss, my friend. She went with a similar crop top that she wore the day we drove in, but this one is a hunter green color, and damn, it compliments her tanned skin tone beautifully. Her hair was done in a perfect side braid, but the wind has caused it to flow in every direction.

If there's one thing I've learned… It's that messy Avery is probably my favorite Avery.

She's just so beautiful when she's her real self. No makeup with her hair wild and free, dressed in casual clothes.

"This is easy for you because you're a track star."

"Running flat city sidewalks and walking up a hill work two very different muscle groups."

She groans, "I don't have either muscle group for this activity."

"Come on, kids," Bill bellows from about a quarter mile away. "We're almost to the top and then we can take some pictures."

"Wait till you see the view!" Cathy shouts after him.

We slowly continue up the mountain. Avery is at my side and I decide to let her set our pace.

"I can see myself owning a house up here," I admit. "This

really is the perfect place to get away from work and the city for a little bit."

"You're practically off the grid up here. I don't think I've had cell service all weekend."

"I haven't either."

She takes a couple of deep breaths in an attempt to calm her rapid breathing from exerting so much energy. "But, you're right. This really would be a perfect place. It reminds me of home."

"Have you talked to your mom lately?"

She nods. "I have."

"That's good."

"You don't happen to know anything about a check that was sent her way?" She stops dead in her tracks, squaring herself in my direction to make sure I'm listening to her. "A check large enough to cover almost three months of mortgage for her."

I grin. "Not a clue."

"Marcus!"

I laugh at her. I can't help it. "You're cute when you scream my name."

"Why did you do that?" she asks, softening her voice.

"When are you going to learn that I care about you, Ave? I care about the people you care about. When your mom and I spoke on the phone about her trip for Fourth of July—"

"You two spoke on the phone? She never told me this? I can't believe she—"

"Stop." She tenses under my palm as I grab her upper arms and level myself down until we're eye to eye with each other. "Do I need to remind you of everything you've been doing for me this entire summer?" Her shoulders relax under my touch. "And you didn't ask for a single thing in return other than to go to real estate school. Which is nothing to me compared to what you've done."

"I didn't…I don't want anything more."

"I know you don't." I press a kiss to her forehead and wrap

her body in my arms, embracing her in the middle of the bunny slopes while the rest of the group waits for us. "You mentioned your mom a few times to me. I thought helping her out would be something I can do."

She pulls her head back to look up at me, glassy eyes as she blinks away the tears. "You're something else."

I swallow the lump in my throat, words threatening to spill out of my mouth and tell her how I really feel about her, admitting to the fact that *I love her* is sitting in my chest.

"I—"

"Marc," Todd yells down at us, cutting off the words I want to say. "What are you two slow pokes doing?"

"We're plotting your demise," Avery mutters under her breath. She takes a step out of my hold and I laugh at her response that he most definitely didn't hear.

We move on from the conversation and make our way up to the top of the mountain about ten minutes later. Avery is out of breath. "That wasn't so bad," she huffs while laughing.

"Riiight." I laugh with her.

"Can you take a picture of us, Bill?" Todd asks.

"Sure can."

Todd and Vivian walk to the edge of the mountain where the beautiful scenic backdrop makes for the most perfect picture. I watch closely as Todd puts his arm around her the way a friend would. Vivian looks like she tenses up and hesitantly wraps her arm around his midsection, forcing the smile on her face as they snap some photos together.

"Let's get one of you two kissing?" Cathy reluctantly asks. I'm pretty sure she's just as onto them as we are.

"No, that's not necessary." Vivian shakes her head.

"Come on, schmoopie." Todd gives a puppy face.

"I'm going to throw up." Avery scrunches her face beside me. "If you ever call me *schmoopie,* I'll cut your balls off."

"I'd never dream of calling you that, baby." She smiles up at me.

We don't know if the two of them actually kiss, but we hear the click of a camera go off as Avery and I intently stare at each other, both of us with smiles on our faces.

"That was a good one," Cathy coos, the camera directly pointed at us. "My favorite one yet."

"Wait, I wasn't ready," Avery whimpers, dragging my arm to the place where Todd and Vivian just were. "Now, I'm ready."

Avery wraps both arms around my waist in a side hug, and I wrap one arm around her shoulders. When I pull her in close to me, she rests her head in the crook of my arm. We smile as Cathy snaps a few photos. *Snap. Snap.* I turn my head towards her and press a kiss to her forehead. *Snap.* Avery looks up at me, and presses up on her toes to meet my lips and sparks fly the way they do every single time I kiss her. *Snap.* I move my body until she's flush against me, keeping my lips to hers. She grips my t-shirt, and my hand finds the small of her back. *Snap.* I dip her down, and she smiles against my lips as I practically make a show out of how we're going to kiss on our wedding day. *Snap.*

"Wow," Cathy says in shock. "That was... wow."

We both snap out of our trance, our eyes finding the group and everyone looks shocked to see what just happened.

"Sorry," Marc starts. "We got a little carried away."

"I'm totally printing these out for you. They're perfect. You two are... I've never seen chemistry like that before. I'm just so happy I got that on camera."

Todd makes a grumble noise under his breath as if he's annoyed.

Avery blushes next to me as if she was just caught doing something naughty. But there was nothing naughty or wrong about what just happened.

I might be sitting on top of a small mountain in New York.

But Avery has me feeling on top of the world.

CHAPTER TWENTY-NINE

Marc

We may have been nervous coming on this trip, unsure of what was in store, but I couldn't think of a better place to spend the weekend with Avery. The last few days have only solidified exactly how I feel about her. I'm head over heels for her and I fully plan to tell her before this trip is over.

"Who's ready for apple crisp?" Cathy asks as she steps out onto the back deck.

We just finished grilling burgers and rib eyes, and the sun has finally started to set behind the mountains. The mountain air is warm, but the breeze makes it feel crisp for the end of summer. Not a touch of humidity in the air.

Avery places her glass of white wine on the table to rub her hands together as if she's ready to dive in. "You know I'm."

"That's my girl." Cathy wiggles her shoulders with a little dance with her red wine swirling in the glass.

Todd looks at Avery with a scowl on his face. It's very clear that he's not having the same amount of fun as anyone else in the house. Vivian went off to bed right after dinner, complaining of a stomach ache or something. I mean… I'd be doing anything to get away from the toad-faced Todd, too.

"Dessert should be ready in about two minutes," Cathy says

as she looks at the kitchen timer she has clipped to her jeans. "Don't worry, Avery… I made sure to bring a tub of vanilla bean ice cream."

Hand on her heart she says, "You are too good to me, Cathy."

"I'm going to get a refill." Bill raises his glass of whiskey. "Anyone else?"

"I'll take another. Thank you." I raise my glass.

Bill retreats into the house and Cathy follows him.

"So, Marc." Todd's tone is dripping with a challenge. "Where did you two say you were getting married?"

"*Sound River Studios,*" I answer confidently. "We're shooting for this spring."

"Interesting." A displeased frown on his face. "And how did you two meet again?"

"What is this–a game of twenty questions?" Avery snickers beside me, shaking her head in disbelief.

"No. I'm just trying to figure you two out. I've yet to see you at a work event once, *Avery,*" he says her name with so much accusation. "And you turn up out of the blue and here you are. Happy and engaged."

"Isn't that what an engaged couple is supposed to be, *Todd*?" she asks, using the same tone he used. "Last I checked, engaged couples should be ecstatic about their future nuptials. I also don't have to attend every single work function."

"It's just that you're…" He pauses as he scratches the back of his head. "How do I put this?"

"I'd be very careful of the next words that come out of your mouth when speaking to my fiancé, Todd."

"No, babe. Let him finish that. I *can't wait* to hear what he has to say."

"You don't fit the mold," he finally says. "You don't fit the type of girl Marc Ford would ever be caught dead with, let alone *marrying*."

I stand from my chair, bringing myself face to face with him. My hands ball into a white knuckle fist as anger bubbles to the surface at the way he's talking about her… to her right now.

"It's funny you say that," Avery says calmly before I get a chance to talk. She slowly stands from her chair and saunters her way to stand next to me as if this whole thing is the most casual thing in the world. How is she not raging right now? Hooking her arm in mine, I'm sure she feels the tension under her touch. "I was feeling the same way about you and Vivian."

"Leave her out of this."

"So what you're saying is that you want *us* to leave her out of this, but it's quite alright for you to butt yourself into *our* relationship?" Avery laughs at him. "How much are you paying her for this summer charade, Johnny ruff nuts?"

"Excuse me?"

"I'm sure if I've picked up on it, that Bill and Cathy have as well. Where is she by the way?" Avery exaggeratedly looks around the back deck. "Ohhhh, I forgot. She wants to get as far away from you as possible, huh?"

"You have some fucking nerve." Todd takes a step towards her.

"I might, but you haven't denied anything yet."

He moves to face me, pointing his finger directly at Avery. "This girl is nuts, Marc."

"My girl's got fire." I smirk. "What can I say?"

Todd lets out a displeased scoff as his eyes bounce between the two of us. "She might. But I'm the one who Bill is going to give the entire company to."

I say nothing as he turns on his heel and stalks back into the house at the same time Bill comes out. I barely hear Todd tell him he's heading to bed with Vivian and he'll see him in the morning.

Cathy emerges right behind him with a wide grin on her face. "Apple crisp anyone?"

———

We're back in the room after being fully stuffed with dessert. Bill and Cathy excused themselves for the evening and headed to a friend's house up the mountain for some drinks on their back deck. That seems to be the thing to do up here.

Avery is bouncing around the bathroom as she washes her face and takes off her earrings. I slip into my sweatpants and sit on the edge of the bed.

"The nerve of that guy to be such an ass," she says from the bathroom.

"He really shouldn't have spoken to you like that. I'm sorry, Avery."

She comes to stand in the bathroom doorway and shoots me a smile. "Why are you sorry? You didn't say it. He did. And trust me… people like him *do not* bother me one bit."

"I know. But I wanted to punch him in the face for talking to you like that."

"He's not worth it." She spins on her heel and is back to doing what she was doing.

I move off the bed, and I quickly find myself pacing with nervous energy. I need to tell her how I feel, and I need to do it tonight. The water shuts off in the bathroom as I stand in front of the full-length mirror and see her emerge from the door through the reflection.

She has not an ounce of makeup on, and she's changed into a silk sleep outfit that looks like a little dress. Honestly, I don't know if it's pajamas or lingerie, but all I know is I want it off of her.

We keep our eyes locked on each other in the reflection as she stands there. She brings her hands up to her neck and seductively tosses her long blonde hair back behind her shoulders, before she pulls it up in a ponytail.

"God, you're beautiful," I say, as I continue to look at her through only the mirror.

She walks up to stand directly behind me, bringing her hands around my waist, her palms pressed against my muscles.

"You're not so bad yourself," she whispers back, before she presses a kiss to my bicep.

My hand reaches over the top of hers and I interlock my fingers inside them, squeezing them as if I never want this moment to pass. I feel all the air in my lungs taken from me as I so desperately want to say the words I've been dying to say to her.

"I want you, Marc," she murmurs against my skin. "This whole day...you in the shower this morning, our kiss on the mountain, the way you wanted to stand up for me... God, I want you so bad."

I swallow the lump in my throat before I bring her hands down below the waistband of my sweatpants until she can feel how hard I'm beneath them. "Is this enough to prove that I want you too, baby?"

She unclasps her hands from mine and rounds my body until she's standing in front of me, not bothering to waste a minute until her hands cup each side of my face and she's pulling me down for a kiss. My body explodes at the touch from her hands, her lips, her body pressed into mine. My hands wrap around her waist, pulling her into me as I try so desperately to erase any inch between us.

"Do you feel what you do to me, Ave? Only you can get me this hard." I bring my lips back down to her. "Only." *Kiss.* "You."

She grins up at me, meeting the pressure of our hips by pushing back into me. "We should probably do something about that, huh?"

I spin her around until she's looking at us in the mirror, palm to her stomach and pulling her back flush with my body. Her hands cover the top of my hand and I begin to trail kisses along her shoulder.

"Look at us in the mirror," I urge, while my other hand moves to cup her breasts over her lingerie. Her head falls back on my shoulder but her eyes stay fixed on me through the reflection. "What do you see?"

"I see the sexiest man alive holding me," she says, almost panting in anticipation from my hands being all over her.

I grip one of her breasts, while my other hand skates its way down to her thigh. "What am I holding?"

"I-I..." she stutters slightly. "Everything. You're holding everything right now."

"Good answer, but wrong," I rasp in her ear. "I'm holding my girl." I bend down and brush my hands along her inner thighs, watching her face through the reflection as her breath hitches. "I don't give a damn about this deal or anything that happens with it anymore. I want— no, I need—to know that you are mine."

Her hand falls back on top of my hand that's between her thighs and she guides me to her core and I realize she's not wearing panties. She guides my fingers right into her wetness. "So take me, Marc."

I thrust two fingers inside of her as far as they can go, and her body jerks while she lets out a moan and her eyes flutter closed. "Open your eyes, baby. I want you to watch yourself come all over my fingers. I want you to see how fucking perfect you are when you come for me."

Her heavy panting fills the room, her legs are already starting to wither beneath her as I finger-fuck her in front of the mirror. She's already close.

"Can I come? Please?"

I pick up the pace, bringing my mouth to her ear. "Since you're such a good girl and asked so nicely." I press my lips to the spot under her ear that I know sets her off. "Come for me."

She does. Wildly, breathlessly and perfect. Moaning my name on her tongue as she loses her footing beneath me, soaking my hand as her cum drips down my wrists. I'm so fucking far gone for her, my stomach bounces with hope that she feels the same way I do.

"Fuck, Marc," she says, coming down from her high. "How do you manage to always make me come harder every time?"

"I lose all restraint with you. Watching you come undone for me is…" I trail off, unable to find the words stuck in my throat. "Fuck, Ave. I need to be inside of you."

"On the ground, sir," she orders.

"The ground?"

"I want to watch all of it in the mirror. I want to see you slide inside me and make me come again until I'm seeing stars."

I lower myself to the ground, close enough to the mirror that both of us can look. She straddles me with her ass facing me, reverse cowgirl. "I'm not going to last in this position." I let out an amused breath, but it's not a lie.

"We have all night, don't we?"

She grips the base of my cock and lines it up with her entrance, lowering herself until I'm completely inside of her. I can see her face off to the side in the mirror and watch as her mouth makes the perfect O-shape when I reach full hilt.

"Holy fuck," I pant, gripping her ass as she bounces up and down on top of me. She rides me fast and hard, and it's taking everything in me not to come within three seconds of being inside of her. "You're fucking dripping on my cock."

"Ahh, Marc," she begins to scream, but tries hard to keep her voice down knowing where we are. "It feels so fucking good."

I buck my hips up to meet her bounce, my eyes never leaving hers through the reflection. Her mouth remains open, breath hitching with every thrust of my hips.

"I'm going to come. I'm going to—"

"That's it, baby," I grunt, holding back my release because I'm not ready for this to be over. And then with one final thrust, I watch her face morph into ecstasy, slowing her pace as her chest rises and falls, with moans of pleasure just pouring out of her.

I pull her off of me as soon as she comes down from her orgasm. "What are you doing? You need to come."

"Oh, I'm going to come." I flip her over until she's on all fours. Horizontal with the mirror so she can watch as I slide into her. "I'm not going to last much longer. I'm going to fuck you hard and fast. Understood?"

"Yes," she whimpers.

I line myself up with her, plunging deep into her with one move. Her back arches and I reach forward to grab her by the side of the throat. I can feel her pounding pulse under my palm. Her eyes roll behind her head in bliss. "My girl likes being choked."

"Like I said, I want to see stars."

Her head tilts to the side to watch every single move as my cock disappears inside of her over and over again. Gripping her neck while my other hand is on her shoulder as I pound relentlessly into her with primal need.

"Fuck," she screams. "Ahhh."

"That's it. Scream, baby. I want to hear your voice echo through these mountains when you come again."

"I don't think I can. I don't think I have another one in me."

"Yes you fucking do," I growl. "Now give it to me. Come with me while I fill you up."

We both make eye contact through the mirror before she does as I ask. Pulsing around my cock, her orgasm shoots through her like a rocket. I pump into her three more times before my own release comes flying through me. Feeling it in every single part of my body, and our eyes never leaving each other.

Unspoken words pass between us.

Her eyes soften as she attempts to catch her breath, while a smile forms on her soft pink lips.

I pull myself out of her, cum dripping from each of us in a messy mix of euphoria.

"Let me get you cleaned up."

She follows me to the bathroom and I sit her on the vanity as I clean her with a washcloth, using gentle pressure.

"I was a little too rough back there."

"Just the way I like it." She winks.

My features soften as my eyes meet hers. "Avery, I—"

"Can you sleep in the bed with me tonight?" She stops me. "I don't want you sleeping on that couch."

I swallow, trying to rid the dryness in my throat as the words are lodged right there that I need to let out. "Is it that you don't want me sleeping on the couch? Or that you don't want to sleep without me?" I smirk.

"A mix of both."

"Good answer." I wink at her, scooping her into my arms and she lets out a yelp. "Let's go to bed, baby."

CHAPTER THIRTY
Avery

I wake up to the sun shining through the windows, my legs tangled in Marc's and my head on his chest. It feels natural, perfect.

There's a small part of me that doesn't want to move an inch and live in this moment with him. However, fear bubbles to the surface. It's something I can't help because of everything I've been through in my past.

Laying here, in his arms, I feel safe and comfortable.

But I also felt that with my dad. A different kind of comfort, but it was there, nonetheless. It was a love that wasn't reciprocated enough to the point he felt he had to leave mom and me without a backwards glance. He left us so easily. He told us he loved us and still left like we meant nothing to him.

Tears threaten to spill over just thinking about all of it–paired with these intense feelings building for Marc—but I blink them back when I feel him move under me. My body tenses and his arms tighten around my arm.

"Morning, baby," he grumbles through half open eyes.

"Morning."

"You're up early. Who's the early bird now?"

"The sun was shining on my face." I smile up at him from

where my head rests on his chest. "I can't fall back asleep once the sun shines like that."

"I'll have to get some room darkening curtains for the bedroom when we get home."

Home.

When *we* get *home*.

I nod before I bury my face into his chest. Not able to say anything back, not wanting to say anything back to that.

There're words on the tip of my tongue, because I can't deny the truth that *I love this man*. I don't know how or when it happened, but I love him with every single fiber of my being.

A feeling so completely foreign to me that I'm questioning if that's even what this is. It has to be though, right? There's no other way to describe how he makes me feel other than… loved.

He's soft, caring, and gentle, despite being downright dirty in the bedroom.

I can't help but wonder if any of this was fake. Was the gala when this all started? I think back to that first date we went on for "practice." Did we blossom from that? Did I agree so easily to this because there was already something budding between us?

I blink away the thoughts because it's not something I want to discuss before we have a long car ride home. What if he doesn't feel the same way about me? And what if our relationship is strictly just sex?

It can't be.

"We should get up and start packing to head home."

His hold on me tightens as his other arm comes to wrap fully around me in a warm embrace. "Just lay with me here for another few minutes, baby. I don't want to let you go."

I hug him back in his tight embrace and I feel his head nuzzle into my hair.

"Lavender." He inhales. "I love that smell."

I let out a soft laugh. "I'm surprised it still smells like that after all the sweating we did last night."

"Are you sure I wasn't too rough with you?"

I lift my head to look him in the eyes, my throat knots. "No, Marc. You were… perfect."

My admission makes him smile. "Are you ready to go for a little mountain run with me?"

"Are you drunk?"

He chuckles. "Absolutely not. I told you I would try to make you fall in love with it one day."

"Unfortunately for you, the only kind of torture I'm into with you is when you're hard and dirty with me. You won't catch me running. Ever."

"I can live with that." He scans my body with his eyes, bringing his bottom lip between his teeth. "Let's go home, baby."

We arrive back at my apartment mid-afternoon. The car ride here was not weird or awkward, despite the turmoil rushing through my head. He didn't stop touching me the whole drive home. If he let go of my hand, it was because he placed it on my thigh.

While it was a nice ride home, it only increased my fear of this whole thing with him. Do I want it to be official? Yes. But I've never let someone close to me before. That thought alone has me ready to run for the hills to avoid the inevitable pain of a man walking out of my life again.

I begin to unpack some of my things while Marc sits on the edge of my bed, wringing his hands together like he's nervous about something. This is it, this is the moment he walks away from me the same way everyone always does.

"I understand you have to leave," I murmur with my back turned to him.

"What?"

"You look like you're ready to tell me you're leaving. If you have to go, you have to go."

I hear the bed creak as he stands up before he's standing

directly behind me. The air in my lungs gets trapped and I can't exhale it out.

"I don't want to leave, Ave. But I want you to come home with me."

"I don't know, Marc." I shake my head, continuing to unpack my duffle bag of clothes. "This past weekend was the last thing we needed to do with Bill for you to be considered to take ownership of Prestige Horizons."

"And..."

I spin around from across the room, throwing my arms out trying to prove my point. "I know we said something in the heat of the moment. I'm just saying, you're under no obligation to keep this up with me."

"You think you're an obligation to me?"

"Wasn't that what this was, Marc?"

"That might have been what this was at first." He stomps towards me. "But you've become my undoing, Ave. I've been running for years from the walls I had built up around my heart, until you came along and broke every single one down."

My mouth parts in shock, tears threatening to spill over again as my body runs cold as shivers skate down my spine. I blink several times to try and keep them at bay. I do *not* fucking cry.

"When my heart was broken all those years ago, I immersed myself in my job. That was all that mattered to me." Marc's hand reaches up to swipe a loose strand of hair away from my eyes. "That's why this deal matters so much to me. It was all I had... until you."

I forget to breathe as my body shakes, the tears spill over the edge. He delicately swipes them with the back of his pointer finger before he pulls me into his chest.

"I don't know when it happened or how it happened, but I'm completely head over heels in love with you, Avery."

I pull back, gasping. "What?"

"I love you. I've said it more times than I can count under my breath. I've wanted to say it for a while now. But I knew you needed time. I know you think you're not wired for it and you claim you have this big black heart and are incapable of love. But I see you, baby. I see all of you. You're so far from everything you say you are."

"How? What?" I stutter my words. Unsure of what to say. "I—"

"Stop." He brings a finger to my lips to shush me. "Don't say it back. I don't need you to say it back yet. Take the time you need to feel it too. But I want you to know that I'm not going anywhere."

As if he can read every fear and worry in my head he says the words I so desperately needed to hear.

I'm not going anywhere.

No one has ever known these parts of me. Every vulnerable side that I've never let anyone see before. The girls are the only ones who know the real me. Men I've had casual encounters with, have never amounted to anything because I just never let them.

But Marc… he's not going anywhere.

"Don't you think we're a little complicated here? Complete opposites? Like we haven't *really* dated to know all of this for sure. Like—"

He stops my rambling when his hands cup each side of my neck and he leans down to kiss me. It's not a soft kiss, it's a powerful all consuming, like he can't live without my lips, type of kiss. I grip his wrists and relax into his arms, the way I always do when he kisses me, and exhale the breath I was holding in.

I open up to him, allowing his tongue to swipe past my lips. Butterflies in my stomach causing chaos as he reassures me with this kiss right here that he means everything he's admitted.

Pulling back, Marc keeps his lips hovered over mine. "I'm going to head home. But I'll say it again for you to understand… I'm not going anywhere. I'd rather do this complicated chaos with you than do easy with someone else."

My eyes flutter shut as I tip my head into his palm still on the side of my face.

"I love you, Avery."

With one last kiss, Marc is out the door.

Leaving me standing there speechless.

Eager to tell him how much I love him.

Fearful for what would come of it.

Worried I might have just screwed up the best thing that's ever happened to me by not saying it back when I had the chance.

CHAPTER THIRTY-ONE
Marc

I haven't slept well since I left Avery's apartment on Sunday. Between telling her how I really feel, and the fact I want her in my bed with me, wrapped up in my arms every single night has had me tossing and turning all hours of the night.

It doesn't help that I've been working out of the Bronx office the last three days, which means I haven't had a chance to see her at all.

It's Wednesday so I'm having drinks with Thomas at Moore's tonight. Oliver is… who knows where. And Logan is picking up overtime since he's so close to nailing his promotion to chief.

"Hey, Marc," Thomas says as he takes the seat across from me at the table. "Not busy here tonight."

"Yeah, for once." I scrub at my chin. "How's it going?"

"Busy as shit. That deal I told you about a couple weeks ago blew up in my face. The building was not worth what we were planning to invest in it. Turns out, it was littered with mold. We pulled out so fast."

"No pun intended." I laugh.

"You're sick." He shakes his head. "How was the mountains?"

"Let's just say when I left there, I was ready to purchase real estate."

"No shit?"

I take a sip of whiskey. "Seriously. Bill was right. It's the perfect place for a getaway from the busy city life. The phone service up there's horrific, but when you need some peace, that's what you need. I'm considering getting a place that's big enough for the family."

"Your family?" He gives me a knowing grin as if he can predict where this conversation is going.

"The *Ford family*, not necessarily *my* future family," I say, emphasizing the fact that it would be a place for anyone to use. "I think once I find something, we can plan a family trip up there. I know a realtor in the area who is checking out some listings with multiple bedrooms."

"That sounds awesome, Marc. Good for you."

"It should be great." The waiter comes and we order another round of drinks. "How's the wedding planning going?"

He groans, "Ugh. Don't even get me started."

"That bad?"

"It's just a lot now that we're down to the wire. I'm glad that we decided to keep it a small and intimate ceremony with just close friends. But even as a small wedding, it's still a pain in the ass making sure everyone is where they need to be. Mom doesn't come in from wherever the hell she is until the day of the rehearsal dinner."

"I've barely heard from her all summer," I admit. "I don't even know where she is."

"Who knows. But I'll warn you." He points a finger in my direction. "She's bringing a date."

"Oh shit. That's…good. Right?"

"I hope so." He shrugs.

"Everyone deserves something good to happen to them…" I trail off.

"I don't like that tone…" He challenges me. If anyone in my

family can read me better than anyone, it's Thomas. "Did Bill make his decision for the company yet?"

I shake my head. "Not yet. But I feel pretty confident after this weekend."

"Then why does your face look like that?"

"Like what?"

"Like your cat got run over by a garbage truck."

"First of all." I laugh. "You should know I'm not a cat man. Dogs over cats every day."

He takes a sip of his whiskey. "Noted."

"Second of all, I think Todd screwed it up for himself bringing his chick along for the weekend."

"How so?" He tips his head to the side in question.

"The guy had no chemistry whatsoever with Vivian. The entire weekend, she was almost repulsed by him. Like she couldn't get away from him fast enough."

"I mean, have you seen the guy?"

"Touché." I point a finger at him and smile.

"How did it go with Avery though?"

I tip my head up over the brim of my whiskey I just took a sip from as the words left his mouth. I almost choke on it, because just her name causes me to lose my breath.

"Fine," I lie.

"Spill."

My palms feel sweaty as I white knuckle the glass beneath them. But again, I know Thomas will be the only one of the guys that understands.

"I told her I love her."

"Fuck." He runs his hands down his face, and frowns.

"Yeah…"

"What happened?"

"Well, she didn't say it back." I let out a displeased scoff. "But can you fault her for it? The girl has never done this before. All she knows of love is her piece of shit father walking out on her mom when she was young."

If I could find the guy and strangle him with my bare hands, I would.

"I can't even imagine walking out on James like that and never looking back." Thomas' face wrinkles in disgust. "The thought of it actually makes me queasy."

"Tell me about it."

"Listen," he says, leaning on his elbows over the table. "No one really understands what she's been through like *she* does. I don't even think Peyton and Kali know this side of her. She puts up a very strong front. From what I hear, she's been through a lot."

"I know."

"She's the type of girl who's wild and free because she refuses to let her past define her."

"What do I do? I don't know how to ease her worry that I won't be like him, assure her I won't walk out on her the way he did."

"I don't have all the answers to that because I know that you wouldn't. You aren't like that." He shakes his head and offers me a smile. "The best thing you can do is have patience with her and continue to build that trust. It's clear that she has difficulty trusting that someone won't walk out on her."

"You're right."

He brings a hand to his ear and leans in. "Can you say that again?"

"You're an asshole." I laugh as I swat his hand down. "But you are right. I know I've to give her the time she needs. It's just so hard. After we woke up the last morning in the cabin, tangled in the sheets toge—"

"I don't need all the dirty details, bro."

I throw my hands up defensively. "Hey. For months we had to hear about your shit with Peyton. Don't start."

"Fine. Continue."

"Ever since that morning, I knew I wanted to spend every

day waking up with her in my arms." I smile at the thought of it. "That makes me sound like a pathetic sap, doesn't it?"

"You've always been a pathetic sap," he scoffs. "But that's what makes Avery so lucky. She's going to realize she loves you too and will come around."

The thing is… I'm almost positive she feels what I feel too.

Deep down I know she's going to come around.

CHAPTER THIRTY-TWO

Avery

"We're coming down to the final stretch, Peyton," Emiline says with a mouthful of spaghetti.

Peyton and Emiline came over to the apartment for a spaghetti dinner and movie night. It's a very much needed girls' night after the week I had. I spent the entire week on edge and I've been looking forward to getting together with the girls to try and talk through some shit in my head.

"Em, if you talk with food in your mouth one more time, I'm going to lose it."

"Relax, Ave," Kali cuts in. "What the hell has got you on edge? Is Aunt Flo early this month?"

"For your information, yes," I say very matter of factly.

Kali puts her hands around her mouth to form a megaphone. "Watch out, New York. Avery Woods is on her shit."

"Get the hell out of here." I swat at her hands near her mouth. "Anyway, Peyton… How's the final stretch of wedding planning going?"

"It's going," she finally gets out from laughing so hard. "I honestly think we're good to go—providing you all have your dresses."

Emiline looks at me and over exaggerates chewing her

spaghetti with her mouth closed before she swallows. "I got mine."

"I got mine," Kali says.

"Mine came in today."

"Perfect." Peyton claps her hands. "Then we're all good to go."

"I must say…" Kali starts "You letting us all pick our own style in the same colors was a queen move right there."

"I agree. You know I went with the deep cut V-neck that shows the ladies." Emiline shimmies in her seat. "Plus, it will piss my brothers off."

"It's *really* going to piss them off," Peyton adds.

"They need to realize I've grown up. I'm not their baby sister anymore. I'm twenty-two and just as freaky as them."

"We know."

"Your brothers are dirty, Em," I add after Peyton.

She scoffs. "You seem to forget I'm always in the group chat when you start going on and on about all of the sex you have."

"Don't act like you're not getting any from someone, Em." She runs her hands through her hair and I see her cheeks heat up red at my statement. "You are, aren't you?"

"No!" she exclaims. "I'm not the type of girl who will do it with just anyone."

"So, there's someone you're crushing on?"

She gives me a side eye. "Crushes are for children, Ave. But if you must know, there's someone I most *definitely* have had my eyes on for a while now."

Peyton, Kali and I all exchange looks before we look back at her and say in unison, "Logan."

"GUYS!" she groans. "Don't bring him up."

"It's him, isn't it?" I stand up from my chair in my rage of excitement. "I fucking *knew* something was going on with you two."

"No. Nothing is going on." She stops me dead in my tracks. "Or at least I don't know what the hell is going on. He flirts with me so hardcore while I'm at work. Because you know… working in the emergency department and everything, cops bring people in. It seems like he's always the one bringing them in. And they always happen to be *my* patients. But he's a typical male, so he flirts with all the nurses. Plus, I don't graduate until the end of June, so I'm not even an actual nurse for him to flirt with."

"I just heard a lot of blah blah blah coming out of you." Kali giggles. "But what I think you meant to say was that you two are flirting hardcore."

"Wrong."

I place a hand on her shoulder. "I've seen the way you two are around each other. Whenever I catch him staring at you, he's looking at you like you hung the moon."

"Oh yeah?" She throws her hands on her hips. "What about you? Miss Avoid-love-at-all-costs."

"Pff. I don't know what you're talking about."

Her voice softens. "I talked to my brother yesterday."

"Fuck." I turn on my heels and walk back to the barstool on the opposite side of the kitchen island. "What did he have to say?"

"He said he told you he loves you, Ave."

The room falls silent. I look at Kali and her mouth is open in shock, then my gaze moves to Peyton whose eyes look like a deer in headlights that's about to get hit by a fast moving car on the freeway.

"He did." My head falls with a nod, and I wipe the sweat forming on my palms on my shorts.

"Avery." Peyton's voice is soft, like she's afraid I'll break if she says the wrong thing. "Talk to us."

"I don't know what to say," I shout louder than I want to. "I fucking love him too. Okay?" Tears threaten to spill over. "And I don't know how to deal with these feelings. It scares the shit out of me and I don't want to be scared. I don't want to worry about him leaving me the same way the last man I ever loved did."

I lose it completely, I break down bringing my hands to my

eyes and my shoulders shake with sobs. I can't say the girls have ever seen me breakdown like this before about anything. Tears pour out of me, and I can't wipe them fast enough.

"I'm fucking scared, you guys," I admit.

"Dammit," Peyton says before I feel her wrap her arms around me. "Shhh. We got you, Ave."

"I'm sorry, I don't mean to cry like this."

"You don't ever have to be sorry with us," Peyton says as she brushes the hair out of my face, tilting my head up to look at her. "It's good that you're scared."

"Why?"

"Being scared means that you have something really great to lose, that you love him so much that you don't ever *want* to lose him."

"I don't want to lose him, Pey. He told me he loved me, and I didn't say it back. What if I already lost him because of it?"

"You didn't," Emiline cuts in. "I promise you that you didn't."

"What the hell is wrong with me?" I sob.

"Nothing is wrong with you," Peyton says, encouraging me. "Your father fucked you up so much by walking out on you that when someone finally tries to give you what you deserve, you have no clue how to respond to that."

"But you shouldn't be scared." Kali comes up behind me, placing her hands on my shoulders. "You shouldn't be scared to love Marc. He's nothing like your father."

Peyton leans down until she's eye level with me. "You deserve to be happy, babe."

"You have no idea how happy Marc has made me, Pey." I swipe another fallen tear from my eye. "He's taken over my life in a way no one ever has."

"Listen... taking chances is a really scary thing. But what's even worse is missing out on the greatest love of your life because you were afraid to take that leap."

"What do you think I should do? What do I say?" I'm

rambling now. "He confessed how he felt about me Sunday and I've barely talked to him since then."

"What do *you* think you need to do?" Peyton asks. "Not what you need to do to please him, but what do you need to do for *you* so that you're able to overcome this?"

I sit there, slightly shocked at the question because it's not something I've thought about. The truth is, this past week apart from him, while he worked out of the Bronx office, gave me a very small glimpse of what it feels like to truly be missing him. However, we work together so there's still that contact with each other.

"I just don't know if I'm able to tell him what I'm feeling yet. I think I need some time away from him to just figure my own shit out."

"If that's what you think, then that's what you should do."

His words play on repeat in my head that he told me in this same apartment… *I'm not going anywhere.* I hope to God that he means that.

I want to give all of myself to him, but I'm still afraid. *My* past is not something he should have to carry on *his* shoulders.

I want to give Marc the love he deserves.

But that might mean stepping away for a little bit to sort out these feelings.

CHAPTER THIRTY-THREE

Marc

I've never had the urge to call in sick from work, until this particular Monday morning.

The sick feeling in my gut has me more anxious than I've ever been before. I even decided to skip the caffeine this morning despite desperately needing it because I knew it would just make my anxiety worse.

I still haven't spoken to Avery other than a few text messages and work emails here and there while I worked out of the Bronx office. Trust me, I wasn't there because I wanted to be, but all of my meetings for the week happened to be scheduled in that office.

Avery never leaves my fucking head. She's the first thought I have when my eyes open and the last thing on my mind when I lay there and stare at the ceiling. I wonder what she's doing, what she's thinking, who she's with. But more importantly, if she's okay.

Let's combine this with the fact I'm going to see Avery walk into the office any moment now and that I have a meeting with Bill at some point this morning because he's *finally* made a decision. Although, he hasn't told me what time he's coming, and that doesn't help my nerves or the situation.

Cue overwhelming nausea.

An hour and over a dozen emails later, Avery is still not in the office. But I hear the door creek open and hope blooms in my chest that it's her, until I look up over my computer monitor and see Bill standing there.

I stand from my seat quickly. "Bill. Everything alright?"

"Of course. Sit down."

He moves to sit at the chair across from my desk, and I take a seat in mine, wiping my palms on my pants as I scoot closer to the desk. I briefly glance over to where Avery's desk is located, in an attempt to find some peace in the storm brewing in my office. She shouldn't be here anyway so Bill doesn't find out, but I can't help but crave her comfort at this moment.

Bill must catch on. "Avery out today?"

"What? No. That's not… I mean."

I feel the color drain from my face, my head whipping between her office and Bill. I'm trying to figure out how he caught onto the fact it was her all along.

"Avery has been your assistant for a while." It comes out as a statement, not a question.

"I may be old, but I'm not stupid." He huffs out a laugh. "All new employee reports still come to my house despite me not having an actual office."

"I-I—"

"It's alright. Don't get freaked out over it. That's not why I'm here."

My stomach falling to the floor below me.

"I've already seen Todd this morning."

I think I'm going to throw up.

"Prestige Horizons is yours, Marc."

My mouth falls open, my elbows fall to the desk, and I collapse against it. Everything I've worked so hard for is finally happening.

"But before I continue, I need you to know something." He leans in until his elbows are also resting on my desk, putting him face to face with me. "I knew from the start that your situation with Avery was a set up. I know that you two aren't engaged the same way that I also know that Todd isn't engaged."

My gaze drops to my hands on my desk. I have no words to say back to him as I've been caught in an entire summer of lies.

"Cathy knew it was fake the moment you two showed up to the house for dinner. Something about the way she hugged Avery. She said it seemed… off. I didn't think anything of it, of course. But the more she went on, the more I also couldn't help but notice."

"I-I'm sorry, sir." I shake my head. "I didn't me—"

He raises his hand to stop me. "None of that. I'm telling you this because from the start of everything until the weekend at the cabin, I noticed what evolved between you two. It might have started out fake, but I don't believe it's fake anymore. Is it?"

"No, sir."

"That's what I thought."

"Avery wasn't just my assistant, though. She's the best friend of my future sister-in-law. But I'm telling you, when I hired her, I hadn't met her yet and didn't know who she was."

"I believe you, Marc. You don't have to explain yourself. The company is yours."

I can't help but sit there stunned. "I don't know what to say."

"I haven't been completely honest with you, myself." His eyes fall to his hands as he interlocks them on the desk. "Todd was never going to get this company."

"Huh?"

"It was always going to you."

I shake my head. "I don't understand."

"You're such a miserable shit in the office." He laughs, and I can't help but join him when he does. "I know it's because you've been alone for so long. Don't forget that I was the one who hired you and you told me your story about your graduation night. I remember because you told me *that* was the reason you were pouring yourself into work. An outlet. An escape from everything outside of these walls."

"I got over that years ago."

"Riiiight," he drawls. "But tell me, Marc. Why does your face look like that?"

"Why does everyone keep saying something's wrong with my face these days?"

"You've got this sad look like your cat died."

I can't help the rumble of laughter that comes pouring out of me, forcing Bill to join me.

"You're not the first person to say that you know? But I'll tell you what I told them. I'm a dog guy."

"Noted." He nods with a laugh. "I have one more thing to tell you."

"Your tone of voice tells me I won't like this."

He shrugs. "You might not. But I need you to fly to Austin this weekend for a week of training."

"I—"

"Hear me out," he cuts me off. "It's standard for executives to have to complete. Consider it a CEO training of sorts. It's a few classes during the week on management training that's more extensive to what you're doing now, finances, employee management and the mundane things that downright suck."

I've wanted this opportunity for so long, becoming CEO in the real estate business—becoming the CEO of *this* real estate business, the one that jump-started my entire career. I'm confident in my abilities to be able to do this, which is why I brought Avery into this mess with me in the first place. I knew I could do it.

But I'm also entirely invested in the man sitting in front of me at this point. If Bill says jump, I'm going to say, 'how high?' So despite my reluctance to go to Austin, I'm going.

I swallow past the dryness in my throat. "I understand."

"Excellent. I'm so proud of you, son."

The *son* out of his mouth has my chest tightening. I have

looked up to this man for as long as I've worked here, desired to be just like him and as successful as he's been.

"That means a lot."

He stands with a nod before he starts to walk towards the door. "I'll touch base with you tomorrow morning with your flight schedule and hotel accommodations. Is Avery going to travel with you?"

"I'm not sure. I'll ask her."

I heard the creak of my office door open, and Avery peaks her head over the side of the door.

"Oh my god." Her eyes go wide. "I'm so sorry. I'll come back."

"No, Avery. Come on in." Bill waves her in. "Speak of the devil."

Her eyes bounce between Bill and me, worry etched on her face as if she's just blown the cover of the whole thing by showing up to work when he wasn't supposed to know.

"It's all good, Avery. He knows everything."

Her mouth parts and she stops dead in her tracks. The color drains from her face like she's just seen a ghost and her eyes are fixed on me. After a few seconds that feel like minutes, she hesitantly continues her walk until she's sitting on the opposite chair of Bill in front of my desk.

"I'm going to leave you to it," Bill announces. "We'll touch base tomorrow."

"Thank you, sir."

Avery watches as he walks out the door over her shoulder, and when the door clicks shut, her face is still twisted towards the door.

"Avery," I say, my voice is hoarse with emotion.

She turns to me and I see her glassy eyes looking back at me. My heart cracks under my rib cage at the thoughts that must be going through her head right now.

She shakes her head, snapping herself out of her daze,

blinking rapidly to hold back anything from spilling over. "How did it go?"

I pause a beat as I look over her beautiful facial features. She's so fucking perfect in every way. Her long blonde hair has a natural wave to it today. As if she had no interest in doing something with it and is letting it hang free.

"He gave me the company."

"That's amazing, Marc. Congratulations," she says without an ounce of excited energy in her body.

"Avery. Talk to me please."

She pauses for a beat. "What does this mean now? For us?"

I launch off the chair to round the desk, bringing myself face to face with her. I don't waste another minute before I grip the sides of her face, angling her head to meet my eyes.

"It means not a damn thing. I've made it pretty clear that I want you. Outside of this entire thing we've had to do this summer. I want you as a permanent place in my life."

A tear trickles down her cheek. I brush my thumb to swipe away and her eyes fall closed.

"Can I tell you something?"

"Always, baby."

"I'm scared," she admits, stepping out of my hold. I allow her a moment to take a deep breath and continue. "I don't know how to navigate this, us, and I don't know how to handle these… feelings."

I wrap my arms around her, bringing her head to my chest. I press a light kiss to her cheek and whisper, "I know."

"I'm sorry, Marc. I never meant lead you on and have you fall for a broken girl like me."

I pull back, brushing a strand of loose hair around her ear. "There is *nothing* broken about you. I don't ever want to hear you say that about yourself again."

"But I am. My dad fucked me up so much when he walked out on my mom and me. I vowed I'd never allow a man the power to walk out on me again. We allowed ourselves to get too deep. It scares the shit out of me, Marc."

"Let me go through this with you. Let me carry some of that fear. Let me show you that you never have to worry about me doing that to you." I press a kiss to her forehead again. "I'm all in with you."

She doesn't reply but offers me a hesitant smile. I can see my words swirling around in her head as if she has to digest them and figure out what she wants to say back.

"Bill is sending me away this weekend for a week." I decide to add in my attempt to break down any thoughts she has. "I have to go to Austin for CEO training. Would you want to come with me?"

Her smile slowly falls into a frown, and my chest tightens with worry that this is it. This is the end. She can't do this with me. My stomach drops so fast it causes me to lose my breath.

"I can't," she finally says.

I nod in response, my throat constricts, taking away my ability to *beg her* to come with me.

She laughs. "Fix your face, boss man."

"Excuse me?" The sound of her laughter is so contagious that it causes me to laugh with her.

"This works out well. You going away for a week allows me to stew in my thoughts. Get my shit together with some space between us. Maybe even start talking to a professional about getting over this deep-rooted fear I have inside of me."

"Yeah?"

"I don't feel like I deserve you, you know. And what it boils down to is that I want to. I want to be worthy of whatever you have to give me. And you shouldn't have to put up with someone who is living a life scared of the possibility of you walking out. You shouldn't have to wake up every single day *trying* to prove it to me either."

"Avery—"

"Trust me on this. Please," she begs, hands gripping my biceps in an attempt to make me understand.

The truth of the matter is, I do understand. I don't want to live like that either. I don't want to live in fear that if I do one thing wrong, it's going to break her. I know beneath whatever is going on in her head, is a girl who's stronger than her fragile exterior shows.

"Ok."

The only word I have in response.

I just have to get through this one week without her and hold onto hope that when I return, we can make this work.

CHAPTER THIRTY-FOUR

Marc

"Why do you look like your cat died?" Oliver says.

"What the hell is up with everyone saying that?" I snap. "I. Am. A. Dog. Guy. I can't stand cats. They shit in gross litter and stink."

"Well… okay then," Logan says behind his glass of whiskey. "In an attempt to defend the feline species here, they are also wildly independent creatures."

Oliver almost spits out his drink at his response.

"You two are assholes."

"But really, what's wrong with you today?"

I direct my gaze to Logan. "I got the company."

Both of them remain silent, their eyes bouncing from each other and back to me. "Yay?" Oliver unenthusiastically cheers.

"He's sending me away for a week to Austin. It's the last thing I want to do with all the shit going down with Avery."

"You still haven't filled us in on that," Logan says.

Oliver throws his arms out in the air to signify the place we're in. "What better place than our Wednesday night therapy sessions at Moores."

That causes me to grin. "Yeah, these do feel like unofficial therapy sessions lately, huh?"

"You all are so damn twisted up with women," Oliver starts. "I don't get it, honestly. Why would anyone want to deal with that? I'm team single for life." He pounds his chest like a caveman with his fist.

"Didn't you fall in love on your trip home from Montana?" I quip.

"That's neither here nor there." Oliver shakes his head. "I got over that quick."

"Right," Logan scoffs.

"We're talking about Marc here. Now spill."

I blow out a sigh. "So, yeah… I got the company. I have to go to Austin, and I asked Avery if she wanted to come with me. But she asked for some space. She needs time to process her shit."

"Either she loves you or she doesn't." Oliver shrugs. "Save yourself the heartbreak. Hashtag team single."

Logan slaps the back of his hand on his upper arm. "Shut up, Ollie."

"You laugh, asshole. But someday, a girl is going to walk into your life and bring you to your knees."

"I wouldn't mind dropping to my knees for her. It would bring me *great* pleasure." He wiggles his eyebrows.

"Cheers to that." Logan raises a glass.

"Where the hell is Thomas when I need him?"

Logan and Oliver both shift in their seats, straightening their shoulders as if they are channeling their inner Thomas.

"I can't stand you two."

"Okay, let's be serious then," Logan starts. "Avery needs space?"

"She's scared. I get that. Really, I do. It just tears me apart. What if space makes her decide that she doesn't want this? That she doesn't want a relationship? You two are going to laugh, but if I'm being honest… I can't live without her. I can't sleep without her. I can't function without her."

"Damn."

"You can say that again." I bring my gaze to Logan.

"Damn," he repeats.

"Alright, here's my advice." Oliver claps his hands. "You don't know what you don't know."

"Solid advice, Ollie." Logan laughs.

"Hear me out. You're sitting here, tearing yourself apart for what? Something you can't control? This is one of those situations where you just have to sit back and see what happens. For all you know, when you come back from Austin, Avery is going to be ready to give you one hundred percent. You're gonna end up looking back at this and being annoyed at how worried you were for nothing."

"You're right."

"Tell me something I don't know. But you have to be optimistic. If you want any sort of chance with her, you have to agree to her wishes. Right now, she wants some space. She didn't tell you it was over. She didn't tell you to lose her number. She didn't tell you to go fuck yourself. There's still hope there. She believes it, and now you need to believe it too."

I can't help but smile at Oliver. "For someone who's hellbent on being single for life, you sure do have some pretty sound advice."

"Just means I'm spending way too much time with you saps."

We all laugh and order another round of whiskey.

"Aside from all of this shit, I forgot to tell you guys the good news."

"Let's hear it."

"I bought a cabin in the mountains."

"No shit?" Oliver's eyes widen. "What made you do that?"

"I fell in love when I was up there. Not just with Avery, but with the serenity of the place. The views. The solitude. All of it. It's the perfect place to escape the city for a weekend or longer. I wanted a second place to call home that we can all use."

"I would *love* to head up there one weekend. It's the only mountain in the United States I haven't been to or blogged about yet. From the sounds of it, it would be a perfect spot to catch some views with my camera."

"Anytime you want."

"Appreciate that." Oliver nods.

"Maybe Emiline and I can head up one weekend." Logan grins.

"I swear on all things holy… I am going to murder you."

He chuckles. "I love getting you riled up."

I shoot him a death glare. But despite these two and their insane antics, I feel like I can breathe a little easier for the first time since Monday.

CHAPTER THIRTY-FIVE

Avery

"Do all your dresses fit?" Peyton asks us.

"Yes," we say in unison. Each of us sounding a little more irritated than the last time she asked us yesterday.

Peyton throws her hands up in defense. "I'm just checking!"

"Take a deep breath, girl," Emiline says. "Everything is going to be perfect. And if something isn't in place, you still have two more weeks to get it together."

"And that's what we're here for. To help you," Kali adds.

"You're right. Ugh, I just want this to be the best day."

"It's going to be," I reassure her. "You're marrying your best friend in the whole world. No matter what the centerpieces look like, whether Emiline's tits are hanging out, or the food sucks, you're still marrying the love of your life."

"My tits will not be out!" Emiline defends herself. "These girls will be tucked away."

We had to skip out on our taco Tuesday night dinner plans last night because Peyton had a last minute meeting down at the shore with the venue for the wedding. She's getting married at a yacht club down there and she's beyond excited about the location being an all-inclusive.

So we decided to get together at her place this morning to go over a couple last minute decoration plans. It all worked out perfectly because my mom was also off last night, which allowed me to have a four hour long phone call with her about the past.

The amount of closure I received in those four hours was worth its weight in gold, almost as refreshing as unpacking my life in my new therapy sessions I started on Monday.

My mom told me all about her relationship with dad and how it was never the best one, how she was actually happy he finally decided to leave. She felt terrible that my only memory all these years consisted of him leaving us for some floozy.

Dad left mom because there was no love in the relationship.

How can someone stick around if there is no love there? They can't.

That's the thought that kept me up all night. He didn't love her. But Marc loves me. He's confessed it. I can *feel* it in my bones that he does.

The final consensus was that he's nothing like my father.

"Take my mind off of all of this," Peyton cuts through my thoughts. "Have you talked to Marc?"

"Cut right to the chase, why don't you."

"You haven't said a word since he left for Austin." Peyton sighs sympathetically. "That was four days ago. It's eating me up inside not knowing how you're handling everything."

"Honestly? I'm handling it just fine. I asked for this. I asked for the space. My plan was to get my head on straight while he was gone and hopefully I can turn my life around from now until then. Unrealistic." I roll my eyes. "I know this. But your girl can hope."

"It's not unrealistic. You were scared and that's okay."

"I still am. He had to go and break the biggest rule."

"Rule?" Kali tips her head to the side in question.

"When I agreed to do this for him, I had three simple rules—no kissing, no seeing other people and don't fall in love with me."

"Hey, at least you both committed to the second rule." Emiline laughs.

"We got something right." I joke. "It's that last one. I told him not to. And he fucking did and it's thrown a plot twist in this whole story."

"But you love him too, Ave."

She's right. I fell head over heels.

The worst part of it all, is that Marc left for Austin without knowing how I feel.

The realization hits me like a dump truck. I can physically feel the color drain from my face and my heart rate spike. *Oh my god.* I'm so goddamn selfish to not think about how he's been handling all of this.

"Em," I gasp.

"Oh gosh, what?" Her eyes widen at the tone of my voice. Her features are laced with concern. "Are you okay? I'm not a nurse yet!"

I shake my head. "Nothing like that. Have you talked to Marc in the last couple days?"

"Yeah, why?"

I swallow past the lump in my throat. "Is he…" *fuck.* "Is he okay?"

"I was hoping you wouldn't ask me." Emiline sighs.

"Shit," Peyton murmurs to herself.

"From the sounds of it, he has his moments."

"What does that mean?"

"One minute he's hopeful that things will be okay when he returns, and the next he's torn apart at needing space from you. When I video called him last night, the bags under his eyes told me that he hasn't slept since he's gotten there."

My heart cracks behind my ribs, and I can feel tears form behind my eyes.

"Hey, ladies." Thomas saunters into the kitchen. "How's the decor coming along?"

The girls remain silent, their eyes locked on me as if waiting for what my response is to Emiline's admission.

I hear him whisper in Peyton's ear, "Did I walk in at a bad time?"

Peyton nods her head.

"Thomas." My voice is hoarse with emotion. "I need your help."

CHAPTER THIRTY-SIX

Marc

THOMAS

What are you doing?

I'm about to order room service for dinner. What's up?

THOMAS

I booked you a celebratory dinner at the steakhouse down the road from where you're staying.

Reservation is for 6:30 pm.

I really don't feel like going out.

THOMAS

Get your head out of your ass. You need to eat, and the meal is already paid for.

I groan from the bed, annoyed as shit to have to leave my hotel room to go get food. But I know the intentions of my brother. He's not dumb. This is a way to get me out of this uncomfortable bed and stop sulking until I get home.

Two more days until I'm home.

Two more days until I can either sleep again, or sulk in misery.

I count down in my head. Nervous energy swirls in my stomach.

Never in my life have I loved someone the way I love Avery Woods. She consumes me. Our chemistry is combustible. She lights a fire inside of me that I never want out. If things don't work out the way that I'm hoping they do when I get home, I truly believe deep inside me, that I will never love anyone the way I do her.

I decide to jump in the shower to wash off a day of meetings before going to this fancy steakhouse that Thomas set me up with. It's hot as shit down here, and I swear there was no air conditioning in the conference rooms. My brain is shot from all the information I had to try to retain too. I without a doubt feel more confident in becoming CEO after these training sessions though.

CEO. What a wild thing to be called now.

I own an entire real estate company.

The fucking dream come true.

The thought makes me smile as I step out of the shower. I throw on a pair of dress slacks and a white button down shirt, leaving the top button undone for a more relaxed look.

Just as I'm about to grab my phone to call a taxi to meet me downstairs, there's a knock on my door.

I don't bother checking the peep hole when I swing the door open.

I'm rooted in place, my jaw drops to the floor, and my body tenses at the sight of her standing here. In Austin. Outside of my hotel room door.

"Avery," I finally breathe out as my entire body relaxes.

"Are you ready for our date, boss man?" she coos.

"What…" I pause. My gaze sweeping her body that's covered in nothing but a little black dress to make sure she's real. Making sure this isn't just the heat outside making me hallucinate. "What are you doing here?"

She steps into me. My grip is still tight on the door, trying to keep myself grounded in reality. I angle my head down to maintain eye contact with her. "I couldn't wait until you got home."

"Tell me this means what I think it means."

"It means, we have a date to get to." She adjusts the strap on her purse over her shoulder. "Let's go. The car is waiting for us."

I blink a few times, shaking myself from the trance I've just been put in.

I don't respond because I'm still in shock. But I grab my wallet and follow her out the door.

"Can you tell me now why you're here?" I finally ask once the waiter has dropped off our drinks. "And how the hell did you get here?"

She giggles in her seat. "Thomas helped me. He threw me on the private jet last minute after I asked for a little help."

I nod in response, bringing my gaze to my glass of whiskey, swirling the ice around the amber liquid a few times. Hoping to god she continues where she's going with this.

"I couldn't wait."

My eyes snap up, meeting her strikingly beautiful blue ones.

"I also haven't been completely honest with you."

My grip on my glass tightens. "With?"

"Can you tell me again what you told me the day we got home from the mountains in my apartment?"

"I said a lot of things."

Her smile widens. "But you also said one very, *very* important thing."

"I love you?" I say with a question in my tone.

Avery's eyes light up at the same time a wide grin spreads across her face. I don't miss the way her cheeks heat up when hearing me say those three little words I first said when we got home from our trip. She sits up straighter in her seat, resting both elbows on the table before she takes my hands in hers and says, "I love you too, Marc Ford."

I exhale a breath I didn't know I was even holding. My chest tightens at hearing the three little words I have craved to hear from her lips. I rise from my chair, rounding the table to crouch down at her knees, my palms resting on her bare legs.

"You mean that?"

"I do." She nods aggressively. "More than I thought I possibly could. I never dreamed of this or wanted this for myself. But you've flipped my world upside down. You made me believe in something I never thought I could have. I want this with you. I want a life with you."

"Fuck, Avery." I grip her hands in mine, pressing kisses to the backside of her hand. "You have no idea how much I've wanted to hear you say that."

"I'm sorry it took me so long to realize it."

"That doesn't matter. You're here now."

With another kiss to her hand, I feel metal connect with my lips. My eyes snap to her hand to realize she's still wearing the engagement ring I gave her, nestled on her left ring finger.

"You didn't take it off." It's a statement, not a question.

"I didn't take it off."

My lips curve up, practically taking over my whole face as tears spring in my eyes at her admission.

"I couldn't take it off if I tried, Marc. I've fought so damn hard to not give into feelings I've had for you. They've been there for longer than I care to admit. You had me trapped in your orbit ever since that first date. I knew then and there that I would never be the same again."

I twirl the ring between my fingers on her hand, kissing it one last time. "Do you want to leave it on for good?"

"What are you asking me, boss man?" I can't help the smile that takes over my face.

"I know I'm rushing it. I know it's only been this summer.

But Avery… I'm so in love with you. I know that you're it for me. For the rest of my life."

She blinks back the tears. "I love you, too."

"And I think my last name would sound really good with your first."

She laughs. "It does have a nice ring to it, doesn't it? Avery Ford."

"And it would feel really weird going to our cabin without you there."

She tilts her head to the side in confusion. Probably assuming I'm just talking about going to Cathy and Bill's place.

"Do you think Cathy and Bill will still invite us up there since they know now we were faking it? God, I loved being in the mountains."

"They might invite us over for dinner if they're up there at the same time as us."

She leans back in the chair slightly, squinting her eyes at me. "Did you drink before I showed up at your hotel room?"

"I bought a cabin." I grin.

Her mouth parts, but sound doesn't come out.

"It feels like our special place. It feels like the right place for when we want to get away from the city. So I bought it."

"Is this that billionaire thing where you buy buildings and shit?" She teases.

"You can say that." I smirk. "But I didn't buy it as a grand gesture for you… I bought it for us."

"How did you know this was going to work out?"

"Remember those random questions you asked me on that first date we went on?" I ask her.

"Yes," she groans. "Don't remind me. I was just trying to make things less weird."

"Can you ask me the questions again?"

She pinches her eyebrows together, sitting up taller in her chair "Okay, I'll play. "What is one thing you've never seen before and one place you've never been?"

"I've never seen anyone or anything more beautiful than you, and as far as a place I've never been... I've never been in love with someone the way I'm with you."

Her cheeks turn a rosy, pink color at the same time a smile engulfs her face. "You're such a goofball. You know that's not a place right?"

"You're home for me, Ave. You have been ever since that first date."

"You're home for me too, babe." She cups my face, bringing it to meet hers. "Now ask me what you wanted to ask me before."

"Be my fiancé for real. Marry me, Avery."

"Yes." She doesn't hesitate with her response. "Yes, I will marry you for real."

She stands up, wrapping her arms around me. The restaurant around us erupts in cheers and clapping. I pull back and I see happy tears streaming down her face.

"Are you ready to kiss me again, Marc?"

"I might die if I don't."

EPILOGUE

Avery

End of December

"Baby, it's time to get up." Marc shakes my body from my deep, peaceful sleep.

My eyes are barely open, but I groan in frustration because it still seems dark out. "How many times do I have to tell you… I don't want to go for a run at five in the morning with you."

A small laugh registers, and I finally open my eyes.

"First of all, it's not five in the morning. It's almost ten."

My body sits upright, and I scan the room, confused. Whenever I sleep in this late, I feel completely disoriented. Like my body and brain haven't connected with each other to the point I don't know how to function.

Marc throws his head back on the pillow and has now entered a full-on laughing attack. "I can see someone thinks it's funny that I have no idea what's happening right now."

"You're cute when you look all lost."

He scoops his arms around my midsection and pulls me down to the pillow with him. I nuzzle my face into his neck and the scent of fresh soap wakes me up fully. My eyes widen as I pull back and meet his eyes.

"You showered already? How long have you been up?"

"I've been up since six. I've lived an entire day while you laid here catching flies with your mouth wide open."

I playfully swat at his arm. "I do not catch flies."

"You do too." He presses a kiss to my lips before he climbs out of bed. "But you really have to get up now. You need to shower, get dressed and we have to head out. Chop-chop."

"I can see you're carrying over your bossiness from last night to this morning, huh?" I smirk.

"You love my bossiness." He winks.

"Debatable."

"You weren't complaining last night when I had you screaming my name for the whole city to hear while you took my cock like the good girl you are."

I feel heat creep into my cheeks, and I bite down on my lip.

He's not wrong. I fucking love it.

"Where're Joey and Chandler?" I ask.

"I dropped them off with Emiline."

Two months ago, I surprised Marc with his dream dog. A French bulldog. He's made it very clear that he loves dogs. After going back and forth on the name, we decided to keep the name he had. Joey honestly just fit him and his little wrinkled up, confused looking face.

Then a few months ago, a cat was rummaging around Peyton's backyard. One night we were sitting around her fire pit and the cat came right up to Marc. I remember so vividly how our eyes widened at the man who hates cats, attracting a fluffy white and gray feline.

Thomas made a comment about how we should bring it home with us. Marc was hellbent on never owning a cat. But that night, the furball wouldn't stay away from him.

Needless to say, we now own a cat. Not just any cat… a grumpy cat that has a permanent scowl on his face.

Once we introduced him to Joey, they became inseparable, which prompted the name Chandler after my favorite TV show.

"I thought Oliver was our permanent pet sitter?" I laugh.

"He's at the cabin. There's supposed to be a winter storm at the end of next week. He volunteered to head up there for us to make sure everything is winterized."

"He could have taken them with him."

"I said the same thing." Marc laughs. "But Em is happy to play with them for a week."

The past few months we have settled into a normal that I didn't think would ever exist for me. After Thomas and Peyton's wedding, I officially moved into Marc's penthouse. Our relationship has been unconventional from the start. How we went from barely being able to tolerate each other, to fake engaged, to real engaged, to living together. We're so ass backwards but neither of us have been happier than we are now.

Every wall that we had put up from our pasts has crumbled. Each of us vowing to protect our hearts at all costs. Never in my life have I trusted someone with all of me, the way I trust him. When I came back from taking some time to work on myself, I saw first-hand the damage it caused him. If I had known it would be that bad… I would've tried harder to stay.

But in the end, it was what was best for us.

I truly believe deep in my soul, that if I had stayed, we would not be as good as we are today. That says a lot, considering it's only been a few months. Everything that we've been through over the summer has just made us stronger as a couple.

"Why do I have to get ready so fast? It's Sunday. Isn't this a day to relax?"

"Normally, yes." His grin widens. "Except we have somewhere to be today."

This equally excites me and annoys me because I like to have a plan for things.

Realization washes over me as I quickly pick up my phone to see what day it is. December 29th. Which means that tomorrow is Marc's birthday.

What is he up to?

I also just finished my first real estate course. It was overwhelming to say the least, but my organized heart loved checking off boxes for assignments due. It's been nice having a break before the next course starts in the new year.

"Are you going to be more specific?"

"Just get ready, baby," Marc shouts as he leaves the room.

I throw the blankets off me and pad down the hall after him. Not even realizing that I'm still not wearing a single piece of clothing from the night before, and Marc is dressed in his Sunday best. Well… for him, it's his best. Dark washed jeans, a form fitting polo and his hair tousled to perfection. Completely ready for whatever he has planned.

"I need to know what you want me to wear and what I'm getting ready for."

Marc spins around, and his eyes burn a hole through my skin as they trail me up and down. "Fuck. You're making it hard to want to leave right now."

I widen my stance, placing my hands on my hips and giving him the best smirk I got, exposing every part of my bare body for him to see. "Yeah? What are you going to do about it?"

He groans as his head falls back, bringing his bottom lip between his teeth.

"You kill me, Ave. You damn near kill me."

"I'm waiting."

"You're going to have to wait until we get to where we're going," he says through gritted teeth. "Get in the shower. We have a plane to catch."

My eyes widen in shock and I gasp. "A plane?"

He surges towards me, removing any distance that was between us. Cupping my face in his hands before he brings his lips to hover across mine. "Surprise," he coos, before he places a delicate kiss on my lips. "I can't tell you where we're going. But I need you to get dressed before I bend you over the kitchen counter which would make us very late, baby."

"I mean… we can be quick? Don't you want some of your birthday presents early?"

"You should know by now that I love…" His fingertips trail from my neck, down my arms until they cup my bare breasts. "Taking my sweet time with this perfect body." He kisses me one last time before he reaches behind me, spinning me around and giving my ass a smack. "Now get in the shower."

"You're a tease."

"Says the girl who strode out of the room buck-ass naked, tempting me with a birthday gift when we have places to be," he shouts as he retreats to the kitchen.

My core throbs as the loss of contact from him, craving a release from the man who sets my world on fire. But I do as he said and walk my little ass into the room to get ready to get on a plane.

I've never been surprised with anything before, so my thoughts run wild as the water cascades down my body. Where in the world is this man taking me that involves an airplane? The longest flight I've taken is from New York to Vermont, which isn't very long.

An hour later, I'm showered, shaved and my blow-dried hair falls freely down my back. I'm dressed for comfort because traveling is the most uncomfortable thing. I opt for a pair of black yoga pants and a loose-fitting sweater. It's light to prepare for whatever weather we're heading into.

"I'm ready, boss man," I announce as I enter the kitchen, noticing luggage is already packed for me and ready to go. Large suitcases too, which triggers a response in my brain that we must be going somewhere for at least a week. Minimum. "Are you going to tell me where we're going yet?"

"Nope." He grins and is out the door with suitcases in each hand.

Marc

Keeping a surprise from Avery has been the hardest thing I've ever done. I knew I would be able to keep it a secret until we landed at our destination because my driver brought us right to the tarmac to board the private jet. I didn't want to have to deal with her knowing during the international check-in process.

Perks of having money is that I can do it all before we even take off.

We're about six hours into our flight and she still has no idea where the hell I'm taking her. She's so damn cute trying to figure out where in the United States we're going. Her best guess is California.

I've had this trip to Paris planned since before Bill named me CEO. She had mentioned it on the very first date that it was her dream. I knew I'd take her one day. I also knew from that first date that I'd do everything I can to make all of her dreams come true. I'd give her the world if she asked for it.

"We should be landing in about an hour."

"Great. I'm going to take a little nap."

"You slept in and you still need a nap?"

"I've been reading this book the entire time. My eyes are

tired." She laughs. "Plus this whole private jet thing you got going on is making flying very comfortable."

"Get used to it."

"I don't think I will ever get used to private jets or this life with you."

"You better, baby. I'm never letting you go. I hope you know that."

She offers me a smile, telling me that this is forever before she dozes off in the chair. Over the next hour, I shoot off a few text messages to my contacts on the ground to make sure everything is good to go for arrival. We're staying at a quaint apartment that has perfect views of the Eiffel Tower that she is just going to lust over.

Seeing Avery smile is my goal every day I get to open my eyes with her wrapped in my arms.

I've never been so deeply in love with another human the way I am with her. She completes me, makes me feel whole. She never ceases to take my breath away with just one look. Whether it's when she first wakes up, after she's showered and ready for the day, or when she's falling apart in my arms after making love—she's it for me.

Asking her to marry me for real might have been a little too quick from the outside looking in, but I don't believe any of our fake engagement was really ever that *fake.* Everything I've felt has been real. It just took us some time for us to figure it out.

When the plane finally lands and she wakes up from her nap, I wrap her in my arms before we exit onto the tarmac. Bringing my lips to the shell of her ear, I whisper, "I love you so much, Avery."

"I love you too, babe." She tightens her hold around my waist. "Are you going to tell me where we are finally?"

I smile down at her, pressing a kiss to her lips. "How about I show you?"

She nods as I guide her towards the open doors. I don't look to see what we're facing because I'm looking at her. I'm always looking at her.

Her eyes widen, and immediately, I see them start to glisten as she takes in the twinkling lights of the Eiffel Tower in the distance as they glow in the night sky. Her mouth falls open, unable to form words before her eyes bounce from me and back to the tower.

"Is this real?" she says, clearing her throat as if emotions are clogged there.

"It's real, baby. Welcome to Paris." I see a tear trickle down her cheek and I brush my knuckles across them to wipe them away. "These better be happy tears."

"The happiest, Marc," she says through a small laugh. "You brought me to Paris?"

"This was your dream right?"

"Yes. I just can't believe you remembered."

"I remember everything you've ever said, Ave. I want to give you every single dream you have. No matter how crazy or insane it might be." I bring my thumb up to her bottom lip and brush across it. "If it puts this smile on your face, I'll do whatever you want."

"I don't need the fancy things in life, Marc." She throws herself into me, wrapping her arms around my neck for a tight embrace. "I have you. You're all I'll ever need in life."

"Thank god you've already said yes to marrying me. Because if you hadn't, I would drop down on one knee right now to ask again."

"I'm not opposed to you dropping to your knees for me." She smirks.

"You're incorrigible, baby. Let's go. There's more to the surprise."

I exit the plane, leaving her standing there gaping at the fact that I plan to drop more surprises on her lap.

"What more could there—"

Her words are cut short when she sees a petite figure emerge from a blacked-out town car waiting for us.

"Mom!" she screams, rushing to her.

See, I didn't miss a single thing she said. She wanted to see the city, but she also wanted her mom to be here. The goal she had was a goal for the both of them to see Paris together. How could I not make this happen? The woman who raised the love of my life deserves this trip as much as Avery does. She raised her to be the strongest, most independent person I've ever met.

"Surprise, honey," Her mom brings her arms around her to return the hug.

"How? What? Is this real?" Avery's eyes snap from her mom back to me.

"The dream, Ave. It wasn't just for you. You wanted this for you *and* your mom too. I feel like you both deserve this trip."

More tears fall from her eyes before she gives her mom another hug. We pile into the town car and make our way to the apartment. I reserved two apartments through the rental company so that both of them overlook the Eiffel Tower. Her mom has a separate one so that she can have her own space and is free to come and go as she pleases. This is as much her vacation as it is ours. She was reluctant to join us. She wanted us to have our space to finally celebrate our engagement. I told her that I wouldn't be taking Avery without her going.

By the time we arrived, it's already late. Avery said goodbye to her mom so she could sleep and we headed to our rental. I had food delivered to both apartments while Avery unpacked her bags.

I watch her and don't miss the fact that more tears are streaming down her face.

"What's wrong?"

"I just... I can't believe you did all of this for me. I still feel like I don't deserve it... deserve you."

"Come here." I pat my lap from where I'm sitting on the edge of the bed. She wipes the tear from her cheek and makes her way to stand between my open legs. "You deserve me, Avery. You deserve everything. You always have. You always will."

She cups my face and crashes her lips to mine with a greedy kiss. I grip her hips as my tongue swipes past her bottom lip and tangles with hers as she steals my breath with each movement of her mouth. She doesn't release her mouth from mine, when she straddles my hips. No doubt feeling the erection behind the zipper of my jeans pressing into her center.

"You owe me from this morning," she pants against my lips.

"Oh yeah?"

"You teased me." She grinds against me, tangling her hands in my hair. "Thinking I was going to get a little morning delight and you denied me."

I glance down at my watch before I shoot her a devious grin. "Well… would you look at that? It's morning here in Paris."

"Barely." She rolls her eyes.

"Still morning, nonetheless." I snake my arm around her back and in one fluid motion, I flip her around until she's on her back and I'm pressed down on top of her. She lets out a squeal of delight. "Tell me what you want, baby."

She reaches between us, urgent to get my jeans undone. "Make love to me."

She lifts up slightly to pull her sweater off before unclipping her bra. Leaving herself exposed to me. Nothing but a heartbeat passes before I press my lips to hers and trail kisses down her neck, to her chest.

"You're so… fucking perfect, Avery."

Her chest rises and falls with every breath she takes. Her nipples harden when my eyes trail down to her chest again, right before I reach down and cup both of her breasts in my hands.

Gently, I lean in to take a nipple in my mouth. My eyes close as my mouth clamps down over them. I take my time with each one, flicking my tongue over each bud until her body wiggles below me.

"I want more." She bucks her hips up.

"Tell me what you want," I demand, my hands still on her breasts.

She reaches her hands to cover mine. Guiding me down her stomach until I reach the waistband of her leggings. She brings my hand inside of them, until I swipe a finger through her wet core.

"Shit," I groan. In one swift motion, I yank the leggings off, and spread her wide open as both of my hands grip her inner thighs. "I need to taste this pussy, Avery. Right fucking now."

The minute my mouth is on her, she arches off the couch. I bring a hand up to press her lower stomach back down with a move that just fucking does it for her. My tongue swipes across her clit with hunger and greed, as I keep my eyes locked with hers, causing her legs to shake around me.

"Marc," she moans my name, begging for more. Bucking her hips into my face as I ravenously lap her core with my mouth. She's already close to teetering on the edge.

"Let me see you come for me, baby."

"I'm so close." She grinds against my face as I suck hard on her clit. I surprise her by plunging two fingers inside of her, thrusting harder and harder, knowing damn well that's what's going to set her over the edge.

"Ohhh, fuck," she cries out. Her body twisting, legs trembling as she reaches the peak of her orgasm. She screams curse words in the air as if she were a truck driver and someone cut her off on the interstate.

I drink up every damn drop of her orgasm before I pull myself up from between her thighs. Her body goes limp as I hover over her, unable to move an inch, and breathing uncontrollably. My lips crash to hers in a punishing kiss, allowing her to taste herself on my lips.

"That's hot," she says.

"Now... I can properly make love to you, baby."

And I do just that.

For hours, I make love to her until the sun shines through the windows and the lights on the tower stop twinkling. I've never felt more complete than I do with her in my arms.

My phone begins to buzz on the nightstand next to us. I quickly realize that I forgot to turn off my Monday morning alarm I have set for work.

I press silence before it wakes Avery up, but I can't help but notice a text message from Oliver in a group chat he started with Thomas, Logan and I a few weeks ago.

My head is foggy from lack of sleep, but I see it was sent hours ago. Which means it's almost midnight back at home. I sit upright quickly to read it, hoping that it isn't an emergency at the cabin. Except his message is not about the cabin.

OLIVER

I FOUND HER!!!!

Apple Crisp Recipe

How to make Cathy's famous apple crisp.
Prep time: 20 min.   Cook time: 30 min.   Yield: 6 servings

Ingredients

- 4 medium cooking apples, sliced (4 cups)
    - choose a tartly sweet apple like granny smith or honey crisp
- 3/4 cup packed brown sugar
- 1/2 cup all-purpose flour
- 1/2 cup old-fashioned oats
- 1/3 cup butter, softened
- 3/4 tsp ground cinnamon
- 3/4 tsp ground nutmeg
- vanilla bean ice cream if desired

Directions

1. Heat oven to 375°F.
2. Grease bottom and sides of 8-inch square baking dish or pan with shortening.
3. Spread the sliced apples in the disk or pan.
4. In medium bowl, stir remaining ingredients except the ice cream until well mixed
5. When done, sprinkle this mixture over the apples spread in the pan.
6. Bake about 30 minutes or until topping is golden brown (apples should be tender when pierced with a fork)
7. Serve warm with vanilla bean ice cream.

Recipe from: the kitchen of my friend Lisa

ACKNOWLEDGMENTS

I don't know where to even begin with this because there's so many people I need to thank.

First and foremost, I need to thank my husband and kids for putting up with me the last couple of months. The timeline for this book was a lot shorter than the first which meant a lot more time each day devoted to it. I couldn't have done it without my husband's support and cheering me on along the way.

Melissa D—My unofficial therapist. My graphic designer. My plot developer. The list goes on and on. Thank you will never be enough for the daily phone calls (sometimes more than once) and you listening to me maneuver my way through Marc and Avery's story. You were there for every single up and down through this process. Thank you for cheering me on endlessly and making sure I didn't throw this document in the digital trash bin on my desktop.

Kelsey—Thank you for allowing me to use text messages you've sent in our group chat as conversation in this book. HA! But above all that, thank you for taking time out of your wild schedule to read this and edit word for word to make this story flow as smooth as it does. You and Brielle have believed in me before I even believed in myself. And it means the world to me.

Carol-ine—My editor. Thank you for always picking up what I'm putting down and making sure that my quick fingers of misspelled words are the words they need to be. And thanks for letting me call you Carol.

Cathryn Carter—I'm really just surprised you haven't fired me yet. You put up with my chaotic brain and organized mess of thoughts and ideas. You bring the formatting to life with these books. I never thought that *my* books could be this beautiful and you have done just that.

My alpha readers—Jessy, Rachel, Lauren Brooke and Tabitha —To say I couldn't do this without you is an understatement. You saw this book when it was at its roughest and every suggestion that you made along the way, just made the end result that much better. I hope you all know that you're kinda sorta stuck with me. [LB, I promise Logan is coming and I'll stop edging you at some point.]

My beta readers—Sam, Corimae, Jackie and Shima—Thank you for gushing over this story and hyping me up as you read it. Marc and Avery are a favorite couple of mine (so far) and I loved hearing your reading updates of you loving them as much as I do. And thanks for putting up with all the rough stages of the book and loving it anyway.

Last and certainly not least—MY READERS—none of this would be possible without you. It feels wild to call a group of people 'my readers' but here we are. You have taken my debut novel farther than I ever dreamed possible. Thank you for every share, every message and all your support these last couple of months.

ABOUT THE AUTHOR

Jenn McMahon resides along the shore in New Jersey with her husband, Daniel, two children, Zachary and Owen, and two dogs, Cooper and Piper. She has spent the last couple of years engrossed in romance books, to now writing her own and sharing them with the world. When Jenn is not writing, she can be found reading, watching reruns of her favorite TV shows (Scandal, Grey's Anatomy and Friends – just to name a few), or petting her dog. She also loves taking trips to the beach with the kids, Atlantic City date nights with her husband, and thunderstorms.

Made in the USA
Las Vegas, NV
04 March 2024